Sketches

from a

Sunlit Heaven

Sketches
from a
Sunlit Heaven

a Novel

by
SARAH LAW

WIPF & STOCK · Eugene, Oregon

SKETCHES FROM A SUNLIT HEAVEN
a Novel

Wipf & Stock
An Imprint of Wipf and Stock Publishers
199 W. 8th Ave., Suite 3
Eugene, OR 97401

www.wipfandstock.com

PAPERBACK ISBN: 978-1-6667-3590-1
HARDCOVER ISBN: 978-1-6667-9355-0
EBOOK ISBN: 978-1-6667-9356-7

VERSION NUMBER 092122

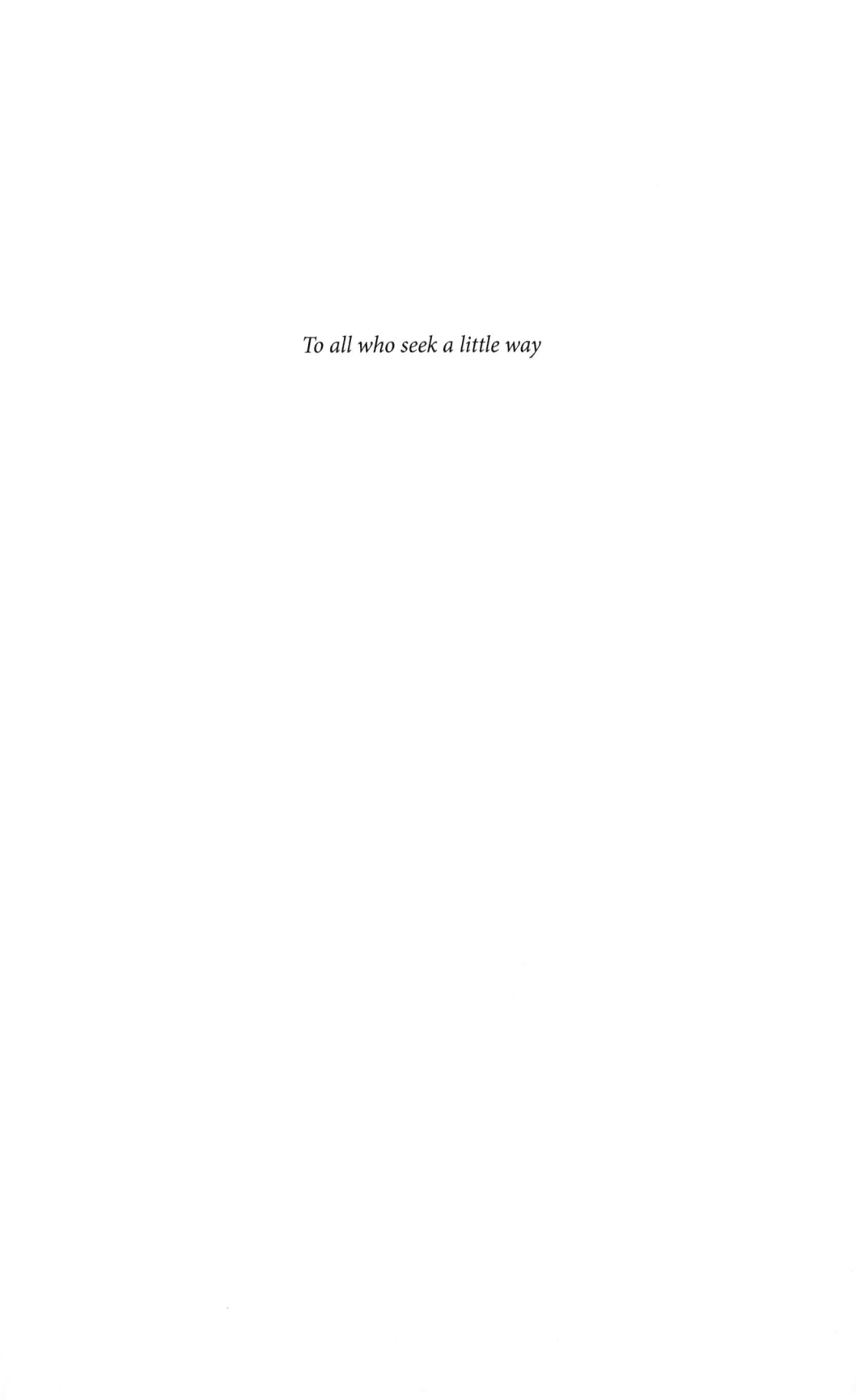

To all who seek a little way

Contents

Acknowledgments

I would like to thank Katie Miller and Sam Treacy for reading early drafts of my novel, and Alison Martin-Campbell, Terri Mullholland, and Neil Smith for their ongoing encouragement and support. My sincere gratitude also to Laura Reece Hogan, Michael Hughes, Marie Laure, and Melaney Poli, for their generous and eloquent endorsements. Thanks to all at Wipf and Stock, especially Brian Palmer for invaluable editing. Thanks to all my friends and family, especially my husband, Kevin. And to Donner and Blitzen, house panthers extraordinaire.

"A Sister's Story," short fiction drawn from an early draft of this novel, appeared in *Dappled Things*, Candlemas, 2017.

First-person narrators in Sketches from a Sunlit Heaven

Thérèse's sisters
Marie. In Carmel her religious name is Marie of the Sacred Heart
Pauline. In Carmel her religious name is Agnès of Jesus.
Léonie. In the Visitation Convent at Caen, where she eventually settles,
        her religious name is Françoise-Thérèse.
Céline. In Carmel her religious name is Geneviève.

Thérèse's cousin
Lucie Guérin. In Carmel her religious name is Lucie of the Eucharist

Thérèse's priestly "brother"
Maurice Bellière

Introduction

What makes a saint? When there is no obvious opportunity for heroic action or the ultimate sacrifice of martyrdom, is it still possible to demonstrate sanctity? We might associate that term with extraordinary spiritual grace and wisdom. If so, how is that sanctity demonstrated, particularly if the saintly person in question lives a short, hidden life? And perhaps equally interestingly, how do those closest to such a saintly soul respond to and recognize her spiritual gifts?

These are questions that I considered as I reflected on the life of Saint Thérèse of Lisieux (1873–97), and as I wrote *Sketches from a Sunlit Heaven*. Conceived as a novel, this book also serves as a meditation on the life and legacy of a real-life saint and on the lives of those closest to her. I have drawn extensively on facts and details of her life and the lives of her Carmelite sisters, as well others who corresponded with her or knew her as a blood sister. I have also done my writerly best to enter into the rarefied world of the nineteenth- and early twentieth-century Carmelite monastery, and to a lesser extent the bourgeois home life of devout nineteenth-century French Catholics. I've considered documents, photographs, and letters, but I don't claim to be writing up history. I continue to wonder about the unlikely fame of the young nun known as the "Little Flower," and the lesser-known stories of her longer-lived contemporaries. But this is a work of fiction rather than biography.

When the idea to write this book first came to me, I knew that I wanted to explore voices other than Thérèse's own. As a writer herself, her voice and perspective come through strong and clear in her autobiographical *The Story of a Soul*, a posthumous publication that has never been out of print since its first edition in 1898. Instead, I wanted to offer fragments of witness from others, echoing in their plurality the gospel accounts of Christ's life; each with its own perspective, but together creating a greater whole than any individually.

I have allowed these fictionalized witnessing voices to take on their own characteristics—some drawing closely on the characters after which they are named, but again not exclusively so. Each has a good heart, personal gifts and flaws, and a unique responsiveness to the paradox of hidden holiness that is Thérèse. Whether or not you are familiar with their historical inspirations, let me offer a very brief introduction to these six speaking characters in *Sketches from a Sunlit Heaven*.

Marie is the eldest daughter of the Martin family, and Thérèse's eldest sister and godmother. She isn't the natural leader of the sisters—that role goes to Pauline. Instead, Marie is a softer, more approachable figure, earthy and nurturing, and whose inner life is tinged with romance.

Pauline is the next eldest sister—prim, trim, a future prioress. She shoulders much responsibility throughout the novel, including an adventure in old age that no one could have foreseen. Before that, she must work through anxiety, grief, and guilt, and participate in the promotion of her sister to sainthood.

Léonie is the middle sister and black sheep of the family. Her spiritual and emotional growth are beset with challenges, and her vocation, separate from her Carmelite sisters, is hard-won and lived out with a hidden sanctity of its own.

Céline is nearest in age to Thérèse. Artistic, intelligent, passionate, and headstrong, she lives longer in the world than her sisters, and outlives them all in the monastery. She must navigate the tensions and pitfalls of creative and religious vocations. She is also a photographer and brings her box camera with her into the Carmel.

Lucie (based on real-life cousin, Marie) is a cousin of the Martin sisters, near in age to Thérèse. A gifted singer, her much shorter life is one of fear overcome through love.

And Maurice, a struggling seminarian, is a correspondent of Thérèse in the last years and months of her life. His voice is literally that of an outlier, but he nevertheless finds himself close to Thérèse's heart.

These six voices cover a span of many decades, from the end of the nineteenth to the mid-twentieth century. The period encompasses two world wars. There is necessarily an acknowledgment of mortality within the text. I hadn't consciously planned for our mortal state to emerge as a theme, but now acknowledge it as integral to the novel. Our recent pandemic has perhaps reminded us how fragile the human condition can be. Hopefully this text and its narratives acknowledge that death is part of life, and of course for some, including all the speaking voices here, it is the gateway to a fuller and more mysterious life. Additionally, I hope that my speaking characters together suggest an individual life is not only precious, but also part of a larger and more significant whole. We are all fragments in a mosaic, gleaming pieces in a jigsaw.

The novel is narrated polyphonically and chronologically, and in terms of its page-by-page structure it takes the form of the sketch, vignette, or fragment. This structure echoes imagery found within its narratives, especially the sketch or photograph, the letter (so important in the preinternet, pretelecommunications age), the mosaic, the jigsaw, and even the fragments of tile from the Roman Forum where Céline and Thérèse once scrambled down for some unofficial relics. I'm aware of more recent exploration of novels-in-flash too, and while I hadn't consciously considered this literary approach while planning my book, I acknowledge its affinities. I also confess my love of Woolf's *The Waves*. I realize that using fragmentary narrative voices asks for patience and attention from the reader; my hope is that each character's perspective remains discernible from within the mosaic, and that the overall trajectory of the novel allows for immersion in the ongoing story, and perhaps for discovering the holiness to be found, however elusively, in them all.

I end this introduction acknowledging a further paradox. While I do consider *Sketches from a Sunlit Heaven* to be a novel, it generally follows the real chronologies of people and of world history. Therefore, I used both research and artistic license to create what I felt to be a fictional world that closely, if selectively, paralleled the authentic past. I'm not the first to have done this for Thérèse: although she is more often imaginatively interpreted in visual art than in literature (which is in large part devotional, theological, or biographical), there are also some literary precedents. For example, Thérèse and Léonie are fictional characters removed from their real-life biographies in Michelle Robert's 1992 novel *Daughters of the House*: I pay homage to this work in the title of an early section of my own. Ron Hansen draws on aspects of Thérèse's story in his 1991 novel *Mariette in Ecstasy*. There are films about Thérèse too, including, interestingly, a 1967 Italian film, *Il processo di Santa Teresa del bambino Gesù* (Vittorio Cottafavi), which comprises the fictionalized testimonies of various Carmelites, including Mother Agnès (Pauline), during a stylized and emotionally compelling "process" prior to Thérèse's canonization. More recently, there is the memorable one-woman play, *Story of a Soul*, by Michel Pascal (2009). Perhaps my own text might find its fit adjacent to these last two works in the ongoing mosaic of creative pieces inspired by Thérèse.

Finally, for all the voices I have evoked and inhabited in *Sketches from a Sunlit Heaven*, these multiple reflections on the life and legacy of Thérèse are also just my own. Thérèse catches at my heart; I find her endlessly compelling but also mysterious; I don't fully understand my own devotion to her.

Hence a fractured and fragmented project seemed suitable. I don't speak for Thérèse, as she has already done this for herself, but I continue to ponder what it must have been like to know her during her earthly life, to recognize her as a hidden saint, and I invite my readers to do the same.

Glimmerings

Marie

My mother bore me on the order of a priest. Mama and Papa were married after she met him on a bridge in Alençon. "Here is he for whom I have prepared you," said the voice in her head. The monks had refused him, just as she had been rejected by the Visitation sisters, so they wed. He presented her with a holy medal to commemorate the day. They took their vows as though consecrating themselves to a diminished but tenacious chastity. They worked, as they must, at their trades, the intricate trades of lace, gems, and clocks. Two years later, a priest chided them to be fruitful and multiply before the Lord. As ever, they obeyed. The first fruit they produced was me. Not a fruit in fact, but a fragment of rock.

Like an uncut diamond, I glint, and I am rough. I have no smoothness to my soul, and I know it.

Pauline

I am straight and slender as an arrow.

The serious second daughter: from birth I am brought up to be a nun.

"Your mama counts on you to be very, very good," says the priest who calls by in a cold cloud of authority.

I nod, alert to the command. I learn to listen and follow, so that I may one day lead. I sit perched on my chair at Mama's round table and watch her painstakingly stitch, stitch, stitch. She makes lace for the grand ladies of Alençon, sends and receives countless packs of silk thread, but too often the women workers she oversees fail her.

"Do not let me down, Pauline," she sighs.

"You're the pearl in her crown," says Papa.

Léonie

Stubborn numbers will not mix.

One, two, *three, three, three.* I hit the oak table with my pink fist. I cannot get beyond it. "Three" is an island, friendless.

I falter early, with feebleness and sickness. I am reluctant to walk or talk. As a toddler I am always coughing. *Hoop hoop, honk honk.* The sound is like a horn, piercing the fog in my mind. Mama prays for me, but her prayers are those of despair. I lack the dark-haired strength of Marie and Pauline, who stand tall, like trees in a garden I must not enter. I am thick-jawed and squint-eyed. No wonder the others do not kiss me.

Léonie, *no.* Léonie, *no.* Léonie, *no.* The word slaps me on my cheeks, my thighs. *Non. Nonne.* I imagine the extra letters softening my scolding, mathematics I cannot understand. Granules of sugar which turn my *tisane* from bitter to sweet.

Céline

I start to draw before I can walk. "We have a little artist," says Papa.

I hazard his face onto the paper with the stub of a crayon in my chubby fist. The thick lines jerk and curve like a boast, and I color him in. I delight in the way my own pressure renders the colors bold, then muted, a ghost of themselves. I color the sea and the sky, each a relentless blue flood. I draw Mama and my sisters, although in my renditions they are bald and float over the world like clouds. I squeal my displeasure at Pepin, our old dog, for pattering over my gallery with his dirty paws. I see myself in the hallway mirror, a pink-faced, whirling girl, and I stamp my feet in a sort of applause.

"Quiet, Céline!" says Pauline. "If you are good, I will teach you how to paint the moon and stars."

Lucie Guérin

I am made of light and song.

As a toddler I rush through the air. Adèle watches from the belvedere, sister-shadow of mine. Papa calls out to me.

"Quicksilver daughter, take care in your flight!"

His brown tobacco smell bears me aloft, like a warm undercurrent. But I outrun even this. In my streaming through the sky, I have become a ribbon, a silvery-white ribbon, like the ones I constantly lose.

"*Ah ha! Ah ha ha! Papa! Papa!*"

My voice is a feather-fine sound-stream. My arms are wings. I am an angel. A butterfly.

Stumble. My little foot, touching the ground, trips up and I tumble. Over and down to the earth; my elbows plough into grass; my knees skid.

"Lucie! Take care, Lucie! Your dress!"

Adèle's voice merges with mine as I cry. I feel pain. I have fallen.

Papa scoops me up and kisses my head.

"Little Miss Mischief. You must wait many years before you fly to heaven."

Maurice

My name is Maurice Barthélémy. I am an only child.

I put on dramas of one and perform them for my father, who applauds me from behind a fog of pipe smoke. I am assisted by the maid to be the hero of my narratives. She fashions me a sword and shield from discarded utensils and pan lids. I become a soldier and vanquish my enemies.

Ha!

Having vanquished them, I don my little black jacket and recite an Our Father to convert them to the Faith. The world responds with a rustle of leaves and the chirping of birds.

"Maurice!"

I hear my mother call my name, and I run like a puppy back into our house.

Daughters of the House

1870–1880

Alençon: Marie

Mama calls me bohemian. She notes my ways: I do not like to be constricted, even as a child. I do not like tight collars and cuffs, the incessant round of washing, brushing, and adorning. Papa gives me a ribbon with a silver medal which feels like a bridle around my neck. I am obliged to wear it for the photographer. To fix my expression like a mask. Then off it is cast. I am not a dog. I am not Pepin, our old hound, who trots along with his brown tail wagging.

"I am quite free!" I say to the maid, Louise.

It gets back to Mama. Luckily, she is amused.

"So, Marie, eldest daughter of mine. Here is your new name, chosen by you. Mistress I-am-quite-free!"

I feel my face burn, but with pride or embarrassment it is difficult to tell. Nevertheless, I do not, on this occasion, answer back.

At ten years of age, already I have witnessed birth and death. There is a war and Papa has brought me home from school. German soldiers live in the basement, an embodiment of childish nightmares. I hear them but never see them. There is a smell of metal and sweat. Mama instructs Louise to guard us closely.

Babies have been born and promptly died. Like the soldiers, they arrive and depart without reason or announcement. I have no wish to die. Nor does my sister, Pauline. I see myself in her, though she is smaller, clearer: I glint; she gleams.

But this gives me my edge. Louise, our maid, is a dark, damp force, pressing us down. Little Léonie suffers at her hand. I, however, will not have

4

her lord it over me. I am quite free. But "Oh!" I cannot help saying. Louise has made a white dress for my favorite doll. The dress is a froth of lace (off-cuts from Mama's table, no doubt) and satin. I twirl the doll between my forefinger and thumb.

"Thank you, Louise."

She fixes me with a stare. I stare back. She thinks I will do her bidding now. I will not. I have completed my schoolwork and tidied my bedroom and I have a right to play. I place the doll in my basket of toys and run out to the garden.

After supper, Léonie and I take the plates back to the kitchen. Léonie is clumsy, so I watch her carefully. She deposits her crockery and turns away to run back to her room and Hélène. I would leave the kitchen too, but Louise detains me with her hand.

"You, Marie—come here, you wicked child."

I prepare myself to outstare her once again, but she produces the little doll with its pretty white dress. I cannot help myself—I gasp and half raise my hand to take the doll back.

Louise takes kitchen scissors and cuts the doll's dress to shreds.

The doll is left shivering and naked.

"And the next time you disobey me, I'll do this *to you*. Don't even think about telling your Mama. She already knows how feckless you are."

I am so determined not to cry in front of this witch who has taken up residence in our house that I bite down on my lower lip and make it bleed. Aware that even this marks a victory for my enemy, I lick and swallow the beads of my own blood. The oily, salty taste surprises me with its strength. It is, I decide, the taste of myself.

Alençon: Pauline

While I am still a child, my guardian angel appears to me, utterly beautiful and dressed all in white. He (or was it she?) takes my hand and leads me into a maze, with dark foliage everywhere. We walk along together, and I feel blessed to be in her company. Eventually we reach a huge meadow bathed in sunshine. In the meadow is Christ on the cross. I kneel down beside my angel just as she bids me. Then my angel disappears.

I am so struck by my vision that I feel the need to share it. But I do not tell Mama, who is weighed down with endless maternities, or Marie, who I fear may dismiss me with a laugh. In the parlor before her nap, I tell Hélène, four-year-old princess, who charms even Léonie with her merriment. I pull her towards me and make her sit on my lap. Our stiff day frocks rustle together, and she wriggles as I speak of the movements of an angel. She knows Jesus because we pray to him every evening together. Recently, she has written her first letters. A big half loop topped with a curl. *J*. But just now, she is not of a mood to learn. Releasing herself from my arms, she slips down on all fours like a baby. Then she's up, coughing for a moment from some invisible dust, and off to find Léonie, giggling at the prospect.

A rawness settles in my throat and my face feels too hot. I am embarrassed by my confidences to a child. I must grow up.

Alençon: Léonie

Hélène is five.

"And feisty," says Papa.

In our little room we fight but find each other to be friends. Younger than me, she does not notice my slowness. We are special sisters. This is how it was meant to be: we are all sets of twin souls, like little angels boarding an ark. Hélène and Léonie share their dreams; we tell stories of hidden treasure and dolls that come to life. I feel a sense of ease: I am balanced against Hélène, my special counterweight. For once I am found equal to my role as playmate.

Then Hélène dies. From this moment I am alone.

Mama weeps and I wonder what my sister-twin has done. I overhear Mama confiding in Pauline: Hélène told a lie on her deathbed. Mama says Hélène is in purgatory because of this. Her voice is a stranger's when she says it, hoarse and afraid. I think it is an adult version of my own voice which cringes and cracks whenever I am judged.

I try to approach Mama, but she is back at her table, separated from me by the tight lines of her dress, the neat circle of the table, the dark swerve of her chair.

Alençon: Marie

The death of Hélène occurs on the same day I turn ten. Despite my remaining clearly alive, according to my plan, I am beside myself with sadness. I dress myself in yesterday's clothes and splash cold water on my face. Pauline and poor Léonie are very, very quiet.

The whole house is chilled. Nobody celebrates.

Mama visits me in my bedroom where I am holding a book of children's stories. These stories bore me—I dislike being shown so heavy-handedly how to behave—and I stare out of the window, wondering if Hélène's soul has ascended fully to heaven or has become delayed, snagged like cotton wool in the long, gray February clouds. Mama sits beside me on the bed. She is dressed in black. Her thin face is, by contrast, very white, apart from the red rims of her eyes. I look up at her and keep my face impassive, as (it being my birthday) I feel I can neither smile nor cry.

"Poor little Marie. This is no way to spend an anniversary. I will have Pauline visit and bring you a cup of chocolate at least." And she stands again, controlling her tears with a great effort.

"I am sorry, Mama," I say, as this is how adults express their support. "I do not believe Hélène deserved to die so soon."

Mama stiffens. But she knows I am still a child, and I mean to say a kind thing.

"The good God calls His angels when He wills," she says, while reaching out to stroke my face with her hand. "My two little boys had no time to sin."

I think of baby Joseph, who used to laugh as Pauline and I danced on the cushions in front of him. But Mama continues.

"Whether Hélène had sinned before she died—this is what I have brought to the priest. Such a young child," and here I sense she talks to herself rather than to me, "but old enough to know when she tells a lie! Oh—" and she turns to me again, "pray for her soul, Marie. You are a bold child too, but please God, you will remain on this earth for years to come. Something in you keeps you stronger than your little sisters!"

I am touched by Mama's words, but now, like her, I worry: anxiety winds itself around my yearning for independence. Am I not good enough for heaven, with this earth-bound strength of mine? I remember little Hélène pestering at Christmastime to come under the covers with me in the chill of early winter mornings, and my reluctance to roll over and give her the warm space underneath my blanket.

I want to be strong, but never mean.

I commit, then and there, always to let my sisters share any warmth I have to offer them; never to let them shiver naked and alone.

For the first six months of my eleventh year, I say my prayers, then slip, in bed, to the farthest side of the mattress, in case Hélène's wandering soul should need safe harbor for the night.

Alençon: Léonie

In the kitchen, Louise raises the rolling pin. I do not know whether she jokes or threatens. The one fades into the other. I am eight: I might as well be a dog. Old Pepin could be my brother, and we could run into the fields together. Louise does not command Pepin; only Léonie. I grip the heavy kitchen door.

Louise looks at me, her hair wrapped up in a blue scarf the color of a bruise. She has her hands on her hips. She holds a dishcloth.

"Léonie, you great fool of a girl, hurry up and help me wash the bowls."

I fear the dishcloth whipping the backs of my legs. I take the cloth from her tough hand. I fold it tightly inside my own. I am lucky—she busies herself with folding and stacking. I stand at the sink and stare into the grayish water. Dull oil flecks its surface. I see murky spots swell and disperse below. I think of sin, and the way it blooms unbidden in my soul. I think of the splotches of hurt that appear on my body after Louise has slapped me. She says she beats the sin from me, forcing it to the surface. The trouble is, there is always more. Léonie is faulty, like a leaky kitchen tap. I am at fault.

"Léonie, hurry up! Stir the fish soup and start to serve. You are making your entire family go hungry. Do you like to cause them such unhappiness?"

Louise's voice is sharp as a blade. She doesn't bother to turn around.

"I am sorry, Louise."

I move to the stove and kneel up on the chair so I can reach, stir, and apportion the soup. Its salty tang reaches the back of my mouth. I must not cough—that itself could cause a beating. I swallow and lift up my arm. I stir, one slow circle of the pan. Then I slop the full ladle into the first bowl and pour.

The family eats. Céline, new at table, swings her legs from the spindly wooden chair on which she has been placed. There is a proud look on her round face. Marie and Pauline raise and lower their spoons in a kind of harmony. Papa resides at the head of the table. His soft face with its beard sets him apart. I think he dreams of the fish that swim past his rod and bait in the early morning. Papa and his daughters. The soup is swallowed silently, but a sort of sweet chiming punctuates our dining. I grip my spoon and clank it by accident against my glass. Imaginary salt already coats my tongue.

Mama pushes her bowl towards me. She has not yet started her soup. "Léonie." She names me as though I am a stranger.

I stare at the square of dishcloth floating like a jellyfish in its pool. The cloth wavers from the bowl's journey across the table. Then it subsides into the bottom of the soup.

I get up to go to my room, my eyes stinging.

"Léonie! Apologize to your mother!"

Pauline has understood the situation with her usual quick wit. But I cannot. In my room the curtains remain undrawn. I crawl under the bedclothes, like a wounded crab.

Les Mans, Boarding School: Pauline

Mama writes to me. I am her chosen confidante; I receive her love neatly fashioned in the squares and lines of her letters. At school, with the Benedictines at Le Mans, we live our days in squares and lines, and Mama helps fill these squares with the words she sends. She has set me well in her intricate plan. She sees I am the daughter with the direct flight to God.

She has a new baby. Her name is Thérèse. Both are unwell. Mama's side aches and she cannot produce milk. Little Thérèse has gone to Rose Taillé—"Cut Rose," Mama calls her—the wet nurse at Semallé. There she will be nourished by a peasant body, solid stock, sure brown hands. But then, Thérèse will be severed from that life and returned to Alençon, a cut flower herself, for her sisters to tend. She will survive: I sense it in a dream. But for Mama herself, I have many fears, and they loom large through all my waking hours. I take up my rosary, devoting myself to its ongoing pattern of prayer.

The answer to my prayer is bleak. Marie and I are recalled from the Abbey school and told to prepare ourselves for the loss of our mother.

Alençon: Céline

I make firm friends with my new little sister, once she is back from Semallé. She toddles and laughs, and I clasp her in my arms. She is a blur of golden light, and she smells of warmth and flowers.

"You are like two little chickens," says Pauline. "Two golden hens in a feathered nest."

She sighs, and makes a thin line with her lips, but looks moved, as though she could arrange nothing better. But soon I realize our hen coup is to be blasted with loss.

"Mama is very sick," says Marie, ushering myself and Thérèse into the playroom and bidding us be quiet as the dolls that sleep there. Our house has the smell of suffering; it streaks from Mama's room; a sharp, dark stain.

"Will she die?" I ask.

Death is still an abstract thing to me; something undrawable, therefore unknown.

"Yes, Céline, I am afraid God wills it so. Papa will be sad, and you must be very good."

Marie makes to embrace us both, but Thérèse wraps her little arms around me, hiding her face from the oncoming grief.

Alençon: Léonie

I ask for the grace to give up my life for Mama's. Then I light a candle to St. Anthony in church, as he is the saint of lost things, and I sense that Léonie is lost. Soon I develop a cough.

"I've offered to die so Mama can live," I tell Marie in the sitting room.

I hope she will be kind, as she has been in the past. She looks at me and tries to smile. Then she sighs and waves me away. I rip up bits of paper in my room and pretend I am a lacemaker, stitching together first Communion veils.

Alençon: Pauline

Papa summons his daughters to view her body.

"Even Thérèse?" asks Marie, hovering helplessly at his side, her face pale and soft against her mourning dress.

He stands on the landing at the top of the stairs and I see with sudden clarity that he is a broken man. "Pauline. Bring all of the girls. They must say goodbye. She is beyond her agony now."

His voice is harsh, without the timbre of calm we have learned to know him by. I usher both Céline and Thérèse up the stairs and into the bedroom. He takes Thérèse in his arms, and anxiety, my constant companion, flares in my heart that he will somehow drop and break her. Léonie sidles in behind us and hangs her head as though she has done wrong.

Mama lies in her bed, as cold and still as the corpse she is. Her eyes have been closed and her hair combed back, but traces of pain linger in the sharpness of her features, the deep lines in her brow, the dark rings under her eyes. The chill seeps into my own blood. I feel small and abandoned. She will never write to me again.

Papa lifts Thérèse up and allows her to contemplate this measure of our finite life on earth. I bite my lip. She is utterly silent.

When he lowers her to the floor once again, Marie takes her hand and leads her, together with Céline, out of the bedroom. The workmen have already brought in her coffin. It looms in the hallway like a door into the night.

Alençon: Léonie

After her funeral Mass, Papa turns to us and says, "My poor girls. You must choose a new Mama."

Céline runs to Marie; little Thérèse to Pauline, who gathers her up and gives her a kiss.

Léonie stands in the draughty hallway, flickering like a ghost.

Formation

1880 — 1882

Lisieux: Céline

Thérèse and I pose for the camera at Madame Besnier's studio. We are both dressed the same, in the patterns sewn for us by one of Mama's former workers. I saw the designs in *le Conseiller Universale* and liked them, as did Marie, who took the magazine from me before I had finished with it. Our dresses, however, are not pink as in the illustration, but a modest blue, with deep, dark V shapes plunging from our necks to partway down our thighs.

Of course, Thérèse, being only eight years old, has no hips to speak of. But I am twelve, and my body has filled itself out with secrets. I stand tall, my legs like trunks in their high black boots. My long hair is tied back. I hold my head up, proudly: a big sister, at last. Thérèse stands close by my side, holding the skipping rope at the photographer's suggestion. I rest my hand on her shoulder. She feels warm and small, a child-version of myself. We hold the pose.

From this strange brown box, an image will come. I am fascinated by the process. Madame Besnier's camera is like a toy confessional, too tiny for its veil, into which are sucked and absolved our hidden sins. After its processing, we will emerge on shining paper, gray, black, and white; immortalized. I think how I should love to do this myself: create art from light and flesh; listen without words and negotiate with time.

A week later the photograph is sent. An accompanying paper describes the process of the silver salts and their darkening over glass to present our likenesses.

"Let me see," says Thérèse as we sit in the parlor, waiting for Papa. I push her playfully away, but she will not be put off.

I take my little sketch book and a pencil and copy our portrait onto the thick cream paper, just as Madame Godard, my drawing tutor, has taught me. I am pleased with the shape we both make together; I outline our heads and bodies as though they are one smooth skyline. Then I mark in the hanging loop where Thérèse holds her skipping rope. I exaggerate its heaviness, as though she were holding the thick cord of an anchor. She returns to sit beside me and see what I am doing.

"You are keeping our little boat steady," I say to her, and, on a whim, sketch a curved deck and a series of waves at our feet. Her solemn expression is full of satisfaction.

Lisieux: Lucie Guérin

Now that Aunt Zélie has gone to heaven, Uncle Louis has moved his family to Lisieux. He visits us often with our cousins. My favorite is Thérèse. She and I play in the garden while the others sit at ease. She has a new spaniel puppy, Tom. He follows her about with his shining brown eyes.

It is a nice game we play. We are hermits, but we live and work together. In the little alcove beside the sycamore trees, we set up our hermitage. Papa lets us take two empty boxes away from his dispensary. One is for the altar and the other is a desk for study and writing. But we don't stay together, because we are hermits. What happens is this: Thérèse prays before the altar in the hermitage. I tend the garden beside it. I do this because hermits do not merely pray, they must also work and grow food to eat. This is what Thérèse says. I follow her direction. Besides, I can see when Adèle or Mama might come down to fetch us. Thérèse likes to be fair, so after a while, I go into the hermitage to pray, and Thérèse works in the garden. She loves the flowers, and sometimes she picks a few small blooms for the altar. She usually chooses asters, daisies, and corncockles. Together they make a bouquet which is white, gold, and blue, like heaven.

Adèle comes to fetch us. "So, the two hermits have finished their devotions?" She has a sly tone. "Time for dinner, if you can bear the company of the worldly, who supply the goods of the table."

She turns on her heel, enjoying the swing of her own pigtails. She has bitten her lips to make them full and red. I stand up—I have been "weeding" in the flowerbed—but am reluctant to follow her in without a reply to put her in her place. Prayer is more important than food, I want to say. But I do not dare. Adèle stops and waits impatiently, halfway back to the house.

Thérèse appears at my side in her lilac dress, her meditations interrupted. In her hands she holds the latest gathering of flowers to be placed on our box-shrine. She smiles at me and marches up to Adèle.

"Here," she says to her, in her clear, sweet voice. "This is for you; the yellow for your hair and the blue for your dress."

Adèle accepts the bouquet, unable to hide her pleasure. I feel a pang of loneliness that could easily lead to tears. But Thérèse comes back to me, and something in her eyes makes me happy again. She takes my hand, and two hermits run back to the world of their family.

The next week, at the Abbey school, I find her at the end of the school day. She is holding a funeral for a dead bird. Some of her classmates mock her for her pains. Thérèse grips her hands together, closes her eyes, and prays. I had thought to sing a little hymn but am scared by her expression, and briefly close my eyes too.

Soon we are walking, step after step, away from the schoolrooms and the playground, and back to our family. My big sister Adèle is ahead of us. She hurries, because she wants to take off her uniform and try on the new skirt Madame Charpentier has brought her.

I ask Thérèse: "What do you see when you close your eyes?"

She looks at me with the slightest of frowns, our dark school dresses adding to her solemnity. "Nothing," she replies. Then she adds, "Though if God wills it, I could see angels. And Mama."

I feel bad, then, that I have caused her to speak of something sad.

Her little hand slips into mine. "I shall close my eyes now, Lucie! I shall walk forward in faith like a blind man. Come!"

So I say, "I shall close my eyes too!"

I shut my eyelids instantly, and raise my hands upwards and sideways, my left still joined to Thérèse's right. For an instant I feel her hand squeeze mine. We walk.

Before the boxes are knocked over and I come skidding down, provoking the anger of the shopkeeper and Adèle's exasperated scolding, I have the sensation of being tall, so tall I am almost a grown-up. A big sister, not a little one. I wonder if Thérèse feels the same, in those moments of marching forwards, when we cannot see one single step in front of us.

Lisieux, Les Buissonets: Léonie

To prepare me for young womanhood, Pauline attempts to advance my prayer life.

"To grow in grace," she tells me, "one must meditate on goodness and humility. One must practice the virtue of self-sacrifice."

But this is a difficult thing for me to master. I am troubled by Christian virtues—they slip through my mind like the sand. When I pray, I see instead my little sisters: Hélène, with a tug of sadness. Céline, bright and confident. Thérèse, with her up-tilted chin and brave smile. When I look in the glass, I try to smile like her. My chin has the same strength, but somehow my smile is never as warm. Léonie's lips are thin and her teeth crooked.

I wake up one morning with the solution to my challenge. I am becoming a woman, so have no more need of dolls: Léonie will give them up. I place my favorite doll on my lap and take a basket, filling it with braids, doll dresses, squares of silk. I dress the doll, Madeleine, in a blush-pink gown, an offcut from Marie's best dress. I kiss her farewell, and lay Madeleine on her bed of finery. I balance the basket on my hip the way Madame Rose used to hold Thérèse as a baby. Then I clatter downstairs. Céline and her little companion play in the garden. They are quieter than I would have been. Thérèse's skipping rope rests on the bench. The girls face each other, playing some kind of guessing game. They turn to look at me, like a couple of golden-eyed cats.

"I am too old to play with dolls," I say, not knowing how else to begin. "Please take from the basket as you wish."

"Léonie. Papa always calls you kind," says Céline. She looks at me. I feel as though I am a sky full of shifting clouds. Then she offers me a smile.

"Please take whatever you wish," I say again. "I am sixteen years old and preparing to be a lady of virtue."

At this, Céline exchanges a glance with her playmate, but Thérèse does not return it. Her eyes are on my basket full of dolls' clothes as if she were suddenly hungry.

Without replying further, Céline steps forward and frowns at the silks and braids. She takes a small cutting of blue silk, and, at my further urging, a piece of braid. She steps back smartly, as though she has received a token at a prize-giving.

I offer my bouquet to Thérèse. She looks at me as though she can see all the beautiful spiritual flowers I would like to gather in my arms and offer to God. For that moment, I do not know what to do. Then she advances with both her arms held wide, her smile as bright as a clear summer's day.

"I choose it all!" she says to me.

And then she says the words again, as though they are a prayer.

I choose it all.

Trouville: Pauline

The school year is complete. Marie stays with her friend from a wealthy family but comes home dismayed by their worldly ways. We holiday in Trouville: the old town welcomes us with its seaside grace. Marie and Papa take Céline and Léonie into town for pastries. Marie has told Céline that this town is full of painters; Céline is eager to espy some. Thérèse prefers to stay with me on the summertime shore. I find a flat gray rock for us to sit on. Despite the late hour of the afternoon, the air is warm; I allow Thérèse to remove her bonnet and place it on the rock behind her. Without any prompting, she sinks into a reverie. Safe by my side, she seems entranced by the water: a broad track of golden light leads to a far point on the horizon, between sea and sky. I look ahead myself and am lulled into a sort of prayer, although I don't know if I can really call it prayer. It feels too pleasant, too graced. It must be a story.

"Look Teresita," I say. She leans against me, her head still turned towards the setting sun on the horizon. "Do you remember the story of the golden track?"

"Mmmm," she replies, warmly, dreamily. I tell it again anyway.

"Margaret was lost in her little boat, then realized that if she followed the golden path of light, into the distance, the frightening far-off distance, she would not be lost at all, but rather sailing directly back home."

She turns her head up to look at me through half-closed eyes; I notice the luminous smoothness of her skin and the faint blue shadows under her eyes. "I know the story, Pauline. It makes me think of heaven, where Mama is waiting for us. Don't you feel like this when you pray?"

I smile at her. Sweet Teresita. And bold.

"I would set out today if I could," she muses. "But would you sail with me—you and Marie? And Céline, and our little cousins too?"

"And Léonie—don't forget your poor sister."

She nods, rather distracted. I feel for Léonie, even though I've teased her like the others: Léonie the Left-Out. Mama's prayers from heaven are helping her no doubt. But she needs yet more. More than all of us she needs the sunlight, labile and fragmented though it is on her turbulent waters.

"The boat carries my soul," continues Thérèse, intoning the lessons I have taught her. "But the boat is life here below. Our lives are made of time, and the boat sales on its track until it reaches harbor."

We both speak together: "*Time is your boat, and not your home.*"

The lines of Papa's favorite poet, Monsieur Lamartine, pressed into our memories. Thérèse loves to recite it, to lead us all as if in the most serious of litanies. I press her closer, smelling her freshness; imagine her yellow hair streaming behind her as she sails towards the sun.

Lisieux, Les Buissonets: Céline

I turn thirteen and start to bleed. I am astonished at the redness, the thickness of the blood. It is a watercolor scarlet mixed with clots of dark paste. I attempt to rinse the blood from my thick cotton knickers, but Elise, our new maid, must have noticed and told Marie. She comes to see me in our bedroom, when Thérèse is out with Papa. I put down my sketchbook but stay seated on my bed.

"Céline, I bring you the rags: you will need to use them at a certain time of the month." She issues me a parcel wrapped in tissue paper. In it are folded gray napkins. "It is something all women must deal with," she shrugs.

I realize that I have been ignorant of an important bodily function for thirteen whole years. Women everywhere, bleeding! And yet for a woman to wear red is bad; it is vulgar: all women, vulgar in their bright painterly parts.

"Are you in pain, Céline? Does your stomach hurt?" I nod; it is true, the cramping is unpleasant. "Elise will make you a tisane," says Marie. "Tell Papa you have a headache, if he sees you are unwell."

She embraces me—I catch her scent of rose water—and leaves. Thérèse comes in soon after.

"Look, Céline—Papa let me pick flowers for Pauline!"

She extends her hand in which are some semi-crushed pink-and-white wildflowers.

"Beautiful," I confirm. "Let's press them and make a holy card for her."

I have said the right thing; Thérèse's face glows with anticipated pleasure. She looks around our shared bedroom and sees the wrapped package from Marie. I get up and place it in the cupboard I use for my towels and flannels. Her eyes follow me, but she stays close to her own bed; her blonde hair contrasts prettily with its burgundy blanket.

"Did Marie come up?" she asks. "I saw her going down the stairs and thought she had been with you."

I nod, but I don't say anything else. She looks at me like the thoughtful little sister she can be. Then she gets up and goes to her shelves, pulls down a box of crafting cards, pencils, and ribbons.

"I will make her a beautiful holy card too," she says. "Even Elise will love it!"

I catch her enthusiasm, and my imaginative ideas start to flow. She is like a little muse to me. We occupy ourselves with the business of sisterly love.

Lisieux: Pauline

I am at early morning Mass at St. Jacques, with Papa and Marie. A sudden insight flickers at my throat and illuminates my mind. In it I find the memory of my schoolfriend, Edith, who died so beautifully last year. She had wanted to enter the Carmelite monastery, but God took her to Himself directly. Now I think: the vocation to enter Carmel was not hers, but mine! An urgent flush engulfs my face, my body. I am afraid to go up to receive Communion, lest I cause the world to melt about me. But I force myself to stand; I feel my lack of height next to Marie, and yet I am a flame that soars to the stars.

Carmel is the most severe of our religious communities. I stammer my request to Papa that very evening: he pulls his beard and looks at me strangely but gives me his blessing—I would not say he was exactly surprised. There is a recent Carmelite foundation in the rue de Livarot. I see its chapel's tall, elegant exterior in my mind's eye, with intense focus, and I remember my own childhood vision of the angel and the cross. I am irresistibly drawn to the enclosed world of these holy nuns and realize Mama must be praying me on from heaven.

Two weeks later, I request entry from the prioress, Mother Xavier, and my future is set. I tidy up my study in the attic and stack my books and pictures. Marie may like the former, and Céline, perhaps, the latter.

Then comes the task of telling my sisters.

Marie sits beside me in the day room. I wonder what transpires in her soul. Her chestnut-colored hair shines in its chignon, her eyes are chocolate-brown, infinitely attractive, but I do not think that they meet the gaze of many. Her days are busy now; she oversees the running of Les Buissonets, the schooling of the girls, and the comforts of Papa. The days of prize-winning for her stories at the Abbey school are far behind her. I am curious as to what inner brooding she is given, and when I ask her, it turns out she anticipates my news.

"Pauline, is it true? You have set a date for leaving us? It will be so strange to be without you in this world."

"Yes, Marie," I say. I smile, but my words sound solemn. "All is arranged. Papa and Uncle Isidore will accompany me to Carmel next month, and of course I would like you to walk with me too. Dear Marie, I will write to you whenever I am permitted. I am sure it will be often, and you will see me often too—each week, after the first month of my postulancy, if it pleases you."

I keep my eyes down on the pretty green rug for much of this speech; if it sounds rehearsed, that is often the way with me. I long for spontaneity, but my mind compiles my statements like a governess at her study.

When I look up, Marie's face is a mélange of sadness and dream. She furrows her full brows as though she has a question she cannot articulate, and chews absent-mindedly at her lower lip.

"I envy you, sister. You have known your destiny from childhood. Mama shaped you; God has chosen you. Your soul is prepared, and your health is strong. To have always known the course of your life—that is a great gift, Pauline, and one for which I—I still long for myself."

She looks down at her hands rather than me at the end of this speech.

For a while I am silent. Marie is my clever older sibling, but she is right in her self-appraisal. She is a hesitant dreamer, reluctant to embrace the future. She blooms into a womanhood that, like mine, has never been sullied by the touch of the world. She is beloved of Papa; she is womanly in a way I cannot imitate, and yet she is slow to learn the will of God for her future. Or perhaps she is slow to accept it, but I do not think she actively resists a calling. Still I ask her: "Perhaps you will take my course in life one day, Marie. You are precious to the Lord, and He calls all His own by their names."

She shakes her head and smooths the gray silks of her skirt.

"Will you marry then, Marie? Raise a family like Mama and Aunt Véronique?"

I have thought her capable of it; there is a solid warmth to her domestic rule which could bring up children well. But at twenty-two, there is no man who courts her: Papa is oblivious to the need for providing such social opportunities, though Uncle Isidore could well supply her with a suitor.

Marie shakes her head again. "Oh no! That's not for me. Besides, I do not care for parties and crowds."

"Will you stay here then, with Papa and the girls?" I think of Céline and Léonie testing her patience.

"Perhaps." But her soft face betrays her with its sag of aversion, and I realize that my Marie is adrift, rudderless. I resolve that I shall pray for her in Carmel. "I will really miss you, Pauline," she says, suddenly animated. "We always knew your future, but to have you leave so soon! Things will change when you are no longer here. Thérèse—"

And here is the unresolved challenge to my departure, a sensitive little daughter who God calls me, it seems, to abandon. I choose my words carefully, more carefully even than before.

"Thérèse will miss me. My heart pains for her. I leave in two weeks and don't know how to tell her. I fear tears, Marie, many tears. And I dare hope she has a vocation too, but she cannot join me as swiftly as she thinks. She must grow up, and you must help her, sister. You are her godmother, after all."

This is true: as the eldest child, Marie stood proud before the priest when Mama's last new-born was baptized.

A rustle behind the half-closed door. A sharp intake of childish breath. Thérèse.

Oh no.

Feet running down the hallway to the stairs. To her bedroom, no doubt. Marie and I stand up and look at each other. We go to the hallway and hear the bedroom door slam shut, followed by a muffled coughing and sobbing. I am frozen with remorse.

"The poor little one is once more losing her Mama," says Marie, quietly. "I am no replacement for you."

Langrune-sur-Mer: Maurice

I play with the boys from the local school, and we march along the street, on a mission to capture the golden apples in the orchard of Monsieur Marais. It's my birthday and nothing dowses my spirits: I laugh at the rough-and-tumble beneath the trees and laugh harder when chubby Robert yells out his warning. "Run, run! Monsieur is coming down the lime tree walk and is threatening to slice you up for pie!"

We scramble through the ragged gaps in the fence; shout our goodbyes in the dusty street.

Arriving home, I see my mother at the kitchen window, just as I knew I would. It is high summer and my mouth waters at the lemonade she will serve, with cakes to follow. In my hand is a large apple, promising crisp sweetness under its smooth yellow skin. But as I tumble into the cool of the hallway, it is Papa who emerges from the sitting room, and ushers me in there.

"Maurice, sit down. Your moth . . . Annabelle and I would like to speak to you before your birthday is out." And then, as if to himself, "It is time, yes, time for us to talk."

I look at my father, his familiar, bearded presence, and am unsure whether to feel excited or afraid. Am I to receive another gift, or the first of my grown-up responsibilities? My heart beating insistently, I sit on my small wicker chair. It prickles my thighs and I squirm, trying to get comfortable.

Mama appears, and instead of giving me my kiss, goes to stand with Papa. She is dressed in her usual cornflower-blue apron, but her face looks serious. I feel a further qualm. If this is adulthood, I am not sure I want it. To make her smile, I hold out the apple I have purloined.

"Ah, Maurice."

She steps forward and takes it and smells it distractedly before dropping it into her apron pocket. Her mouth makes a sort of smile but seems to stop in its tracks. I feel afraid.

Papa clears his throat. "You are a big boy now, Maurice—eleven!—and we need no longer keep life's complexities from you when it comes to questions of your—ah—parentage. The truth is, the truth is," and here Mama takes his hand and gives him the same broken smile she offered me, "that your mother and . . . that is, Annabelle, my wife, and myself . . . we are, as a matter of fact, and legal truth . . . yes, legally, the fact is, that we are your aunt and uncle."

"I don't understand, Papa. Do we have aunts and uncles coming to visit?" Perhaps this is another unexpected tradition for when one has a big birthday. But already, my sense of self has started to feel hollow. And Papa—the man I have known my whole life as Papa, is continuing.

"Your dear mother—no, not Annabelle—your dear Mama, Marie, was very weak after childbirth. I'm sorry to tell you she died one week after you were born. It was very sad for your father Alphonse, who, ah, realized that the best, yes, quite the best thing was for Annabelle and I to receive and rear you as our very own. We were, you see, married, but without the happy addition of a child. And—well!—a boy like you, we were happy to have you live as our son."

Before I can process this, Mama has come and knelt before me. I inhale her familiar smell, of honey and bread and love, and then she is embracing me in the warmth of her body, and she is weeping, and, inexplicably, I am weeping too, as though stung by a bee.

"We are still your guardians, oh! For as long as I live, Maurice, I will think of you as my only son!" she whispers into my hair. But I push her away. Something like ice has got into my veins, and my lips have turned to snow, and all my body is as a jagged rock. I stand, struggling for breath.

"Who—who—" I hear myself stutter.

Papa speaks again. "Your mother is Marie Bellière. Your father Alphonse Bellière. Your name is Maurice Bellière, not Barthélémy, though if I could suggest—"

But I do not wait to hear the suggestions of this man I had thought to be my father. With a surge of unutterable panic, I run from the room, run from our little house onto the dusty side street and, senselessly, back to the gaps in the orchard fence, where I stop, cold and dizzy, and am promptly sick. I wipe my strange-feeling mouth with my stranger's hand. I have thrown myself up. I am alone, and have lost my mother, even my own name. My legs shake and betray me. A boy is a sham; a boy is but a lonely ghost seeking reparation.

Vocation

1882—1886

In Carmel: Pauline

The door to the community enclosure opens: I pass through it to my place among God's living saints. This new family presses towards me, a flock of tall women in full brown habits, thick white wimples, and long black veils; my heart beats fast despite my immense efforts to remain serene.

Mother Xavier emerges from the gathering of nuns in this passageway between world and cloister. Her aristocratic profile looms into a sort of solemn portrait.

Here is a true Carmelite, strong within and without.

Almost unconsciously, I exert an extra level of control over my trembling self and raise my chin to echo her bearing. She embraces me with a light, dry encircling. Then, "To the choir," she orders, and leads me there herself.

In the comparative darkness of the nuns' choir, I am dizzy, until I am able to orient myself by the large grille at the far end that separates us from the public chapel. Another nun appears soundlessly at my side and gestures for me to kneel down. Beside her flowing gestures I feel clumsy; cramped by my worldly skirt and jacket, blinkered by my bonnet. Looking to my side, I am aware that there are wooden stalls, in which the other Carmelites are seating themselves. One face is visible to me, kindly and elderly, with eyes like glowing gold. Of course: old Mother Rose-Chrétien. Foundress and presiding spirit; I know her from the painting in the visitors' parlor. Instantly I feel warmer, as though I have been acknowledged by a beloved schoolmistress.

I close my eyes and begin the serious business of self-sacrifice, and I thank God for offering me role models for my path. Inside my soul, the two faces of Mothers Xavier and Rose-Chrétien, respectively abrupt and gentle, regard each other across a polished floor.

Later that day, I am assigned to the novitiate and find myself under the tutelage of Sister Bernadette. Her face and her approach are both soft; softer than I had allowed myself to hope for. I do not know that this is altogether for the good. At twenty, I feel old for a postulant: too old to be molded with ease to the regime, but too young fully to acknowledge the finality with which I have severed myself from everyone I know.

Lisieux: Marie

With Pauline gone, a fuzzy hunger agitates my soul. I go, unscheduled, to confession after cousin Adèle urges me to speak to a visiting priest.

"Marie, he is a holy man," she says.

Together Adèle and I attend his homily at the great Lambert textile factory, two ladies sitting at the back in our gloves and respectable high-necked dresses. Afterwards, I join the queue of penitents at the neighboring chapel.

Kneeling in the confessional, I remain buttoned up. It is dark. His voice is wood and spice. I have around my neck my black velvet ribbon, holding its silver medal to my throat. I feel like a doll. I sense his eyes gleam briefly. I smell wax and dust motes. I admit some peccadillos: I have felt aversion to my sister Pauline's religious vocation. I have been uncharitable towards poor Léonie. I have stayed too long over my morning chocolate. I entertained a flash of envy seeing Papa stroke little Thérèse's hair in the morning light. I fall quiet. I have not done much wrong—I have not done much at all.

He absolves me, without extra comment, with the briefest of penances—a Hail Mary, an Our Father. I say the prayers immediately, by rote. Then I leave for home and examine my hands. They are smooth in the shade.

The next day I sit at my dressing table, examine my face. My skin is puffy and pale, my eyes and brows brown. My hair is dark, soft. I am the eldest and the tallest. But I look as I feel: as though I am barely awake. I am as dozy as an early morning bedroom, the curtains heavy and never yet drawn open. I am twenty-three years old.

The second time I go, he challenges me. "Who *are* you, Marie? I would like you to show me your soul."

I do not know what to say to him. Should I confess to reading novels? Some priests would counsel against this, sternly, but when I tell him he only replies, "And who do the stories call you to be? Do you answer the invitation? Are you pleased to be asked?"

I tell him I imagine my own adventures, sometimes, of gypsies, foreign princes, deserts, and forests. I do not know what possesses me to do this. I have told no one else such things: not Mama when she lived and I was a sallow schoolgirl, eager to be befriended by the beautiful and wealthy. Not neat-minded, postulant Pauline. Not Papa, though he might be more inclined to laugh at me than take the books away. Not Léonie. She is frightened of gypsies. Perhaps I could have told the girls; bedtime stories for Céline and Thérèse. But godmothers should be beyond reproach, so I have kept my love of romance to myself.

"I have no penance for you," Father Pichon says after long deliberation, "but this: write to me the story of your soul. Tell me your life and the dreams of it too. And I will respond to you, not with fantasy, but with the truth."

Upon my promising him, he absolves me, more solemnly than before.

He leaves the confessional soon after me and we walk, sharing a vibrant silence, towards the light of the open chapel door.

In Carmel: Pauline

Silence is the first and foremost lesson: silence which pools out and blesses the whole community. It graces but does not blur; the silence sharpens us, makes us acutely aware of the moods, movements, and mistakes of every sister. Even if we are not present, any disturbance of the silence ripples out and causes subtle distortions of the Carmel's profound well of silent prayer. Catholic daughter, convent educated as I am, I have never known such silence: the very composition of the air is weighted with it. The longer I breathe in such silence, the more it seeps into my bones and my blood; I open my mouth and silence immediately fills it.

I open my heart in prayer and am filled with a subtle nothingness, an elixir.

We maintain silence throughout the Carmel: conversation is forbidden in the choir, the cloister, the gardens, the refectory. Each nun kneels for hours in her cell, becoming one with silence itself. We chant our Latin psalms in the choir, creating a trellis of fine-spun song around which the silence twines and blooms. Twice a day, we meet in the warming room where we may speak, while sewing or patching or other light tasks. Once a week we gather for the Chapter of Faults. We attend confession with Father Youf, where we are expected not to take too much of his time. Once a month, we have a private meeting with the prioress. This too must not be regarded as an indulgence. Mother Xavier sits in her office like a queen, but has little concern for her new recruits, and my instincts lead me to question nothing and keep my eyes downcast. She would rather we remain silent.

I learn to listen for the ringing of the bell: a high, silvery sound which is operated from a small room to the side of the choir. Sister Bernadette writes down the coded tintinnabulations for me in a sequence of lines and circles, as though each pattern of peals is something between a musical phrase and a line of verse to be scanned and transcribed. Still, it is only through attention to the sounds of the bell that I gradually internalize each call, to the chapter, to meals; and my very own arc of sounds summoning me to prioress or novice mistress. The bell itself is a silver-tongued nun, a sacred, bodiless presence, framing the portions of our daily silence with her filigree peals.

Otherwise, we communicate through sign. Bernadette teaches me this graceful and limited language of gesture. To touch a finger by the border of one's veil is to refer to the novice mistress. I practice on my as-yet-invisible veil. Bernadette smiles to encourage me. When I see a sister gesture to me with her arm raised and thumb touching forefinger, I am invited to approach. A folding and opening of the hands signifies the library. To lower my brow to my palms, the infirmary. Gardening is indicated by a raking movement. The doctor (who examines us through latches in the parlor grille) by two fingers resting on the pulse. The laundry by a two-handed scrubbing gesture. This one makes me laugh.

"You may talk during your work in the laundry. Many of us appreciate a song and a joke there," says Bernadette.

Some of these signs I pass on to Thérèse, thinking she would find them amusing. A sign at a time, for our few moments at the end of the weekly family visits in the parlor. I search for her heart through the opened grille, hoping for a smile. But instead of being entertained, she mimics each one with a solemn expression. Tears glaze her eyes, but do not fall.

Lisieux, Les Buissonets: Marie

While I puzzle over how to write my life for the good priest, Papa takes his two grown-up daughters as travel companions. Paris beckons—I wonder, and am a little afraid of, how the real city will match what I have read in the newspapers and novels. My mind teems with secondhand adventures, with black-clad young men who offer me flowers. I hug Thérèse.

"Uncle is looking forward to having you, and little Cousin Lucie too," I tell her. I note how thin and sad she looks but try to block this from my thoughts.

We have barely alighted from our coach when the telegram comes, not from the priest, but from the doctor. Papa and Léonie both frown; no doubt for different reasons. I lift my hand to my brow to assess my own expression, when Papa speaks: "We must return to Lisieux. Teresita is unwell, she is hysterical." Then he looks at me; his frown has developed into fear. "Marie, you must be mother to the girl now."

I am Thérèse's godmother, and my duty is clear. I read the telegram.

"Papa, let us go back immediately. I will look after your little queen." I mean my voice to be clear and warm, but there is a catch in it. Léonie and Papa look at me; Léonie still trying to understand the situation. Papa has the bright sparkle of a tear in his eye.

On our return I go to her room at once. Thérèse raves, and I feel the chill of an impossible task. She calls for her mama, and she does not mean me. I discover from Céline that in our absence, Uncle Isidore sat with the girls and talked about Zélie, his much-loved elder sister—our Mama who is dead these six years. Thérèse was seized with a shivering from which she has not recovered.

Her face is contorted; an agony no ten-year-old should suffer. She twists in the bed as though she is tortured. She cries—she cries out—she sees what is not there. I sit with her, as do Léonie and Céline in turn. Céline watches her sister intently, seeking a sign of the bond between them. Léonie is quiet at her bedside but delivers her reports to me like a little nurse.

She cries. She cries out. The bedroom has some innocuous black nails from which holy pictures could be hung—to Thérèse they have become the grasping fingers of the devil. Papa goes to her the instant he returns from any outing. But she stares at her king in terror. She sees a panther at his throat, set to shred them both to bloody tatters. She tries to warn him, before a howl of horror comes from her poor frame. She calls for her mama. She sees what is not there, and it is dreadful. Once, she throws herself from her bed and it is a miracle that she does not break her own bones.

She cries for me. "Marie! Marie!" I go to her. I take her hot little hand, but she snatches it away. "Marie! Marie!"

She does not know me.

"Perhaps her sight is blurred," suggests Céline; something I had not considered but am willing to believe. I go downstairs, out onto the terrace, out of the house, and stand on the drive in the sharp spring weather, in my soft slippers. The pain in my feet is misery. I have never taken to pain; I will never be a saint, mortifying myself in the hope of pleasing God. I look up at Thérèse's window. Léonie has carried her to the glass, and out she stares, her face moon-white and pitiful, her hair a cloud of sorrow. I wave and attempt to smile at her. She does not acknowledge me at first, and then, inauspiciously, her face crumples into tears.

The doctor is called. St. Vitus' Dance, he diagnoses. "The girl will pull through if she survives the present crisis. Give her cold compresses and salt-water baths."

I think of Mama's contempt for doctors and the way they failed to save her; of Mama's pale face, her body drenched and dunked, again and again, in the waters of Lourdes that afforded her no cure.

"God willing. She is a determined child. She misses her sister Pauline," I say.

Doctor Notta pauses at the door.

"Ah yes. Mademoiselle Martin, who entered the convent in the rue de Livarot last month. She will no doubt be concerned."

"Pauline knows that her prayers will be of more help than her presence, especially as Thérèse recognizes no one," I respond, though I know he is right.

Another moment's pause. "No doubt," says Doctor Notta once more, doffing his hat.

The dance of a saint, says the doctor. But I fear more the work of the devil.

Her face is pale and her skin clammy. She wears a clean nightgown, but a sour smell persists. I bring her a glass of water—she must be parched. Her eyes glint at the sight of it and she screams. Poison! She knocks the glass from my hand. The water spills and the glass hits the bedpost and shatters. Thérèse shuts her eyes, puts her hands over her ears and screams again; a prolonged, piercing, one-note torment for us both. The pieces of glass glint like distorted diamonds.

Papa enters the bedroom and stares aghast, as though his jewel cases have been vandalized by a demonic force, and all his precious stones cast to the ground. We get on our knees to gather up the fragments.

When Papa has left, Thérèse is no better, but has fallen back, whimpering, onto her pillows. For a horrible moment I fear she might be dying. Beside myself, I fetch Léonie from her room and Céline from the company of the maid. I kneel back down on the floorboards and gesture for my sisters to pray with me. Together we face Our Lady of Victories, to whose church in Paris Papa has sent money for a novena. Her white face gazes down, calmly and blindly. Clearing my throat, I search in my mind for the Memorare.

Despise not my petition, but in your mercy hear and answer me.

Léonie clutches at her rosary. Céline nudges my elbow and gestures with a tilt of her head towards Thérèse. She is silent. Her blue eyes are open and looking up at the statue of Mary. I hold my breath, listening to hers.

She smiles.

Thérèse, our beautiful child. Her eyes turn to us.

She smiles again, less certainly, but for longer. The whole room is full of grace.

"Marie," she says softly. "Marie."

In Carmel: Pauline

Thérèse visits the parlor with Marie, and soon all the sisters hear that the Virgin has come to her aid. Mother Xavier, softened by the ardor of a child, humors her.

"We have a little visionary!" she says.

I simply thank God that she lives. But the others murmur together in the cool of the cloister.

"What sort of miracle is this? The child could not say whether the Virgin was dressed in blue or white! Whether she had gold or red roses on her feet!"

As the questions reach her, Thérèse bites her lip and wipes away a tear, mortified by her own bold claims; I should not have encouraged her to tell her story.

In a few weeks my headaches start, and I wonder what sins I have committed. Deep in the back of my mind, I know: I have neglected the young soul who called me mother, and guilt nags and jolts at my temples.

I am at the Chapter of Faults. The community has gathered in the chapter room, on the first floor of the cloister buildings, next to the dormitory of St. Elijah. Sister St. John is zelatrice this week. Her role is to point out the faults of others, so that Mother may correct them and mete out penance. In my stiff blue dress, I am already a penitential presence, a worldly bruise in the good brown earth of Carmel. There is a faint scent of sweat and fear. The room is well-lit with oil lamps, as if to root out sin.

Sister St. John leans in towards Mother Xavier, who sits with her customary regal presence on a wooden-backed chair, the only one in the room. Older sisters are allowed to rest on benches at the chapter room's sides, while the rest of us kneel in uneasy discomfort. Mother's face is sunk in shadow; her head remains slightly lowered as though she contemplates her own hands at prayer.

A large sister gets up and moves heavily to the center of the room, only to prostrate herself on the bare wooden floor.

"My mother and my beloved sisters. I beg you to forgive my carelessness in the choir, and my even greater laxity in the refectory. I have caused you all distress and I have wasted the community's time. I ask for a severe penance, as my continual faults deserve."

"Sister Cecile. We have noticed your difficulties in punctuality. Please stir yourself to a greater effort for the sake of your sisters. You will fast for the remainder of the week and keep watch with our sick sisters in the infirmary, in place of recreations."

Mother's voice is neutral but never loses its sharp clarity.

"Thank you, Mother."

Sister Cecile gathers herself and shuffles back to her previous position.

I feel a chill. My skull throbs as though a cap of ice has forced itself under my tightly bound hair, and its pain is seeping across my brow, into my eyes. I gasp and raise my hand to my head, pushing my bonnet aside; I immediately realize my error.

"Pauline. You are unwell?"

The community's eyes are upon me: I am the relief of the evening.

"I am sorry, Mother Xavier. My headache has returned. I failed to accept the suffering sent to me."

"You are still weak." She does not mean physically. "So recently retired from the concerns of the world. Accept the pain as your work for the night. By doing this, you save souls, and offer reprieve to priests."

"Yes, Mother."

Self-consciously, I prostrate myself, feeling uncomfortable and exposed with my uncovered head. My skull pulses with the stress of being the focus of attention.

Mother Xavier detains me at the conclusion of the meeting by a deft hand gesture.

"You will report to me immediately after breakfast if the headache is still there. Consider this an act of obedience. Do not, however, expect to be excused of your tasks."

"Yes, Mother," I offer again.

"A Carmelite is a strong soldier," she says. "You must expect injuries and cherish them as honorable scars. But Pauline," she adds, regarding me intently, "pain is the least of our battles here."

The next day, in an effort to atone, I visit the infirmary of the Holy Face. There I find Mother Rose-Chrétien. She has been transferred to the soft bed of the aged and ill, yet she is so full of peace that a visit to her bedside has an aura of refreshment to it, as though one had visited the Blessed Sacrament in its tabernacle.

The room is comfortable and warm. I approach the bed, which has curtains pulled back that can be drawn to separate the occupant from the spaces around her when necessary. The infirmary contains a desk and a low table on which can be placed medicines, water, and a wash bowl. A window on the far side looks out onto the garden, backed by chestnut trees. There is a scent of soap with a note of sweetish sickness. Inevitably I am reminded of poor Mama, but here all is calm, welcoming God's plans.

Mother Rose-Chrétien's face is soft, and her eyes lowered in prayer. She raises them as I approach. She smiles, and it is as though she has always been smiling. She is wrapped in a white shawl which seems to intensify her smile.

"Pauline," she says.

"I am here," I reply, lamely, but I find myself smiling too. "I don't wish to tire you, Mother."

"Nor I you," she says. "How are you finding our life?"

"As I expected . . . and . . . different, too. All the sisters seem so experienced."

"And yet, some disappoint?" She looks at me, amused. "We are just human souls, Sister Agnès." She has learned of my new Carmelite name. She leans forward then, looking more solemn. "One day, dear sister, you may even lead us all. But first, you must forgive us, as you must learn to forgive yourself."

Lisieux, Les Buissonets: Marie

A knock on the door to the room I have designated as my housekeeper's office. I am running through the total cost of our provisions for the month, aware of my own profound disinterest in the task. I look at the clock, one of Papa's, on the little mantelpiece. It is only half past two—it seems as though I have been at my task for hours.

"Come in!" I cry, torn between annoyance and relief at a distraction. Then I brighten. Could it be the priest?

It is Thérèse. She has been crying, and sidles into the room with a white handkerchief crumpled in her hand. Contrasting with her embroidered floral frock, her face is a picture of misery—red around the nose and eyes, and pale in the brow and cheeks. I suspect what is coming, and although my heart pains for her, I feel a kind of despair for us both that she is caught in such a never-ending cycle of anxiety. She is strong-willed but pure as a lamb. Only Pauline matches her in determination.

Yet here she is, terribly upset again at—likely as not—precisely nothing.

"Marie, I am so sorry," she gasps, clutching the handkerchief like an inadequate toy.

I beckon her to me. "Come here, little goddaughter. Tell me what's wrong." She comes to my side, full of shuddering sobs. "I do not like you to be so worried, there is no need for these tears!" I touch her cheeks where the tear tracks glisten. Her skin is soft as a flower in the rain. She exhales deeply and rests her head against my shoulders.

"I need to go to confession, Marie. Will you please take me?"

"Thérèse, you went yesterday! And you spent a lot of time in the confessional with Father Laurent. What could you have possibly done between then and now?"

She looks at me and is almost cross. "I have done nothing but sin!"

Her voice wobbles, and the tears start again. There is no use in teasing her out of her unhappiness. I must unpack it, like a set of papers from an officious supplier of household goods.

"Tell me, then. Let us review these famous sins together." And I turn my chair away from the desk and the clock, and gesture for Thérèse to pull up another chair and sit at my side.

"I don't know where to begin," she says. Her shoulders sag.

"Begin at the beginning," I say. "When you returned from church yesterday, what happened?"

"I banged the door shut," is the immediate reply. I know then that this list has been rehearsed already. "And I didn't say grace properly. I thought uncharitable things about Elise, and I didn't thank her for washing my new coat. I looked at myself in the glass and thought—and thought I looked nicer than Céline. And I didn't answer Céline when she called for me from the sitting room. I knocked my prayer book off the bedside table through my own carelessness—again! And oh! Marie, I tried to say the rosary but kept thinking about the dress I would wear at the next meeting of the sodality of Our Lady!"

She pauses to sob. I do not, however, believe that she has finished her woeful recitation. But this—this is more than enough.

"Thérèse, my little girl. This must stop! These are the symptoms of your scared little soul. They are not sins; you must not give them such weight!"

But her face sets in a stubborn impasse.

"But they *are*, Marie! Pauline would understand me. You do not! Everywhere I go, everything I do—I sin!"

And I hear a great despair. More even than when Mama came back from Lourdes and knew the Virgin had not granted her request to live. More than all the voids and failings of my twenty-four years. In the face of her weakness, I am obliged to become strong.

"Listen, Thérèse." I take her onto my lap—she is not so big that she resists this gesture of babying. I encircle her in her dress, as though she were a bunch of flowers. Her blonde hair spills down against my own dull dress. "Pauline is in Carmel now. I am your godmother, and what I am going to tell you is for your own spiritual health and for the good of the souls who surround you. We are a family given to God, and as faithful Catholics, we are members of a wider circle yet." She has stopped her crying and she listens, as though to a kind teacher granting a story instead of a punishment. I grasp for inspiration. "Now, as a godmother, little sister, I will tell you what to do. You will go with me to confession once a week, no more, no less. There you will ask your questions and receive absolution."

"When shall we go? This evening? Pauline would always take me whenever I asked—"

"Not this evening. Tomorrow, perhaps. But first, I will listen to your so-called sins. Only the ones that appear to me to merit that name will you confess to the priest. Not the others, Thérèse—because they are phantoms of your mind! The devil's minions try to tempt you to despair. But I am here to tell you that they are no sins. If I am wrong, then the Good God will find no fault with you, because you are merely obeying me, as a goddaughter should. Do you understand?"

She does understand. Her body relaxes against me, and she sighs away her fear. I dislike the connotations of demanding her obedience. As if I am any kind of guide to the spiritual life! But here I see it necessary, another household duty. Thérèse, newly compliant, newly content, convinces me that the poisonous state of scruples may be lifted from her. She obeys a representative of her beloved God; she does not then have anything to reproach herself for. I, who am so rebellious, am her means of deliverance. Have I too been given a lesson in the benefits of obedience?

I would not go so far as that.

*   *   *

I continue to send my letters to Almire Pichon. He replies, swiftly, encouraging me to seek his counsel. He says my soul is fine and delicate, and in need of direction—his direction. I hold off from discussing our correspondence with Adèle. But still, I feel the urge to introduce my new spiritual director to the family; those who still remain at Les Buissonets. Eventually the moment comes, and I defer no further.

"Papa. He is a good man. I would like you to meet him—and he has asked to meet you all."

Papa stands by the fireplace. Thérèse and Léonie are writing in their copybooks. Each is writing slowly for different reasons. Léonie because she finds all schoolwork difficult. Thérèse because she is uninterested in class-room sums. Céline sits slightly apart from the others, an open sketchbook on her lap. She makes wide, sweeping strokes with her pencil. Does she draw a tempest?

"This Father Pichon. Does he know of our Pauline?" asks Papa.

"Yes, Papa. And he knows the Carmel."

"Then he is welcome. Arrange a visit, Marie. You know the schedule of the girls." And as an afterthought: "Perhaps Céline will paint his portrait." Laughing gently to himself, Papa retires to his study.

Thérèse looks up at me and inquires, "And will we be writing stories of ourselves to the good father?"

"Don't be impertinent, Thérèse!"

She notices more than is good for her.

Father Pichon calls at Les Buissonets to pay his respects before leaving for Canada. He will be gone for three months. His long black soutane brings a fresh, cold smell to the house. His face is carved ivory with flashes of French fire.

"And you, Marie," he says to me, after warmly commending Papa for his daily attendance at our Cathedral of St. Pierre. "When I return, will you also be committed to daily Masses? How will my Marie decide her future?"

My Marie.

This priest, more than any other man, owns a part of me. And this makes me think of who owns him.

I write to him with the ardor of a lover. Not in anticipation of sensual pleasure, not like the heroines of the novels I indulge in, dreamily, in the sitting room, after the household accounts are more or less complete for the day. Although an unnamed sensual flickering persists, perhaps, in my soft body's alcoves. But I write with a burning in my heart that he has kindled. I write of dear dead Mama and the friends I have lost, through fickleness, through the failures of human constancy, through my own distaste of pom-posity. I write of the Maudelondes; of my failure to pique any gentlemen cousins' interests despite Uncle Isidore's promptings; my instinct to nurture others, my failure to long for marriage and maternity.

I write of my soul as a boat becalmed. Rudderless. Basking in half-light.

And now this burning, which will not die down.

But neither does it rage. I still do not know where my life should go. Except to Calais, on a set day in August, to meet the good father upon his return, and learn of my destiny.

I present Papa with the unusual request. He is quiet as he considers it: a trip to the coast, with all the practical outlay this entails. He places his coffee cup down; it chimes on its saucer tunefully, like a sort of bell, and he turns to me with an affirming smile.

"Yes, Marie. I too would like to welcome the wise father home. He is doing much good to this family by his prayers, but his presence would be welcome too. Especially now."

"Especially now, Papa? You are well? And Uncle and Aunt, they are well?"

Papa regards me steadily and strokes his trim white beard. "We are all well, my diamond." This is reassuring news. But he continues, "You, Marie, are the precious stone still looking for your final facets. Father Pichon cuts through your uncertainties in a way your family cannot, and I thank him all the more for this."

My face flares with the burning that his name inspires in me. But there is no more time for talk, as Céline and Thérèse tumble through the door, ready for songs and praise. I smile, already imagining our trip.

* * *

Calais. The salt and oil of the place. The cold and wind. Calais is a rough edge, a torn-off line of land. I imagine its ragged body aching to be healed. But a cold sea separates it from its better half—I wrap my heavy blue coat around myself and shiver. He has not come.

Papa returns from his promenade along the front. Léonie is with him, looking down at the wet stone pathway, as though practicing custody of the eyes for some future cloistered life of her own. We wait and he does not come, and we wait, and he does not come. The vessel from Canada has long alighted and whatever business a man must conduct before disembarking and emerging from the harbor could never take this long. I say silent prayers and think of his latest letter, itself long awaited, folded carefully away in my reticule. A letter which urges me to consecrate my life to God in the most complete of ways.

Papa eventually turns and abruptly announces a retreat to our lodgings.

In my humiliation I think that Almire must have his reasons. Like God, the pain caused by his absence is more than a test; I tell myself it is a grace. I sleep, eventually, treasuring this idea, the letter beneath my pillow, and the story of a vocation tucked away in a bruised corner of my heart.

In Carmel: Pauline

"Mira. Meeeeerrraahh!" The unmistakable sound of Sister Anne calling for our miscreant animal. Mira is not like Tom; she does not come when called. She does not respond to command unless that command constitutes an invitation to dine and is accompanied by an appetizing smell. She is brown, black, and white, a true Carmelite cat—though how she passed her novitiate with such a poor show of obedience is anybody's guess.

Mira is here on the sufferance of Mother Xavier. But rather than suffering the creature, she indulges it like a daughter. And Mira, the canny animal, knows this; she fawns on her unlikely patroness. No one is as good as Mother Xavier, although in true cat fashion Mira also tends to prefer those sisters who like her the least. I confess I am among this number; I dislike unpredictability in any form. Mother Xavier sits in her prioress's office and Mira scratches at her door. Let in, she nestles, no doubt, on her forbidding mistress's lap, fed a small corner of cheese rustled up from under Mother's habit, or perhaps the torn-off fish skin from the evening collation. No doubt she considers herself especially talented, especially loved, for capturing the heart of one who is otherwise so gruff.

Before I know it the bell sounds, summoning me to Mother. I am surprised: it is late in the evening and the Great Silence has officially begun. I make my way down the dormitory stairs, still wearing my newly professed nun's habit and veil, and, after hesitating, my cream mantle too. If Mother wants me perhaps it is to run an errand. It turns out that I am correct.

"Sister Agnès. I have been calling for you," she says unnecessarily. I kneel and kiss her long brown scapular in penance as I have many times before. "I need you to climb up to the convent roof."

"The roof, Mother? Now?" Perhaps repairs are needed; but this is the realm of the workmen, surely?

"Yes, *now*, Sister. Quickly too. Mira is trapped up there and the night is cold. Please coax her down."

I know better than to question my order a second time. "Yes, Mother. Right away." I rise to my feet, bow, and go towards the door, my thoughts scrabbling for the right way to deal with this request in the same way my hands and feet will soon be scrabbling over the uneven slates of the Carmel's roof. Then I hesitate. "Which roof, Mother?"

It occurs to me that the flat tiles over our garden-facing hermitage cell would be a lot easier to navigate than the high angles over the dormitory block.

"Use your initiative, Pauline! But for Our Lady's sake, hurry up. Go to the door at the top of St. Elijah's staircase, and make sure Mira is in before you come down. You are young and quick, and she likes you well enough. And—wait!—when she is in, go to the kitchen and prepare her a saucer of milk. Remember to add sugar. Leave it in the cloister outside the refectory. Sister Anne will help you if you must have help, but I want that cat back before Matins."

She inhales and snaps her fingers, and I know better than to linger.

Out in the dark on the roof, I crouch in the cold on the flat tiles just outside the attic door. I dust off slender skeins of cobweb, wrap my mantle around me, and utter a prayer that is more gripe than beseeching. The sky is ink-black and tiny stars resemble the flecks of light I experience before my worst headaches commence.

"Come on, you spoilt animal," I mutter under my breath.

I see nothing and hear nothing; Mira may be sheltering behind the dome of the hermitage, but I am hardly inclined to crawl out there to see. The absurdity of my situation strikes me and tires me. If I could just laugh with someone—I think of my Thérèse. Would she be amused at this ludicrous turn of events? Or would the solemn turn of her soul these days forbid any note of mirth? I wonder how she would respond to such an indulgent, irreligious command from our prioress, Christ's representative in the convent. And Marie—would Mother Xavier think thus to command her?

"Mira!" I call out. "Mira!"

The cold, dark night answers me with its nothingness. My breath plumes in futility.

Then a cat shoots past me and down the stairs, a shadowy, animated blur.

I utter an inchoate prayer of thanks and return to the dormitory. Surely Sister Anne can sort out the ungrateful creature's milk.

I dream all night that Marie is lost, and that I stand shivering on the convent roof, calling and calling her name.

Lisieux, Les Buissonets: Marie

Our letters resume and inform the fabric of my days for six more months. In Lisieux I cross the rue de Livarot, empty basket over my left arm. I have been to see Pauline—Sister Agnès, my solemnly professed sister. She no longer conceals from me her hopes that I will join her—the older sister following the younger.

I cannot help but feel a lack of ardor in my soul.

"Follow me," say Pauline's eyes.

"Fly to her," say Pichon's letters.

I think how proud Papa would be of his eldest daughter.

A rough diamond jostling in a jewelry box.

"My Marie," says Almire.

"Yes," I say. "One day."

I am to call into the dressmakers before returning in time to speak to Céline's art tutor. I give myself over to momentary daydreams.

"Fly to me," says Almire.

"Follow him," says Pauline.

"Love is the king of the heart," says Adèle.

Later, I sit in the garden at Les Buissonets, and the April sun shines warmly on my back. I have put my hair up, but done it shoddily, and can feel tendrils of brown curl down over my neck, while further wisps slide over my eyebrows, distressing and framing my vision. I shut my eyes, and in a milky-brown nothingness contemplate my future.

I breathe, slowly, consciously, in and out, the warm air filling my lungs, then flowing from my body like a song. It is the middle of the afternoon, a Saturday. Céline is at her painting; Thérèse is probably with her, reading or sitting in her serious silence. Léonie I expect is asleep. It is her way of blocking out the pain of not knowing her place. The air is mild though, it is patient, uplifting, like a balm—the sweet balm Adèle gave me as a birthday gift last year. At some point soon I must get up and return to the house.

Almire reads me like a book; he draws a story out of me. A book of my weakness and failures, but a book containing chapters of which I am still proud; a hidden core of freedom flickering within me like a flame.

Don't hide this flame, he writes to me. *But don't squander it in the gusts of the world. Nurture your flame in the oxygen it craves. Consider carefully where that pure air might be, dear Marie. Hasn't someone flown there before you, letting you sense your own calling on the breeze?*

These are his words. His voice is wood and smoke. The jut of his chin is slim and shadowed. His eyes are full and fine. To this one priest I have written the story of my soul. I see that it is incomplete, and yet it feels as though it is drawing to a close. Is this how it is when one must make a great step to a new life? Nearby, a dove starts her rhythmic cooing. How simple it is, finally, to understand one's calling.

Alençon, Convent of the Poor Clares: Léonie

Pauline the Carmelite scales the heights of perfection. And now Marie, too. Her boat sails into port at Carmel, slowly but surely after all. Little Thérèse is desperate to follow. She walks around our house as though she is a holy hermit, except when Céline draws her out of her sadness. Poor Léonie is alone. But then I realize: the future is spelled out in my epithet. Oh! It is decided.

Poor Léonie will become a Poor Clare. I will bear my vows like a crown of thorns.

At Alençon, while Marie is saying her farewell to old friends, I stammer my request to the mother superior of this convent where I once prayed with Mama. She looks at me with strong dark eyes. She bids me approach the convent grille.

"Are you willing to sacrifice your life?" she asks. Her breath smells of metal.

"I am willing," I confirm.

She accepts me on the spot. Without further ceremony, two sisters receive me at the door to the side of the convent parlor. Before a word is said, I am presented with the gray dress of a postulant. I struggle into it all by myself. When Papa comes to collect me, I am on the other side of the grille. His shocked mouth tries to form the words of a blessing. Marie's mouth sets into a line.

The next day he brings Thérèse. She looks up at me in my drab dress and little brown veil. For a moment I am puffed with pride. I tell her, "Look into my eyes, little one. Poor Clares observe close custody of the senses. You will not see them again." And then I add, "Unless you join me here one day."

She steps back, with her shoulders tense and hands stuffed into her blue coat pockets.

"Pray for me, Léonie, please," she manages to say.

But the cold is dreadful. No children—not even ghostly ones—run in these corridors. The food is meagre bread. No talk: just sign after sign I cannot hope to understand. The sisters direct me with sharp-slicing hands. Léonie is the dunce in this mathematical faith.

There is little sleep to be had. I lapse into a feverish doze in the hard chapel pews. One moment, I think Louise has come to scold me. Another, Mama. Then darling Hélène, calling out in her own childish pain. The rash on my chest starts to spread up my neck and then flares onto my face. I cannot stop crying. Mucus and blood stain my postulant's sleeves.

Papa collects me the next week and takes me home to Les Buissonets. Marie has left for the Carmel. Céline and Thérèse remain. They each hug me, carefully, as if I might break.

"Your pretty blue eyes," whispers Thérèse. It's the kindest thing I've ever heard.

In Carmel: Marie

Pauline greets me at the door to the community with a light hug and a serene kiss. But her clear gray eyes are full of joy, and I easily detect the excitement beneath her controlled demeanor.

"Finally, my Marie, you have come to us," she murmurs, before the decisive movement of Mother Xavier summons me from the group of welcoming sisters. She receives me with outheld hands, but I cannot clearly tell the feelings underneath. I notice I am taller than her by an inch or two—but even close up, Mother Xavier seems the more statuesque.

All my ambivalence about the aristocracy rises up into my throat. I press my lips firmly shut—I am a woman now, not a tale-telling schoolgirl. I have made my choice freely and fly to God Himself, undeterred by His chosen representative.

The choir is dimly lit and leaves me . . . I cannot say inspired.

I go through the rituals of introductions and a tour of my new home—my new life, in fact. The cloister seems impossibly restricted. But the garden welcomes me in its verdant way. I note the potential for vegetable growing, flower tending, the wildness of the meadow and hidden joy of the hen coop.

"You won't get any work with the chickens," says Pauline—Sister Agnès, as I should now call her. "Sister Benedicta has looked after the chickens for nearly fifty years. I doubt even Mother Xavier could get her to share her territory."

I laugh—is this allowed?

Pauline reads my mind: "The gaiety of the Carmelite is proverbial, according to our seraphic mother," she says, alluding to Holy Teresa of Avila. "Little wonder we must laugh, when you get to know all our faults and crooked ways—and still, we are called to this life."

She takes my hand as she speaks. I look around: we are at the far end of the grounds, and the day is warm and reassuring on my face once more. A calico cat sleeps in a sunlit spot on the grass.

"That's Mira, Mother Xavier's cat," says Pauline.

But whichever way I turn, I see the high enclosure walls which keep us prisoner. God's prisoners, I remind myself. Protection from worldly distraction. Still the high walls feel like yawning shadows that remain, whatever the position of the sun.

This first day passes, made up of bells—I am to have my own sounding sequence—and routine. I am made to feel accepted despite the sustained silence officially broken only by recreation and liturgical acts. I start to admire these women's habits—no fripperies. Even more obviously, no anxieties as to daily choices. I start to see a freedom in restriction. My inner life is, surely, still my own.

Pauline walks up to the dormitory with me after Compline. It is the time of the Great Silence; we do not, must not, speak. But at the door to my cell, she takes my hand again and kisses me quickly on my cheek, reaching up on her toes, nimbly, to do so. As she does so, a little spark of happiness settles in my soul. I smile my goodnight and shut the cell door.

My cell has a wide window which looks out over Lisieux and beyond the town to the Normandy countryside. I stand by the glass and drink in all I see; my body sighs and relaxes at the unrestricted view. Houses, become increasingly small and simple, twinkle back at me—their own glass windows reflect the gleam of the setting sun. Each is touched by the same great light; each reflects its glory. The whole scene is overflowing with visual harmony, suggesting mutual, infinite expanse. *In some of these shining houses live my poor worldly friends and their families. In others, unknown saints. I will have many hours to imagine these various lives.*

Almire was right. Carmel is the home of the blessed. He has written to say he longs to see me here, that he will come to preach and hear confession, and I long to show him how right he was. I am touched by this last gift of the day; touched, finally, to the point of a heartfelt glow.

Conversion

1886—1888

Lisieux, Les Buissonets: Céline

Christmas. Léonie, returned from her ill-judged attempt to join the Poor Clares, retires to bed with a nauseous fever. The rest of us attend midnight Mass at St. Pierre's Cathedral: Uncle, Aunt, Adèle, Lucie, Papa, Thérèse, and me. Bishop Hugonin celebrates. The congregation teems with all the great and the good of Lisieux. Our tiredness and excitement create a bright delirium; with the shimmer of incense, the gold vestments of the priests, anything seems possible. All receive Communion. With a sudden pang, I offer mine for Mama and our departed little brothers and sisters: soon we will be another year away from them. Kneeling in our pew, I glimpse the fluid forms of the Maudelondes returning to theirs, further back and on the other side of the central aisle. Henry is with his sisters, immaculately turned out in his military coat, a slim young man with impeccable manners and mien. He catches my eye and raises his hat and his brow, and inclines, slightly, towards me.

Papa insists we walk back home. The sky is crystalline and finely studded with lights. He walks with a deliberation borne of stubbornness and fatigue; his face looks as pale as his hair and beard in the monochrome brushstrokes of night. And Thérèse, Thérèse is tired too, but she does not know it. In her eyes the Mass is a great romance, the Communion a long-awaited kiss from her prince.

"I used to think my name was written in the sky," she says to me, slipping her arm through mine as we turn off the rue Saint-Marie towards Les Buissonets. I squeeze her arm.

"Perhaps it is," I say. "There are enough stars tonight for all of our names. If I had my sketchbook, I would draw them for you."

She takes this in good humor and sighs with a dramatic satisfaction, her breath a fine visible mist in the cold. I wonder idly whether I would sigh with such pleasure should Henry kiss my hand, and I imagine, equally idly, that he might be rather eager to do so, but I do not share this thought.

Ahead of us, Papa coughs, and I return to the present moment. "We'll be warm at home, Papa," I call out to him. He grunts but does not turn back to join us.

Only when we are indoors do I realize the extent of our father's fatigue. Removing our coats, we make our way to the sitting room, where Elise has set the fire glowing orange and red behind its grate. On the little table will be a tray of sweets and Papa's brandy bottle, its amber glass glowing in the firelight. But before we partake, there are the Christmas slippers to attend to, something which still seems to bring great joy to Thérèse, despite her aspirations to maturity at the age of thirteen. It will fend off moodiness at any rate, just for tonight.

The slippers are waiting on the small table between the hallway and sitting room. Within their red-gold fabric are neat little gifts which Elise and I have wrapped at Papa's request. Each Christmas Eve, Thérèse unwraps the trinkets and is a child again, playing before her family, basking in paternal love. Thérèse is just behind me when we hear:

"Not this childish thing again. It's the last year of it at any rate, thank God."

Papa mutters, but he does not mumble, and we both hear every grudging word he says.

I feel a sharp horror in my stomach as I struggle for a breath. But Thérèse—dear Lord; Thérèse will be devastated. She heaves between happiness and tears at the best of times; this will sink her, and she will drag Papa down with her. I turn, but she has already run up the stairs to our room. Papa has proceeded into the sitting room, apparently without a care that he has said such wounding words. Sometimes I fear this sudden streak of severity in him, which comes so close to cruelty in its pronouncements.

But it is Thérèse to whom I must go. I have held her many times in recent months as a crying jag plays itself out. I might not be able to hear her sobs as I ascend the stairs after her, my best dress rustling as I go, but I can feel her misery. There will be tears, without doubt.

At first, she keeps her back to me as she stands at the foot of her bed. I realize she is looking at the little crucifix which hangs in shadowy dignity over her iron bedstead. For a flickering moment, I accuse her, silently, of wallowing in her pain.

"I'm so sorry, my darling. Papa is just tired; you know how he gets. Don't go down just yet. Would you like to pray the rosary?"

I know she wouldn't, but it is something to say, and would offer a justifiable pause before our descent. But then she turns to me. There are tears in her eyes, but she does not let them fall. She wipes them away with the back of her hand and somehow her whole face is shining.

What now? An outburst of temper?

But then she smiles, just as though she has recovered from another childhood fever.

It is a soft smile: no anger. It is fresh, and light. Her whole demeanor is uplifted. Even her long fair hair glows as it haloes her face and flows down her back.

"I am fine," says my sister. "I am going down to Papa. I am so happy, Céline," she continues, and rushes up to kiss me. "And I love you so much!"

And with that she skips down the stairs, light as air. Before I reach the landing, I hear her in the sitting room uttering cries of delight as she unwraps the little gifts. I go down and enter the room to see her kneeling at Papa's feet; he sits next to the fireplace in his great leather armchair, smiling at his little queen, brandy glass in hand. It is as though nothing even approaching resentment had passed through his mind.

"Céline!" calls Papa, reflecting the warmth of the fire beside him. "Come and join us before the fun is over!"

She calls it her conversion. Who am I to judge? The kiss from her prince, her infant king, has marked her somewhere deep inside. Suddenly there is a strength that has been missing since Mama's death ten years ago. Bold, baby Thérèse has reawoken as an adult. On the sitting room wall hangs my painting of the Nativity; its dark oils drawing the eye to a wondrously glowing cradle. Papa and Thérèse echo its miracle, forming their own bright cameo.

*   *   *

She does not want to marry; not ever marry, apart from to her Jesus. But she wants to save as well as sacrifice. She wants to mother souls. At Mass, she clutches a holy card in which the Magdalene kneels and weeps before the Cross.

"How thirsty He is," she says, tracing a flow of invisible blood from His crown of thorns, down His naked body, and into the parched ground. "I would like to quench His thirst."

I think how little she resembles the fallen woman in this poorly drawn picture; the one a redeemed penitent, the other little more than a girl, innocent as dew. But it is great sinners that she seeks. For that, she must look further afield than the Carmel and Les Buissonets' dwindling circle.

"Céline! Look—never have I seen such a lost soul. Come and tell me how to pray for one so needing grace."

She has this week's edition of Papa's *La Croix*. On the first page, the double photographic portrayal of a man, much younger than Papa: straight-faced, impassive. Short dark hair, a hint of dark beard about his solid features. Dark eyes drilling towards us, the casual viewers of his condemnation. My skin prickles. There is something about him that excites as well as disturbs.

The man is Monsieur Pranzini, and his trial is one of life or death. Pranzini is a seducer, a fraud, a bigamist, a dangerous man. Now he is charged with murder, the murder of two women. He stands trial in Paris and is the front-page headline of every newspaper in France. Women in the public gallery swoon at his smoldering gaze. Little wonder that I sense a stirring in my body that is other than an impulse of pure grace.

In my own way I need to pray as much as does Thérèse.

So this we do. We sit in the garden with our rosaries, offering their mysteries for Pranzini's soul. After early Mass at St. Pierre's Cathedral, we slip into the Lady Chapel, light our candles, and bow our heads in prayer. Distracted by a lingering tension in my neck, I steal a glance at my sister. She is utterly still with her head raised higher than when we began our intercessions, eyes softly closed. I see her brown lashes grace the pallor of her skin. Her blonde hair flows down the back of her deep blue jacket. The golden skein of its surface catches the morning light. In her right hand she holds her holy card.

We do not tell Papa the object of our fervent prayers. "For Léonie," I imagine myself explaining, should a discreet lie be necessary.

Pranzini is found guilty and sentenced to hang, as we feared he must. The day following his hanging we return from early Mass together with Papa. He retires to his study, calling Elise for hot coffee. When the study door is shut, we slip into the sitting room where the new day's *La Croix* rests, freshly folded on a side table beside Papa's empty armchair. Together we seize the paper, and resting on an arm of Papa's chair each, turn hastily to the execution report we know will be within.

"Oh, my God!" gasps Thérèse. "He answered my prayers, Céline—look!"

And she looks at me with ecstasy. Together we read the report: the words blur and haze as I picture the events described. Yesterday, led shackled from La Roquette Prison to the guillotine, unrepentant, our Pranzini was offered the crucifix. Unaccountably, he kissed it. Thus, this lothario flew to his maker in a last, late, flare of grace.

For Thérèse, this is more than an answer to a prayer. It is confirmation of her vocation. Spouse and mother triumphant, within the heart of Christ.

"My first child," says Thérèse, her face set to an invisible sun.

*   *   *

Later in the belvedere, we sit and watch the sunset. The golden red rays are from the heart of God, the heart of Christ. We bathe in it. Prayer flows around us, holy water. We breathe in; it is supplication; we breathe out; it is abandonment to the Divine Will. Time stops and pools in our opened souls. Thérèse looks at me and knows all that I know. I look at her and find her a purified essence of myself. I am a papery twin to her living voice; she's an angel; imprinted with her outline, I stumble towards His outspread arms, even as she's transfigured in His blazing light.

I am surprised but not astonished when she turns to me one afternoon, and, catching my hand, cannot contain her secret, which is no secret at all. "I am called to Carmel, Céline; I am called to enter soon. I know it—I am all His now."

"Oh, Thérèse," I say. She has bloomed like a wildflower, according to His season.

"I cannot remain in the world. Carmel is the desert where God wishes me to hide myself."

She is so vivid, in her fourteen-year-old body; her flesh full and her breathing heightened. In her green velvet dress, she is the spirit of His spring. I know that she is utterly sincere. It is, to her, as though her life depends upon it.

"Papa will be sad." I state the obvious. She looks out onto the garden. Papa is there, resting on the far bench.

"Yes. It will be a hard thing, leaving Papa."

"You should ask his permission," I remind her.

She replies, smoothing her hands over her hips: "I will tell him I am called."

When she tells him, he picks a flower for her, a white aster from the garden. Its roots are intact. She shakes the soil from it, places it in her copy of *The Imitation of Christ*. I capture the moment on the canvas of my heart.

All that evening, his mouth is set, and his eyes fixed in the middle distance.

In Carmel: Marie

I find myself flourishing in the freedom of Carmel. First as postulant, then novice, in my stiff white veil and my rough brown woolen tunic and scapular—a uniform without insignia, or any insignia but God. Novice Mistress Bernadette smiles at me indulgently. Mother Xavier smiles much less generously, but I sense that she waits for me to find my feet, making my own mistakes along the way. I allow my soul to expand in Carmel's many silences. I cannot regret my decision—my thoughts remain my own, even kneeling in the choir, and I cannot think God forbids me them. Moreover, I am freed, forever, of corsets, frills, and parasols. Perusing the Rule, I find sisters are only required to wash their faces weekly! Perhaps with good reason, as cold water is our only means of ablution. But even cold water is a sort of release—bracing, salutary against the summer's heat. In my unlikely prison, I am alive.

In the afternoon the bell peals a complex sequence of chimes; short and long and short again. I recognize my sound and that of one other; we are summoned to Mother Prioress, so I dust down my hands and my habit from weeding in the courtyard and go there forthwith. Blinking to adjust my eyes to indoor light, I find Pauline already in place, sitting demurely in front of Mother's great desk. I wonder again how she manages to look, in her habit and black veil, so small and so controlled. Her eyes slide towards me as I pull up another chair at Mother Xavier's gesture of invitation.

"You are hard at work, Sister Marie," says Mother, dryly.

I nod. "I let up with the gardening for a day and all the weeds spring back."

Mother regards me, her gaze opaque—I must have been impertinent. But then she smiles, and uncommon beauty flashes from her features. Not for the first time I think she must have been extraordinary as a young woman. There is a portrait of her in the entrance to the library, and I had unreflectingly thought it exaggerated to please her; a young Mother Xavier, prioress even then, but smooth-faced, with liquid-brown eyes, elegant nose, and rose-pink lips. Now I think it must have been more accurate than I had credited; she must have broken hearts in her worldly years—perhaps she does, in her own way, even now.

"A fine sentiment. One you should share with Father Youf," she says, still seemingly amused. "He would no doubt agree with its moral of unceasing vigilance."

"Oh! I didn't mean—" But Pauline gives me another glance, as if to say, *For goodness' sake, agree*; and so I do. "Thank you, Mother."

"Sisters Agnès and Marie. We must consider your particular situation. Little Thérèse is eager to enter our Carmel. This young soul is like a daughter to me. And," she says, pushing a number of clipped-together letters sideways on her desk, "your dear father is generous to a fault, offering a third dowry of ten thousand francs to our humble foundation."

I poorly suppress a gasp at this vulgar talk of money. But Pauline does not flinch. "What an honor this is to our family," she says, smoothly.

"Nonetheless, Agnès. There are concerns also. As you know, St. Teresa herself counselled against more than two blood sisters in any one community. We would be unable ever to consider our young postulant for a position as choir sister, while you both remain here. She would have no vote, no say at Chapter. And secondly, her still extreme youth concerns us. We have a strict Rule here, as you know, and keep admirably," she nods to Pauline, "and you, Marie, are discovering. But how will such a child—she is not yet fifteen, no?—cope with the fasts, the long hours of prayer, the daily grind of labor?"

With this, Mother Xavier sits back in her tall prioress's chair. Her expression has changed to one of expectation: expectation, I dare to think, of being entertained. If she wants us to disagree, she may succeed, although I am reluctant to air our differences in her presence. But before I can think of some platitude to ease us over a conflict, my sister is speaking.

"Mother Xavier, I must plead for Thérèse. I am convinced that she has blossomed this year." Pauline sits up, even straighter than before. Her voice takes on an edge which for a moment I cannot place, until I realize that she echoes the tones of Mother Xavier herself. "She claimed to have a vocation to the Carmel as soon as she knew about mine. We know this. But now it has become the truth. She is still young, but her heart is here, and I wonder what good will come of preventing her from entering this year, or next. She could join us after the Lenten fast."

"Good, good," says Mother Xavier. Then she looks to me. "Please, Marie. Speak freely to our concerns." And even though I cannot trust her, I am obliged to find my voice.

"I—I am hesitant for her to join us. Dear Pauline, you were already here in Carmel when she was ill. Believe me. It was beyond frightening. And it was only three years ago. Yes, she is older now, she is almost a young woman. But when I entered, she was still crying at the slightest criticism. I listened to her scruples again and again; you should have heard some of them. She would worry herself to death here! And we would be worried to death over her also."

I stop myself and raise both hands to my face, pressing my fingers into my own soft flesh. I fear I am only making enemies.

"Good," says Mother Xavier again, unexpectedly. She regards us both in her inscrutable way. Does she mean to divide, or unite us? "One thing I can guarantee. I may have treated her as a pet in her younger years. She has been charming in her visits to the parlor. But she will get no such softness from me in the cloister. Can you imagine the unrest that would cause among the other novices? Even you, Marie, would find it unfair. The girl would be obliged to do her penances just as any other Carmelite."

She refers not only to the fasts and the Chapter of Faults, but of the little whip in every nun's cell, the practice of self-flagellation we call the discipline. I doubt I am the only sister to avoid the practice—but I also doubt Thérèse would shirk it.

"She is ready," says Pauline. "I am sure of it."

Silence settles into the room like so much convent dust.

"Very well," says Mother Xavier. "I thank you for your thoughts. Let us ask the Blessed Virgin for direction. I myself think that the time may indeed be right," and she fingers again the letters on her desk. "But still, we may have opposition to overcome. You may leave."

She looks at us sharply and the interview is over.

Outside, Pauline beckons me into the garden, and we slip through the cloister door beside the infirmary to get there. It is unlike her to flout the general silence, but I calculate there is not much time before Vespers. We walk until we reach the chestnut avenue, with its short quiet passage through the shelter of the trees. The light is always dappled here. I feel the summer sunshine touch my face.

Pauline slows her walk. She turns to me seriously, her thin face looking both pink and pinched, her hands, under her scapular, plunged into her capacious tunic pockets. Unlike me, she never seems to perspire, even in the hottest months. Slowly she says: "I do know, now, Marie, how much pain my coming here caused her. But even when I left her, I thought her vocation was a true one. As did Mother Xavier. She recognized Thérèse's calling long before we recognized your own. You know, she's been writing to her since Thérèse was ten years old."

As I walk with Pauline, I have the impulse to confess I am still waiting for my own vocation fully to manifest. I suppress the impulse. Instead, I reply, "Pauline, if nothing else, think of Papa. He has been so brave, but this—this will destroy him. He loves Teresita beyond all of us; she is his great consolation in a world of loss. He needs her for many more years yet. I miss his hugs, his sounds, even his smell, and I was older than her by nearly ten years when I left Les Buissonets. But Thérèse! She does not realize how sad that parting will make them both. We really must not act on her whims, no matter how desperately she wants to be cloistered. When the grille is between us and the outside world, nothing can reverse it."

I step on a twig: it crunches as it breaks.

Pauline reaches for my arm and squeezes it briefly. "I know," she says, quietly. Then she takes her hand away. "Your perspective is human, Marie. Anyone would understand it. And you are right about Papa. There is a frailty to him that concerns me a little more each visit. Living with him daily, she will not have noticed it—although I think that Céline has. And yet . . . His ways are not our ways. I have to believe this. Such is our life! Senseless—to the world. But filled with God, even if we hardly feel Him while we live." She looks at me, emphasizing this last, distressing, thought. "Thérèse has changed this year. Since Christmas she has found an immense strength. I see it in her face. I believe the time is right."

We walk back. She is Pauline, full of lists and plans. She tells me that Thérèse is to petition Bishop Hugonin, and, if he refuses, Papa will take her to Rome with Céline, to plead her cause at a Papal Audience. I listen and am amazed at the boldness of this scheme. I must trust her to be right. I tell her so. I tell myself that I can quietly care for her here and attempt to offset the full rigor of our Rule. But now Pauline is confiding to me that Léonie tries again with her own vocation, this time with the kinder nuns of the Visitation, and my heart twists with hope for our misfit middle sister. And we turn the talk to general things, to painting and sweeping and the health of Mother Rose-Chrétien. Mira slinks ahead of us, hoping to access spilled milk in the refectory, or a patch of late warmth outside the dormitory staircase. We return, entering again that dappled interlude before our little garden and the flagstones of the cloister.

Paris: Céline

We set off on pilgrimage to Rome. We take the train, and travel, travel, travel! But Thérèse's only goal is to kneel at the feet of the Holy Father and whisper her petition into his Holy Ear. Pauline urges her on from behind the monastery enclosure. I have seen her letters with her tight, neat script. They are like little plays which Thérèse must learn by heart. I see her murmuring Pauline's thoughts as though on a string of beads. *It is God's work*, writes Pauline; *you are God's prop; I am His prompt.*

The bishop and the convent chaplain balk at Thérèse's young age, but my ardent little sister is more stubborn than they know. She *will* be a Carmelite. If she has her way, she will be in Carmel by the end of the year; a fourteen-year-old girl engaged to Eternity. Unable to contemplate the event in reality, I wonder instead: How would I paint such a moment? For this reason, as much as for Thérèse's own holy call, I embrace the torrent of sensations that travel brings, hoping one day to paint them all.

Before we join the others on our pilgrimage, we visit our capital. Two days in Paris and my head spins. Here is the Louvre, the high temple of French art. I am with Papa and Thérèse; and both defer to my opinion of each painting. I will visit again, I am sure of it: Papa has murmured that funding, an apartment, may even be arranged for a talented daughter called to study painting. I tingle and quake at the thought. But Thérèse? Given her will, she will travel no more. She shadows me in good-natured quietness. I do not know how much art she sees. Papa draws her close; he raises the exhibition map before her face, attempting to shield her from the risk of painted nudity. But left to peruse this new art unfettered, I have seen astonishing things. I am looking at genius and, for the first time, I think my own girlish efforts so much firewood; poor straw barely fit for a blaze.

Here is a Renoir, newly mounted. For a moment I think, arrogantly, nonsensically, it is a portrait of me. How could that be? The head of a woman, perhaps just twenty years old; but how weary and dream-laden she seems. This is how I feel, but never how I would publicly pose. Yet here is the posture, with her left hand propping up her heavy head. Such rich colors, and such brushstrokes! Thérèse and Papa are engaged in conversation; I do not think it is about art. I turn back to the modestly framed canvas and feel myself diminish in stature before something so compelling, so utterly modern. The rich blue of her dress is echoed in the blue—deep and heavy—above her head, and in the blue shadow at the line of her palm. This woman's skin is the most beautiful translucent tone. It shines, almost, though I know it to be technique. I lean in, discerning ghostly blue tones under the pink of her complexion. She is a breath away from living. Ah! Perhaps she is me after all. She is sad—and she wears a slim wedding ring, the cause of her pain. But these pearlescent shades, the fullness of her flesh—how can the critics miss its power? I have heard that they misread such splashes of light on human skin as putrefaction. This seems to me to be pure ignorance. I long to explore the style in my own work.

Perhaps it takes someone who is both a natural subject of such art and a painter herself to be touched by this creation in her own living core. Mother of God, Guardian Angel: see how very proud I am! See how much I still have to learn, to fashion myself in the shadows of humility. I am cross with myself, yet pleased, obscurely, with my private thoughts.

I emerge from my trance and soon we leave the Musée. It rains, and this is the one thing we are inadequately prepared for. Yes, we will dress for the Pope, but for the weeping heavens—no. Papa suggests we buy new raincoats in the neighboring Galeries du Louvre, so in we go, huddling with Parisians and other tourists who entertain the same thoughts. I look at their faces; their worn, wet complexions; the pink, peach, gray, blue, making up the dermis of the human body. The smells of damp materials, weary shoppers, mingle like a swirling landscape of paint. Inside them all is a woman resting her head on her hand.

Papa generously ushers us to the ground floor, where he orders two raincoats, and they are fitted and purchased. And then, with time to spare before dinner at the hotel, we ride the new, steam-powered elevators to the top floor of the Galeries, for no reason but novelty and pleasure. I look at Thérèse and find her entranced. In this enclosed space, removed from the bustling floors, we move upwards and the swirling in my stomach reminds me of my involuntary physical response to young Henry Maudelonde's interest in my drawings—in my person. Thérèse must feel this swirling too; of what does she think?

She has her look; her lips pressed together, sweetly suppressing a secret.

The next day we begin our pilgrimage proper. We are perhaps two hundred in number—such grand people, so lively and so loud! And never have I seen so many holy priests. We travel to Italy, and after the venerable cities of Milan, Venice, Bologna, onwards to the holiest of worldly cities: the Vatican itself, where hundreds of priests say their masses and hear the sins of penitent pilgrims daily.

The train carriages are like plush salons in incessant, literal motion. They are far from quiet. What prayers there are are murmured among the commotion of the other pilgrims and the clatter and rumble of the train. We are crossing France so fast it seems the country is a blur; we fly from Paris; the worldly heaven of Paris and its art. Papa holds the newspaper to his face in the way he held the map for his youngest daughter at the Louvre, shielding himself from worldly chatter.

But as the days progress, I see that these priests are as flesh-bound as we. Not in their dress: black soutane, sash, and hat is the order of the day. But their laughter!—I had not conceived of the unbridled laughter of priests. I had not conceived of them breaking into raucous bursts of hilarity any more than I had Jesus Himself. At the Swiss hotel this morning we saw them—not fasting for the souls of their pilgrim flock but consuming hot coffee and brioches from the hotel kitchens. They are a range of ages: some, like Father Révérony, will have taken this pilgrim route many times. Others are less habituated to holiday ways. Father Joubert, for example, who is perhaps ten years older than I, hovers near Papa as we wait for our carriage. His frame is tall and slim, his hands long and pale. He sees me apprising him as though for a drawing. I do not reach for my sketchbook. His face flushes a pinkish sheen. I look away quickly and seek out Thérèse, who is turned away from the milling crowd about us.

At the end of the day she comes to me, her pale face troubled.

"Céline! We must pray before we sleep."

I look at the clock on the mantelpiece of the hotel's sitting room. It is already late in the evening—nearly ten o'clock. The collar of my day dress itches at my neck. The day has been long, full of winding streets and river water, and tomorrow we depart for Milan. Papa has not yet retired but sits in one of the less-comfortable chairs, reading from a small book which I am sure is devotional. He looks tired; his face is gray and his hair white and increasingly sparse. The unwelcome thought comes to me that soon he may fall into yet greater frailty. And that, with Thérèse set to enter Carmel, and Léonie her unreliable self, it is I who shall remain to care for him.

"I will pray with you, my little saint. Shall we pray for Papa?" I offer, thinking that she too has noticed him worn down with travel and age. She bites her lip and gives a nod of assent, but I know that this means she had someone or something else on her mind. "And of course, for the Holy Father in Rome to assent to your request," I add, hazarding a guess.

"No, Céline—I am in Jesus's hands now," she surprises me by saying. "It is the priests, Céline! We must—we simply must—pray for priests." And she grasps me by the hand. I don't fully understand her argument, but I see she is genuinely distressed. "See the good fathers on our pilgrimage?" I look around me, as though priests may have slipped through the doors and walls of the hotel lounge without our noticing. But Thérèse continues, "They are just as weak as us! I had not known how urgent the Carmelite vocation truly is. The priests who must guide us in the confessional—who must welcome the body of Jesus at Mass—they are tempted by the weaknesses of the flesh from morning to night each day!"

I begin to understand her distress. To her, to us all, the priests have always been presented as spotless, beyond reproach. We already know that we must pray for them as a courtesy, offering them the respect to which, by nature of their office, they are due. But here on our pilgrimage we see priests of all ages at all times of the day. We see them laugh and eat and drink, sometimes to obvious excess; we see them doing little to disguise their preference for one pilgrim over another; we see them dispirited, irritated, tired. But the weaknesses of the flesh! I suppress the smile of an older sister. I have noticed Father Joubert lingering at the dining table, smoothing back his hair while he looks at Papa and myself. He is a man, and not the first man to have looked at me so. I cannot think, however, that this is what Thérèse has noticed. She would be a lot more agitated if she thought of such masculine weakness as that.

But I do not tell her this. Instead, I squeeze her hand and assent to her plans. We retire to our room, where pretty twin beds remind me of our shared bedroom at Les Buissonets. Thérèse loses no time in dropping to her knees by her bed, crossing herself, and beginning her earnest solicitations into the ear of the good God. I am, despite my current cynicism, moved almost to tears. She is so very pure, this little sister of mine. Her heart is like a clear stream, gleaming in the sunlight. Even the priestly foibles she has witnessed have merely caused the waters to ripple. I kneel down beside her and resist the impulse to take her into my arms.

The next day, through the Alps, our steaming train plunges into pitch-black tunnels, causing even the world-weary travelers among us to gasp. Beside me, Thérèse shivers with mute terror. Then the subsequent rush into light such as Lisieux has never seen. Even the air is liquid gold. God's painting is more modern than the Paris Salon, more ancient than the hills.

Caen, Convent of the Visitation: Léonie

Not for me the grand international pilgrimage, or the glory of a youthful vocation. Not Léonie. Never for Léonie. Instead, here I am: Caen. The Visitation. This convent is a place of unearned grace. A lighthouse on a rocky coast. I am allowed to test my own vocation again. I have found the strength to turn to where a hand is outstretched for me.

My cell here is quite beautiful. Plain and light-filled, just as I wish to be. A basket chair and a soft gray blanket for my bed. From its windows I see the tall spires of the Abbaye-aux-Hommes, St. Stephen's Church. Strong buildings from the centuries when men's faith was as firm as the earth itself. I also see the inner courtyard of the convent. There Christ hangs crucified on the central column. My new world turns around His presence. But even the light in which He suffers here is softer.

The nuns here are quiet, of course, but they smile. We look each other in the eyes. I am new, and when I get lost, I am retrieved and kissed better with a kind word, with a blessing. My heart expands with hopefulness. I write to Thérèse and send her my poor pieces of wisdom. Sister Marianne finds me a small map of Italy so I can pray for her progress with Céline and Papa as they go to the Holy Father. I did not ask them to remember me there. I am happy to be forgotten.

But, day after day, I forget too much. I get lost too easily, even when the layout of the convent and cloister is simple enough for a blind child to navigate. I am perpetually lost. I step into the cloister and cannot find my way. I turn a page in the breviary and do not see the prayers the others say. I lose my footing. I lose my confidence.

I stay in my cell.

I sit on my chair and worry at my needlework. I prick my fingers. I rub blood into my eyes.

I get into my bed and pull the gray blanket up over my nose. In the warmth of its fluffy cocoon, I forget myself. I fall profoundly asleep.

Bologna: Céline

After the glories of Venice and Milan, we arrive at Bologna. The echoing arches of the station are thrumming with life. Our party begins to alight, in search of rest and sustenance. The steamy smuts of the train disperse to reveal hundreds of young men.

"They are students from the university, come to welcome us," says Father Révérony. He seems in a good mood, considering his responsibilities as the bishop's representative. Papa is in good spirits also; in his morning coat he walks on ahead to the luggage carriage. Thérèse and I prepare to step down onto the platform. But it is difficult to know where to step as the young men surge towards the train with their rapid, eager, Italian tongues a-clatter. I see sharp chins and gleaming brown eyes, rich brown hair, and Adam's apples tender as sand dunes. The aromas of tobacco and coffee, masculine flesh and the hum of men's blood, the grease and oil of the train: the scent of dangerous pleasures indeed. I inhale, I drink in this vivid scene.

I step off the train and onto the platform and the students stand aside to let me pass. I prepare to walk like an embodied prophet into the heaving streets of Bologna. I am missionary and miscreant, lady of the manor and twin soul of a future Carmelite. Rapid impressions of all my possible futures flicker through me, affix themselves in the niche between my memory and my imagination. I am going to expand my spirit here.

But then I realize that I am a lone pilgrim on the crowded platform. Thérèse is not with me. I whirl about, looking for a girl in a blue dress coat, a girl with a sky-blue bonnet and long tresses blonde as a meadow in the sun. She is not there. My throat burns with panic. I have lost her. Papa entrusted her to my care, and I have failed him. I strain my eyes, begging God to help me find her. She wills to be gone from my side soon enough: she must not be lost to me now.

As I take increasingly rapid steps back towards our carriage, I see her. It is an extraordinary sight. She steps off the train onto the platform but instead of the surging crowd parting as it did for me, a young man in a long gray coat detaches himself from his group and steps towards Thérèse, reaching out and taking her in his arms at the instant of her alighting. I see, and I cannot comprehend, my pure saint of a sister in the full bodily embrace of a suitor. She looks, at this instant, not like a plumped-out child, but a young woman, full of curve and beauty. The man lifts her, infinitely gently, onto the pavement, and takes a minimal step back, still holding both her upper arms as though he means to embrace her once more. I do not see his face, but his demeanor is confident, virile, instinctive.

My heart is in my mouth. What reversal of fortune is this?

But as I watch, swift reversal follows swift reversal. Thérèse lifts her face up to the young man's own and although I cannot discern her exact expression, I know it in my soul. Bold, chaste, forbidding—any physical fears masked behind the dark glass of her calling. *I am an ark, a cenacle*, I seem to hear her sing. *Touch me at your peril. I am an unscaled tower.*

Backing away, the unknown young man retreats from his flesh-and-blood Beatrice and drifts off into the general melee. I have reached Thérèse myself now. She looks at me, dazed; a little disoriented, as though she has lost her bearings in a flash of unexpected light. I take her hand, make soothing talk of writing to Pauline tonight. She follows me as bidden, saying nothing, though her breathing comes harder than usual and her hand grips mine unusually tightly.

She has preserved herself, just as miraculously as St. Catherine of this city; later, we visit this saint's remains and find her stiffly upright on a throne; a white smudge on her desiccated chin marking a kiss from the Infant Jesus—the only one she ever received in the course of her earthly life.

Rome: Céline

Rome. The whole motive for our travels; the climax of our mission. We take in the sights of this historical city. Secretly we dream of the blood of the martyrs. At the Colosseum, we both slip through the barriers and, gathering up our skirts, clamber down to the arena floor. We should be solemn, but we are too excited even to offer a prayer. We scrabble for relics, for mementos; I find some dislodged fragments of tile and give Thérèse a piece she treasures like a blessing. Later at Mass, I clutch my little fragment as though it is the singular part of a sacred mosaic. My thoughts wander: it seems to me that life in this world has the fragmented nature of just such a mosaic. We are all parts in the whole vast design. Each soul lives through the mosaic of her days until her picture is complete. I think of the Carmel and its own jigsaw of souls, and of Thérèse as the tiniest piece of their story.

The next night Thérèse and I sit together on another hotel bed. It is the Saturday evening before our audience, and we look through Pauline's letters once again. Her words gleam with lucid encouragement. But it's different when you're really here, and not directing from a room removed.

In the Vatican, one settles automatically into a state of hush. We walk as a party towards the audience room, the *Sala dei Palafrenieri*. We have received Communion at Sunday's High Mass, after evening confessions, at which neither of us revealed our bold intentions for the next day. Father Révérony must have had his suspicions though, as he repeatedly reminded our pilgrim group to keep silence in the presence of the Roman Pontiff. Thérèse looks gorgeous, if a little pale, her fair hair fixed and flowing smoothly down her back. With her stiff black dress and black silk mantilla, she is already a nun: a doll dressed as a nun, I catch myself thinking. The party is solemnly expectant. Papa joins the gentlemen at the back. A serious-looking young lady from our group proceeds us, thin and tall, like a high-class governess.

The Sala is gloriously grand, *trompe-l'œil* statuesque saints residing within their illusory alcoves. The ceiling is somber and heavy, and the floors comprise polished islands of darkness and light. When the Holy Father enters, we strain to catch our first glimpse. A slight figure in white robes with a red cope ascends, slowly, painfully, his throne at the front of this hushed, ornate room. His Swiss Guards carefully usher us forward. Father Révérony takes his place at the front of the line, ready, no doubt, to monitor us carefully. I see Pope Leo, seated and unmoving, at the same time as Thérèse, who can't help but cast me a quick look, and her lips form the shape of a swift silent "O," as though to exclaim at his great age and fragility. I share these thoughts but also have my own, which I try, superstitiously, to hide from her: our own Papa, as he reaches his own old age, will resemble this cadaverous Holy Father more and more.

The queue forms and steps forward in orderly fashion. The younger women are first, and this includes us. In a carefully orchestrated procedure, each pilgrim approaches the Pope, kneels before him, bows her veiled head, receives over it a hovering papal hand and an inaudible blessing, and immediately rises to return to the back of the room. There are a few persistent whispers from the older women waiting their turn behind us, but the grandeur of the place absorbs any stronger attempt to sully the silence, drains the merest thought of any such attempt. And yet—this is what we are here for. A pretty pair of Trojan horses among the obedient faithful. I feel my own heart thumping in my chest.

Thérèse, however, is first. Of the two of us, Thérèse is always first.

I whisper to her. "Speak!"

As though in a dream, I watch as my little sister approaches His Holiness, Leo XIII. As instructed, she kneels, demure, before the papal presence. But as he lifts his right hand to bestow his blessing, my sister discards the script—or rather, seizes upon her own script, the lines approved and finalized by Sister Agnès of Jesus, safe within her monastery walls. Thérèse raises her own hands and places them, gripped together, across the papal knees! At the same instant she speaks, or rather, chokes out her request:

"Holy Father! Please grant permission for me to enter Carmel before I am fifteen!"

She is, I know, on the verge of tears. If my heart is hammering, what must hers be doing? Yet she keeps her position and raises her face to he who could change her whole future. The moment catches in time. Some pilgrims have noticed and there are some sharp intakes of breath. Father Révérony, momentarily stunned by Thérèse's boldness, springs into action. In an instant he is by the Holy Father's side, murmuring obsequiously.

"Your Holiness, this child wishes to enter a convent. Her superiors are looking into the matter."

His apologetic tone affects amusement. Behind that, I hear his blunt anger. The Holy Father looks again at his supplicant, and offers the platitude,

"Well, well, you must await the decisions of your superiors, my child."

And so it should have ended. What else could he have said, knowing nothing of my sister's soul? But Thérèse, now off-script, shows of what mettle she is made. Instead of rising she grasps his knees harder; her voice only she raises.

"Holy Father! If—if you would just say the word, everybody would agree!"

Immediately two Swiss Guards step forward and pull her to her feet. My throat closes in fear. I think she will cry out. But in this moment the Pope makes an attempt at salving the distraught girl before him. Slowly he says, "My child, you will enter, if it is God's will."

And then she is dragged away, weeping, all her strength spent.

And now, in the wake of this scandal, comes my turn. My limbs move without volition and soon I kneel where she had pleaded. The papal hand is held over my head. And I too speak: I hear myself say, "Holy Father, a blessing on Carmel, I beg you." This at least he could grant us. But he looks at me with the incomprehension of a deaf old man.

I stand and walk away before the Guards are able to seize me, or Father Révérony stab me with his glare.

There is no exalted talk this evening. Papa received his blessing, introduced as "the father of two Carmelites and a Visitandine." No comment was made about the two desperate daughters who accompany him to Rome.

He holds his silence with us too tonight. Thérèse is mortified and weeps as abundantly as the rain that falls all day; there is no helping her, and only sleep will give her peace. I test the memories of the afternoon against my heart and feel a ragged tearing pain. I am ashamed; of myself, yes. Of whom else, I am not yet able to say.

The journey back is slow and somewhat painful. Papa reprimands some of our fellow pilgrims when they chatter on through a proposed rosary. Nevertheless, Thérèse retains her civility, at one point even charming Father Révérony when she is obliged to join his carriage to the station. As for myself, I continue to drink in the Roman light; its blazing fires and its sensual shadows, and I feel my own body refracted into vision.

A little while after our return home, all barriers are lifted to Thérèse joining the Carmel, just as her own heart has insisted: one more Christmas, one more birthday in the world, and she enters at Eastertide. Papa is pale as news of the bishop's permission arrives, and I wonder, just momentarily, whether he senses his own looming mortality and wishes to protect his little queen from sensing the same.

Caen and Lisieux: Léonie

At the start of the year Papa comes to fetch me. His face is full of love and hurt. Sister Marianne sits with me in the visiting room while Papa talks to Mother Prioress. "You have a saint for a father," says Sister Marianne. Her smooth complexion soothes me.

"Before he was a saint, he was a jeweler," I tell her. Then I add: "I'm like a broken watch that is returned to him again and again."

She smiles her little smile and takes my hand. The light shines through the January clouds. It is weak like me. "You are a yearning soul," says Marianne. She is careful with her words. "Your time will come."

Papa emerges and extends his arms towards me, taking my faulty self back into his heart. "You will be able to help Thérèse," he says.

"And she will help me," I blurt out in return.

Thérèse and I form our bond. It is a strange bond, during these cold months—her last months in the world. We are both stubborn souls, but her stubbornness is sweet and simple. Léonie has merely stayed stuck.

"I could enjoy myself before I step into the enclosure for good," she tells me. Her golden hair is tied back, her pretty face serious. "But Léonie! I want to be a nun—even here at Les Buissonets."

I am a failure. She awaits her winner's prize. But just for now, we are both nuns in limbo. I try to explain this thought to Céline. She flares her nostrils and turns back to her painting. It is a painting of a dreaming child.

Thérèse withdraws to Pauline's old attic room. She wants to mortify herself. She orders her life by the ticking of a clock. But I, I make myself walk mile after mile. Sometimes the air is full of spring. Thérèse would see the corncockles and the tulips. Léonie sees the ruts in the roads and the bent stalks of broken weeds. Léonie sees the blighted trees. But in the poverty and woundedness of the land, I also discover a need I might meet.

The needs of the poor and dying are not sweet—but still, they are simple. I bring food, water. I dress wounds and soothe simple hearts with set prayers. I am clumsy: I drop and forget my supplies. But it does not matter. An hour's walk brings me to Marthe. I see that she does not have long to live. She has no daughters. Her house is a hovel—brick and mud. Inside, its one room now serves as her sickbed. The house smells of blood and bodily waste. I take off my jacket, roll up my dress sleeves and clumsily tie on my apron. I clean the room and take out the slops. Gently, I change her clothes—Céline would call them rags. I peel them back like skin from rotten fruit. She is barely aware of my presence, but this I am used to. Once she holds my wrist with surprising strength while I wash her with a damp cloth.

"Your name," she says, in a low, firm voice.

"I am Léonie," I reply.

She does not have the breath to thank me. I leave her bread and a blessed candle. I bundle up her stained sheets and dirty clothes and carry them back to Les Buissonets. No one says anything to me about them. Perhaps Elise thinks I have soiled myself.

When I return the next day Marthe is dead. The bread is uneaten, but her scrawny right arm is stretched out, hand open and extended. Perhaps her guardian angel came to take her.

I wash her cold, white body again, stuff wads of cotton between her legs, and dress her in the fresh nightgown I had brought her. Some children come in while I work. I turn to them sharply.

"Fetch Monsieur Durand," I tell them. He will collect the corpse and arrange with the priest for a quiet burial. Before I leave her, I push her hands into the prayer position on her chest and wind my black rosary beads around her fingers.

Lisieux: Céline

In January Thérèse turns fifteen, and all she wants to do is fly to her convent cell. She has been told that as she is still so young, she must wait until the Lenten fast is over. Despite herself, she crumples with impatience. I soothe her, after my own fashion.

"Live a little," I suggest. "Come to the town with me. There is a new patisserie on the boulevard Fournet. We can have hot chocolate; bring some cakes home for Papa and Léonie."

She is not persuaded. She retreats to Pauline's old attic studio, treating it like a monastic cell. It seems she must do penance even when she has already gained her victory.

I go to the town myself, meeting Adèle and Aunt Véronique, who, embracing me, declares that Lucie must visit Les Buissonets soon. We call at haberdashers, stationers, milliners, and yes, the patisserie. Adèle is immediately at ease and selects sweetmeats for us all.

"We'll get something for Thérèse," she says, concerned to show she cares for her stubborn little cousin. "And Céline, you will visit us this Saturday, with or without your sisters! Come—wear your plum dress and new hat. The Maudelondes are away, but—Albert will be visiting us; he wants to meet you; he knows you paint and would hear your opinions on the Paris exhibitions."

She smiles; it is a fait accompli. Of course, I will come.

* * *

Albert Quesnel sits in the corner of the cluttered sitting room like a large, black spider. I have given my coat and new hat to Simone and patted down my hair and skirts. He sees me and folds himself upwards, then forwards into an almost indiscernible bow.

"My very great pleasure, Mademoiselle Céline," he says.

I offer him my hand. He takes it in his own and there is a moment of hesitation before he raises it slightly and bows further towards it. But does not kiss it. I feel myself to be a rare drink; a glass raised and lowered in ritual salutation. Before long Adèle and Lucie both come in and settle down for the semi-polite sisterly exchange of the Guérins. Albert discourses surprisingly well, after our awkward opening. He is an informed gentleman, and I find myself genuinely interested in his reports from the art world of Paris.

"The next exposition, Céline—if I may—promises to be of particular interest to those following the new light-centered portraiture set in the natural world," he says, his tone casual, inviting.

"Indeed," I say. "It seems young Monsieur Monet will continue to surprise us with his unusual brush strokes."

Drawing on my own recent visit there, I am more than able to keep the conversation going. Albert mentions the new art emerging from Giverny. Out of the corner of my eye, I see Lucie leaning forward in her tight day dress; and Adèle choosing rather to watch my reactions. She hopes to play matchmaker with this new caller.

"You are of a family truly blessed with religious vocations," Albert says. "Two sisters in the Carmelite monastery here, in Lisieux. What a great honor for your father." This I can't deny. "Yet his other three daughters remaining at home to care for him—what an even greater comfort."

"Not three for long, Monsieur Quesnel." Cousin Lucie can't help herself from joining in, like a quivering dot of light in our vignette.

"Surely you are not also called to the sanctified life?" he says, turning to me.

"We are all called to live the sanctified life, whatever our circumstances," I say to him, reflecting on many conversations I have had with Thérèse, and indeed with myself. "But it is my youngest sister, Thérèse, who has heard and responded to the call to Carmel. She enters there this year."

Saying it to him, I am stirred into a new sense of pride. I imagine painting Thérèse on the eve of her departure, a seated Thérèse, looking into the fading sky from the belvedere; a girl dressed in grace, giving her life to God. How would Albert receive this notion? As a symptom of delusion? But in fact, he is pleased enough with my earlier response.

"I am deeply moved by her commitment," he manages. "And by the spiritual and artistic gifts of your whole family." He hesitates. "Mademoiselle Céline, would you permit me to call on you for a further extension of our conversation? My soul benefits from your vision. Please do not deny me this pleasure."

I feel myself blush. Stupidly so, as my attraction for this man is negligible, compared with the pull of my soul towards light and canvas and painters' palettes. Yet it has been a pleasure, of a diversionary sort, to converse with him, and so I agree with a forced but gracious smile to his request.

At night in our bedroom, Thérèse is so quiet that I know not whether she wakes or sleeps. Perhaps she does neither, but is wrapped up in the jealous God who can't wait to take her. I imagine a man's breathing—Henry's, or Albert's—accompanying my thoughts as they dissolve into dream.

*   *   *

All too soon April is upon us. Uncle arranges for a final photograph at Madame Besnier's studio before she enters. Thérèse sits with her hair up, her hands folded, and her eyes full of anticipatory joy.

On the designated morning we attend Mass at the Carmel. The white light of Easter week makes the chapel shine; it is adorned with both sunshine and flowers. Behind the Carmel's choir grille are Pauline and Marie; I can neither hear nor see them, though I strain to catch a glimpse of a cream mantle and a whispered smile. Léonie fidgets with her dress collar. Papa looks straight ahead at the Virgin and her lamps. After Communion he bows his head as though it is the heaviest thing in the world.

At just gone half past eight, Father Youf gestures to us that Thérèse should follow him to the side entrance for postulants. She steps into the small passageway at the end of which is a heavy door. There is no external handle. She knocks. This is her dream come true.

This is the moment she leaves the world for ever.

She turns from Léonie to me, and I step forward for a final embrace. Her body in its dark blue dress and cape pushes itself against mine; I find her warm cheek and press mine against hers; I am crying, but I brush the tears up and back into my hairline; this is her moment, but oh! I have never felt such a tearing pain.

"Céline," says Thérèse, her voice bright with sudden fear. She does not say any more. I step back against the cool of the wall, my legs trembling and uncertain under my dark skirt. But no one looks at me. Thérèse has turned to Papa and, kneeling, asks his blessing. Our Papa kneels down before her in his long black coat, as though the weight of his loss is too heavy to stand. He lifts his shaking hand to the side of her face.

Then Uncle steps forward to ease him to his feet, while Canon Delatroëtte hovers over them, frowning. Thérèse rises, and at the same time the door opens, and she floats through it into the enclosure, and I think I see Pauline and perhaps Marie, but before I can make contact or mouth a greeting, the door is shut and Thérèse is gone.

Lisieux: Léonie

Gone. Thérèse is gone. Céline and Léonie remain. Alone, I know Céline may open any door she pleases. Léonie *non*. Léonie *non*.

Enclosure

1888—1890

In Carmel: Pauline

Mother Xavier permits me to be the first to greet her. We wait in the shadowy passageway; I know that Papa is receiving his little queen's farewell blessing. Then the door to the enclosure opens. My heart swells with pride, with a sense of achievement.

She comes in wearing her dark dress and navy cape and I pull her towards me. I am struck by her fullness, her warmth and her weight: my vast child fat on a world she has abjured. I am relieved to see her so sturdy; our ways are so hard at first. I breathe her in; she is baby-sweet still. Just slightly, she stiffens and waits to be released. Of course. The others. I kiss her lightly on the brow and step back as she smiles and then turns to Marie.

I glance through the side door out into the world. Papa, humble gentleman to the last, has stepped back, no doubt to offer further prayers with Céline and poor Léonie. But a shadow remains; I see Canon Delatroëtte stand square to the door. He clears his throat and I place my black veil back over my face and turn towards him.

"Sister Agnès, you have quite a family here now," he says in his hard, low voice.

"Yes, Father," I reply. "We are truly honored by our sisters' callings."

He sighs and I detect a fatigued irritation.

"Yes, well," he mutters. "You and your prioress have chosen to accept this schoolgirl into your order. Let us pray you don't regret it in the months and years to come."

In Carmel: Marie

Her blonde hair falls below her shoulders. She looks round-faced, but still somehow fragile. Her blue irises in their pools of white are huge; they shine. My heart twists with a profound joy and pain. I am, after Pauline, the second to embrace her.

"My little one, my goddaughter. I am so happy to see you," I say.

"Marie," she replies, her voice a whisper. I smell the hint of rose water on her skin; we are so unused to the world's fineries. I clasp her soft body to my own, as if trying to fill her up with warmth, and then release her.

Mother Xavier lifts her hand and soundlessly snaps her fingers. "We will proceed to the choir," she declares, just as she had to me. "Young Thérèse. Our Lord awaits you there."

Thérèse at once turns to obey this new, powerful mother in her life. Mother Xavier looks at her latest postulant with a sort of troubled love, already perplexed by her new daughter.

Lisieux, Les Buissonets: Céline

It is evening, and the light fades as though never to return.

By my side is my sketch book. I will not go to Madame Godard's lesson this month, but I am compelled to mark the day with my art, somehow. In the sketch book I have been drawing lines and curves. The lines resemble pear drops, tear drops, diamonds; shattered gems. Cross-hatchings of gray and black. Each stroke darkens, like a black veil falling over what had once been bright. I press harder than usual with my pencils. One I break.

Tom patters into the room and places himself desultorily at my feet with a noisy, impolite, doggy sigh. Papa's prized clock ticks away, obstinately, on the mantelpiece. Léonie is no doubt sleeping, but I am too agitated to follow her example.

There is a sound at the front door. Elise must still be here, as I hear steps and then the door opening. A man's voice. A caller for Papa? But Papa retired to his study immediately after dinner. It is his way of shutting out the loss. Perhaps our second cousins, the Maudelondes. Henry with his mysterious charm.

A gentle knock against the open sitting room door.

"Monsieur Albert Quesnel for Mademoiselle Céline," says Elise, her voice a mix of deference and curiosity. And in walks Albert; tall, dark, and gaunt-looking in the evening light.

"Monsieur Quesnel! This is an unexpected pleasure. Please, sit down."

And he does, in the chair beside the settee on which I sit with my open sketch book. He seems nervous, but perhaps he is just slightly breathless from his after-dinner walk. "Papa is in his study. I should—"

"Please, do not trouble him," says Albert. "Monsieur Martin is a contemplative man; I would wish to respect his nature." He risks lifting his dark eyes to mine, and offers a lopsided smile, which I return in kind. "You have been working on your art." He gestures at the open page with its mismatched lines. "You are dedicated to it. This is a wonderful thing, Céline."

And he smiles at me again, as though I am his great hope for the future of the cultured world.

I shut the book and clasp my hands together primly in my lap.

"May I offer you some refreshment, Albert?"

"Very kind of you, Mademoiselle Martin."

I ring the bell and Elise reappears with Papa's brandy bottle and glass on a silver tray. Albert pours himself a very modest measure. He smiles still, but his hands shake a little.

He settles back into his chair and asks me about my day, politely indifferent to the sparseness of our sitting room compared to that of the Guérins. I tell him that Thérèse entered Carmel this morning. He nods, as though this is a known event, a fixed date in the cycle of the liturgical year. And, it turns out, a good day to make a proposal of marriage.

"This is a year of great changes and brave decisions for your family. Won't you join me in making your own great decision and do me the honor of becoming Madame Céline Quesnel?"

And he gives his half-smile again, draining the small brandy glass and setting it back on its tray. Tom raises his head and quietly whines before lowering it back between his paws.

The grays of the evening swirl through the room and gather together on my sketch book before pouring themselves into my heart. My throat is scratchy and my eyes sting. I imagine pronouncing my marriage vows to Monsieur Quesnel in a gray gown, unpinning my long gray hair on our wedding night so that it falls about me, becomes me, my body vanishing and the hair collapsing like a dry nest to the floor.

I know that I cannot marry him. But where have I gone?

"Monsieur, such a kind, kind offer!" I must let him down gently. "I am so very touched and honored—if you knew what your words meant to me!" And the gray seeps into my mind, and I am stumbling in a fog. "But I am afraid I must disappoint you. I am so very sorry. Only this morning, I had determined upon a—a vow of celibacy! I have just written to my confessor who has been urging me to take this step; a small step, I know, compared to my darling sister, but one I feel I must take, in hope of one day securing my own certain calling, whatever that may be."

Even to me this sounds prolix, long-winded. But Albert has the grace to hear me out. Presently he nods, as if to himself, and rises.

"You do me no dishonor, Mademoiselle, and I am forever grateful for your honesty in this and all our intercourse. In fact, I had spent many hours in prayer this week before coming to you with my humble request this evening. It may be that the good God has spoken to me through you. I too have been meditating on the possibility of a vocation." His tone is even, but underneath, brittle. He moves towards the still-open door and gestures with his hand for me to remain seated. "Do not be surprised, Céline, if you next hear from me from the grand seminary of Sommervieu. And rest assured of my continued intercession for your happiness at all times."

And with this, he bows slightly, and is gone to his future without the prospect of a wife. Tom sleeps on, satisfied there is no need for him to accompany Albert into the hallway.

I sit in the encroaching darkness, with a dreaming dog, and wonder why everyone is called but me. It is true that Father Pichon once suggested I take a yearly vow of celibacy, but even this plan is suspended, the delay of an abstraction. In agitation my hands find my sketchbook and open it again, on a blank page.

A fresh page, I tell myself. I will see what might emerge in the empty light of morning.

* * *

Absence flows in to replace her. In our room, her copy books, stacked neatly on the desk. I leaf through them—brief sketches of faces and flowers, without the benefit of my own artistic training. Still, they are Thérèse and hold a kind of fragrance of her. In the bureau drawers, some linen and chemises. All owned by absence now. A hollowness scoops deep into my heart.

And Papa's too. His leg still drags from an attack of vertigo last year. I fear his fragility; my mind plays, unbidden, a foreboding of his death. I remember how Thérèse, years ago, had a vision of him veiled in a gray cloth. He struggles—to rise from kneeling in prayer; to sustain conversation at dinner; to remain living with his remaining daughters. Léonie is aware, under her glaze of indifference. We exchange glances, but who knows what they might mean?

Then one day he is gone, as abruptly as his convent-seeking daughters. Elise wakes me without my morning coffee, to tell me that Monsieur Martin is nowhere in the house. He has left no note and told no one of his plans. She is anxious; her mousey hair escaping her cap, and her pale face taut. I try to calm her. Papa likes to travel, to walk; perhaps he has gone out to fish? But his fishing rod and bag are still in their places in the conservatory. Perhaps, then, he is visiting a poor family in Sant Desir? But this suggestion rings hollow, even to me. It has been many months since Papa bestirred himself to active charity.

By the middle of the day, Uncle Isidore has joined Léonie and me in the sitting room. Reassured by his broad-chested presence, we speculate more fully.

"Papa fears another war," says Léonie, rather brusquely. As always, her blank expression doesn't fit the worry in her voice. "He told me last week that his weapons were primed."

Alarmed at this information, we check his room. His guns are in place, unloaded and on their wall brackets. Uncle Isidore strides back and forth across the sitting room floor, once knocking the low coffee table as he passed. I imagine how Thérèse and I would giggle if she were here and circumstances different. She has imitated Uncle so well before, incongruously planting her hands on her hips and lowering her voice: *Well, well, what have we here!*

Hours pass.

Finally, in the late afternoon, a telegraph comes. Uncle reads it, his pince-nez in place. I am frightened by the deep frown through which he regards us. However: "Louis is well," is the first thing he says. "He has been found in Le Havre. He is confused and unable to explain to the doctor attending him there how it is he travelled so far."

Léonie gives a little shriek and twists her hands together. "Papa is safe!" she says. "Will he come home today?"

"Is he able to rest there?" I ask. "Must he return tonight? Or should we go to fetch him ourselves?"

"I will go there," Uncle Isidore replies. "You girls will stay here. It will agitate him less and allow him to rest on his journey."

Léonie is satisfied with this reply. But something in Uncle's choice of words makes me increasingly uneasy.

Les Buissonets: Léonie

"Good Léonie," he says before he disappears once more, "You are my eldest daughter remaining in the world. You must have your say with the house."

He pats me on the arm before going up to his room. Céline has the eye for comfort and color, not I. But Léonie can sense the wounds. I know when a room is wounded, and when a chair is sad. Léonie knows about Papa's hurting heart.

Now his heart has wandered from his world.

His absence is an agony. "Must we tell Thérèse?" I ask.

"I will go to the Carmel," says Céline. "He will need their prayers."

She leaves, and I pray for Papa alone. I sense his lostness. I see his haphazard journeying as a zigzag slash of scars. Three days pass. I think of the blank time that comes after Jesus' passion.

The fourth day brings a letter:

> *Please send eighty francs.*
> *Yours in good faith,*
> *Louis.*

The mark is from the general Post Office in Calais. Céline finds the letter almost as upsetting as his departure. I tell her it shows good sense. I know not every request can fully be put into words. Uncle and Céline set off to bring him home together this time. Left alone, I sit down on his empty leather chair, wishing to comfort it.

I sense the flames before I hear Elise's screams. A toxic warmth, like a sweat, creeps under my skin and breaks through to its surface. The stiff gray stuff of my dress prickles. I cough and cough again, trying to shake off one of my fits of despondency. Then the screams come.

Les Buissonets burns.

Elise runs through to me. I smell smoke in her messy hair and maid's apron.

"Dear God, Mademoiselle Léonie! You must leave!"

She plucks at my sleeve, as I sit up, rigid, in Papa's armchair. But I cannot answer. My throat has turned to a burning coal. I must have fallen into hell. I am at fault. I am the fault-line through which the fire has come.

"Léonie!"

"I—I am coming, Elise." Somehow, I am standing. Elise pushes me through the sitting room door and pulls me by the arm along the hallway. Smoke is starting to fill the ground floor. My breath is scratchy and hard. The hallway has stretched itself into an endless corridor; like the cloister at the Poor Clares of Alençon; I cannot tell where it goes and if it ever ends. Endless burning, endless death! It is as much as I deserve. I wonder whether this will be my last thought.

Suddenly we are in the bright, cold, open air. Elise and I bend over, panting for breath. When she stands up her hair is loose and her skirts smudged, but she has returned to herself. She explains to me that a neighboring cottage had caught fire earlier in the day. Being of poor material and straw roofing, it was transformed into an uncontrollable blaze. Then the wind flung burning clumps onto the trees at Les Buissonets. The trees dropped their flames onto our roof.

I am horrified all over again. I turn and run into the pathways beyond Les Buissonets' entrance, taking the smallest and poorest of tracks. Marthe—I will go to her, take shelter. But oh—she has long been received into the good earth. I crouch like an animal in the dark. Hours later, cold and hunger bring me back.

It is the end of a nightmare. Céline greets me in tears at the front door, and I run like a child into her arms. The fire has been extinguished; firemen have attended and left, and Papa has returned, like me. He sits slumped in his armchair, attended by Uncle Isidore and Doctor Notta. They mutter together of fits and fugues. I hear the clink of the brandy glasses. I see the flicker of tamed flames behind the sitting room grate. I sink into a singed chair and listen to its sorrow.

Lisieux, Les Buissonets: Céline

The damage to Les Buissonets echoes the damage of its master. Papa raves. He has one foot in another world; a world of phantoms, demons, and pain. Doors slam upstairs and soon his voice is to be heard. Anger! Curse words he would never utter when sane. I listen on the landing to his barking interrogation of the nothingness in his room, imagining the shapes of these devils he confronts. My hands grip the bannister. I am more alone than he.

Doctor Notta attends. He is as discreet as one could wish. He says nothing of the sorry state of this home once filled with daughters and laughter, but climbs the stairs in his dapper black suit, doctor's briefcase in hand. He knocks on the door of Papa's room and promptly enters. The door shuts firmly behind him. From downstairs, I hear the murmuring conversation of two gentlemen, with nothing amiss except the intimate location of their persons. Then Papa begins his barking once again: a shocking staccato, where all his life he has been even-toned and gentle.

When the doctor emerges, all is quiet. I guess, from the open bag, that Papa has been given a draught. I show Doctor Notta into the day room and sit at an angle to him, smoothing my skirts. Léonie appears at the doorway, and after some hesitation, joins us, hovering behind me.

"Your father has had another attack. I have given him a sedative, which proved highly effective." His own face is gray and parched.

"Thank you, Doctor," I reply. "He has been very tired of late and these fits of temper exhaust him extremely."

Not to mention us, I add, silently.

"He will sleep for several hours," says Notta, "and afterwards you will find him much more tranquil. I will leave the medicine with you, and suggest you dispense a further small dose before bedtime. It will not do for Monsieur Martin to return to his agitated state." He looks quickly at Léonie and back to me, before licking his lips neatly and continuing, "Particularly when there is little help for you to call on in the night."

"Oh, what is to become of him? He has always been so kind to us," blurts Léonie, suddenly stepping forward.

"Indeed, he has," replies Notta. "And this is precisely why we must do our best to return his kindnesses. It is our duty to provide him with repose, with peace and tranquility, using all the medical power at our disposal." He stands. "I will visit tomorrow evening. I will leave more drops and a further prescription here meanwhile."

He sets a brown glass bottle on the table, scribbles on and tears a page from his notebook. Then, snapping his bag shut, he turns to leave.

The next day, and the day after that, all is quiet.

But the day after that Papa raves. He raves with his voice, but oh—far worse—he gains access to his guns and stands at the window, brandishing his heaviest weapon against an invisible assailant. Uncle tries to talk him down but finds Papa has locked himself in his room, as well as his own distraught mind. By the time the doctor arrives a certain calm has been restored, but all of us know that things will never be the same again.

Still, I did not understand quite how decisive Uncle Isidore and Doctor Notta would be. Within a week all paperwork has been completed and Papa is admitted as a long-term resident at the *Bon Sauveur* Hospital in Caen. He is diagnosed as being of unsound mind and of danger to his family if he should remain with us unsupervised. Therefore, he is to take up residence to immediate effect, with family visits strictly rationed. We must not overwhelm and destabilize the work of the good sisters there. The good sisters!

"But he was only trying to protect us," Léonie says to me, stiff with shock. I pull her to me, smelling her fear, and for the time being all her spiky resistance, and all my fiery impatience, melt away as so many petty impurities. I do my best to comfort her, and in so doing, try to soothe my own terrified soul.

At the Carmel, Pauline and Marie receive the news with visible distress. Then Thérèse comes forward and I have to explain to her that she will be an orphan at her final vows; that our dear father will be led where he does not wish to go.

She surprises me with her response. "It is his final trial, Céline," she whispers, after a pause. "It is his road to glory."

I do not contradict her. She has a slight smile and tears in her eyes. I see her as a timeless portrait, her pale face swathed in her white veil, the whole proportioned into little squares by the exactitude of the parlor grille. I close my eyes. The image remains.

A few weeks later, Léonie and I have been installed in a boarding house in Caen. Uncle Isidore makes longer-term plans for us to move in with him and Aunt, Adèle and Lucie, and blend in with their family's social and cultural life. Kindness and authority blend together in his soul's gruff palette, but his gestures, his brushstrokes, are one-note, unsubtle. I doubt that we will ever dwell in Les Buissonets again.

Caen: Léonie

Papa moans in a low voice as he is wheeled back into his room by a *Bon Sauveur* sister. Céline tells him that we travel to Paris with Uncle Isidore and Cousin Lucie next month. Then she tells him that his eldest daughter takes her life vows in the Carmel soon. His diamond, Marie. He nods and raises his hand in a shaky blessing. I would rather stay with Papa than journey to Paris, but neither he nor I are given any choice in the matter.

"Come, Léonie. There is nothing more for us to do here today. Papa must have his rest."

Céline links her arm in mine and leads me away from the great hospital building. We return, by prearranged carriage, to our boardinghouse in Caen. We share a room, twin beds with dull coverlets, and a thick window onto a small brown garden. All is ugly and discordant.

Sharing is unfamiliar to me. I have not shared my bedroom since my childhood years with Hélène. Céline is more used to the idea—but I am no Thérèse. Léonie does not gleam with holiness. I am no longer young. But here we are, thrown together in this long crisis.

Without speaking, we sit facing each other on our separate beds. We wear similar plum dresses. I guess my chignon, clumsily applied in the morning, is even more lax and loose than hers. I feel awkward and angular. Céline is soft and attractive. Her thick brows frame her creamy complexion. The sickly scents of the asylum remain in my nostrils—a blend of flowers and fear. Food will be served downstairs, and we should eat, but my stomach feels tightly knotted, just like my clasped hands. Céline makes no effort to move. I sense the terrible tiredness of us both.

Still we do not speak. The light gradually fails. Céline and Léonie dissolve into the night.

Paris: Lucie Guérin

Paris. The vastness, the sounds of the place! They enter my body and make it vibrate, like crockery on an unstable kitchen surface. At any moment, I might fall to the floor and smash.

Such is the condition of my soul. Papa and my cousins Céline and Léonie are unaware of my perilous state. Papa brings them to distract them from family sorrows—their sisters lost to Carmel; their father lost to the double confinement of *Bon Sauveur* and the prison of his mind. Sadness surrounds them like a dreary song.

Cafés. Galeries. Pavilions. Everywhere, worldliness. Danger! Fear! Céline does not see this, because she is an artist. She responds to colors, shapes, and lines. This is not even her first visit. She knows how to navigate the world. Léonie is aloof as ever, awkward even in her overcoat and bonnet, her jaw firmly fixed.

Everywhere, unholy celebration. One hundred years of France's shame: the bloody revolutions which cut us off from grace. The bloody sins for which we still atone. Papa ushers us past the streets which writhe into raucous life each evening. We go instead to the church of Our Lady of Victories, site of our family's particular devotion. We all light candles to the pearl-white statue whose head bears a slim halo of stars, and whose smile cured Thérèse of her childhood sickness. Here she is large and silent and—I fear to say it—apparently blind.

To be blind is to dwell in grace's safe shadow. What I have seen has brought down a pall.

Buildings, as though some demonic energy has scooped up houses of business, commerce, and bodily sin, and gathered them into a Babel of exhibitionism: the Paris Exposition. Here the gardens of Spain, and here the pavilions of India. Here a village of Africans who stare at Papa and me as we promenade on the far pavement, still visible from their barred gate. One dark-skinned woman in her sparse cloth garb follows me with a piercing gaze, grasping the grille as firmly as any nun in her parlor. My head spins, and my heart hurts for her trouble, for all their trouble. There is shame here, too. The shame is for us.

The Louvre. This great hall of art houses images of horror. Nudity! Flesh: the sins of the flesh. My own skin flushes and shivers at the exposure. Here are women without shame: arms languorously extended above heads, beyond chaises longue. Legs exposed. Thighs spread. The artist's studio is where these perversities flourish. The man paints, and the woman lies on the altar of his gaze, without the sacrament of marriage or confession, oh! My head spins with the thought. And Céline is schooled by these people?

Back to the *Galerie D'Apollon*. Gold upon gold in an echoing house of sin. Here the portraits are of the plump, worldly, indolent. I scuttle on over the broad floors like a mouse.

In the women's washroom, I push up my dress sleeves and pour cold Parisian water on my wrists. I am stained beyond washing.

Papa in his whiskers and jacket waits for me outside the plain black door. He sees I am concerned, but he cannot know how troubled. He takes my arm at the elbow and guides me towards the exit. As we walk along the hallway, he pats my forearm with his hand. He makes me feel safe as he always does; his breadth and stability anchor my fluttering thoughts. But despite his firm faith, I do not want to confide in him.

He whispers in confidence to me: "Is it your time, little one?"

I am not shocked by this. In our family Papa is doctor and medical almanac. But I shake my head and tell him I am only tired. There is no shame in the ailments of the body, and the female body is frail. But there is a great shame in unseemly sensuality, shame in abusing the vulnerability of others. I have never been brought up to be comfortable with this.

At night, I write a short letter to Mama. Then I refill my pen and write to Thérèse. I think of her in the cool of Carmel. Of her face, smooth and happy in the convent parlor. Of our years of playing hermits and blind beggars in Lisieux. I write as through in penance for enormous crimes, crying a chorus of sobs as I write. I have cut myself off from the devout life, and Thérèse has been protected when I—I have been ruined! I tell her that Holy Communion is a banquet from which I have excluded myself, and that I do not expect her to understand why I feel how I feel. I am soiled and shorn of song. I seal the letter in its envelope and am bereft.

Her reply is swift, swift as an answered prayer. I am so astonished at her admonitory confidence that in a surge of renewed hope, I announce to Papa and Céline that I wish to attend Mass at the earliest possible opportunity. They look at me as though I have burst into an aria.

Even now, my vocation is emerging like a crocus from the frost.

In Carmel: Marie

I watch Thérèse shiver as she sweeps the black and white tiles of the cloister floor—a task with which I am very familiar. I know the burning cold which attacks the hands, naked on the rough broom handle. How the freezing numbness spreads throughout the body until it feels as though one's bones will never again be warm, and all the surrounding flesh is so much cold jelly. It is November, and our Normandy winter is only just beginning. While

I watch from the entrance to the antechoir, Mother Xavier appears as if from nowhere—in reality, from the shadowy recess before the prioress's office—and stands before her newest novice, gesturing to the window ledges. I know without doubt that she scolds. My little sister kneels before her and kisses the edge of Mother Xavier's long woolen scapular in penance. Mother turns and strides back towards her domain, like a spider who has bitten and laid aside her latest prey. Unless I am mistaken, Thérèse wipes away a tear. I am amazed she does not sob out loud. I step forward to console her.

"Are you cold, Thérèse?" I cannot help myself; years of ingrained concern do not subside under our new regime. The prioress is cold in ways more than the spiritual. Thérèse seems to attract her attention: always her censure rather than any praise. Thérèse looks up at me, and just for a moment I think I see a blue tinge to her lips and a drawn look to her previously plump face. "Poor little sister," I murmur, drawing nearer to her. I carry a basket of scraps for mending at the evening's recreation but think to set it aside in order to embrace her.

Her eyes continue to seek mine. She gives me half a smile, but she does not speak. In fact, she places the broom aside and I realize she is about to prostrate herself, a vicarious penance for my breaking of our silence—where I intended compassion, I have merely inflicted further hardship. But then the bell sounds: the ring sequence instructs all professed nuns in the cloister and courtyard to use their full face-veils; a workman must be present. Thérèse slips into the refectory. It will soon be time for her to set the places anyway. At least she will be warmed by the heat from the kitchen. Pulling the great black veil over my own face I peer through its gauzy cloth and make my way to the garden sheds, where there is also privacy, albeit little heat.

I ponder the future of a nun who is so intent on becoming a living rule, of martyring herself to obedience, especially when we have a prioress so capricious that the other novices refer to her as The Wolf. Left to draw my own conclusions, I have long decided that even in Carmel, rules are for interpreting rather than blindly obeying—an insight I have shared neither with Almire, nor Pauline. One must be free to discern one's limits, even as a nun. Perhaps only little Mira would agree with me: Mother Xavier's fêted cat, who is even now rubbing herself on the hem of my habit; she who will neither obey any rules, nor tell any tales.

In Carmel: Pauline

She rebuffs me. I attempt to shadow her the way I did Marie, in these first clumsy months of postulancy and novitiate. She is assigned to setting the tables in the refectory and I follow her in, holding my pencil and paper in a pretense of stock-taking and cupboard-checking.

"We may speak; Mother permits it," I tell her, wanting to catch her downcast eyes, trying to smile. She does not respond. Not even to me. "Tell me how you find our life, my darling. Céline says you have written the most beautiful letters."

She ceases her activity of breaking the bread and placing a chunk at each sister's place on the wide trestle tables. She hazards a look at me, and though it is ostensibly serene, I feel stung by an obscure distress. What have I done?

"I am well, Sister Agnès," she replies quietly, though her face is pale. I bristle at the formality of her using my religious name, though I remember well how I clung to order and formality in my early years here—how, in truth, I cling to them still. She returns to her task. I feel a flicker of annoyance. I think what else to say to her.

"Did Mother Xavier permit you to use the fur-lined slippers?" I inquire. Uncle has taken on the role of generous guardian since Papa has become so unwell. Solicitous for Thérèse's wellbeing in our unheated cells, he has arranged for some items of comfort for her. She does not answer, but I sense an increase in tension as she moves to the other table. I contemplate offering to help her, then decide she would be happier completing the chore on her own. But inspired by Isidore's benefaction, I add, "You know, you could take an extra blanket from the bedlinen cupboards. It is no sin to look after—"

"Pauline! I am quite well. But I must finish my duties. I have a meeting with Mother before second collation. As you know, she does not care for unpunctuality . . . nor has she given me permission to speak to you."

At this she looks directly at me, and her blue eyes burn me like ice. I take a step back; I had not expected this. Tears, yes. Questions and requests for hugs and help. But instead, there is a sort of stubborn willfulness, something which I have never before felt from her with such force.

I murmur a platitude and take my leave without attempting to embrace her. As I return to the little procurator's station by the warming room, I think I see Mother Xavier standing behind the narrow window of her prioress's office, like a soldier with a bow and poisoned arrow.

Dream of Céline

I dream my little sister leaves me once again. This time, not to the enclosed sanctuary of the Carmel, but into the dark forest. It's evening. There is a chill in the air, and whatever foliage populates the forest, it emits an odor of metal and blood. Has there been battle here? I recall Papa's tales of when the Prussians came to Alençon. Thérèse, though, has gone, I cannot speak to her! A numbness comes to my face, to my right arm, as though a part of me has died. No one is about, and yet I cannot follow my little twin. Some invisible power holds me apart.

With all the ghastliness of nightmare, I know what is to happen. A single, dreadful scream. A sword-slash, supernaturally magnified. A plunge through her dress into her poor flesh. A severance of such finality I know it to be death. Thérèse has been martyred. Oh, but this is her dream! To leave her family and offer up her life for her God. To be cut down in battle; to be slain like a sacrificial lamb. Thérèse, Thérèse, think of those you leave behind! I am burning, but it is with envy as much as grief. Why can I not die in battle? I am embattled but snagged in paralysis, a poor caught fly in fortune's sticky web. I can't even scream.

Something stirs behind me. I turn around, and realize I am in the middle of the forest, not caught at its edge at all. A child approaches me: Thérèse? But no, it's a boy, about twelve years old, dressed in brown overalls and apron; a cobbler's assistant, I realize with my dreamer's knowledge. Look, he even holds his tools, a weathered leather bag and an awl covered in mud. But his face! Framed by dark hair, it's pale, round, vacant. I think he must be lost. With a sudden kick he tips me to the floor, as though I am the cheap statue of a saint. Then he kneels by my side.

I am paralyzed, but bizarrely ecstatic. He is going to kill me! The boy slams his awl into my throat. I am going to die! Then his small white hands reach into my face and start to gouge out my eyes. Exquisite pain! These eyes, twin vanities, will be scooped out and flung into the dirt; and I will be the most worthless artist in the world, but the finest of God's martyred daughters.

I awake. I am in bed, back in our lodgings at Caen. My numbed arm is folded underneath my fetal torso. My throat is raspingly dry, and my face pressed into the sour-smelling pillow: a failed Cecilia, unable either to sing or die.

In Carmel: Marie

Carmel holds us to the wheel of its Rule. The hours and days turn and oblige us to work and to prayer. We spin our own little stories out amidst its turning.

As the days get colder and shorter, so do the tempers of some of our sisters. We are a full house at the Lisieux Carmel, and the skills and temperaments of those who form our family are far from perfect. But some things are beyond petty—they are ridiculous! Squabbles over who must tend the pathway to the hen house. Ill-tempered clattering in the kitchen. Whisperings over the disordered books hastily replaced on the antechoir's shelves. Worse still, Mother Xavier herself seems to relish the discord. Requests for her to resolve an issue are likely as not to fan its flames. I wonder how far Thérèse herself has become aware of this.

In the workroom I come across Sisters Aimée and Marie-Joseph literally tugging at opposite ends of a piece of bedlinen.

"Sister, this linen is needed for the infirmary!" hisses Sister Aimée, her forearms bulging with the strong muscles of those accustomed to manual work.

"I am the linen mistress and I say they are neither aired nor ironed!" hisses Sister Marie-Joseph back, several tones higher and louder.

For a moment I feel I am back at Alençon or Les Buissonets, where I would have bustled in and stopped this nonsense, whether it was a spat between Céline and Thérèse, or the bullying of that awful Louise who made Léonie's life such a misery. But instead, I clamp my mouth shut and inhale the wax and incense of Carmel. Then I remember what I can do. I walk—I almost manage to glide—up to Aimée and Marie-Joseph and drop immediately to my knees, and from there prostrate myself onto the dusty wooden workroom floor. Surprised that another sister has approached so close without their noticing, Aimée immediately responds to my gesture by falling to the wooden boards also. Dust specks swirl in the afternoon light. They rise up as Marie-Joseph joins us on the floor. We all rise too, and I bow deeply to my superiors in this stiff religious life, before leaving to recover myself in the garden.

A few days later I am folding blankets in the linen storeroom. Again, I overhear Aimée—this time she is gossiping with Marie-Philomène. I still myself and try to catch her words.

"That great oaf of a girl! To be wealthy doesn't help when it comes to weeding the vegetable patch! It was bad enough when they let in that older one, Marie," says Aimée. I swallow and burn from the double insult to our family. "I like our little Sister Agnès, I have to say, but Marie—what a contrast. Dreamy like some witless wife in a novel!"

"*She* never had a vocation anyway," replies Marie-Philomène. "I heard she was bundled in here by her confessor. They didn't know what else to do with her. At least you can't say that about Thérèse. Now there is a soul with a calling. But they say the father lost his mind when he gave her up."

At this, I feel my face burn and my eyes start to sting. With an effort, I remain silent.

Aimée harrumphs in reply. There is the sound of ceramic jugs clinking together. The jugs for our cells, holding cold water for the quick splash of face and hands I have come to relish before our hours of community prayer. "Well, Sister Thérèse certainly doesn't have a calling for housework. I caught her picking up the breadbasket for the refectory tables this morning. She'd managed to trip and scatter the bread all over the floor."

Marie-Philomène poorly suppresses a snort of laughter. "She's clumsy alright. And not the slimmest novice I've ever seen either. Shouldn't she be wearing the broken bread around her neck?" This is one of our traditional mortifications following spills or breakage.

"I would imagine our dear Mother Prioress would be willing to make her eat up all the bread she spilled as a punishment." Aimée pauses here, for thought. "If she finds out of course. She is not kind to her new recruit. Who is zelatrice this week?" This despised, rotating role among the professed sisters involves making a note of whoever has disobeyed a rule, no matter how trivial, and making this transgression known to the prioress. Not that we aren't all obliged to accuse ourselves of trifling sins in the weekly Chapter. But the zelatrice, true to her name, goes above and beyond in causing shame for the culprit and salacious entertainment for the rest.

"I don't know. Bernadette, I think."

"Well, she won't spill the beans will she—unlike her goat of a novice."

The nuns both laugh, and I sense they are getting ready to move on. But before they do, Sister Marie-Philomène speaks again. "You know, I saw her in the oratory last week. It was in our spare half hour before evening collation. She was in there touching up that fresco she's been doing since she got here, the one with all the angels. She didn't see me, but all the same, she was smiling this most beautiful smile."

"Well, perhaps she was pleased with her painting," dismisses Aimée.

"Perhaps. Though I think . . ." Marie-Philomène trails off with the effort of this thought, "I think that she has something. I have never heard her complain or cry. And I like her face. For all her puppy fat, there is something very calm about it. Very . . . kind . . ." Struggling to articulate her insight, Marie-Philomène gives up.

"If you say so, Sister," says Aimée, with an exaggerated sigh. I doubt she will ever be receptive to such thoughts anyway. The two women lapse back into silence as they head out into the cloister.

At Carmel: Céline

In the visitor's parlor I spend precious half-hours with Thérèse. She is coming up to her profession; to taking her life vows. Her soul spins, and I sense it. At one moment she is full of childish joy and writes her invitations with a flourish, imitating the wedding invitations of Adèle and Francis. At other times I sense an intense loneliness in her heart. And then she asks after Papa and her voice quails, and her face, framed in its snowy veil, is full of sorrow. She will be as good as an orphan at her veiling ceremony. But I have something to show her, both image and text.

"Here," I say. "The Holy Face, a devotion from our Parisian Carmel."

She takes the card; stark and monochrome, unlike the pallid daubing of some holy art I have seen.

"Thank you," she says, then takes a sharp little breath. "He suffers, Céline—look how bruised and broken He is, and how beautiful."

I nod; I have spent many lonely evenings contemplating the face; sleeping, or dead; His eyes are closed. It is a portrait that I long to paint one day.

"How like—" She speaks slowly, as the thoughts are formed.

"How like Papa," I finish for her. Our eyes meet through the grille, but I cannot sustain her gaze. "And look, He gives us bread from His word." I pass her the text I have copied from Isaiah. The suffering servant. It is He; it is Christ; it is Papa—

"It is for us—it is for all of us," says Thérèse, having read the passage and folded the paper into a smaller and smaller square. And she adds in a whisper, "It is for me." Sensing that these words mean more than they seem to, I remind her of her long-cherished name in religion: Thérèse of the Child Jesus. She bites her lip. After a pause she says with disarming sweetness, "You know my desires are limitless, Céline. As for my name at profession, I will take it all—everything he offers."

As I return to the easy comfort of Uncle Isidore's, I wonder what new calling I have ignited in her, and what share I may have in it, wherever I am finally directed to live out my days.

In Carmel: Marie

A knock on my cell door.

"Deo Gratias!" I call in response, as I am required. I am writing a letter to Thérèse, to slip inside a holy card I have made for her profession. The door is pushed open and Thérèse herself slips in, white veil glowing in the evening gloom, dark habit loose as a nightgown. "My darling Sister Thérèse," I say, trying not to appear concerned. But she is unsuccessful at hiding her own agitation. "Whatever is the matter?"

"Marie," she begins, her lip beginning to tremble. I get up and embrace her at once, and for once in this house, she yields. She lets out a half sob—I know she is exercising control in limiting the outburst. She is thinner than I thought. I hold her gently at arms' length and contemplate her face. It is pale. Her eyes are rimmed with red.

We could be back at Les Buissonets and she a young girl with scruples once again. But it is not a scruple so much as one great fear which crucifies her now.

"I have no vocation, Marie!" she manages to say. "I have been distracted—I have been afraid. I blaspheme if I say my vows, knowing all my flaws. Whatever shall I do? Uncle will have to collect me, as Papa cannot. I have let down Mother Xavier again—and again. She will never accept me. I am not sure whether she ever has."

With this, the tears recommence, and she can no longer speak. My goddaughter weeps with her desolate thoughts; at only seventeen years of age, hers is an exquisite desolation.

In the end I take her hand and lead her out of my cell. We go downstairs and stand in the cloister walk, gazing at the heavens.

"Mother Xavier tests you because of our life. She tests you a great deal, perhaps even too much, because you are a strong soul." She looks at me full of a pain I think I understand. I want to tell her that she must be kind to herself, to draw solace from her own inner world. But this is no time to cultivate sedition. "If He does not want you here, He will tell us now," I whisper. "But look how many times He has led you through doors that would be locked to any other soul. Your distractions are so slight I believe they only charm Him. Now you are seventeen and of an age to be His spouse."

We wait in the soft September evening. There is no thunder, no lightning; in the distance, I think I hear birdsong. I wonder whether to tell her that I have never experienced anything like her own ardor—I have barely felt my way in religious life, dimly perceiving one step in front of another, as if holding up a candle that flickers in the night. But this evening is not about me, and perhaps that is the best gift of all.

After what feels like many minutes, her hand squeezes mine and finally relaxes. Her breathing is easier; soon she will be released from her turmoil—I know my goddaughter.

"Perhaps you are right, Marie," she says. "Mother Xavier tests me to strengthen my soul. Papa is absent. But God is not. And besides, if I adopt the name of the Holy Face, I must accept that His eyes are closed."

She looks at me as though I have enlightened her, and I am relieved, but later I am bemused by her additional choice of name, the way she weaves innocence and suffering into a coat of arms. The romantic design is all her own: my little Sister of the Child Jesus, and of the Holy Face.

In Carmel: Pauline

Her hair is cut and falls in its full gleaming length to the floor in St. Baume, our little clothing room beside the choir. The stiff toque and cloth wimple are placed on her shorn head in readiness to receive the full black veil of profession; the white attached for the last time. Sisters Bernadette and St. John help her prepare. She has written her profession day vows on letter paper and folded them inside her robe, in the pocket near her heart where her profession crucifix will also be placed. She will go to the choir for a half-hour's silent prayer, and then upstairs to the chapter room where strewn flowers outline the space on the floor where she will prostrate herself, before Mother Xavier accepts her vows. I pull her to me for a kiss and cannot resist cupping her face in my hands for a brief moment of intimacy. When she does not push me away, I know my own heart begins to be healed.

She looks me in the eyes; her gaze is not searching, but full of an emotion partway, perhaps, between fear and love. "Pauline, pray for me," she whispers.

"You are ready," I whisper back, releasing her to the Carmel. "He calls you by your name."

When she has gone, I collect her swept-up hair, and twist it into a soft rope, inhaling as I do so the scent of childhood, flowers, and precious memory.

In Carmel: Marie

In the chapter room, she prostrates herself in the cruciform shape of those who are to take final vows, and I have to stop myself running forward to scoop her up and ask her where it hurts. Instead, Sister Bernadette intones a hymn to the Virgin, and Sisters Marie-Joseph, Marie-Philomène, and Aimée cast their handfuls of half-crushed rose petals: sheer grace, sheer love, shimmer in the air.

At Carmel: Léonie

Doors open. Doors close. The paralysis in Papa's legs is complete and irreversible, and so he returns with us to Lisieux. Uncle Isidore will be his guardian, and we his nurses. Uncle and Céline make extensive arrangements to bring him to the Carmel. His cloistered daughters greet him in the visitor's parlor, the grilles pushed back for close family members who are ill. Céline steps forward, but I feel unworthy. I stand behind him as he trembles in his invalid's chair. Pauline is the most composed, but I think Marie and Thérèse are shocked, now they see his condition for themselves. Thérèse wears the black veil of a professed nun. She is nearly eighteen.

He makes a great effort himself and lifts his right arm, pointing upwards. "In heaven," he manages to say. Until we meet in heaven.

The grille and the visitors' doors are shut firmly behind us.

Trials

1890 — 1895

In Carmel: Pauline

The chill seeps into the bones of Carmel's sisters and into its very bricks. As the year ends, there is no respite to be found save the weak comfort of the warming room. Mother Xavier has the sense to suggest that each nun take an extra blanket to their cell; I suspect that the more ardent sisters do not avail themselves of this opportunity, Thérèse being one of them. How she does not shiver herself to death in the choir is a mystery to me. Her teeth chatter intermittently, despite the resoluteness of her jaw. Wrapped tight in my own habit and mantle, I sit in my choir stall and fret over her youth.

Worse is to come as influenza sets in. Old Mother Rose-Chrétien is the first to die. Her death is as gentle as her life. But no sooner have we laid out her body in choir than Sister Fébronie takes ill. This is swiftly followed by another sister, and then another; the whole community succumbs. Marie coughs and becomes feverish at recreation, and so, more worryingly, does Thérèse. Mother Xavier beckons to me before we file in for Compline.

"Sister Agnès. A crisis is upon us. I myself feel increasingly unwell. Please, take two blankets to your cell; this is an order; we cannot afford to lose your strength and capability." She coughs as though to prove her point. "I do not wish to emulate our blessed sisters of Compiègne. There must be no community martyrdom here at Lisieux."

And indeed, there will be no executions here, but before long nearly twenty nuns have taken to their beds. Sister Aimée and I minister to a recursive row of sweating, shivering sisters. Thérèse shivers too but insists on playing her part. She rolls up the sleeves of her tunic and folds up her scapular, as though we are harvesting hay in the meadow.

After a week it is obvious that this harvest is of souls. On New Year's Eve, Sister Marguerite dies, delirious, calling for her mother. Doctor de Cornière certifies the death while holding a handkerchief over his mouth. On his way out, he offers his respectful greetings to Sister Thérèse who is about to turn nineteen.

The next day it is as if she has had a premonition. She goes into Sister Angelique's cell as though in response to a ringing of the community bell that only she can hear. When she comes to me her expression is solemn but markedly at peace.

"Our Sister Angelique has left us for Jesus. She was wearing her mantle and great veil. I closed her eyes and lit the blessed candle. Shall I inform Sister Elisabeth?"

Elisabeth is our new turn sister; already we rely on her to run messages and make arrangements. But how sad for us to plan another burial. I try to muster some words of comfort.

"What a birthday you are having, my darling," I tell her.

She inclines her head and when she looks at me, eyes clear and chin slightly lifted, I have no doubt of her soul's mettle. She no longer needs my coddling. She has not needed it for many months; she is conforming to the Rule in all its simplicity and strength. Looking out onto the cloister garden, I see the falling snow start to settle, its pure crystals blanching out the foibles of the past. I make a note to write to Céline of how our little sister has grown into one of the strongest nuns of Carmel.

Céline: I long to be with her again, to share some human warmth and the gifts of her artist's vision. But like Thérèse, I must be patient: our intrepid sister-in-the-world tends to Papa's prolonged debilitation, to Léonie's religious vacillations, and otherwise lives according to the pleasure of Uncle and Aunt, passing through her own trials there.

La Musse: Céline

Since Isidore came into his inheritance, we share this great Normandy holiday home and its forest of a garden, with the Maudelondes, our grand second cousins. Usually, Isidore and Aunt Véronique like to alternate with the elder Maudelondes, whose grown-up offspring, our childhood friends, take their own vacations elsewhere as often as not. Léonie and I have tagged along in recent months, poor sisters from a little offshoot family that is both an embarrassment and a badge of spiritual pride. But suddenly, Léonie leaves us once again for Caen. She tries again with her vocation; always stubborn, neither succeeding nor rescinding her hopes.

Left as sole Martin daughter in the world, I find myself marooned at La Musse. Before I know it, I am playing an unspoken game of romance with Monsieur Henry Maudelonde. The young man's eyes have followed me for years, as mine have noticed him. He trains for the law and promises to do well in life. He politely kept his distance when Papa had his first attacks, and now asks smoothly after his welfare, careful to minimize any distress for me. I assure him that Papa is well cared for and is easier to look after in his paralyzed state. It is true: his agitation has lessened, and a kind of beatific passivity is now his normal demeanor. He is taken to the gardens by day, wrapped well against the elements, and sleeps long and calmly at night, thanks to the doctor's drops.

Henry is a man of the world. And yet I like him; I always have. He is strong, slim, and comfortable in his own self, in a way that Albert Quesnel was not. His hair is a lustrous chestnut brown, and he sports a moustache and a smart cream collar. In the garden room, he crosses his legs and leans forward in a flirtatious manner that is at the same time entirely polite.

"And what of Céline's illustrious career? Does she follow her heart in following her art?"

"I do continue, Henry. I have been—encouraged—by my small exhibition at Madame Godard's studio."

Secretly I am proud of the compositions I have completed these last few years. Their subjects are modest—simple figures and still lives—but I have worked on their light and color until I see something of love in them.

"You have sold your paintings?"

I blush at the suggestion. My body prickles with embarrassment and pleasure. "I have not," I reply.

Though it is true that some suggestions were made there of a future contribution to a Paris salon. Papa himself, before his confinement . . .

I surprise myself. Have I not yet given up this dream? I press my lips together, then cast a glance in Henry's direction. He returns the smile I have not realized I am offering him.

"And your famous camera. Is this another of your many creative talents?"

So, he knows about my latest acquisition. Of course, our cousin Lucie has also been learning photography. Perhaps she has told him about our joint enterprises of family portraiture. I hope he is not put off by young women who roll up their sleeves and handle boxes and tripods, and are neither afraid of splashes of sulphide solution nor the darkroom's mysterious processes. I smile some more in spite of myself.

"I have taken some plates of the family," I admit to him. "I do not re-gard them as art though—merely markers of face and figure. I prefer my oils. It takes a painter to describe the soul—"

I blush, having given too much of my private thoughts away. But Henry merely raises his eyebrows and nods. He leans further forward, clasping his hands together.

"You use the latest lenses?"

"I have the Darlot, yes."

We talk further. It is extremely pleasant. He does not ask me of my cloistered sisters, but of myself. The bell rings: Aunt Véronique requests my company at afternoon tea. Henry, ever the gentleman, stands. He turns to me before he goes.

"Would you do me the honor of sitting beside me at dinner tomorrow night, Céline? I have already suggested to Uncle and Aunt—"

"Of course," I demur without thinking. How easy it would be to place my hand upon his sleeve as he departs.

Caen, Convent of the Visitation: Léonie

Mother Marie de Sales is my former novice mistress. She looks at me in the wood-paneled parlor.

"Oh Léonie. What shall we do with your yearning soul?" Yearning. The same word my only friend at the Poor Clares used to describe me. "I cannot think other than that you are called to be among us," she continues. My heart leaps a little, despite my life of failures.

"I have always wanted to be a true religious," I say, using my old, awk-ward phrase. I am sure I sound absurd, but this is the case in community or in the world. If I am known and accepted for the absurdity that I am, then perhaps I can be happy.

"And what of your father? Does he give permission?"

I bite my lip, but I have prepared my answer. "He is very ill, Mother. Too ill to be our guardian. My Uncle, Isidore Guérin, has promised his per-mission, if you accept my vocation as a true one."

Mother looks at me as though she searches still for the right response. The boxy frame of her Visitandine's veil accentuates her forward angle. Her face is soft, but her gaze is sharp.

"Is this the time, Léonie? Is this God's time for you to come to us?"

I want to answer her, but Léonie has never been good at telling the time.

La Musse: Céline

"It is indeed a cold season, even for our hardy Normandy," observes Henry, leaning closer towards me than is strictly necessary; I smell his cologne and the subtle musk of his tobacco. He has taken off his jacket and sits beside me in a waistcoat and loosely fitted shirt. The dining room of La Musse is full of laughter and affection, despite the chill outside.

Both aunts are engaged in lively conversation further along the table; lively but vacuous; their tinkling laughter echoes the clinking of our knives and forks. This dinner is an extended continuation of nuptial celebrations: Cousin Adèle and her bearded beau, Francis. She looks prettier than ever, her delicate features and widely set blue eyes all the more alluring against her beautiful teal gown. Francis expands to fill his seat with a benevolent masculine presence. His voice booms across the table. He is largesse personified.

The scallops are served with a mushroom-colored sauce. Isidore's avuncular voice can be heard as he summons the sommelier. I drag the tines of my fork around the expanse of my plate, imagining that I am ploughing a miniature field.

"Yes," I reply, somewhat belatedly. "And I hear it is worse at Deauville. Freezing fog is a hazardous thing."

I stop myself; I do not mean to adopt the tone and topics of a querulous spinster—certainly not in front of Henry, who persists in his impeccable courtship of me.

"And your dear sisters? Warmth is in scarce supply at the Carmel, I think."

I frown; but his concern seems genuine, so I cannot take offense. "Yes, it is hard for the Carmelites. I do not think that their sainted Spanish foundress anticipated the Normandy winters when she devised her rule. But they are well. Pauline sends the community's regards to your dear mother as well as the happy couple—"

"You must miss your little Thérèse. She too is well?"

"She feels the cold, I know. Pauline wishes she would take advantage of an extra blanket or a foot warmer, but" I shrug, "she is young, and believes herself strong."

Henry pauses before continuing to dine. I lift my heavy crystal wine glass and take a sip of the strong, warm liquid. Lucie once confirmed to me that red wine has blood-strengthening properties. I imagine pouring red paint onto a wide, white canvas, infusing the whole with its clots and tints. Under my own rose gown I feel hot, a little damp. But Henry is speaking again.

"You create art with your meal, Céline. More proof of your gift. I hope you continue to nurture it away from the dining table."

"You know I do, Henry. I have my little studio at Uncle's in Lisieux."

"And from where do you draw your inspiration?"

"From the world around me—from past paintings, those of the masters—"

"And the new holy pictures from the studio of St. Sulpice?"

I glance at him. He looks at me. I cannot tell: Does he tease, or merely inquire?

"I—they—are very popular. I am sure they do much good to many souls."

I think of that studio's increasingly sugary portraits: simpering children and vapid Madonnas. But I am too proud, perhaps. Such art—if it is such—is successful; even austere Carmel receives their latest catalogues with enthusiasm. Thérèse has fashioned her own holy cards from some of the worst exemplars. I shake my head. My opinions should not be shared. But Henry has turned to his other neighbor, a friend, I believe, of his mother, and I hear him guffaw at some tale of childish inconsequence. I lift my glass again, fortifying myself to endure the rest of the meal.

As we file from the dining room Henry approaches me once more. In the shade of the hallway, while some neighboring ladies depart in their carriages, he gently touches my upper arm. Immediately my whole body comes alive. I turn my face to his. I observe his strong chin, his moustache, his light brown eyes, his rather thick lips, as in a daring portrait. For a moment all my other senses cease, as I contemplate him. Then I feel his proximity again and hear him murmur, "I asked Aunt Véronique if I could kiss her beautiful niece. She said she would never forbid a connection, if it was to your agreement."

I am stunned by this speech. And yet, it is what I have been waiting for—my whole life, perhaps.

Before I know it, he has led me into the deeper shade of an unoccupied sitting room. He closes the door behind us—gently, silently—the noise of departing guests is muted, but still audible. He places his lips upon mine and his hand comes to rest upon my back. I close my eyes and am as if swept along by a great wave. Washes of color crash over my soul and flood my body in a way I have never known. My world dissolves and reforms as a fiery entity, a comet or shooting star, defiantly brilliant in the face of a cold dark cosmos. My heart is as if plunged into a pulsing sun. Then I return, partially, to the moment and hear him exhale through his nostrils, and feel his lips pressing harder and coaxing my own to open against him—

Henry.

It is too much. I break the kiss. He releases me from his embrace, and I take a step away from him.

"My dear Céline," he says—it is a strange tone he has, between a groan and a gasp, "I must beg—"

But I raise my hand. I do not want to hear him beg.

I do not know what I should say. I know I should speak. But what is language in the midst of a torrent? From the look of him, Henry has now reached the same conclusion. We stand facing each other in the dim light of the sitting room. And then the moment is lost. Adèle is in the hallway calling for me; we are obviously the last to depart and by now they are anxious for their conjugal privacy. Conjugal. Married. A state of life to which I am called, or not called—I do not know. I think of Thérèse, her cool little hands holding mine through the parlor grille. I smooth down my hair and my skirts, and with a final awkward glance at Henry, tall and half-obscured in the low light, I reach for the door.

I sleep little after this encounter, my heart a flailing parchment in an intemperate gale; my thoughts smudged paint, a distressed palette of emotions. I do not share my quandary with anyone. I cannot.

A few weeks later I resume my correspondence with Father Almire Pichon. I outline my current state of life and remind him that I am the unworthy sister of three Carmelites and a Visitandine postulant. Before I am next due to meet with Henry and the Maudelondes, Almire has arranged for me to solemnize my vow of celibacy, which I make before the old priest at St. Jacques's Church after morning Mass: I am unsure even that he knows my intention, such is his mumbling in the confessional.

Now I am a vessel sealed. But oh—what flammable elements have I discovered within my own poor form.

In Carmel: Pauline

I am given my new role after the chapter meeting, where I made sure to award myself a bouquet of egregious faults. With my familiar headache pressing like an inner crown across my brows and the back of my head, I accept the results of the ballot and step forward to become prioress. Though he is far away from Lisieux and from all of life's cares, I seem to hear Papa speak to me, just as he used to.

You are Paul the prince just as much as Pauline the pearl!

Mother Xavier presents me with the prioress's crozier. She will retain the title of mother; indeed, by the fixed angle of her jaw and the narrowed slant of her gaze, she lets me know that the office itself will return to her before too long; in six years perhaps, or more likely three. She has ruled this place like an empress, and ceding authority, even for a single term, is anathema for her. And yet the sisters have seen, perhaps, in me, somebody who will attend to the Carmelite Rule as though her life depends upon it.

"Mother Agnès. May Our Lady guide your heart, Jesus your soul, and the holy prophet Elijah your will," she says, before stepping back into the gathered ranks of our community.

I barely remember to bow to her, and then I do so with all the fervor of a new postulant. I offer a quick prayer to Elijah. Make me as a man like you, I pray. So that I can take up the sword of leadership, I who am so small and scared, always, at the back of my mind.

As prioress, my duties are more mundane than spiritual. I am given the keys to the large office, with its imposing desk, where I shall become bookkeeper and chief business correspondent. And I must appoint a mistress of novices, traditionally a position given to our outgoing prioress. Even as I enter the prioress's office for the first time as Mother, I wonder how I will solve this first, most immediate conundrum.

There is a knock at the door.

I straighten up. It must be Mother Xavier. Perhaps she wishes to distill some wisdom into her successor. Perhaps she already wishes to start her work on my fall. I prepare myself to begin a new period of tense diplomacy between us. But it is not Mother Xavier.

Thérèse's face appears round the door, and she steps humbly into the room. She is pale, and she seems pensive, but she smiles at me, and I step towards her in gratitude. She permits me to take her in my arms, and it is I, the smaller woman, who feels enveloped in her love.

"You have shown yourself worthy," she whispers to me, her woolen habit folding itself into mine. "He calls you by your name."

She echoes my own words to her on the day of her profession.

"You appear like an angel to comfort me, Teresita."

"I will always help you. Marie too. You are our shepherdess!"

I pause. It is too easy to exchange pious platitudes, and I do not want our moment of genuine connection to be dissipated. The weak evening light shines in through the office's narrow window. It just touches the feet of the statue of the Virgin who graces the mantlepiece opposite.

May Our Lady guide your heart.

I have an idea. I gesture for my sister to sit down, and I come to join her on the chairs before my prioress's desk. I take her hand. It is cool.

"Sister Thérèse. May I ask you a discreet favor?" She acquiesces with a slight nod of her veiled head. "Mother Xavier will take the role of novice mistress by default. But we have several novices currently, and—" I decide to risk a minor indiscretion, "I wonder if she is entirely suited to the challenges of the role. If she were to have a young nun helping her, one who has recently navigated the waters of the novitiate herself, what a blessing it would be to—to the community." I squeeze her hand. "Would you take on this role, my sister? There may be certain, ah, temperamental issues to bear in mind . . ."

But already she has understood my whole dilemma and answers it directly. "Of course, Mother Agnès! I am, I am your—your little brush. You and Mother Xavier will paint the broad strokes as directed by the Holy Spirit. I am no such artist. But as your little brush I can fill in all the gaps—I know these little sheep of yours, having so recently been one of them. I am no artist, but I love to paint—I would love nothing more than to paint the colors of holiness according to your outline." She is smiling again, although her eyes are cast down, as though she is receiving an order. I am about to thank her when she looks up at last. "Oh Pauline!" she says, as though saying something daring, but absolutely right. "Are we not like Mama and her lacemakers? I will work the smallest patterns, knowing you are safeguarding all the designs." Impulsively she leans in and kisses my hand, and then rises and makes to leave, bowing briefly as she exits the door.

I stand up myself and move over to the window.

"A start," I murmur. Though the start of what is still to be determined in my mind. The start of a soul's rise to glory is the silent answer I give myself, and I do not think for an instant that this soul is my own.

La Musse: Céline

July. Papa sleeps. He has fallen from bed once, over a week ago now, so we have Uncle's kind servants, David and Rebecca, watch him constantly. Isidore has suggested a new bed, one designed for invalids, but I say it will disturb him when he has become used to his remaining little pocket of the world.

In the early morning, I write to Thérèse. It is a task made strange with the subject matter I wish to broach: my possible future without her. A future which, despite her abandoning me for Carmel, she will not countenance without a struggle. I have already experienced the effect of her fierce prayers, stumbling numbly about on the dance floor at Henry's engagement soirée. I swallow down the bitter fact that he found new love so easily.

This time it is not a question of marriage and family. I accept I have a call. But might it not be the case that a conflicted soul such as mine is called to work out her vocation in the world? I have Father Pichon's latest letter open on the writing desk before me, dipped in its shadows, even as I date and inscribe my own endearments:

> *Céline, great sacrifices are required for those who wish to travel the world for the salvation of souls. I cannot promise you the martyrdom you long for at the Mission in Canada, but neither can I exclude it. One thing is certain: your path is unique, and so must be your cross.*

My darling sister, I write. Then abandon my pen and put my head in my hands, feeling the strain of my tight cream cuffs. The heavy clock on the side cabinet ticks. I decide I must say something and strive for a balance of generality and hint:

> *I fear, in my heart, I rely too much upon your graces. Oh! Thérèse. I have been thinking that I must prolong my separation from you, if only to make our heavenly reunion all the sweeter. Forgive me. Your Céline who loves you.*

I do not think for a moment that she will accept this proposed course. But I have no more time. Today I am indeed to be a voyager, spreading my wings wide, if only in the grounds of La Musse itself. My box camera and its tripod await me downstairs, like a patient servant, an apprentice.

Sometimes, although I shall never admit it to Father Pichon, art can indeed be a salvation from distress. Not for Papa: he is beyond creative expression now. He can only offer himself, his near-completed life, in all its colors and tones. But for us, the remaining younger ones, a project has been set into motion. Lucie and I have not always been the closest of cousins. But she is talented. She sings like an angel, as well as throwing herself into this new art of the photograph. This morning we embrace and share a conspiratorial smile, knowing what images will follow.

Adèle and Francis will join us. Francis is so good-humored, his moustaches almost twirl of their own accord at the prospect. And Father Joseph! The good Doctor de Cornière has let his priested son come out to play. Father Joseph is in fact the experienced one, having visited the New World. But I am the artist; I set the scenes; I conjure the tableaux. We are "going to the Andes." In the clear eye of the camera lens, the many lush acres of La Musse are exoticized, as, in a way, are we.

As far away from Carmel as it is possible to imagine.

Farewell! Stout Uncle Isidore joins in the first photograph, shaking Francis's hand as we depart the grand doorway of La Musse, travel cases in hand. In the cases are cloaks and provisions, as though we were off on a real holiday. Lucie and I wear similar dresses: full-length and tasteful ivory, with deep blue cross-body sashes minimizing our bosoms but accentuating our waists, all small. Adèle's dress is similar but of slightly duller material: the dress of a married woman. Here we all are, reveling in the monied habits of secular leisure. Aunt Véronique cannot keep still, despite my telling her more than once about the importance of holding her pose. She stands at the top of the steps to the house and keeps turning her head to survey us all. She will come out as a whitened blur, a woman without a face.

Farewell, La Musse, farewell. One day soon I shall be saying that to you in earnest. Although to what adventure, if any, I do not yet know.

Off we go to explore one hundred acres of verdant ground; ground transformed through our fancy, and through the artificiality of the glass plate, into the very Cordillera Mountains! There is laughter. Francis leads the way, shooting gun held aloft. Adèle and Lucie follow him with little rivulets of merriment and song. Julie, on her half-day away from toil in the kitchen, follows along. I stroll, for a while, with awkward Father Joseph.

"A glorious day," he observes. His voice is thin.

"A beautiful day indeed," I say. "But you must have experienced true heat in Chile; far greater than this."

He nods as he walks. "Ah yes. God's earth is not always so pleasant for us missionaries. Our adventures must be all for Him, or we risk a scorching!"

I am not surprised his talk turns pious so quickly. He is little at ease with the ladies, despite his travels and his learning. A scorching? It's hard to imagine him succumbing to sinful temptations. He must be a very literal man.

"Ah, how are your dear sisters?" He cannot help himself inquiring, though I had hoped for a day away from talk of them.

"They are well, Father," I am obliged to reply. "Although we all think ceaselessly of dear Papa as he comes to the end of his . . . earthly pilgrimage."

Father Joseph is comfortable with talk of impending family death. He offers me a selection of pious platitudes. I suppose that he has experience of such situations. They are common, of course. Everyone needs a priest at such a time.

I make a mental note to avoid his ministrations when Papa's exile ends. Bridges. Rivers.

"Let's start here," says Lucie. "Let's get on the bridge and make up a story. I know! Let's fish. Céline, borrow Francis's gun. You can shoot!"

So we do. I set up the camera, with its polished lens, pushing the tripod legs down into the rich earth. Francis helps me with the equipment, needlessly, but he is a man and likes to oversee our endeavors.

"Careful Céline," he advises, cheerily. "Keep your beautiful dress as spotless as your soul!"

He beams at his own clumsy compliment. I smile back at him, having wiped my hands on my handkerchief and stowed it away in the little hip pocket under my sash.

"I'll set up the glass plates," I say. "Julie, could you hold up the lens cap on my signal? Let's pose on the bridge as Lucie suggests."

I feel shy asking Francis for his shooting gun, but he presses the long, cool weapon into my hand and guides me by my elbow to where the others stand over the sluggish water.

"Closer together!" says Lucie, eyes bright, as though she conducts a choir. "Father Joseph, lean over the bridge and imagine you see flying fish. Adèle, here—take the net, ready to scoop."

Adèle takes the proffered net but stands rather stiffly, a residual, default resistance against her younger sister. Lucie doesn't care; she gestures me into the center of the group and pushes me against Francis, who seems suddenly huge and warm in comparison to his travelling entourage. Lucie poses, pointing with the whole of her left arm to the water. Pressed between Francis and the bridge rails, I clutch the shooter against my body, then tip it away so it points to the water, in parallel with Lucie's extended arm. But I keep my face turned towards Francis, mutely aware of his physical proximity. He beams at me. His left hand touches my body. Our eyes lock and we smile. I am suffused with a warmth like an electric current rippling up and down my sash and spreading over my breasts and hips. Despite myself, for a fleeting moment I think of Henry, and realize that this is what it is to be a wife. This is the life I have already given up.

We hold the pose. Julie is expert at counting the required seconds.

Afterwards I work hard to disguise my dazed emotions, as if I had looked directly, and unwisely, at the sun.

*   *   *

And then the sun goes out. Within a week of our photographic excursion, Papa is dying. His hair and beard are already blanched in death. His breath is ragged, irregular. He no longer looks or speaks. I dip and wring the cloth and press it often on his brow. I think that from the slight relaxation of his breath every time, this is comforting to him. Francis visits briefly every hour, lifts, taps, and hums. That is his trade. Adèle, too, although her presence is a peculiar sort of absence. She is a proxy sister, a phantom of my real family. The others are all gone.

I pray, after a fashion. Then I look at him, my moribund father. I now assist with his second birth, the long years of illness having come full term. I have a feeling that I must in some way push him out of earthly life, and into heaven, as the completion of my role. Papa: strong as a giant, gentle as a mother. His face shines. The face I have washed with my cloth and my tears; for twenty-five years with my tears. I unfold the damp squared cotton, half expecting to see his image on it. The whiteness of his hair and beard. A suffering God.

When he dies, I sense a shower of gold dust sighing its way up to heaven.

I take his photograph and develop it without Lucie's fluttering help. He is utterly still: it is an excellent portrait. His hooded eyes closed. His face all white and light. On his chest, the heavy crucifix from his bedroom at Les Buissonets; it anchors him in his final sleep.

Caen, Convent of the Visitation: Léonie

I have become Sister Thérèse-Dosithée of the Visitation Convent at Caen. My angels in heaven—Aunt Dosithée, and now our dear Papa—seem to smile at me. Their prayers make up for our divided family here on earth. Céline comes to my taking of the habit, but is unhappy the whole day. I see her plump face pinched at the lips, as pinched as could be.

Still, her face is not pinched like mine. Her jaw does not jut.

Even now my skin begins to itch.

As a Visitandine I once again rise at five-thirty, having slept seven hours through the night. The order is kind, kinder than the Poor Clares, kinder than Carmel. As I am a weak soul, it is kind to me too. Chapel and quiet are interspersed with work periods and recreation. The scent of candlewax and lilies sweetens my heart. Our convent is like an open shell, with prayer radiating from the choir stalls. One day it may be my privilege to sit within those stalls. But I am just as content to be a novice, polishing the pots and pans. One day I may tend our sick sisters as I did Marthe. It is only when I dream that I think I am back at school. But at school I was expelled for failing to keep the rules.

Two, three. *Two, three.* Numbers piled up, stopped, collided together. A white pain like a lance to a boil. Bad dreams taunt me in the kindness of the night.

Thérèse, however, loves that I am here.

When she was little, I would sing her songs and hymns. My cracked voice pleased her. I was like a bird feeding her chick. Her lips would take little bites at the words. Now I think it is she who feeds me with her letters; her words are soft and sweet so that I can digest them. She tells me to forget myself and remember only Jesus. She reminds me to renew my resolve with each breath, and each heartbeat. Oh, if this were my only task, how happy I would be. But the community's prayer book is heavy in my shaking hand, and the strict novice mistress's orders come thick and fast.

"Sisters, we must be diligent in the service of Our Lord. One of the ways we do this is by practicing alacrity at our prayers. The service books guide us through the Divine Office. We must honor and follow this guide, set by our foundress in her wisdom and mercy."

We novices rustle our papers and prayer books.

I see myself failing. Sister Thérèse Dosithée struggles to understand the fast-flashing pages. They hurt her with their flight of words. My fingers pull the pages over and over—clumsy, at fault.

The eyes of Mother Marie de Sales are on me. She raises her brows, very slightly.

Léonie, you have lost your place. My fingers rise involuntarily to my headband.

The itching intensifies. I think that a ribbon of red-raw skin must frame my face more boldly than a wimple.

I have lost my place.

Worse, I have lost something of the faith of my family, my sisters of blood and community. At the Mass I stare as the priest raises the white flat sun of the host. I see nothing but a tasteless wafer. I taste nothing but old paper. I know this thought is very wrong, but it stretches like a shadow over my poor faith. I scratch at my own soul, trying to wake her.

Lisieux: Céline

And now I am spinning, spinning, like a top free from its leash. I visit the Carmel and, walking alone to the parlor, feel a huge mesh of pain in my heart. Thérèse grasps the grille and implores me with her stare, black veil flung back, her face urgent with hope. It kindles the same urgent hope in me. She says little but bids me fit my hands over hers and pray in a trembling silence.

Later I speak with Pauline. She is the expert. "I do not want to presume," I say to her. "I cannot expect miracles."

Yet of course this is exactly what I expect. After all these years, it is practically my birthright, should I wish to claim it. And suddenly, I do.

Pauline's look is studied; her face has its sharp look. Does she doubt my vocation, when Thérèse never has? Is she embarrassed by the stream of blood sisters to follow her into this sanctuary? She reads my mind: "A fourth

Martin sister is not, for all of the community, a welcome event, Céline. After Thérèse . . ."

"Who has been exemplary, or so you tell me."

"She is an angel," replies Pauline, drawing herself upright. Her voice is clipped, precise. "But nevertheless, there was friction at the start. And now once more we push at the rules, we seek to bend them for family members." She sets her lips firmly; they are a bar to her heart, just as the parlor grille is a bar to the community beyond it.

"Pauline—I mean, Mother Agnès—I know you are right. I'm a tag-along and I can't be given full rights. But, oh! Pauline, if you knew how I felt . . ." Here I stifle a tear, a hot streak of self-pity and frustration. "I am sick of the world. I am so tired. I would accept any position. Pauline! I would be a postulant forever, even wearing those hideous blue bonnets until I am an old woman!"

Pauline smiles: she can't help herself. But neither do I help myself with such remarks. I try again. "Surely you need another sister at the turn, along with Elisabeth? With my knowledge of the world, I could interact with it to your benefit; I could shop, clean—"

"Oh, you will do your share of cleaning Céline, never fear. But I hope for something a little better for you. I am proud of you, and of the sacrifice of self you now hope to complete in Carmel. You have suffered and loved for us all, little sister. I will speak to our choir nuns and find a way forward. If nothing else, we need your art. I wonder even if you should be allowed to bring in your photographic materials."

At this my heart leaps.

"In this modern world," she continues, "your skills could supplement our portrait work and would bring great pleasure to the sisters. Well," she corrects herself, "some of them."

"I would do whatever I could to serve the community," I assure her, formal again.

"And of course, Thérèse has set her heart on you finding your vocation among us. You know she would be your novitiate angel, and in all but name direct your soul here? You would not find this . . . uncomfortable?"

Just for a moment our eyes meet.

"I know it. She has written me the most beautiful letters. She is a part of me. Her wisdom would complete my calling."

"Humbly said," concedes Pauline, though she continues to look at me as a problem to resolve.

I go back to Uncle Isidore's and recreate my prim sister's features in a deft sketch. *Agnès the Merciful*, I write underneath. Then I go downstairs for some strong wine, and find a letter from Henry Maudelonde, and his new bride. They have returned from their tour of southern France. I gulp the wine and feel its numbing flood inside my chest and through my suddenly shivering body.

Two days later I receive word from Almire Pichon.

Fly, then, to the harbor where He bids you seek your salvation. You have labored long in the field; He bids you refresh yourself with joy.

This is recapitulation. For Marie, the flight to Carmel was at his bidding. For me, it is a disappointment to him. Such is the misdirection I arouse in men, and they in me.

Adèle pretends to be short of breath. She has always done this, since childhood, when something displeases her. She straightens her back and pats her hair, looking distinctly unrelaxed on the sitting room chair.

"This is rather sudden news, dear Céline."

I hear her out. I am rash, I am hasty. I am an ingrate, after all the months Uncle and Aunt have devoted to my wellbeing. Lucie will miss me; it will put her development back for years. I am practically committed to the Christmas parties. Plans have been made. I fade away before this noisy wall of worldliness.

"And Céline, surely you want to at least experience a little freedom, a little fun, for once in your life? Francis and I would be so happy for your company. And I know we are not the only ones. Henry and Hélène, Aunt Brigitte: you are so cherished! Please don't let us down—yourself down."

"Adèle, my dear cousin. I am so sorry. But I have no choice: a vocation is a sacred calling and can no longer be deferred."

I parrot pious words, unsure that I believe them myself. Adèle knows it. She will not hear them. She wants a friend, to balance her married life with the continuity of female companionship. She turns away, defeated.

"Your cousins—all of your cousins—will be very sad," she whispers.

Dream of Céline

The day before I enter Carmel, I dream that I arrive at my apartment in the rue de Rome. Berthe, the maid, shows me to my room where my valises have been placed. My camera and my box of palettes and brushes have been delivered too. The art box rests on a large side table the color of dark sand. The room smells strangely, though not unpleasantly; a sharp, musky perfume. Perhaps it is of varnish and Parisian tobacco. None of the walls are walls, but grilles with long dark curtains drawn across them. When Berthe opens the window shutters, raw light fills the room. Different to the light at Lisieux, yet not the stained city light I was somehow expecting, and holy, yes, blessed and blessing me in its own way, which must also be God's. I quiver in response.

I turn again to find there is no shortage of mirrors. I consider myself in the nearest one, in my black travelling dress and gloves. My face has a new sheen to it, a tone, though pale as always, that I don't quite recognize. My features are soft, but my eyes match my brows, firm and dark. I am twenty-six years old, a spinster, and an artist. I have come to Paris with the knowledge and backing of Uncle Isidore and the blessings of our late Papa before he lost his mind. I have come to follow my dream and my calling, and to paint the heavens, my ringless hands clutching my brushes.

I have come against the express wishes of Thérèse.

An envelope on the side table. I open a letter from Henry to find a single pressed rose: deep pink and full-petaled, with a single black thorn attached to its stem. From Thérèse, I have received nothing.

I haul out my easel and set it up against the light, select my brushes, and mix my paints. I paint myself and Thérèse as we were in Madame Besnier's photograph; side by side, my body an elongated promise, and she holding up her rope as though it were a noose. I paint us again and again, creating unknown colors to depict a nameless pain.

Lisieux: Léonie

I have been expelled. Like a stillborn lamb, I am pulsed out from the Visitation before my final vows, before my hidden life properly begins. Mother Marie de Sales, my one-time friend, stands firmly at the door. It opens and I fall, flailing, back into the world.

The world receives Léonie back like a familiar bruise. At Aunt and Uncle's house, I am terribly alone. Céline has flown to Carmel. My clever artist sister has gathered her talents and vanished. Cousin Lucie flutters through the house like a lost butterfly, desperate to follow Céline into the monastery, not sparing me even a glance. Uncle is pained at his own daughter's vocation. He is just as pained at the absence of vocation in his clumsy, hopeless niece.

I visit the Carmel and sit in the chilly visitor's parlor. I am back in my dress: the tight velvet bands and puffed shoulders I hate. I am no lady and have no right to parcel myself up as one. My lank hair is gathered up. I took pleasure in pulling it tight at my temples. This is one mortification I am allowed. My reddish scabs throb, as though I have played clumsily with a crown of thorns. I sit, a visitor. Always a visitor. The walls here are high and white. Opposite me the great double grille, black squares within black squares. I am in a prison of my own. A prison of exclusion.

The inner boards clank back. First Céline. She is a Carmelite postulant, and I am a nothing. We have traded places since the time of my entering the Visitation. There I was the bride and she the guest. She speaks but it is a mere noise. Céline does not have the sweet tones of Marie and Pauline. Her spirit always had more salt to it than theirs. And yet she has become one with them, finally. I think of Henry Maudelonde and his new bride, and for an instant imagine Céline as that woman. A multitude of Célines splay out in my mind, as though they were a pack of playing cards. Painter. Nurse. Wife-and-mother. Teacher. Sister. Genius. Bully. She finishes speaking, and means to be kind, but I cannot meet her gaze.

There is movement behind the grille. Pauline and Marie. Pauline's neat step. Marie with a kind of swish. I smell a mixture of wax polish and boiled vegetables, and see Marie wiping her hands with a cloth. Pauline has come from her prioress's desk. Perhaps they have met to discuss me first: Léonie the schoolgirl who must leave and leave again. And then I sense Thérèse. She glows rather than steps or rustles, and I imagine her soft skin against my own sharp features. Tears like spilled soup drop onto my lap.

In Carmel: Céline

In no time at all I am a novice nun, utterly drowned out in white. White down to my ankles. White collar tight as a dog's. White cuffs, chaining the wrists. White my face in the sheen of the sacristy plate. Bernadette bids me take a discreet look. White my blanched heart. White my knuckles and nails.

The community prays and I prostrate myself. White and a veil of gauze placed on my head. White the candle: a straight, slender bone.

I have given a general confession and am absolved from my own inner world.

White lies, white lies.

In the refectory, a great bouquet of lilies is placed at the end of the bench where I am to sit. I look at the card. It is from Henry, with his warmest regards. Lilies for the marriage table. A waxen betrothal.

A flicker of white fire. A blenched flame; weak blade without sun, without earth.

Thérèse comes to me in the courtyard, holding a glinting thing. "Céline!" she says. "This silver sword is yours."

It is a prop from a play, she tells me. She is, in a reversal of our previous roles, my protectress and guide. She will teach me how I must fight and die and still continue to live.

I grasp it for dear life.

Discipline

1895—1896

In Carmel: Céline

Another night burning. My face pressed against the rough pallaise. I dream, and in my dream, Henry presses his cheek against mine, and my skin burns from the roughness of his bristles.

"Now," he whispers, "you will never know what I could have given you for Christmas."

His voice is a blurred whisper. The sound of my own is nonexistent as I try to respond. Then we are on a bridge at La Musse and my hands clasp Francis's rifle. I think, *This time I will shoot it, and the bullets will ricochet along the river until they are beyond the bounds of place and sound.*

"You are ill-rested," says Thérèse at our scheduled meeting. It is early afternoon, and after the stodgy meal too early to be called dinner, my mind is slipping and my body twitching with exhaustion. So, I sit with her, in the antechamber of her cell, aware of how my white veil contrasts with her superior black, and do not feel like talking. The door to her inner room is just slightly open. A streak of sunlight spills through it onto the antechamber's wooden floorboards.

"Have you reported to Mother Agnès?" she inquires. I shake my head and bite my lip. She is to all intent my novice mistress, and I must listen to her experienced voice.

"Then you shall do so immediately before recreation this evening. You have much work to do, Céline—Sister Geneviève—and I do not mean sweeping the refectory floor."

"I'll do it," I mutter.

"Look on this as a sweet opportunity for you to practice self-discipline. The harder it is for us to control our own tempers, the more Jesus likes us to try."

I stare at her. She stares back. Her gaze is as opaque as her veil, but she wears a very slight smile. She seems to catch my thoughts.

"For example, your expression. Here is something that is simple to do: adopt an expression of peaceful composure. And yet it is very hard too. But consider how this simple, difficult thing can be a work of charity in a community of nuns."

"Thérèse, I fail to see—"

"I know! I too failed to realize the effort it would take to raise a smile. But think—God sees us and longs for our loving response. Our sisters see us and all the while they may be hurting in body or soul. Through these hurting sisters, God needs us. More than ever, Céline! Remember, when I was so weak that Christmas—"

"You were marvelous. I have never forgotten it."

She looks at me more seriously than I intended her to. "It wasn't me, Céline. I was given a gift." She stands up and, taking my hand, bids me rise too and face the little statue of Our Lady in the corner of the room. "Let us ask her, Céline. Let us pray you are given these gifts too."

We stand a moment in silence. I imagine Our Lady looking at us: two little sisters, holding hands just as we used to; seeking a favor. But I struggle with this new Thérèse, so lucid in her purity. We are together again, but our souls are far apart.

The door opens slowly, and novice Sisters Anne of the Trinity and Mary Magdalene come in. They line up behind us, falling automatically into place for what seems like a communal act of worship of the novitiate. Barely missing a beat, Thérèse begins a Hail Holy Queen. We all join in, my voice loud against the soft piping of the others.

In Carmel: Pauline

The rap on the prioress's door is so imperious that there can only be one visitor.

"Deo Gratias!" I call, bracing myself for—it is difficult to say in what way I have provoked her disapproval, but disapproval it certainly is. I run over my recent administrative actions: a nervous assiduity has kept me to all the written tasks of my role as Mother Prioress. Nothing in the intricate running of the Carmel has been left to chance: I have overseen budgets, building work, the progression of novices, the appointments of hebdomadary, bellringer, zelatrice, and tierce. I stick primly to my obligatory monthly conversations with every sister, absorbing the petty minutiae of their inner lives and doling out a myriad of spiritual platitudes. Where I lack Mother Xavier's flamboyant personality, I have kept rigidly to the Rule. But I continue to feel too small for my office: even my voice sounds thin and girlish in this room, still so indelibly associated with her, rather than myself.

Mother Xavier flings open the door and strides towards me, her habit flapping around her. I rise from my desk, never so aware of my lack of height. Unconsciously, I clasp the symbolic prioress's key that hangs from my cincture, willing its hidden iron into my soul. I see her face redden as she starts to berate me.

"Pauline, what in heaven's name do you think you are doing?!"

"Mother Xavier, I—"

"You will not answer back to me, *Sister* Agnès!"

The insult is crude. And it riles me.

"I am, for all my many faults, Mother Prioress of this community," I snap at her, surprising us both with the force of my anger. "I beg you, with respect, to honor the Rule of our order and address me as such."

I cross my arms over my scapular, seek to dampen down the insistent thudding of my heart.

Mother Xavier tilts her head slightly backwards, as though she is a horse refusing a hurdle, or a fine lady assaulted by an unpleasant smell. The nostrils of her aquiline nose flare in distaste. She will have her say. "You, Pauline—Sister, Mother, what you will—have brought our Carmel into disrepute *all on your own*. Whatever were you thinking of?! You cannot disrespect our chaplain. He is the guardian of our souls! You place our life at risk. Never mind in the next world, I'm thinking about this one!" Her voice booms.

I would not have been surprised if she had spat at me here. But she does not. Instead, she continues to stand stock still.

I begin to understand the foundation of this particular altercation. I sink back into my chair—my prioress's chair, safely behind the large, wide desk—to consider it. Mother Xavier must have spoken to Father Youf; she had no business doing so, but of course the two have a long history of official discourse, and it would be surprising if their regular chats had not continued in some way. And the subject of their conversation must have been my recent budget review. And now the reason for her attitude is plain. I have reshaped the budget; I have made cuts; I have sought to make savings; taking my responsibilities as prioress seriously, I have been frugal, and I have been firm.

I have, in particular, cut the excessive discretionary funding for the chaplain.

In my review I noticed it had increased by two thousand francs over the last three years. This seemed misapportioned to me, and I had taken a mathematical pleasure in returning it to the basic stipend it had previously been. I made my calculations with a smart gray pencil and savored the complex chart of rows and columns which bloomed, like a trellis, with the flowers of my planning. Even as I completed my plans, I thought how proud Mama would have been of my painstaking work.

But it is one thing to make plans and another to coordinate their execution. Mother Xavier is speaking again; her voice rises once more to a confrontational pitch. I hear myself answer, my voice becoming more direct, less subservient. Inside I am quaking.

"You are a disgrace to your family, Pauline!"

"I am a Carmelite and I obey the Rule of this house. You—"

"I should never have let you enter! You were too old, too malformed for our life. And see what family misfits you have brought in your wake."

This slur on my blood sisters causes me to gasp.

"I came according to His call. I act according to His word. My sisters—"

"Your sisters are the least of my problems with the Martin clan. It's *you* who are the problem—you weak mouse! You, among all your pathetic tribe, need the support of the priest. You are frightened to cough! And what do you do?" Mother Xavier is now directly opposite me, leaning into the heavy desk. Without looking down, she picks up a sheet of paper, which happens to be a letter from Uncle Isidore, and rips it violently in two. "You prevent him even from having his morning coffee. Oh ho! He will take some convincing to absolve you now." Satisfied she has hit home, she makes as if to sweep out of the office. It is a mercy: my shaking is surely visible by now, and my mouth too dry to remonstrate further. But she cannot resist one last hissing stab at my soul. "And Agnès, I counsel you to go and confess your utter cowardice and unfitness to lead us."

She has gone. Silence reverberates like the aftermath of a slap.

I sink back into my chair and put my head in my hands. The probability that Mother Xavier will move on from this confrontation far sooner than I does not console me. I am shivering. I have disgraced the office of prioress, and I have disgraced myself.

That night, I undress in the dark and take the discipline in my cell; a practice I have been discouraging among the other sisters. As the little whip's hooks catch and tear my back, pain's white fire blenches the ongoing fear in my mind, that God flashes His ire through His more seasoned superior, who will return soon enough to her rightful domain.

The next day I find a folded paper pushed under my cell door. It is from Thérèse.

> *I love you so much. Every trial you endure burns as an offering in my heart and the heart of our Spouse. Every tear you shed, every beat of your heart, saves souls!*

The words are clumsy and profound at the same time. After a few moments, I refold it and place it carefully in the pocket under my scapular, next to my heart, beside my vows of profession, and a little blonde twist of purloined hair.

In Carmel: Marie

I watch our worldly Céline as the initial rush of being here fades for her. As after any intoxication, she will be left with heaviness about the heart, perhaps a sense of frustrated regret. I make quiet arrangements to encounter her in the kitchen.

I am preparing the baskets of bread to accompany our midday meal, which will be the usual thick vegetable soup and cheese. She enters in order to wash her hands and fetch the broom. She catches a glimpse of herself against the vast silver pans in the center of the worktable. She pauses, no doubt appalled at her distorted reflection, and seeing me watching her, grimaces. I laugh, and in doing so, allow her to laugh a little too. I signal that we may talk.

"I will never be at home in these brown sacks we are obliged to wear," Céline confides, exhaling as she does so. "If our bodies are made in God's image, why must we reduce ourselves to looking like beggars?" Céline is Céline—I hear her out. I doubt she feels as free to express herself in front of Pauline, or Thérèse. "I no longer feel beautiful," she finally whispers. "And I am convinced my soul is even less attractive than my body." I would tell her that I think she is beautiful, but it is not my eyes or appraisal she thinks of. If I were to write a story, Céline would be the bold heroine of a romance.

"You miss Henry," I tell her, after a short pause, without expecting her to deny or acquiesce. "It is normal. We are women. We all bring our lost lives into the Carmel with us. It is their sacrifice which makes us strong. This is what He asks."

I gesture to the statue of the Sacred Heart—I partly know and partly guess how much she suffers from this sacrifice. Of all of us, it is Céline and I who have noticed men; men who are flesh and muscle and blood, warmth and gesture and gaze. And though I do not say this aloud, Céline bites her lip and nods as though she hears me anyway. I decide to make myself vulnerable, but not through physical prostration.

"And Almire. What of him? Does he still speak of seeking French souls for his mission?"

She stiffens slightly, then raises a hand to her white veil, unconsciously thinking perhaps to push back her hair. Do I surprise her using his name? I have called him thus in my heart for long enough.

"I do not hear from him. He remains in Canada, I think. He works hard, far too hard though, Marie. His sight is poor."

"I knew as much. He once told me he had four hundred letters to write in a week."

Céline raises her dark eyebrows. "He is gifted. It comes at a cost. But," and she thinks of me, perhaps for the first time, as a friend rather than a mother figure, "you and he were close. That will never change. We deal in eternity here. The past remains, like a photographic plate—or perhaps you would say a letter in its envelope." I think of the letters that flew between us. "He was your director first, before anyone else in the family. You drew him in. He drew you here. Whereas I think that, in the end, I only baffled him."

"He has a special gift," I tell her. "He molds his hand to the soul he directs—even yours—and makes his words fit her world." Céline nods. She has her own doubts and desires. "Don't be distressed at who you are," I tell her, perhaps rashly. "God loves you just the same." She smiles again, a little easier with herself. "And what, after all, is sacrifice, if we do not have the clear sense of what we are giving up? For me it was always nothing more than a dream, a romance in my mind, but you came so close to—to the blessed state of matrimony."

She looks at me now as though wounded, and I question the judgment of our conversation. But then she smiles, and it's a genuine smile, even though her brown eyes gleam with un-spilled tears.

"Thank you, Marie," she whispers. And then she adds, "You have had to make your sacrifices too."

After she leaves, I sense the relief of a chafing I did not know I felt. I think, for the first time, that I am no oddity here, after all; how can I presume to know the hearts of my female companions, the hurts and losses that paved their way to Carmel? To love and renounce that love is a spiritual path that might lead to a heaven of sorts—here, we are practiced in the arts of love and absence. We bleed together and we grieve together. But we continue to love. This is, in a way, our calling. I continue to prepare the refectory bread, feeling my belted tunic and scapular lighter than before.

That evening, I write him a letter, the first in a long time. He is a man, yes, and I am a woman imprinted with his voice.

In Carmel: Céline

For all my sacrifices, I have one unique role: I am the sacristan of faces and forms. Pauline, true to her initial promise, has appointed me Carmel's photographer, duty-bound to record our feast days and professions and general activities.

"She should give you the cellar under the sacristy," Mother Xavier suggests, and I wonder whether, although she is out of office, she yet considers herself the prime subject for my studies.

Pauline agrees, and Marie helps me set it up. I am not immune to the tacit disapproval of Sisters Aimée and St. John, and many of the others, who likely think it a Martin family vanity project, if they have any understanding of photography at all. I am given cracked basins, a dusty cabinet, a spoiled trestle table, and an old oil lamp to find my way in and out. The room smells of dust and damp, and soon, of the sulphide solution that draws each image from its glass plate. Thérèse visits me there one evening at my invitation.

"It's my new darkroom," I explain to her. It's a warm enough spring day, yet I think she shivers a little. I wonder whether she would like to know my process but decide against explaining it for now.

"It will be nice to think of you working here, while I prepare the vessels in the sacristy," she says, taking my hand. She is really cold, and I place both my hands over hers. But she is thinking, and carries on speaking; seeing the occasion, perhaps, as an opportunity to teach as much as to be taught. "We will both be preparing a place to be filled with light, Céline! You with your science of light draw images from hiddenness—I polish the vessels in preparation for them to receive our God . . ."

I embrace her, seeking to impart a little warmth. This is more like the sister I love. "We must work together, if you are willing," I say, inspired by an idea. "Together we can make something for Mother Xavier's profession anniversary; the important one, fifty years—not next year, but the one after that." Privately, I relish the chance to work with my sister on a long-term project that is *not* the painful reformation of my soul. "You can write the verses, Thérèse. I will take the photographs with my poor old camera. God willing, we will find the time, little by little."

She smiles, broadly, at this, and I smile back in relief; she is genuinely interested. I think we might have a bit of our childhood alliance back after all, creeping in like sunlight through battened-down hatches.

Meanwhile I set up my work. For all my humble words to Thérèse, I have a good box camera; Madame Besnier herself would have little finer, and I think that my twelve-year-old self would be pleased to see me now, at my photographic work within the enclosure walls. My initial efforts—set up in Carmel's little meadow, a respectful distance away from my first subjects, are hardly definitive compared to Cousin Lucie's and my own theatrical set pieces at La Musse, but my confidence still blooms with what I start to achieve. The camera fits twin glass plates, so each occasion allows my subjects to pose for two exposures. I place the plates upright or lengthwise depending on my intended composition; clean, clear glass, facing outwards. Behind the camera, I slip under the dark cloth—I joke it is my future profession veil—and carefully lift the lens cap, sometimes enlisting another sister while I slip into the tableaux I have created. "Hold still," I like to say. I take photographs in the cloister, the courtyards, the meadow, and the chestnut walk. The sisters hold still for nine seconds. Except sometimes they don't, despite their hours of training in the art of contemplative stillness.

No matter. I retreat to my drafty darkroom when the opportunity next arises. The more I work at developing the slides, the more I think of Thérèse's analogy of preparing the vessels in her beloved sacristy above. I roll up my voluminous sleeves and pin back my veil—sometimes even removing it from my scraped-back hair in the privacy of my work. I titrate my commercial salt solution into the water and pour over the plates. The images emerge and, in the dimmest possible illumination, become intensely clear: a second's worth of hallucinatory power. The moment they start to fade, I remove the glass plates and rinse them in plain water before slipping them into my second basin filled with a hyposulfite of soda. As I do this, I become the sole preserver of memories, of dreams that would otherwise sink into oblivion; I have something of the sensation of stopping time itself, of retrieving the ephemeral seconds of our lives from the strongroom of eternity.

When the white on the glass of the slide is gone, it is time to let the light in. I turn up the gas lamps and sometimes even bring the slides upstairs to expose them to sunshine. The procedure is finished. I return the slides to the darkroom, ready to apply citrate paper the next day. Thus, despite my previous dismissal of this art to Henry, I paint my new portraits with light and time.

In Carmel: Pauline

Céline sets up her box camera in the laundry room.

"This is hardly the setting for a dignified portrait," I say to her, not for the first time. But in this one area, she assumes her independence, and I allow it, as I sense it saves her soul from a latent despair.

"It's not that I disagree with you, little mother," she says, adopting the informal moniker by which I am now persistently called. "But the camera can provide a glimpse into our life as well as our spirit. We are not proud, and if I am to record our commitment to humility, then I should take the photographic lens even to the hard tasks of the community."

She knows what to say to me. I incline my head: yes, then.

The rinsing is scheduled for the afternoon work period. It's another warm June day and the laundry house has its own humid climate, in contrast to the fresher air of the garden and cloister walk. Céline has already situated everyone where she wants them around the high, shallow pool of rinsing water. I can't help but smile at the crushed gaggle of nuns, many of them high-spirited as schoolgirls for this brief period of misrule. The laundry is always hard work but combined with the "posing" expected of them when Sister Geneviève—Céline's new name in religion—is taking photographs, the women have adopted the air of a recreation rather than an hour of hard physical labor. A few of the sisters are singing; it's one of Thérèse's songs, her sweet words melded to a popular tune so that everyone can join in, re-gardless of the quality of their musical education. Thérèse herself is looking around pensively, also smiling, but less openly than Anne, Magdalene, and Martha, her little novices. A quick glance at Céline confirms that she's nearly ready to take the image. Sister St. Luke is primed to lift and then close the lens cap, which will allow this scene its immortality. To the extreme right, I notice old Sister Stanislaus peering with solid curiosity at the apparatus through her little wire-rimmed spectacles. If she continues to keep this still, it will be a fine image of her.

Some of the nuns have already started the task of pushing and beating the laundered linen with wooden paddles. I look at Thérèse again. Because Céline plans to slip beside her for the photograph, there is a gap to her left which makes her look slightly isolated within the group. But not so sepa-rated that she is immune to Marie-Joseph's clumsy slapping of her paddle onto the sodden cloth in front of her; several sprays of dirty water catch her veil, the side of her face, her mouth.

After all these years my first instinct is to step in immediately and is-sue a reprimand to Marie-Joseph—not that there is any realistic hope of improving her general behavior. A "primitive," Céline recently named her in one of our less-successful conversations. I draw a breath, preparing to release a sharp word or two. But something holds me back from my in-tended course of action. I watch as Thérèse closes her eyes for just a fraction of a second. Then she turns to Sister Marie-Joseph, not to reprimand her, but to give her the warmest of smiles, as though she is delighted to have discovered her so nearby. Marie-Joseph, touched by any kind of spontane-ous friendship, gives her crooked half-smile back. Then, encouraged, she returns to her clumsy pummeling. Fleetingly—so fleetingly—Thérèse's eyes meet mine. I notice the perspiration on her forehead, a further indication of her physical discomfort. I wonder what sort of grace I have witnessed.

Céline bustles into her place and plunges her hands into the rinsing pool.

"Still, my sisters!" she says.

They do her bidding; the camera does its nine seconds of work.

In Carmel: Marie

At recreation, we linger, with the tacit consent of Pauline, a rare pleasure during her time as prioress. Supper has been excellent, with the fish and potatoes kindling a sense of satisfaction despite the Rule warning us against the pleasures of the table. There has been wine; small glasses of a floral white presented to us by Uncle to celebrate his own daughter's entrance into our little ark—stiff in her blue dress, little Lucie kneels in a corner of the warming room, her eyes darting about as though in wonder. Céline sits beside me, and at last seems at home in her habit, the bulk of her white veil untroubling her as she dabs at a small ceramic on which flourishes a lily. Pauline, for once, is in a relaxed humor too. She sits, still neat and straight-backed, facing us, her mending basket at her feet. I have a list of garden supplies to complete for the procuress but allow myself to sit back in my old habit of daydream. I am aided immensely in my reverie by Thérèse. Flushed with the pleasure of having Céline and Lucie here, perhaps, she recounts some childhood exploit at which it is impossible not to be amused.

"And then—do you remember, Céline?—Victoria found the bread in my sweaty little hand. *And what is this, my scamp? You steal rations from the table? Oh ho! Wait until Papa hears about this!*" Straight away, she rushes to the next part of the story. "Papa, of course, leapt to my defense. He thought I was saving scraps to feed to Tom: *My children are of good heart, Victoria. You yourself receive many gifts from them.*"

And through her voice Papa's own tones can be briefly heard. But now, we are at Deauville with the friends of Aunt and Uncle, and Thérèse offers a gentle satire of their worldly ways, before returning us to the loving tumult of Les Buissonets once again. I cannot help it, I laugh along with the others, while reliving our memories as though they were a series of moving pictures, watched by us all. Céline's face is shining with pleasure—and so too, I notice, is Pauline's. I think how good it is for her to forget her burdensome role if only for a while. She seems to bear the office of prioress well, with considerable dignity in the face of an ever-present Mother Xavier who waits to resume the position next year—she regards it as her own, merely leant out to our dear departed Mother Rose-Chrétien's protégée. But I know Pauline of old and can see the strain that has inscribed her features. I am reminded of Mama, harassed to the end of her life by all her lacemaking concerns.

As we stand and draw our family reminiscences to a close, an idea strikes me.

"Pauline—Mother Agnès," I say, "you *must* ask Thérèse to write down some of these stories. They are priceless! Think of all the pleasure they will give us in the years to come."

Pauline draws herself up to her diminutive highest and breathes in as she considers. Then she breathes out and her eyes give a rare twinkle. "I agree, Sister Marie. Thérèse—please write down your childhood memories. You have already shown yourself adept at turning a pretty verse for our Carmelite sisters. Here is your work for me and your blood sisters. Take a clean copy book from the recess in the procurator's office, and use the time after second collation, or whenever you are freed from other duties."

Thérèse, for a moment, is silent. Then Céline collides with her, offering a clumsy hug.

"Do it, Thérèse! It's an order from your prioress—and besides, I can't wait to read them, now I don't get letters from you anymore. An account of our childhood years together would be perfect!"

Thérèse catches Céline's hands and takes a demure step back. But she is smiling. "Yes, Mother Agnès, just as you request."

She bows and slips away into the evening's silence.

In Carmel: Lucie Guérin

I flounder like a new girl at school in this stripped-down world.

I entered Carmel with the love of my parents—even gruff Papa—at my back, and the warm draw of Thérèse and my other cousins ahead of me. Thérèse has several times taken me by the hand.

"I knew you would come," she says, in a poor attempt at a whisper. "You complete our family here—how happy I am for that."

For fleeting moments, especially at recreation, it is indeed as though we are a family together once again.

But even with this safety-net of cherishing, I stumble so easily into fault. This afternoon I slop the cider as I carry an overfull jug from the kitchen to the refectory. The spilled liquid stains my dress and its acrid smell spreads across the refectory floor. Even though the refectory is empty I make myself lay down in the spill, as penance. Wet and uncomfortable, I push myself up and kneel in the mess, putting off the moment I must fetch bucket and mop. I cry raw tears as I gather myself together, and then I go to Thérèse and cry some more.

"I can't get the simplest thing right," I say.

Playing hermits was so much easier than living in this tightly structured community.

Thérèse listens thoughtfully and offers me her smile. Then she turns away, and searches in her workbasket for something.

"Here, Lucie," she says, her words bright with triumph. "Take this little shell." She passes me an empty mussel shell, its nacre-colored insides gleaming in the light.

"Why—I—" Her gesture is a mystery.

"It's to capture your tears, Lucie! Cry if you must, but our Spouse does not want His bride weeping with remorse when she could be smiling with love. Come—remember how much I used to cry until I became a Carmelite and lost my self-regard. I have not grown up—oh, no—I have grown smaller. That is why I give you the shell. Look, it makes you smile already. God is not harsh—He is love and mercy. He wants you to see how silly your fears really are." Despite a fragility to her voice, she fills me with her confidence and care. I am astonished at how she is still herself, but so much more herself than she was before. "See—you understand me at once," she adds, warmly. "What a good nun you already are."

I love her then more than I can say. I hold the shell to my eye and its cool substance is like a little caress. At the same time, I picture my own ridiculousness. A tear, in fact, slides immediately into its new little barque—whether it is a tear of sadness or laughter I am not able to tell.

The bell sounds. Thérèse is summoned by Mother Xavier, and immediately stands. Her levity is replaced by defensive solemnity. I try to catch her sleeve; my fingers brush briefly against her habit as she departs. I wonder then if, despite her soothing words, she still sometimes sheds tears of her own.

In Carmel: Céline

I find Thérèse in the outer chamber of her cell, where she normally instructs the novices with her serenity glimmering like a supernatural veil. I must have surprised her, even though our meeting has been prearranged.

I am coming up to profession, and my soul is as crumpled and recalcitrant as ever, so Thérèse begged permission to help me further with its ironing. But instead of finding her waiting, I find her red-faced and distressed. Her little desk is disarrayed, and her copies of our Rule and yearly almanac, and several sheets covered in her own writing, are scattered on the floor. If I had not witnessed her iron self-control over the last year, I would suspect her of having swept them off the tabletop herself in a fit of pique.

"Thérèse! Are you alright?" All of my old impulses to protect and connect with her rise to the surface. Perhaps someone has hit back at her. Even I—especially I, in truth—have had to bite my tongue when her lessons in perfection came too hard and fast. She rubs her face, rises, and steps towards me, and then makes to prostrate herself in apology for having been seen so distraught. Quick as lightning I reach out to prevent her. "Please. Tell me what has upset you so." And then I add, "If either of us are to be upset, it should be me, not you!" Her eyes flash fire then. I gesture for her to sit back down, and she does. I draw up one of the other little wooden chairs and sit facing her. She wipes her eyes with a cloth from her habit's inner pocket and clenches it with her fist.

"She tries my patience, Céline. She always has. But this—this is too much. It is not a thing to use to test the soul! She goes too far. She should be stopped!"

She breathes heavily. I have no doubt about who she is railing against. My only thought is this: Why has she put up with her for so long?

"Mother Wolf earns her nickname then. When has she ever not?" I hope to raise a smile from her, and I almost do, but then another flush of rage rises in her face. Does she lose her temper at last? I want my little sister back so badly that I start to consider what I can say to provoke her further, in the manner of breaking through a prison wall. "What has she done?" I ask. "Does Pauline know?"

"Oh yes," mutters Thérèse. "She knows. She knows because Mother Xavier returns to the prioress's post at Advent; the elections are foregone. But that's the thing, Céline. She wants to delay your profession, so that she can be the one to hear your vows. And be in all your precious photographs too." There is a tearful note to her anger. "Marie tells me she does it to strengthen your patience, but it's wrong!" And her eyes plead with me now, in the way they did when I still sat on the other side of the grille in the visitor's parlor. "I want you here Céline, forever! You *are* ready, and yet I fear the devil still . . ."

I understand her then, and my response is, despite all decisions made, conflicted. Why the rush? Does she continue to fear I will fall away from Carmel? I visualize myself winged and flying away, like one of the strange Russian paintings I once saw in Paris. Then I dismiss the image from my mind.

"I am willing to wait, Thérèse. After all, I am already here."

I seek to reassure us both with this. She nods, sniffing still.

"It's just unfair, and I—I have been tried by her, Céline, for so long. You would not believe . . ."

"Everybody knows how hard she has been on you. But it's not just you. Did Pauline tell you about the time she had to go up on the roof to rescue her cat?"

She does smile at this, and I am relieved. I shift back in my uncomfortable chair. I wonder, not for the first time, why Thérèse is so concerned to meet this woman's approval, even when she doesn't occupy the prioress's role.

"You know, Céline, my difficulties with Mother Xavier were excruciating when I entered Carmel. I loved her like a daughter does a mother, like—I don't know—I wanted to please her so badly. Any sign from her, any glance, any smile—I would have to hold the handrail of the dormitory stairs to stop myself from bothering her sometimes, I was so—so attached to her."

She smiles a little more now. A sad smile for her younger self, I think. For a sixteen-year-old girl charmed by an imperious older woman. I feel a further twist of understanding along with my sorrow. She had never told me.

"I am your novice, Thérèse," I say, resisting, now, the temptation to egg on her flare of temper. "And that is the important thing for me. Even after my profession—whenever it is—I will remain your novice. I thank God for it. You have saved my faulty soul."

She is calmer. "We are all faulty, Céline. But the Rule is a rule of love." She suddenly coughs. "But I love you too much to let her break you; to break us apart."

I squeeze her hand and notice again how ageless she seems—both woman and child—and still a fresh source of unbreakable grace.

In Carmel: Lucie Guérin

To mark six months into my novitiate, Mama and Papa send us a gift, and I feel as excited as a child at Christmas. The case arrives and Mother Agnès gives permission for the novices to assist with the unpacking. The case is delivered into the warming room, Cousin Marie supervising, with her tough-tender voice and gestures keeping us in check. A basket is discovered inside the case. And inside the basket, a little hand, a little white foot.

"Careful! Don't break it!" Marie's voice calls over the commotion.

My novice friend, Sister Magdalene, shows rare energy, and she and I push past Thérèse to behold the revelation. There in the wicker basket is a child. The Divine Child. Our child.

In a way, this moment should belong to Thérèse, Thérèse of the Child Jesus and her blood sisters. But I am glowing with pride. For once, my heart is light and woven into patterns of intricate joy, like the lace which lines the basket; the sunlight which shines through the lattice windows. Yes, my soul is as bright and white as the swan's-down gown and sheet of this wax infant. He stretches out his arms to me and I am drawn into Him. I am one of the family. I am Lucie of the Eucharist. Look at his blue, blue eyes. And the hair! Blonde and soft, true baby's hair.

"Have you seen? It is your hair, Teresita," says Marie, forgetting her attempt at sternness. "And look: our own Mama's lace lines his bed. And Thérèse, this gown is from your own—your beautiful bridal gown."

I think of Thérèse at her clothing; the gorgeous swan's-down in which she went to her betrothed. Mama must have saved the material, all these six years. Did Marie know? She never said.

Thérèse positions herself at the basket's side. She has her customary smiling serenity, but her eyes are clear and full. Is she crying? No tears fall: she does not need my little shell. She picks up the child with an indefinable emotion. Magdalene and Martha continue with high-spirited comment, though always with a glance to authority—in this case, Marie. Will the doll come to the refectory? Should it receive Father Youf's blessing? Surely new flowers should be ordered for the crib! Céline joins us, standing behind Thérèse, who is quiet. Older sister behind the younger. Novice behind her mistress. Céline forever oscillates between the two roles.

Thérèse touches the strands of blond hair, smoothing them softly away from the baby's face. She lifts the doll as though it is a real infant which would delight in being raised high, held secure, in the unearned celebration of being alive.

"Look!" she says. "Ah, look at our child."

Sisters Magdalene and Martha are suddenly silent. I look up at the infant in its beautiful white garment. For an instant I have the strangest feeling of being at the moment of consecration in the Mass.

Then, with an intake of breath, I feel embarrassed by my thoughts. Have I sinned? Surely I should not be thinking such things. I *must* have sinned. But I catch the glance of big Cousin Marie, her cheeks red and her eyes kind, and her tough tenderness catches and holds me like a hug.

Suffering

1896—1897

Normandy: Maurice

"You should write to the Reverend Mother of the Lisieux Carmel," says Father Du Barre, my spiritual director.

He leans back in his armchair, and reaches for his cigar, positioned expertly over a small bowl on his side table. I shall always think of Du Barre as associated with ease and tobacco. Prayer swirling from his soul just as the smoke drifts from the glowing cigar-end, now moving to and from his mouth, like part of a personal liturgy.

"Would she want to hear from the likes of me?" I can't help asking.

It's all very well for Du Barre to moot such a possibility, but I am surely so severely disconnected from French society as to be nothing but a nuisance. As for becoming a member of the priesthood, I have many more leagues to go, including my imminent military service. Nobody hides that from me. But Du Barre surprises me.

"Probably not, Maurice. Mother Xavier is a high-born woman, and rumor suggests she has lost none of her blue blood during her years of enclosure. She is still something to be reckoned with when it comes to sacred—ah—politics in the Bayeux diocese. Even when she's not officially Mother Superior, she still rules the roost. A queen with her own kingdom, indeed." And he chuckles to himself. "But I meant: write to her and ask her to assign you a sister, one of her pure-hearted nuns, who will pray for your soul—and remind you by letter that she is so doing." He looks at me, assessing my reaction. "These Carmelites sign up for the life to pray for priests, Maurice. You couldn't do better for yourself than to get one of them on your side. They're lightning rods of grace."

This is my spiritual director at his typical best. Enigmatic, mocking, serious. I see why he is good at advising coltish young men such as I. I see, also, the devout priest below the worldly exterior. I nod.

"Sounds wonderful. Just what I need," I agree. "I'll get a letter sent off today."

Du Barre smiles, and puffs away on his cigar. "That Carmel is one to watch," he says. "They've had some good women enter there recently. Oh, you always get the rough ones from peasant families—they're tough, so they're good at holding out with the lifestyle. But Xavier has got some sophisticated souls joining her in there too. One family—would you believe it—sent in four sisters, and a cousin to boot!" His face indicates he can hardly believe it himself. "That Martin family—the father's dead now, of course, but the uncle, Guérin—Monsieur Guérin, writes for *La Croix*—he's a big lay voice for the church. Keeps the good sisters in fine wine too, I don't doubt." And he chuckles again. "Of course, she shouldn't have allowed it—all those blood relatives, I mean—but that's what I mean about Xavier. You won't get one up on her in church matters very easily."

Bearing this caveat in mind, I write and send my letter.

She responds immediately, and in the affirmative. I will be assigned her best sister, who begins her intercession for me at once, and will write, herself, after the Carmel's Lenten restrictions. She signs off with a calligraphic flourish, her flawless bloodline informing the signature's vigorous balance.

In Carmel: Céline

Every so often the novices—and their assistant novice mistress—demonstrate their playwriting and playacting skills. It is the second time Thérèse has written a play for her childhood heroine, Joan of Arc: and this time, she not only writes her, but *becomes* her, under the gaze of our enrapt sisters. Thérèse is Joan is Thérèse. I play the part of Barbara, the saint who flies to visit her in prison. She lays her head on my breast (so strange that this is not her hair, but the brown tresses of an old wig!), and I comfort her with my winged arm. Joan-Thérèse in her dungeon, chained to the wall, and steadying herself for the flames of martyrdom. I arrange for photographs of this Sister Joan.

"Look to the heavens, Thérèse," I call, double-checking my camera box and its two-slide glass plates.

"Truth to tell, Sister Geneviève, I see nothing but empty skies," she replies, in her quizzical fashion of late. But she does as I bid and directs her gaze upwards. I capture her nicely, I believe.

"Let us pose together, now," I say, resuming, with a certain amount of pleasure, my deft commanding stance from those last weeks at La Musse.

Just for today, I am the manager, the artistic director, and Thérèse is under my supervision; the tables temporarily turned. She is no fool of course; she will recognize my pride and serve it up to me later, seasoned with Carmelite morality. But for now, this does not disturb me. We are held together in the eye of the slide; sister spirits in our play-act of French hero-ism. Pauline stands, then, and clicks her fingers: enough.

Bernadette and I remove the plywood panels signifying Joan's dark night, and Thérèse comes forward in her card-and-paper costume, all wooden sword and starry eyes. She comes to face the flames.

And my God, they nearly take her.

A whoosh of oil and flame and her left side is alight. The sight is shock-ing. Pauline and Marie rush to their feet in an instinctive response to save her; the other nuns following more or less immediately. In a slow couple of seconds, I realize what has happened: the gas flames from our heater, masquerading as the martyr's pyre, have leapt to life, enticed by Thérèse's flammable warrior's robe. A horrific panorama threatens to unfold but—thank God!—never does. Thérèse is pushed to the side, her actor's weeds ripped off her; Pauline wraps her in her own cream mantle, as though she is an infant, miraculously upright. I rush to join my siblings in their rescue attempt, knowing I am superfluous, yet unable to abstain.

Sister of mine, how you scare us. How you scare me!

Less caught up in the practicalities of rescue, I am able to witness her face, her gestures, her spontaneous expressions in the microcosm of time during which her life is in the flames. And I see there no terror, no confusion, no distress. Only her half-raised arms, her ever-present, quasi-stubborn smile, and the tiniest widening of her eyes, as though she's caught a glimpse of someone she loved.

And fire is her theme now. It slow-burns its way into her verse. Some-times I see her face flushed, though my intuition holds that she shivers more than ever in the night. I watch her at Adoration, sneak glimpses of her profile as we kneel in the choir. Periodically I catch her eyes, steady and gleaming, as though still seeing shapes in the flames, the monstrance a kind of gilded furnace through which angels tread.

She comes to me with the old ardor in her eyes, ready to share it.

"I have written it—my act of consecration to merciful love, Céline. Come to the oratory with me. We have Mother Agnès's permission."

She must have charmed her: Pauline is usually so cautious in respond-ing to spiritual requests that go beyond the Rule. But soon she will hear my vows of profession—this is thanks to Thérèse's insistent diplomacy too—so I suppose she regards this as a sort of final preparation.

When I kneel with her, I am convinced she is possessed by Eternity itself. She says the words of her act and her voice soars like a bird, and her body trembles as though drenched and drunk on this unknown God of love who searches so fiercely for a home.

In Carmel: Lucie Guérin

Evening recreation. Little Sister Anne and I are kneeling in a corner of the warming room. Sometimes, despite Thérèse's injunctions, it's nice to share the hour with a friend. It's December; we're both tired but excited about the weeks to come. Our baskets are on the floor before us. Each is filled with mending to be done. In the corner of mine I also have paper tucked away, as it's high time I wrote to Papa. I don't share this with all the sisters. They probably assume I've already written to him; such is the wealth of edible gifts which he sends in. I recall the sensation of juice from our winter pears, cool on my chin. The litany of produce for which we offered thanks after collation. I remember living at home and being terrified I had committed sins of gluttony. Or ungratefulness, lacking in charity towards my parents. Things are simpler here. We are simply grateful for what is given.

Mother Agnès and newly professed Sister Geneviève sit together also, I notice. Their heads lean towards each other like the statues of our Holy Mother Teresa and John of the Cross on the mantlepiece. Under them the heat of our little fire warms us after supper. A glow of happiness in the December chill. Pauline, seated, is like Teresa. A figure of wisdom. A tight-wound dynamo. Céline is the one who tends the flame of art.

Tonight, Céline looks pale, her normally smooth brow creased in tension. I hear Sister Thérèse's name but nothing else of their conversation.

"Where is she?" inquires Anne of the Trinity, speaking in an agitated whisper.

"She is in the sacristy," I reply. "She wanted to clean the chalice before the visiting father's Mass tomorrow. She told me she didn't like to be rushed."

Anne seems satisfied with this information.

"I've seen her polishing," she confides. "She takes her time. I've seen her look inside the empty chalice when she's cleaned it, too."

I frown at this information. It seems an odd vanity for such a strict sister. But Anne provides the gloss: "She told me she likes to see herself reflected in the place where God will rest. So that she knows how powerfully God will also dwell in her."

The thought pierces me with its beauty. But inevitably, it disturbs me too. I know I would hesitate to meditate in such a way. Our hours of mental prayer are strictly defined. But who knows this more thoroughly than Thérèse? Then I think: she has not looked well for some time. Perhaps this is her way of bolstering herself so that she has the energy to continue with her tasks, not the least of which is continuing to advise novice Sister Anne, and me.

Then the door from the cloister opens and Thérèse comes in. She is breathing hard. She does not melt into the background as usual, but stands before us, a fragment separated from the whole.

"The cellar under the sacristy," she says, and her voice scratches with anxiety. "I heard a noise."

Her face has a flush, but it doesn't disguise her underlying pallor. Agnès and her sister stand at once, Marie of the Sacred Heart going swiftly to stand beside her. Mother Xavier sits upright in her central chair, and, assessing the situation, places her knitting back in her basket.

"Sister Thérèse," she says, "compose yourself. You have come to us. There is no need for agitation."

"No, Mother Xavier. I am sorry. But I thought I could hear someone moving about, and I knew Sister Geneviève was here, so—"

The unspoken fear of an intruder hangs, silent but tangible, in the suddenly cooling air. Behind this, there is another fear, flickering in Thérèse's face, and felt, at the least, by those who know her best.

"I did call out, but nobody answered. It was not Mira, Mother."

Mother Xavier nods. Mira, who is old now, generally spends her days sleeping beside the warm vents outside the kitchen.

Pauline steps forward. "Mother Xavier. Should I fetch Father Youf?"

Our chaplain lives in the house adjacent to the Carmel and could, in emergencies, be roused by a bell. I picture him reading his evening newspaper.

"No, Agnès. We will not disturb him on a whim. But take Sisters Geneviève, Aimée, and . . . and Lucie of the Eucharist back to the sacristy and see what you can hear yourselves." Mother Xavier looks at my companion with a glint of authority. "And Sister Anne of the Trinity will go with you."

Thérèse looks relieved. But she will be embarrassed to have disrupted the recreation. She inclines her head slightly, smooths her habit with her hands and turns back to the door.

"Not you, Sister Thérèse. Please take a seat—take Mother Agnès's chair and tell me again what you heard." Then this: "Let us see what your little family can find in your wake."

After perhaps a second's hesitation, Thérèse obeys her without a glance to Pauline or Céline. She coughs as she sits.

In the cloister Mother Agnès signals to us that we may speak; so we do, quietly. "I want us to visit the outdoor room first," she says.

So, we do. We turn right, instead of left towards the sacristy and its cellar. The outdoor room is in the far end of the cloister, directly opposite the chapel. It contains our haymaking and other gardening equipment: tall raking forks, buckets, hessian aprons, and a row of watering cans. In the dim light it smells of mold and fresh earth combined. Of metal and wood. At Céline's signal I take a pitchfork and give it to Anne. Then I take one for myself. Anne giggles despite—or because of—the tenseness of the situation. Like me, she is remembering our acting roles as devils, casting the silhouettes of the pitchforks onto a screen in Thérèse's Christmas play last year. Sister Geneviève takes another rake, but passes it to Aimée, and Pauline bids us hurry.

"I said that door should be locked," mutters Céline, thinking of her equipment.

A burst of gentle laughter comes from the warming room. But we don't rejoin the community; we carry on along the cloister, turn left and past the chapel and choir, in order to reach the sacristy.

It is dark, but nothing disturbs the repose of chalice, plates, and vestments. Each seems to rest easy in its place. Thérèse is careful like that. Pauline raises her oil lamp and immediately shadows loom across the walls. Just like in our Christmas play, my rake is a devil's pitchfork. Céline's shadow is unnaturally elongated, her shovel bent into a black reaper's scythe. Involuntarily, Anne of the Trinity and I step closer together. As our pitchforks converge and recede in Pauline's inadvertent shadow puppetry, I sense her febrile energy merge with my own. We are frightened, but wide awake.

Pauline moves around the room. The shadows of us all circle the walls, a ghoulish, moving image. There is nothing substantially untoward. Gesturing almost invisibly to Céline, Pauline moves towards the door to the cellar below. With her profile thrown into sharp relief she descends the staircase, still holding the lamp aloft, and with Céline, who knows the cellar room well, directly behind her. The rest of us crowd at the top of the stairs. I hold my breath.

Silence. Then the steps of the two sisters as they return from the depths.

Pauline speaks. "Nothing," she says. "Sister Thérèse may have heard something, or it may have been nothing. She has been unwell and the extra sacristy duties may have taxed her too far. It is possible that she took fright at a mouse. Let us return to the warming room, thanking God for our safety and praying for our little sister's full return to health."

As we exit the room, I look back one last time and think I see a final shadow loom beyond the farthest bench where the chalices are placed.

Normandy: Maurice

She is balm, she is sweetness. She is mother and sister. The opposite of shadow: this nun is a bright light cancelling my darkness. Thérèse, Sister Thérèse. Soon she not only prays for me but is permitted also to write. Her hand is simple, upright, and true. Her voice is a breath inside my breath. She tells me, in all innocence, the story of myself. She turns me to prayer, into prayer, and through prayer makes me her own. I become simpler, whittled down. A stripped twig, a stretched-up branch. She is a bird, trusting my branches. She is my branch, rooted in God.

She writes. I write. Antiphon and chant flutter over France.

And then I fall.

"Maurice, you scoundrel!" Bertrand slaps me across the back, simultaneously with his verbal assault. "Let's get more wine down your gullet!" He slaps two tankards of dark red wine onto the stained table. The tavern is crowded and noisy. Sharp, barking laughs punctuate the air; air that is fetid with foul language and soldiers' sweat. "You had rifle practice with old Fougard today? Bet you wanted to shoot him in the balls by the end of it—here, Lissand, come join us, you randy goat!" Bertrand addresses his last comment to a short, squat, brown-haired man who had been trying to get one of the barmaids' attention through persistent leering and gurning. "Little Bonaparte! Bet you like them unwashed, just like our dear departed Emperor."

Bertrand attempts to make some gesture that is at once lewd and indicative of rank. He falls across the table before he succeeds. I laugh—an ungallant guffaw. My head swims and my body swells with a rough warmth. I gulp down the acidic wine and belch loudly.

"Haaar!" responds Bertrand. "Let's give the girls a song."

Then we're chanting, raising our mugs, and cheering indiscriminately. The *Marseillais* reaches its crescendo, descends into fragments of folksong, marching-song, hymn. The concerted effort putters out with little groups of soldiers launching into their own bold chorus lines. The wine pushes my blood down and around my arms, legs, chest, lifts me out of physical exhaustion, and I goad Lissand into a marching tune; ra *ra* ra *ra* ra ra *ra ra ra*; slap and spittle over the sanded floor and out onto the street we go. Coarse jacket fabric round the neck. I smell my own sweat mingled with his. *Ra ra ra*; brothers in arms; brothers at play, *ra ra*. I never had a brother, another boy to knock about with, push and punch, roll in the gut of the world, the playground, the gutter. I land in the gutter with Lissand.

"Bellière—Lissand—you crazy dogs—I know what you need—"

Bertrand goads us with his rifle and for a moment I think he will shoot one of us. I care little for the prospect, but I care little about it. Wine is my only care; wine and the blood pulsing into my hands, feet, cock—my God, what have I become? A long streak of piss against the wall.

"Get your rifle fired by the end of the night, Maurice—" Bertrand is saying; pushes me into the open doorway where the warm red light welcomes us, soldiers all, and an old woman points me towards a much younger woman who has appeared like a miracle at my side.

The warm red light receives us like a womb. *Sandrine*, I think she says, and for some reason this is unbearably funny for us both, and laughter runs down our bodies like children in a bath; naked and innocent before a roaring fire, children clinched together in a small tin tub, hot ripples between and within our innocent skins; soft cloth fallen to the ground and onto the pillow of her breasts and nipples with aureoles like roses and given to me like a kiss. The blood-wine surges through me like dark lightning; irrefutable, unstoppable. She smells of earth, sea, fish, and blood; I bury myself in her flesh.

The next morning, I limp towards the confessional in the unknown church. An old woman scurries down the side-aisle, casting me a swift glance and, seeing from my stained uniform that I am a soldier, continuing swiftly towards the street. I enter the dark little cubicle and draw the musty curtain across, concealing myself from the world.

A faint noise as the small panel between the priest and myself slides open. My mouth has never felt so dry, my head so painful, my soul so foul.

The priest clears his throat, signaling me to begin.

But I cannot begin.

In Carmel: Marie

I dream of letters falling from the skies.

Upon waking, something tells me this might be Thérèse's last retreat. The thought emboldens me, as it has on a previous occasion, to present her with a request. I find her in her room, in the antechamber where she sees the novices. They must have just left her, because she sits in silence at the small table on which is placed the Rule and the shortened daily office, and also an almanac for the year. We are already in autumn. This world of exile seems to spin on its axis a little faster for each year we endure on its ground. I think of saying this to her, by way of a little holy conversation, but remember that where Pauline would join me in the safe language of polite sighs and pious sentiments, Thérèse has a distaste for such pleasantries. So instead, when she has signaled me to come in, I tell her what I see: that she looks extremely tired. She smiles, faintly, but genuinely enough.

"The novices often challenge me to a duel. Today was one of those days," she says, her voice husky. Then she stretches her arms slightly, sighs, and smiles more fully. "I like to think of myself as His warrior."

"I know," I say. "I remember your play."

"He takes us at our word sometimes," she affirms. "I'll recover. Or not, as He wills." I pick up her last clause, as perhaps I am intended to.

"You are not well, my darling."

"Sister Marie," she says gently; she would not reprimand her godmother. "I am as you, His spouse; and I obey the rules of His house."

She coughs, mildly. I do not want to push her, not about this, not today.

"I have a request, Sister Thérèse," I say. "You are going on retreat next week. A whole week of silence and prayer with no tasks to interrupt you. You don't always love your retreats, so don't pretend to me that you do. But you come back from them full of light."

"Do I?" she says. She smiles a smile straight out of her childhood—happy and anxious in equal measure. "It's true I wrestle with my soul more often than not when I'm secluded so heavily. I would be happier if I knew, really knew, exactly what it is He wants of me. Not really a soldier, not a missionary, not a martyr, not—" she hesitates, "a priest. So what am I, really?"

I am puzzled. "A nun! You just said so yourself—His spouse, called to prayer, the hidden life. Is this not enough for you?"

She looks at me and is more serious. "No. It is not, Marie. There is something more I can be for our God of mercy and love; something—I can almost taste it and yet—I cannot put it into words, what I mean. Not yet."

"Well," I say. "I shall pray for your intentions."

"Thank you. But Marie, you wanted to ask me something, I am sorry—"

"A favor for me. And perhaps, from what you have just told me, for you too." I approach her and take one of her hands. "Would you please write your thoughts to me in a letter? I don't mean notes of Father Youf's homilies. I'm afraid to say I think I've heard them all before. I mean the lights you get, you know, when you pray. I would love to hear your prayers. Would you write them down for me? Not in a poem, although I love your poetry. I mean as if you are talking to me."

We don't speak together that much, not here—I suppose we both knew it would be like this. But I still miss my goddaughter in Les Buissonets. That's why I persuaded Pauline to order her to write about her childhood last year. She never disobeys an order—partly thanks to me.

If she feels pressured by my request, she doesn't show it. But neither does she show any inclination to talk further.

"Of course I will, Marie," she simply says. Then she adds, with the slightest of secret smiles, "You know, I have many letters to write."

Lisieux, at the Guérins: Léonie

She writes to me, as I hide away at Uncle and Aunt's, and tells me the story of my unkempt soul. She takes me as if by the hand.

> *No matter what you have done—and fall you will—there is nothing that the good God will not forgive. A child who runs to her mother's arms will be received with joy, Léonie. The mother knows this child will fall again! But what can she do? She must forgive, every time she is taken by the heart!*

I stare at this note. Its upright cursive script contrasts with my own awkward style. It makes me think of childhood, of Léonie's sad girlhood. My sour days under Louise's rule. The pain of her hand and the terror of her words. Then, release when Louise's spell was broken and Mama learned, before she died, to know me. But this mother described by Thérèse is bigger than the mother Léonie remembers. She is bigger and warmer and enfolds us all.

How can Thérèse understand this, when she hardly remembers our own mother at all?

When I reply I assure her of our prayers. I ask again after her health although she always tells me she is well. The very next time she writes there is a new quiver in her handwriting. It is now much more like my own, with its hesitancies and weakness. But Thérèse is never hesitant.

Normandy: Maurice

I muster my poor spoiled courage and write, begging for her prayers. Only then can I start to hope again. I wait for the mail every day, shunning my military companions, and dreaming once more of missionary lands.

When the letter comes, it is absolution; more powerful than the absolution I sought but could not feel in the confessional. I am dizzy with the grace she assures me I am already bathed in. Grace is all elements: sun, rain, wind; the dawn and dusk, the flames of the fire, and the stars; perpetual lamps in the sky's wide sanctuary. God's love pours out upon me, and her hand bids me to lift my face to the source.

In my joy at understanding I can so quickly be forgiven, I imagine her my priest, and myself the unworthy penitent, vulnerable to the sway of self-love far more than she. What a strange idea: a young woman who is a priest! I can almost see her at the altar, her soft hands raising the host, becoming a lightning rod of grace, becoming a sacrament in her very being. I shake my head and start to rub the stubble of my newly growing beard. I would cause scandal to say such things, even to Du Barre. And yet—I sense no disquiet from God, nor even in myself.

In Carmel: Pauline

We are in the warming room; the last to leave before Compline and the Great Silence. She kneels at my feet as though she is still the *Benjamin* at Les Buissonets. Then she tells me she has long felt unwell, that she coughs blood and believes she is dying, and I cannot bring myself to speak. Even in the dim light I can see the pallor of her face and wonder how I did not know before. It is late October, and the world gently, relentlessly falls: leaf by leaf, breath by breath.

She tells me that I should not concern myself with her body, her envelope. That I am her little mama, that I can read the letter within, the story of her soul, as though I had written it myself. And yet she had not told me, sent no early missive of this news.

Shock is like a bitter ice when one is expecting soft sweets.

In Carmel: Marie

Céline and I are in the office of altar bread. We have worked here, she and I, in the quiet spaces of the week, taking our allocated time slots and co-inciding every now and then. We do not speak much—but she will offer her observations on the heat of the oven, on the purity of the flour, and I respond with my smile. Sometimes I'll reply too; I sense I am permitted to transgress the Rule for the good of family. Sister Geneviève is still my adoptive daughter, and I am sensitive to her many moods. My little infractions don't seem wrong, although I would not make them with Thérèse. She does not need me to.

Today we make the breads alone. I inspect the ovens for cleanliness and dust away any grits with a feather, as our manual instructs. Céline mixes the fine flour and the gaseous water flowing from the small side pipe. I can tell from her heavy-handed pounding and pressing that she is unhappy. She bites her lip and frowns, giving herself a look of simultaneous youth and weariness. "You are worried about Teresita," I say.

"I sleep badly, Marie," she confesses, pausing to wipe her brow and leaving an unintentional smudge of flour there. "In my dreams I see her dying and I am beside myself. I have seen too many members of our family die."

I, too, pause, and look at her, acknowledging what she says. Geneviève, young in Carmelite years. Céline, old enough to remember Mama's dreadful dying, and the only one of us to nurse our father to the very end. Then I think back to dear Hélène, passing so suddenly at five years old; and further back to Melanie-Thérèse, dying because of a neglectful wet-nurse.

"I know it, Sister Geneviève. And I know what it is like to lose a blood sister."

She stares back at me, and I think this must have been the wrong thing to say. I have never been renowned for my tact. But Céline knows I mean to stand at her side in the face of the unthinkable. She sighs and continues:

"I am angry, Marie. And I am ashamed of my anger. That she should press so hard for me to be by her side in Carmel, and now, after three little years, it will be she who leaves!" Céline's agitation is palpable. Her rhythmic pushing and shaping of the flour and water becomes spasmodic. "I understand Pauline's vexation at her secrecy. Thérèse has been ill all this year and told only The Wolf. Why would she do such a thing?"

I let silence soothe us a little, before trying to calm her with my words.

"Remember one thing," I say, "She is Thérèse. God has possessed her for as long as she could breathe and babble. He possesses her now. I will show you the letter she wrote to me in her last retreat. You are not the only one she instructs in this house. And now, it may be her gift to us to show us how to die. It will be a hard gift, but one day, we will be thankful for it."

Her eyes widen as I speak, but she remains mute. Then she turns and pours the flour-water into the molds, where, plunged into our oven's heat, they will find their fixed form; impressed with the initials IHS and our cruciform God. The press creates big and small discs, formed in pressure and constraint. Later we will cut them with our sharp compass-blades. The large for the priests to use at the celebration; the small for the communicants. Each year we make thousands and parcel them up to sell at the turn. They are, in more ways than one, our livelihood.

I see Céline staring at the press in the concentrated way I have known since her childhood. She says to me, slowly: "Marie, I *must* preserve her. Like this press, I must capture her image in a way that allows us to have her with us. I will photograph her. I will photograph us all. The photographs will serve for my paintings in days to come."

"You have many photographs, Sister. Of all of us! You have made good use of your box camera, you and Cousin Lucie."

But Céline is not satisfied.

"I must do more. Thérèse is burning up in her fire of love. I must press her living image to the glass. While there is time—oh Marie, that flower Papa gave her; she showed it to me the other day, paper-thin with the roots fallen away. She said it made her happy to see it nearly destroyed, as it signi-fied her own fragility."

At this, I feel a sudden breathlessness and raise both hands to my throat. The cloth I had been clutching drops, abandoned, to the floor.

*　*　*

When we take the photographs, we are out in the Lourdes courtyard. The weather is bright but bleak: it is November. Thérèse, pale and quiet, stands against the tall table on one side. I whisper to her to rest against it when she needs to. I doubt that she will, though she just gives her half smile and nods. Céline sets the camera and poses us: Cousin Lucie joins us in her white veil and saddened face: it is her childhood companion and novitiate angel who is dying, and our cousin is no fool when it comes to medical matters. I stand on the far right, holding the little press and the dry wheat bread sheet, as though to imprint there and then the face of Jesus. Pauline stands more cen-tral to our group, holding the small circular cutters which release the hosts into their singularities. Céline, having given her meticulous instruction to Sister Aimée, joins in an action pose as she places the large compass cutters against the priest's host.

Thérèse remains on our far left, behind her table. She places the hosts into the chalice—echoing her much-loved duty as sacristan. Of course, she must pause nine seconds for the camera, and pause she does, holding the host with a tender gravity. She looks at the lens with her ebbing strength. Céline arranges for two exposures, as she always does. She retreats to her darkroom under the sacristy. Lucie goes down to help her.

Later we look together at the developed images. We are in the warming room, before official recreation. I take care to guide Thérèse into a comfort-able chair. Uncharacteristically, she agrees, and equally uncharacteristically, she expresses an opinion on our newest portraits.

"This I like," she says, placing her finger on the second of the photo-graphs. The one where she stands to the extreme right of the sheet, almost out of the frame, and her face solemn. "I like to work, to work for Him. Céline, Marie, thank you! This picture shows my truth—and my desires."

"You are a little priest!" says Lucie.

Then that immediate glance towards me in case she has said something wrong. So soon before her profession, and still, she doubts! But Thérèse looks at her and smiles her old, slow smile, her chin jutting slightly forward, and lips pressed together, as if savoring their secret.

In Carmel: Lucie Guérin

I am professed: a pauper transformed into a princess.

My hair is shorn. It falls in feathery clumps to the floor. I prostrate myself in the chapter room, and then Mother Xavier receives the fifth member of the Martin clan as I kneel, place my clasped hands in her lap, and recite my vows. Pauline assists in the pinning of my small black veil. The moment is so extraordinary I seem to hover above it, already a spirit.

In the public chapel, a family ceremony. I am clad in the cream cloak and full black veil of a Carmelite. Finally, I graduate into my new home. Papa blesses me, his eyes shining behind his spectacles. I inhale his tobacco smell as he embraces me for the last time. But I know that our bonds are as strong as ever, that this is, in some ways, Papa's Carmel as much as mine.

Céline photographs me as I kneel in customary fashion in the courtyard, my eucharistic moniker displayed as a vivid image in my hands. It is hard to sustain my smile, but not because of fear: I am more dazed with the finality of the rites. I am wholly His now. Scared for so long of receiving the sacred host, I have become its dedicated angel.

In our extended recreation, Thérèse brings her papers. She has written me a poem.

"Sing it, Lucie!" she urges me.

But I am worn out and still shy under my new veil. So she sits up and does her best to recite her own words: I notice again how her voice has changed, is low and cracked when it used to be sweet and clear. She speaks of our vows as weapons, of myself as a warrior. Poverty my sword. Chastity my shield! Obedience my flag of victory.

Her voice tires extremely. Swelling with love, I stand up and take her song sheet after all. I sing out the lines to a popular tune. My newly consecrated voice peels around the warming room and out into the cloister, where I imagine it dancing in victory around the courtyard. My very breath is a long sword.

When I look, Thérèse's eyes are bright like Papa's were in the chapel.

This soldier goes to war then. But armed, and not alone.

In Carmel: Pauline

I do not know how long she will remain with us. Though it is spring, she struggles to breathe, and her voice is changed: now husky and rough when once it was a smooth, sweet fluting. Mother Xavier acknowledges my concerns but declines to discuss them.

"She is a strong soul," she tells me. "Let us concern ourselves with the saving of souls who lack even an ounce of her strength."

We both read *La Croix*, so I guess to whom she refers. The most tortured of souls. A woman too.

Her name is Diana Vaughan. A Palladian victim, the abuse she has suffered at the hands of her fellow Freemasons is terrible to read. Too terrible to imagine. I am so glad that Papa was spared their details while on earth. Still, he can help us now with his heaven-bound prayers.

I feel in her my suffering opposite. I flew to the Carmel; she was dragged into an infernal family of demons. I serve and lead in response to prayer and the promptings of the heart; she was abused and defiled by those possessed. The devil's claws drew her blood; and yet she has somehow escaped. Isidore brings us the day's papers, but I am already aware of the ongoing scandal, as though by osmosis.

"I want to help this poor girl," he says, ever the provident uncle.

"We help her with our prayers. Even now we are partway through a novena to St. Joseph," I assure him.

But, as ever, the power of his thought weighs upon me.

"Send her a holy card," says Mother Xavier.

I set to work preparing one.

The next day I speak to Céline and Thérèse, inviting them to my cell's anteroom. We sit and I show them the photographs from the Joan of Arc play, before that fire broke out and scared us all.

"Sister Geneviève, these images are beautiful," I tell her.

"Thérèse makes them beautiful," she replies.

Thérèse herself attempts a smile, despite her breathlessness and the pallor of her face.

"We should send them to a soul who has experienced her own imprisonment."

"You mean Diana," says Thérèse, perceptive as ever. "Yes. I would like to offer her our love."

"This one, I thought," I say, pointing to the image of Thérèse-Joan leaning against Céline-Barbara, the plain wall of the Lourdes courtyard as background. "I have made some touches to the light, Céline, I hope you don't mind." She doesn't admit to minding, of course. "We will send it with the assurance of our prayers. Perhaps one day we shall see Diana in the parlor."

"Or the novitiate," says Thérèse. "There is no limit to God's mercy, if He is allowed to pour it into us."

"Who stops Him, then?" responds Céline.

I tense up; I don't want an argument here. I know there have been sharp words in the novitiate, despite the novices knowing their assistant mistress is unwell. But Thérèse doesn't retract. Instead, she burns with her simple message: "We do."

In Carmel: Marie

We are at supper in the refectory. The U-shape of the trestle tables is populated by hungry nuns. Soon it will be Lent once more, our season of austerities. But today Mother Xavier has authorized a cup of red wine for each sister. I sip mine gratefully. It warms my throat and radiates outwards to my whole body. I feel myself glowing under the rough cloth of my habit. I glance unobtrusively around and wonder whether the others feel a similar radiance. My thoughts, swimming somewhat in this unauthorized reflection, return to the lectrice of the week. Sister St. Luke reads from an obituary notice from Nantes of a Carmelite who died in her forties.

"Her last words, to her devoted Mother, were of her great love for the Divine Mercies reflected in nature. 'How I will miss the birds, the trees, the very blades of grass!' Yet she remained abandoned to the will of God until her last breath."

I lift my spoon to my mouth, swallow hot soup, and follow it with a bite of bread.

Cough, cough.

It is Thérèse. From the corner of my eyes, I see her raise her napkin to her lips.

Cough.

She holds her breath. The refectory settles back to the sound of cutlery raised and lowered. Sister St. Luke returns to her reading.

Cough.

She tries to clear her throat, but another cough takes her, and then another. She breathes in, a labored rasp. A choking noise, a cough. A phlegmy, hacking cough.

I raise my eyes and look at Pauline, whose gaze meets mine. We cannot help it. Thérèse cannot help it. The cough is a little demon, grasping her viciously under her wimple and scapular. She tries to stifle it, to swallow and suppress it, but she cannot. I do not even try to look away. Her face is red with shame at the disruption she is causing. The noises of dining cease, as does Sister St. Luke's narration. At last, Thérèse looks up towards the prioress, her face a desperate appeal for help and for forgiveness.

"Sister Thérèse!" Mother's words are like a rap on the knuckles from an impatient schoolmistress. "Would you please just leave us!"

Her chair groans and scrapes against the tiles as she immediately stands. She coughs still, though she tries so hard to keep her mouth clamped shut. She bows and for a moment I wonder if she will try to prostrate herself. I want to help her, but without a further glance she leaves the refectory. I hear her cough as it recedes along the cloister and is absorbed into the stairwell.

A sustained and strained silence ensues. Then, responding to the snap of Mother Xavier's fingers, Sister St. Luke turns the page of the obituary circular, and begins to read once more.

In Carmel: Céline

Eastertide. And atheist Leo Taxil arises to taunt us. We read, three days after the event, of his speech at the Paris Geographical Society. Instead of revealing Diana, he declares she never existed, and instead reveals himself a wicked fraud, and—oh, horror—projects Thérèse and myself as images of public mockery across the great hall. The sophisticated audience sees us and laughs. But they do not see us. They see pale girls playing dress-up. They see gullible Catholic women. They see the foolishness they want to see. But they cannot know her heart. Anyone who had the slightest hint of how it burns would never do this. But the world is wicked, and she is dying for it.

She says nothing; she saves her precious breath. But she tears out the copybook pages in which she had transcribed some of this so-called convert's prayers and walks slowly to the compost piles at the back of the hen coop. When she comes back, she looks at me blankly, her eyes dark.

People can be very cruel. I knew it with my head, of course—not so much in my soul. This must strike her too. But we cannot converse as we used to at Les Buissonets, so I let her return to her needlework for Sister Marie-Joseph. She takes her workbasket back to her cell, shutting the door behind her.

In Carmel: Lucie Guérin

Thérèse appears beside me in the warming room. Her face is pale and there are beads of sweat on her brow and upper lip.

"Lucie, I beg of you. Look as though we are talking this evening."

Protect me, say her eyes. *Protect me from prying nuns and from expending energy which I no longer have.*

So I help her, she who has taught me everything I know of this consecrated life. I murmur softly for both of us throughout the hour. Thérèse nods and sways as though in response to my words, though her movements, which seem pained enough, are no clear response to my bland anecdotes of life in the kitchen and refectory. In her hands she clasps some small squares of paper trimmed with lace. Holy cards in the making—they stay unmade.

After the hour I help her to the dormitory stairs.

"Thank you, Lucie," she manages, with a forced smile that does not convince. "I will be better tomorrow, perhaps." Neither do her words convince.

It is little surprise when, two weeks later, Mother Xavier dispenses Thérèse from all her work duties. I write to Papa and Mama with the news. We have officially been told nothing but coughing and such weakness in a young nun leads us to whisper our conclusions. It is surely Phthisis. The tubercles must have spread. I catch my reflection in the dark glass of the refectory windows after supper; I look sadder than the Virgin of Sorrows.

Entering Life

1897

In Carmel: Pauline

I am thirty-two years old, a cloistered nun for twelve years. When I left the world, Thérèse was nine. I realize her pain then as our roles are now reversed; she is leaving for heaven, having kept her imminent parting as silent as a swallow on the wing.

Through the night I dream fitfully. Thérèse is a doll I have dropped on the floor and Léonie has claimed for her own. I search out Marie to complain and have her soothe me with anodyne words, but she tells me Mama has died. I squint at the balance ledgers of our Carmel, wondering whether I can buy Thérèse another body. It needn't be a china one, perhaps a papier-mâché torso, wrapped in petals. Envelopes sit on the prioress's desk, addressed to me. My God, every one of them is from Thérèse, in her natural, heavenwards handwriting. My hands are wrapped in bandages. How can I open them?

At one o'clock in the morning, I rise from my pallaise, put on scapular and sandals, and wrap around me the long cream mantle of a Carmelite. Lighting the lamp with difficulty (cold fingers rather than a bad lamp) I take the unprecedented step of moving along the dormitory corridor and knocking on the cell door of Mother Prioress. I am uncertain whether I am asleep or awake. Perhaps I sleepwalk, for my mouth is dry and the seconds stretch and contract in an uneven pulse.

Mother Xavier opens the door. "Agnès."

She seems unsurprised. Like me, she is wearing a white cap and the robe of our habit but is veil-less. Was she even sleeping? An oil lamp burns steadily on the small desk in the antechamber to her cell. There are papers on the desk, a quill and inkwell. A candle also offers its glimmer, placed in front of a small Madonna and Child in the corner opposite her desk. My skin prickles. She looks at me inscrutably and beckons me in. I dip my right forefinger in the holy water stoup and bless myself.

"Sit, daughter."

I sit on the visitor's stool. She in the chair. Her features dip and darken in the night.

"Mother, forgive me for the intrusion. I have sinned against obedience in my breaking of the Great Silence, and against charity in my disregard for your—"

"It's about Thérèse, isn't it? Nothing else would ruffle your feathers in such a way, Agnès. In fact, I have been expecting you these last few weeks." As always, she can wrong-foot me in a second. But hold, Pauline. I am here for a purpose, neither to remonstrate nor receive motherly comfort. I am here for Thérèse. For the dream letters unopened within their envelopes.

"Agnès, any mother would be heavy with natural sorrow given the illness of their youngest daughter. You and I share that burden, in many ways."

I swallow my frustration, and some of my fear. "I am grateful for your warmth and care towards our whole family."

She raises her left hand slightly. "Sister Thérèse has borne her sickness with exemplary grace. We must look forward with her to her heavenly reward, which is, alas, soon to come."

She waits for my response. I pause to gather my courage.

"Mother, I am full of longing to tell you what burns in my heart."

"So I see, Agnès. Well—it seems the time is right."

A trace of irony laces her eloquence. I take a deep breath and embark on my mission.

"Mother, when I was our unworthy prioress, I asked Sister Thérèse to write down her childhood memories. I did not mean for her to take them as an order, but such is her zeal that she committed herself to writing the story of her life. She did not remind me of my suggestion until the completed manuscript was presented to me in high summer last year."

Mother Xavier folds her hands and seems to frown.

"Sister Thérèse obliged you in your whim."

"Mother, you are right: it was a whim. And burdened with the duties of our office, I did not even open her copybook until you resumed your natural role as shepherdess of your flock, and I found a few moments of the day to attend to personal matters.

"I was amazed at what I read. It was beautifully written—full of grace! I have never read of a soul with such purpose and clarity—this from Teresi—from a sister in spirit and in nature, who is so young, so quiet, so unassuming in our daily life. I would like to offer you this text, Mother, as you are just as much a mother to this graceful soul as I."

So far, Mother Xavier seems unperturbed by my words. The candle glows in front of the perfect miniature mother and child as I continue.

"I approach you at this unusual hour with an equally unusual request. But such is my conviction that Divine Grace operates in Thérèse's words that I must share with you my thoughts. Her copybook for me mostly recounts the holy atmosphere of our childhood home. As you know, our father was a saint, and raised four of his daughters to be given to the Carmel. His sacrifice was completed by the total self-offering of his final illness and death. All this she recounts beautifully. But most beautiful of all is her account of her first year here—as befitting the spiritual beauty you have built within its walls."

Mother Xavier remains silent. For a moment I think I am still rehearsing back in my cell. The words unfurl from my mouth, betraying their polished origins. And having set the pace, I must continue.

"Mother, my request is this: Sister Thérèse is too humble to continue her memoir on her own, without another request from one whom she cannot disobey. Her work is no longer trivial. I think it is of great importance to our Carmel. And also, dear Mother"—and here I must be as diplomatic as our Holy Foundress herself—"as a community circular must, so sadly, be written for this dear sister almost certainly within the term of a year, what better way to have material than to have her write, both for you, and for the wider community of Carmelites throughout our suffering country? Such a text would be a spiritual gem."

I have finished my plea and await her judgment. I have gambled, have taken a great risk—not only with the future of Thérèse's words, but with what she has already written. It would be entirely within Mother's power, and not entirely alien to her character, to confiscate Thérèse's *Springtime Story* and put it on the fire, as a fruit of vanity sprung from misuse of office.

Silence reigns as it has always reigned in this deep hour of the night.

Mother Xavier sits in the chiaroscuro of her lamplight. Half her face is like a burnished wooden carving. The other half black as our veil, as the curtain between priest and penitent. I cannot hear her breathe. I am, however, painfully conscious of my own breath as I await my sentence. No doubt this older woman is turning my information over in her mind.

After a long pause, the span of at least seven Aves, she speaks.

"You may not believe it after our previous disagreements, but I recognize your quality, Pauline. You came to Carmel with a true vocation and have been strict with our rule and modest in your manner. Yet you are still fearful. You like to stop a good way within our boundaries, and no doubt you have found some of my own ways not without risk or question. This has worried me, more than a little.

"Now you are experiencing great sadness, and great love. Yes, natural love, for your little Thérèse, to whom you have been a mother longer than you have been Agnès of Jesus. Do not fight this love, Pauline. It is God who shaped our natures, and your nature is one doubly purified by prayer and suffering. Your mission to love will be twice necessary here.

"As to the matter of the writing. This is an unusual situation. Sister Thérèse excels in obedience, but I too see the workings of grace. She is a beautiful soul, *Mother* Agnès. And a hidden one. I will tell her she must continue with her personal history. When the time comes, you will fashion her words after the manner of a spiritual testament, in language that befits circulation among our sister Carmels. You will do this with my full confidence. I thank you for bringing this cause to my attention."

I am overcome with relief and gratitude. I make to stand up and wonder how to phrase my thanks to this unknown Mother Xavier, full of compassion, who sleeps within the proud superior. But she makes the gesture with her hand again.

"One more thing. Yes, you will do this, Agnès, and you will shape your sister's writing so that the whole is of one body—and is dedicated to me, entirely and only to me."

In Carmel: Marie

I am on my way back from the garden sheds, having done some good weeding this mild June morning. It is still some time before our first meal, and my stomach has started to grumble. Perhaps I could slip into the refectory, where some of my latest herbal tisane still sits in its jar on the ledge beside the kitchen door. I pause in the sunlight, surrounded by scents of the natural world blooming into fullness. The air is still and clear, and I catch a duet of lilting laughs from the alleyway ahead; though not strictly countenanced, this young women's laughter is as light and uplifting as birdsong. I feel a lightness in my own heart too—my body is a thing of nature after all, and my heart takes part in its harmony. Though I know there is sorrow to come, God sometimes gives us these honeyed tastes of heaven. I turn into the chestnut tree-lined alley myself and see a solitary nun in an invalid's chair, soaking up the sun in the recess at the alley's end.

I know from the bend of her veiled head that it is Thérèse. The invalid chair is familiar too—it was Papa's. She is not hunched in pain or in prayer but is writing in a copybook. This would seem odd did I not know that

Mother Xavier has tasked her with continuing the memoir Pauline commissioned from her some years ago—years when she was in such good health that she was considered for our foundation in Saigon. I remember how my heart had clenched at the thought of her departure. Now she faces another departure, so much more final. Our cemetery is not far from where we now are. I shiver, despite the warmth of the sun. But at such moments I have learned to counsel myself.

Remember, in the end, that all is love, Marie.

Thérèse's words from her winter retreat echo on in my soul: how much I have to thank her for. While I still feel the old tug to approach and coddle her, just as at Les Buissonets, to soften her grief and assuage her scruples, I acknowledge how little she needs my advice now.

Nevertheless, as her blood sister, I am entitled to a kiss, and just as I am about to step into the dappled alley towards her, one of the two now-visible novices beats me to it: novice Anne breaks into a fluid trot towards her assistant mistress (I am sure she still thinks of Thérèse as such, despite Thérèse's dispensation from her duties). Sister Anne's white veil flares in the afternoon light.

"Sister Thérèse! It is so good to see you out in the fresh air! Do you sketch our miraculous Virgin?" She refers to a little marble statue of the Madonna nestling at the end of the alleyway.

Thérèse lowers her arm and lifts her face towards her visitor. Her gestures indicate ease and welcome.

Not waiting for a reply, Anne continues, "I hope you are not feeling lonely while Sister Mags and I are busy bees elsewhere. But look—I've brought you some flowers from the meadow to brighten your day. Here!"

The meadow is our little square of grasses and flowers situated between more orderly lawns and the laundry room and hen coops. Anne tumbles some flecks of blue into Thérèse's lap—I think I see corncockles and forget-me-nots. And now here is little Sister Magdalene, who adds to the haphazard bouquet. I am fond of these young souls, and think to join the little party, but Anne nudges her friend at the sound of a summoning bell, and they head off towards the cloisters and their duties.

By the time I reach Thérèse myself, she has tidied the flowers away into her habit pocket and is holding her handkerchief to her mouth. Coughing gently, she meets my eyes and smiles.

"Are you alright, my darling?" I resist the urge to place my palm against her brow.

"I am, Marie. It is all—grace."

Her voice is quiet but composed. Shadows from a passing cloud flow over us before the sunlight blesses her again.

Normandy: Maurice

I ask for her photograph, and I do not seek Du Barre's permission for the request. Where this boldness comes from, I am hard-pressed to say, unless it is her own; she lends me the strength of a man—of a soldier, in fact—a strength I lack.

In another life, I imagine myself her suitor. A life where she is less pure, but I am more so. Where letters lead to an exchange of images; cards to gifts; promises to trysts; walks along the promenade to comfortable hotels; tearooms to sitting rooms; a glance to a smile; a smile to a fingertip kiss; a man's hand to the soft skin of a woman's face, and—ah. There I must not stray; I cannot stray, for the sake of her love.

My sister in Christ, I write. *I would love to see your eyes while you remain with us in exile.*

The envelope comes quickly. It is July. I remove a fine layer of tissue paper from the photograph and see her features for the first time. *My grand look—or so the novices tell me*, she has written, in pencil, on a little square of paper that accompanies the image.

She kneels in a grassy corner of the convent, the wall behind her no doubt separating her from the world around. She wears habit, veil, and wimple, as expected. The long ivory mantle of the Carmelite falls from around her shoulders. She holds up two large holy cards: the two images which signify her names in religion—the Child Jesus, and the Holy Face. It is hard to judge her height and general size due to the voluminous habit and the lack of referents within the photograph, but I estimate her to be a few hands shorter than myself, and to be of reasonably broad physique. All of these things, in my imperfect way, I had imagined for myself.

But it is her face that draws me; renders me weak and exalted with fresh recognition. Her jaw juts slightly, subtly forward, as though she dares me to love her through all the barriers of society, propriety, time, space, life—death. Her mouth is fixed in the merest hint of a smile, lips slightly parted. Her eyes—dark eyes—stare straight at me; not for a second do they waver; not for a second did she fail the camera's orders. Above these eyes, dark brows, and below them, dark shadows, and creasing of the skin. Her cheeks are not gaunt, and yet they are drawn. Did I not already know, I would have been unable to estimate the age of this woman. But I do already know; and more than I would wish to.

She is twenty-four years old. She is a dying nun.

At twenty-four, had she been born a man, she could have become a priest.

As it is, God calls her to Himself, and for that, she must give up the little life she was given. Her letters have prepared me as best they can, and I have written to her both my anguish and my blessing. What more can I do, being bound, God willing, for the missions?

In a fever of longing, I imagine being already priested, taking the train to Lisieux, and a carriage direct to the Carmel. Would they let me through the enclosure to see her? I would kneel at her bedside, take that pale, thin hand, lower my head to kiss her, feather-light, strong as a eucharistic prayer. I would offer her the host; I would offer her viaticum. The angels would guide my hands as I touched the crown of her head, her brow, the sides of her suffering throat, and made her well; light streaming through us like a grace.

On the other side of the little note, a further message. Ah—I had not noticed, rapt as I was in my self-celebrating vision. In pencil once more, more obviously shaky than on the reverse. A request.

> *Would you please save me the trouble of requesting a holy martyr's relic, and send me, while you still live, a lock of your hair?*

And her initials, and a mark where her pencil must have grazed the paper as it fell from her hand.

So I do as she asks. She is my queen, and I her knight. She will never be mine; I will, therefore, forever serve her. Or, she is my priest, and I her penitent. She my saint, and I her devotee. I snip the locks from my skull, above my left temple. I push the inch-long brown hairs into a fold of white paper, fasten it shut with a pin, and send it with a letter which thanks her, and thanks her again, for her prayers.

In Carmel: Céline

We gather around the cross in the cloister courtyard. The novices and newly professed support her as the summer evening gathers in. She strews rose petals onto the granite base of the crucifix, as has been our custom, the custom she established, these strange and wonderful years. As I arrange for a photograph, the others kneel at Thérèse's feet. For a moment or two she holds her pose, but then lets the petals scatter, and her hard breathing continues. Although imperfectly suspended for the camera lens, the moment strikes me as one of infinite clarity, a radiance painfully exposed; even while she has already turned towards eternity.

In Carmel: Lucie Guérin

Doctor de Cornière has been visiting.

"He looks like a man of the world, with his jacket and his hair smoothed back like that," comments Anne of the Trinity.

The doctor orders vesicatories. I wash the cups afterwards, imagining their burning rims pressing down on my sides, back, flanks.

Céline, who has moved into the nurse's station, poorly suppresses a sigh as I return the cups but leave them in full view of our patient, who is currently sleeping. I go and spend time before her beloved statue of the Holy Child, my face hot.

Marie emerges from the infirmary, her apron bunched up in her hands. She is visibly upset.

"Tell me, Lucie: Would you allow your child to suffer when she has been an angel her whole life? How many pearls does a heavenly crown need?"

"She suffers for others, Sister Marie," I offer, aware of the reversal in our usual exchanges. I have heard Mother Xavier extol the virtues of suffering well borne, though I wish I had not.

Marie snorts in what looks like anger.

"Let them suffer for themselves!" she says. "Céline is right. Some people do not deserve her suffering, nor would they receive it with any grace if they knew that she was offering it." I think of Monsieur Taxil and heretic Father Loysell, for whom Thérèse has prayed. "There is merit in an act of mercy also," Marie adds.

Later I return to her bedside. She sleeps on, peaceful in her rest.

"We are giving her the morphine syrup," confides Céline, forgetting my earlier clumsiness. "She is barely aware of it, but takes whatever Pauline tells her to. There is no shame in easing her path; we are the hands of a merciful God," she adds, a slight shake in her voice, from anger or sadness or both. "At any rate, if we are at fault, her purity remains. She will intercede for us one day, knowing the intentions of our hearts."

Lourdes: Maurice

I travel the country to beg God for her cure. This place is awash with pilgrim groups. I have joined a Normandy cortège as the least consequential of participants. I am nothing but a stretcher-bearer and feel all the more genuine for this. I stand beneath the horse-drawn coaches of the indisposed and monied, assisting in the carrying of invalids to the source of blessed water, the springs miraculously divined by our Blessed Bernadette. Most are women, older women, tightly bound in their black frills. Each I bear with as much love and dignity as I can muster. Each I imagine as a type of Thérèse. How I wish I could bear her frail body here; with what love would I carry it to the Virgin's healing streams!

But perhaps there will be no cure for her. All I can do is pray, and, poor seminarian that I am, I can barely manage a single Our Father. Instead, I try, and fail, and try again to curb my will, my despair in myself; and to offer all for love, confident that God asks nothing more than this simple trust in Him. This is my prayer. Each invalid I guide into the cold Lourdes water I offer up as intercession for her peace. All the while I think of her. She is my conduit to Christ Himself.

I help to lower these poor patients into the freezing baths of a desperate faith. They rise up drenched and shivering and dare not speak their fears. Our Lady has healed them, or she has not. Who knows the hearts of the dying? Who among us knows their own heart in all its frailty and pain? And I think to be a priest: but it is she who bodies forth the infinite graces and suffering of Christ. It is she who teaches me not just to accept her dying, but to carry on living.

In Carmel: Marie

Céline exhales and wipes her brow with the back of her hand; her face is a pale moon of sorrow. The sleeves of her habit are rolled back, and her tunic pinned up as though for heavy manual work. Over her habit is an old apron. It has been washed frequently and recently, but still the pinkish-brown bloodstains are traceable on the once-white cotton. We are in the doorway of the infirmary of the Holy Face, where Thérèse is confined to bed.

I make the sign for the doctor—two fingers tapping the pulse on my inner wrist—and raise my eyebrows. With a slight shake of her head, she indicates no. But then, she unexpectedly makes two signs herself. The first, a hand scribbling in the air: writing. Then hands pressed together in prayer and immediately raised and spread wide: priest.

Céline is writing to a priest? Is it Almire?

No. She shakes her head again, reading my mind. With a quick glance towards the room's interior, she indicates its resident, Thérèse. And then, breathily mouthing the words, she tells me, "Monsieur Bellière." Yes, I have heard about her task of writing to this would-be mission priest. I look into the room, not wanting to disturb her.

The bed has been moved so she can look out into our little garden beyond, and a band of sunshine graces her covers. She is propped up on her pillows, and wears the short white veil of the invalid, as though she is a novice again, preparing for her next set of vows. Already she seems wrapped in a profound quiet.

A shiver of curiosity arises in my mind. This seminarian, chosen to be the subject of her prayers—what graces he must be receiving, even now. But does she write to him with the ardor I wrote to Almire? Does she wait, and wait, and wait for his word? She has never met him, to my knowledge. Do they exchange images? Does she long to hear the sound of his voice? Dear God, any comfort to her is surely allowed by now. And I hope a little—inchoately, selfishly—for my own final days to be accompanied by a fine image of one who guided my life through his strong, sparse words.

"She writes him long letters," says Céline in a low voice, "very long. She takes several days. I do not know where she finds the strength. It drains her and sustains her."

"Does he respond with wisdom?"

But why should she need his wisdom?

Céline shakes her head again.

"She says he is her little adopted brother. I think she guides him, as she guided us in the novitiate. Only," and Céline hesitates, but seeing that I have never censured her, continues, "with a little less severity, and a little more sweetness."

Later, sitting by Thérèse's side as she endures the evening in a half-conscious struggle to breathe, I see the photographs pinned to her dark bedside drapes. Photographs, not of her sisters, but of three priests, as though her yearning for brothers has multiplied during her mortal sickness. Here is Father Roulland, our missionary priest recently posted to Asia, plump and resplendent in his clerical satin. Here is Monsieur Bellière. He is young! He looks askance from the camera and his face is slim and callow, with a long, soft beard. And here is a third photograph, noticeably creased and less in focus than the others. It is Théophane Vénard, dead these four decades; beheaded by the Chinese; it is said that he went to his death with a heart as light as a bird released from its cage.

"She finds great consolations in Théophane's martyrdom," Pauline explains to me in the cloister walk. "He will be a saint one day—his soul was full of joy." She sighs, then forces her thin lips into a smile. "As to Maurice Bellière, she has a lock of his hair under her pillow." She looks at me as if in confidence. "I believe she will follow him to the African missions after her death, such is her zeal for his soul."

I look out through the side door to the green of our garden; beautiful, but enclosed. Yes, her soul is like a letter; luminous and blessed. Released from its envelope, she will soar across the world.

In Carmel: Céline

I take my nurse's apron off one morning, after washing her fragile frame. She comes back from wherever she had been in a reverie and turns her face to me; she is still childlike despite the sketch of pain beneath the skin. She contemplates the little rips and stains on my habit. Automatically I start to smooth it down, as though I were still in the world and my gown had got crumpled with sitting too long.

"Poor little sister," she says; her voice weak and hoarse. "In heaven you will get your shining robe."

But something in her words doesn't feel right. My instinct is to comfort her. I wonder whether I should wind up the odd little musical box that Léonie has unaccountably sent her.

"We will all rejoice in heaven," I say. "The skies will be perpetually blue, and Mama and Papa await us." Then I add, "And the Blessed Virgin herself awaits you."

On this last point I know I am bold. But the woman who mothered God himself must surely do more than dispense graces from a golden throne. Thérèse, with all her daring, would not deprive me of this idea. In other circumstances, we would talk about it, draw it, paint it, pray over it. But she is unhappy, and it is from more than physical distress, which, dear God, is dreadful enough.

"These thoughts of heaven," she says, between rasping breaths. "They . . . do not move me, Céline. I have lost my sense of such a place."

"Thérèse, my darling. What are you saying?"

"I—I—no longer believe in that sort of heaven. It—it is a trial He has sent me." She stops to cough, and her previously pale face takes on an uneven purplish hue. "Do you remember the journey to Rome? The train plunging into those tunnels dark as night?" I nod. "Jesus has placed me in such a tunnel. I see no light ahead of me."

Moments of that journey's blackness and terror rush back into my soul. I start to understand just how much Thérèse is suffering.

"But surely you have received help. From Father Youf?"

Even as I say it, I realize the unlikeliness of Thérèse receiving support from our irascible chaplain. Graciously, she shakes her head.

"I do not—see him over this matter. For one, I do not wish to be told my soul is imperiled." Despite her condition, we share a grim smile. Father Youf tends to predict the worst for his penitent sisters. We have had more supportive counsel from our visiting priests. "But last year he bid me write the creed to keep near my heart. That I did—in my blood." She gestures to the paper folded on top of the gospels that rest on her side table. "And

Mother Xavier," she adds, falling back onto her pillow, "she understands her little daughter. More . . . than I once thought." And here she offers another little smile. "The darkness shines in its own way, perhaps."

I leave her with this thought, bewildered at how I might ever paint such a concept.

In Carmel: Pauline

I write to her while she still lives.

Before I flew here, she would climb on my lap and ask me if she had been good. Sometimes, I was strict with her for the sake of strictness; like Mama, I believed that a disciplined soul is pleasing to God. I think now that I could merely have loved her. And there is such little time left.

We dance around each other in our words. I am still shaken by her months-long secrecy, the secret of her impending death! And she, so grown up that she is graduating from this life at twenty-four, like the youngest of priests. I fear she cannot quite take me back into her heart.

She calls me a scared soul and tells me she is unafraid, that she will be a missionary yet, returning to spend her heaven blessing this earth. I sit at her bedside and catch her words as though they are tears. I absorb them into my soul's paper. I am no longer her teacher. She teaches me: how to pray, how to smile, how to live.

How to die.

The infirmary is flooded with late summer sunlight.

I can't help it; the questions come. I am a clumsy pupil. As though I am preparing her for another first Communion, I question her. So close to death, such a wise pupil; my concept of catechist and student are blurred.

"When will you die?"

"On any day God asks."

"Would you rather die or live, should God allow it?"

A pause while she gets her breath. "Neither! Only His will," she manages.

"Of what will you die?"

She looks at me, struggling either to laugh or reprove, I cannot tell.

"Little mother. I am dying of death!" Then she adds in whisper, "But entering life. . ."

I write it down. The paradoxical nature of her words doesn't escape me, but perhaps their hidden meaning will emerge. The sunlight gilds all things, even as it dims.

In Carmel: Lucie Guérin

On the feast of Our Lady's Nativity, we gather for an extended recreation. Thérèse is not with us. I sing the final stanza of her song, the one Céline calls king of all her poetry: "Living on Love." She lives on little else now.

I visit her later to let her know, but she is full of distress because she has forgotten Sister Martha's birthday, her thirtieth. I promise I will send Martha her best wishes, but she insists on writing a shaky little note with her stub of a pencil.

When I visit her a few days later, she is distraught for a different reason. Somebody—Sister St. John?—informed her that she was not considered much of a nun because she had never had to suffer.

"How can she say that?!" I can't help myself, brandishing a mental sword in my cousin's honor.

"It does me good, Lucie," she manages, recollecting herself. She points to the ruby-red cordial by her bedside. "Looks delicious, doesn't it?" A fit of coughing stops her talking. I am reminded of the pretend potions we used to make from leaves and berries when we played hermits at the bottom of the garden and think to distract her with the memory. But she gets in first with this: "Such medicine can be more bitter than sweet."

Even now she teaches me, pointing to truth behind easy beliefs.

Finally, she receives extreme unction, Communion. Céline and Sister Aimée help her swap her sickbed cape and veil for the toque, wimple, and short black veil. An unwell-looking Father Youf shuffles in, placing the vessels on the table at the foot of her bed. From there he turns to face her and raises his right hand in absolution. Lit up perhaps with the intensity of the moment, Thérèse is more animated than she has been in a while, as though eternity has started to shine through her frail frame.

Between breaths she tells us, "It is life that I go to—there my mission will begin."

Public Chapel, Carmel of Lisieux: Léonie

We are summoned to the Carmel. The light in the public chapel has faded. It is dim and flickering, like my own understanding of faith. But I know Thérèse is dying. There is nothing to be said or done. I sit at the front before the ornate altar. To my right, a dark drape covers the great grille. Behind it is the nuns' choir, but I sense it is empty. Uncle Isidore is beside me, stooped over in prayer. Aunt Véronique sits at my left side. Her crystal rosary gleams alongside a handkerchief of Alençon lace. We pray for her soul, for her sisters, and for ourselves.

I half expect a flutter of wings—I yearn so very much for a sign. She has promised me that one will be sent: a sign made of love. A sign that heals all the hurts of the past. I pray stiffly, holding myself back from great howls of grief. Léonie, a stiff sister in her stiff body.

We hear the bell. It is loud and insistent like an angry teacher.

At the age of thirteen, she showed me how to punctuate. I remember her happiness as I slowly progressed. She understood for me the written word is like a cage—a frightening prospect, a trap. She helped me on my own terms. A soreness in my throat catches me unawares. I would like to help her flee her cage. I bury my face in my over-large hands.

Time passes.

My stomach rumbles, rudely. I swallow down my shame.

The bell again.

Perhaps if I count. I pull my own poor rosary from my handbag. One, two, three. Our Lady come to me. The infantile rhyme loops around in my mind. I offer it to God, having nothing better.

Uncle Isidore shifts back in his chair, and Aunt does the same. She lays her hand on my shoulder. She is not cross with me. She is terribly sad. We are all daughters to her, and to lose one is the worst pain that can be felt. She has lost and regained me twice in recent years. Léonie, an adult daughter, helpless as a child.

The evening comes on. All the vigils I have attended well up into my mind, like blood which cannot be damped down.

In Carmel: Céline

All these hours she has been in her agony. I reach over and place the ice on her burning dying lips and she looks at me with eyes full of suffering. I rub the ice gently on her mouth and the suffering mingles with solace, and as she looks at me her gaze reveals a sheen of love. And mustering all her strength, she tells God that she loves Him, and oh! looks up, rapt, as if glimpsing a world of pure light.

Then her soul slips away, and her head falls back.

The community is summoned; they are mere background hatching.

I stumble out into the cool of the evening, and the skies are dark and dull and drizzling.

A single, anguished, sob escapes from my lungs.

The world fades away and I think I can see stars.

Public Chapel, Carmel of Lisieux: Léonie

And then there is movement. Turn sister Babeth approaches us from the back of the chapel, with a note in her hand. Uncle stands. Aunt turns her head and reaches for my hand. Uncle reads the notes and passes it to me, and Aunt puts her arm around me as we read together in the dim lights of the chapel.

> Our angel is in heaven. She left us at half past seven, at peace after crying, "My God, I love You!" Then a long last look of bliss. Oh, what did she see!

The neat words blur on their paper. I grope after their meaning. Did she, oh, did she find her way to joy?

In Carmel: Lucie Guérin

After the death Céline rushes out to the garden, and soon afterwards Marie of the Sacred Heart joins her. I look at Pauline, ready to take my direction from her. But she kneels, mute as a statue, at her sister's bedside. The others are as though suspended in a liquid: swaying slightly, caught in prayer, distorted by grief.

Only Thérèse is at peace; her head still on the pillow and turned slightly away. Silence blooms from her body; silence hard earned after such terrible weeks.

After some time—I do not know how long—Mother Xavier snaps her fingers and rises. Automatically we rise in her wake—apart from Pauline, who remains kneeling and who has covered her face with her hands.

"We will pray the litany for departed sisters in the choir—at once," says Mother Xavier. Her face is stony set.

Of all the deaths she has seen, this is surely the hardest. But a death is a birth in the house of Mount Carmel.

Of all births, the hardest and holiest.

In Carmel: Céline

The next morning, I try to acknowledge her new state.

"She is in heaven," says Marie, pale, reassuring herself as much as me.

I look at Thérèse's face. It is smooth and dry now and framed once again in her full toque and veil. The trace of a smile plays on her lips, as though she dreams of her beloved meadows. I would beg her to share these dreams with me, but her eyes and mouth are closed.

"I will take her picture," I say, suddenly sure of what must be done.

"Here? Another hour and we will take her to the choir."

"I know. But look how beautiful she is. Let me take this for us, and for Pauline. And for Léonie, so she can see her in the infirmary." I nearly say, "on her deathbed," but I think better of it.

I set up the camera by her bedside and expose the plates to the room's thin light. As I do so, just for a moment there is the scent of violets. Then I take them down to my darkroom, as though I have collected her last smile in their chemical layers.

It is one of my most beautiful photographs—only a photograph of course, not the living display of soul through flesh. But the stillness of the dead ensures there is no blurring of her features. There is a clarity to the image that surely catches at the heart, whether you knew her in life or no. Idly, in my meditation that evening, I imagine a future Pope kneeling in front of this photograph one day, as though at the bedside of a much-loved saint.

Two days later, I take her last image. In the choir the light is more muted, and Thérèse herself has aged with the gravity of death. Her brows and lashes have darkened, and her cheeks have sunken. Her skin, by contrast, is as white as marble, as untouched ice. I shiver as I operate the camera. There is a majesty to her, inhabited by death, that I have not seen before.

"Pray for me, little one," I whisper, touching my fingertips to her cold lips. "Remember what you said about spending your heaven here below."

* * *

Le Normand: Death Notice

It is with great sadness we have learned of the death, last Thursday evening, at the Monastery of Our Lady of Mount Carmel, of a young woman who offered all her youthful years to prayer and sacrifice. Mademoiselle Marie-Françoise-Thérèse Martin gave herself to the consecrated life at the tender age of fifteen, becoming Sister Thérèse of the Child Jesus. After ten years of cloistered life this angelic soul went home to God, and we hope with great fervor that she received the heavenly crown that her pure life, and terrible final sufferings, surely merited.

The funeral will be celebrated Monday morning in the chapel of the Carmel.

Le Normand offers to the family of Sister Thérèse of the Child Jesus, to the Mother Prioress, and the other nuns of Carmel, the homage of its respectful condolences.

*   *   *

You are invited to assist at the service and burial of
Marie-Françoise-Thérèse Martin
in religion
Sister Thérèse of the Child Jesus
who fell piously asleep in the Lord
September 30, 1897
in her 25th year.
It will take place on Monday, October 4, at 9:00 a.m. precisely.
Pray to God for her!

From:
Mademoiselle Léonie Martin; Monsieur and Madame Isidore Guérin; Monsieur le Docteur Francis La Neele and Madame La Neele.

Lisieux: Léonie

In the cold, we climb the hill to the top of the Champs-Remouleux Cemetery in Lisieux. I lead the mourners. I am her only close relative still living in the world. My mourning dress and thin coat button me up in blackness. Inside my black gloves, my hands are cramped and freezing. Uncle walks behind me. Every so often I hear him clearing his throat. The plain coffin is borne by Francis and the funeral directors until it reaches its resting place. Thérèse rests inside, relieved of all the pains of adulthood.

"The Carmel's own burial ground is full. I have made arrangements for a generous plot in the town's cemetery to be set aside for them," Uncle has explained.

He has buried his grief in business. It seems wrong that Thérèse is forbidden from sleeping within the enclosure she loved so much.

"Won't she be lonely?" I say.

But I will be forgiven. The bereaved are allowed their clumsiness.

"We will visit her, my darling," murmurs Adèle, treading delicately beside me. "We have that privilege now."

As I cast my handful of soil over the grave, I whisper to her: "Sleep tight my little one. You and I have been returned to the world without our willing it." And then I add, "Léonie will never stop praying, praying we are brought back home."

At Sea: Maurice

We set sail for Algiers; the ship takes me direct to my unknown future, and the autumnal sea is deceptively calm. I left Marseilles with the blessing of my mother—of Annabelle. My heart twists: I have done her so many disservices small and large. This woman who adopted me as her son and made him the joyful center of her family life. Annabelle Barthélémy has not found my vocation to the missions easy. But some sweet soul has eased her qualms through their powerful prayer, and I do not hesitate to guess whom.

Here it is late evening, and I stand alone on the deck. We have many passengers, some travelling for trade and civil duties, others, like me, bound for the missions; but all have now retired. Something keeps me alert and awake. The air is fresh and rich with the scents of ocean-borne travel: salt, oil, a brisk sense of human finitude within this relentless, restless geography of water. The night is also inky black and rich. Both elements harbor eternity and it is as if I am already sailing there.

I am beginning my life all over again. Once landed at Algiers, I will join the White Fathers at Maison-Carrée, their nearest outpost for my novitiate. I will don the white robes and the heavy wooden beads of a missionary. My possessions are necessarily scant, but I bear a few papers: a brief guide to seminary life in the order, and my letter of admission to the Fathers. And also, carefully hidden in their precious envelopes, wrapped in a soft scarf of my mother's, are the letters of my dying saint, my sister. In time she will join me; even now the envelope of her body unseals itself and her soul flies parallel to mine. She promised to send me her crucifix. I take the promise both literally and spiritually.

Such thoughts. I hold the cold deck rail with my left hand and the right I hold up to the night sky, hailing it, shielding my own soul from heaven's dazzling darkness.

Legacy

1898–1912

In Carmel: Pauline

Céline and I sit late in the anteroom to the library, oil lamps lit and blankets over our knees. We face each other across a pitted wooden table. Around us are scattered notes upon notes, one long letter, and two school copy books.

Thérèse's writing is overlaid with ours as we consider how to recreate her in word and image. The work seems endless, and a sweet pain like no other we've experienced. Huddled in her habit, Céline turns over a page, and in the inadequate light I think I see Thérèse's face as she bends to her task. Returning my focus to the papers in front of me, I take my pen and cross out some of her lines, correcting the grammar, excising the awkward. I am simply correcting her homework as I've always done. In my tiredness I forget she is dead. And then I remember.

But much is to be done. Primarily the dedications. All must be altered for Mother Xavier. I take the eraser and remove my name from the first dedicatory page. Far from dismayed, I experience a little flash of pride that although my name is removed, my hand edits the whole.

Then the phrasing. I fill out those sentences which trail into childishness. I mute the endearments. Prune the exclamations.

Then the adding.

"Céline, do you remember the time Thérèse gave her last *sou* to a poor old man? The year before Mama's great suffering?" Céline looks at me with a cautious expression. Of course, she does not; she would have been seven at most. I continue: "I think we should include it."

No reply, but she nods. Then she scores a fluid black line on a scrap of squared paper.

Now the difficulties of cutting. I read of Thérèse's temptations against the faith with a sort of horror. These words are very far from sweet. My throat constricts at them. I know full well that if another sister had confessed such thoughts to me during my term as prioress, I would have sent her straight to confession and marked her down as a danger to the community. Apostasy is a serious thing in an enclosed community. It infects, spreads. And my sister's habitual sweetness would make the revelations of her blackness of spirits all the more shocking. She writes of her oncoming death as a night of nothingness, then retracts her own statement, fearing to blaspheme. The term makes me shiver even now. I look at Céline: she knew of her little sister's terrors, by the end. A persistent whisper in my soul tells me Thérèse found her way to God through this very darkness, but I dare not quite articulate my thoughts.

How Mother Xavier first took this passage is a mystery, but her acceptance of it as part of my sister's final trial attests to her own brand of spiritual toughness. I sit up straight and pull my own woolen habit into shape. No: these strong words are not for others to read. I take up a scrap of paper that Céline has abandoned, trim it, and paste it over Thérèse's haunted thoughts.

Day after day, Céline and I work on the reconstitution of our lost sister. She struggles with her grief but recently has sought to salve it with a new drawing, what she calls her oval portrait of Thérèse, inspired by a group photograph from years ago. Thérèse excised and highlighted. Her young face pensive, as though gazing into her own future—and ours. Her veil falling in seemly—and seamless—fashion. Her mouth dainty in prayer. And I—I shape and dovetail her manuscript, where Thérèse herself was ad hoc, sometimes ragged. I labor to fashion an oval of a text, smoothly written, and rising to a beautiful point.

Such is my need to remain her teacher. To help with the homework of her whole written life.

In Carmel: Marie

"Marie," says Pauline, sitting down next to me on the bench outside the infirmary wall. We face the little meadow Thérèse herself would have looked at from her sickroom window. It is evening, and the sunset casts a deep gold on the autumnal scene. "Céline and I have read Teresita's letters to you, the ones you were inspired to ask for two years past."

"From her last retreat?"

"Yes. They are beautiful—they sing more clearly than ever."

"I know," I acknowledge. I have noticed, throughout all the rigamarole of death, just how alive and fragrant her soul still seems to be, especially in letters such as these.

"We would like to include one in the extended circular, with your permission. They will do much good for souls. If I am right, they have already given you the great grace of peace."

Her voice, like her body in its tidy habit, is prim. I think carefully before responding to her.

"It has taken me time—a long time, as it always does—but I think I understand her now, what she was trying to do, to say to me."

I keep my tone low, deliberate and even.

"She must have loved you very much to find the strength for these words."

I wonder then if my sister is jealous.

"She loved us all, Pauline. I asked her for a flower. She gave me a bouquet. I am sure she intended me to share my gift."

Pauline looks relieved. "I thank you, my darling. I knew your generous heart would agree." And then she continues, expanding on her plans. "Marie, I should tell you that we think that her first retreat letter should be the text with which we end the manuscript. It is both beautiful and certain. I have edited all her words as she herself asked me to do, but even so, her own declarations make the finer song. She is indeed love in the heart of the Church: she is nothing but love."

"Well, dear Agnès of Jesus," I tell her, "you are free to edit the manuscript as your heart dictates to you. I think that your new task may be one of promoting the memory of our little sister. She entrusted herself to you. You may have much to do in response to this trust."

"I hope not!" Pauline says, wincing under her veil at the prospect of a new burden.

And yet I sense the blooming of a call for her; a new call within an old vocation. The rich light gilds her face and hands as she reaches out to touch me lightly on the arm. I place my own around her slender shoulders.

Lisieux, with the Guérins: Léonie

Thérèse's book is in my hands: *The Story of a Soul*. Light and clean and beautiful, just like her. Pauline said it was first to be called *The Springtime Story of a Little White Flower*, but I prefer it as it is. Simpler. It could be a child's primer—I should still profit from it if it were—but it is her voice as she flies towards heaven. It is more than just the story of a soul. It is a huge heart, confidently placed in my own poor hands.

Les Buissonets. The Abbey School. Carmel. Songs of love.

Does she mention me? Yes. Léonie is the least, the last, the littlest. But my blue eyes—she remembers them. The songs Léonie sang to her when she was so strangely ill.

I have learned that to be the least is the best of all.

I tuck her last note to me into its back pages. Go to open the windows wide.

Letters to the Carmel of Lisieux

Dear Mother Xavier, I write to you as unworthy Mother of our little Carmel in Tours. It is my pleasant duty to thank you unreservedly for arranging for the circulation of The Story of a Soul. *We have read it in our refectory over this past month and I can say that not one sister has been left unaffected by the angelic perfume that emanates from its pages. Many tears have been shed at the account of her passing, including tears of my own. Again, I wish to thank you for your generosity in sharing your knowledge of this beautiful daughter of God's love.*

*   *   *

Dear and Holy Mother, please, forgive this written intrusion into your sacred enclosure. I must confess to you that my sister, who is a novice of the Carmelite monastery of Dijon, has passed on to me your publication, The Story of a Soul, *which tells of the beautiful life and holy death of your daughter in Christ, Sister Thérèse of the Child Jesus. I have never felt so strongly that an angel is watching over me from heaven, and I believe this angel to be her.*

*   *   *

Dear Sister Agnès of Jesus, you do not know me, but I feel that your beautiful, beloved Sister Thérèse of the Child Jesus has contacted me from beyond the bounds of this our exiled life. I have prayed to her at a time of great darkness and despair and have twice been sent roses that I believe to be supernatural in origin. I write to you now as a testament to my gratitude for all you did for this sister while she shared our earthly existence. My belief is that, in her transfigured state, she shares it still.

*   *   *

Dear Sisters of the Carmel of Lisieux, I enclose an offering of 4Fr for you to light a large blessed candle for me in front of your portrait of Sister Thérèse of the Child Jesus. I would like to thank her for granting my prayers. I have never known such strong intercession from any other member of the company of heaven.

*   *   *

Dear Mother Prioress, after long years in the wilderness, I have returned to the Holy Catholic Church through the writings and heavenly intercession of Sister Thérèse of the Child Jesus. In a vision, she has asked that I donate 100Fr to the upkeep of the Carmel of Lisieux. I humbly request that a small plaque be placed commemorating my offering at the door to the enclosure through which she entered as a young angelic soul, and through which her body left as the glorious remains of a saint.

In Carmel: Pauline

Mother Xavier looks at me over her reading spectacles.

"Mother Agnès. You have seen these letters?"

She pushes the latest batch towards me, over the large but increasingly cluttered desk. It is early afternoon and I have been summoned by my bell when I should be in the laundry. These days, though still brusque, her manner with me is less brutal than in the past. She seems smaller, and the skin on her face and hands has a sallow tinge. Her gaze, however, still burns.

"Yes, Mother Xavier. The correspondence shows no sign of abating."

"In fact, it increases, Pauline. Daily! The only consistency is of its tone, but even that is increasingly fervent. According to some of these testimonies, our departed Sister Thérèse now has the power to manifest money and cast out demons."

I cannot disagree with her. I share her concern over the more out-landish testimonies. But there is something wonderful about the stream of letters too.

"Sister Thérèse has struck a chord with little souls, both without and within the monastery. We have new novices who inspire us all. Sister Marie-Ange is particularly—"

"Yes, yes," replies Mother Xavier. She cannot gainsay this: already two beautiful young women have joined us as postulants because of Thérèse's memoir, which, with Uncle Isidore's funding, we have published and made available to the outside world. "But these others, it would seem, all feel the need to write to me requesting our material or spiritual support. They all want a little piece of her! I hope, Agnès, that you will help me turn back the tide of these missives before the little ship of our Carmel sinks under them entirely."

I nod my assent.

"Of course, Mother Xavier. Sisters Geneviève, Lucie, and Anne of the Trinity will be pleased to assist us."

"And Marie of the Sacred Heart?"

"She will help us too; I am sure of it."

"She has been less concerted in her zeal for the publication of your sister's writing."

"She provided us with the third part of the completed text, which complements the first two memoirs so well, Mother. She offers her help to Sister Geneviève during her long hours at her easel. She cares for the novices and our white veil sisters. She has helped us with her prayer."

Mother Xavier regards me again. How very tired she seems.

"Prayer is what we are here for, dear Agnès. Prayer and penance. It is my hope that you and your . . . sisters keep your focus on our primary call-ing. As did Sister Thérèse herself. We are all in need of mercy, are we not?"

Caen, Convent of the Visitation: Léonie

I am not here on my own merit: I have none. Nor am I convinced that my renewed welcome is an act of pure charity, though it feels like a miracle.

"How is your dear sister—your Pauline?" is the first question Mother Clémence puts to me. "I am so delighted that she writes to me. Your family is truly a talented one."

Mother Clémence bids me be seated before her great desk. There is a smell of soap and ink and candlewax. I am able to smile. This new mother has a manner that I like. She knows who she speaks to: Léonie the misfit and nuisance. But she is kind and makes to include me.

"I mean you also, Mademoiselle Léonie," she adds. "You have been with us before, and your faithfulness to our order is humbling. And more than humbling. I believe it is a sign and one I shall not ignore." She reaches for a letter neatly folded and filed in her desk's letter-rack. "I have here Pauline's recommendation—Mother Agnès, we should say."

I catch a glimpse of familiar script, extremely small and neat.

"Pauline knows of my desires," I say. "And of my failings."

"She says that your dear departed Sister Thérèse had an unshakeable belief in your vocation as a Visitandine."

"It is true. Thérèse was full of confidence."

I think of her letters to me. Has she found a way to help me from heaven? I feel an easiness in my ribcage, as though I have newly learned to breathe. As though I could bear even my doubts with joy.

"She is full of confidence still," says Mother Clémence. Her clear eyes regard me as she smiles. "And so am I."

In Carmel: Céline

More and more the audience grows.

Mother Xavier has, perhaps for the first time in her life, fallen ill, and so Pauline resumes her role of prioress as though she never left it. And I, too, have claimed my role in Carmel now. Céline—Sister Geneviève—twin-soul of a future saint. I tell myself again and again that she has not really left me. She guides my hand, bids me hold to my sword: I will not let her go.

In my new attic studio, I lay out my photographs, these images of sepia women. I am not downplaying my skill, no—never!—for it is from God. But this is not quite art, and it is not for prying eyes. People who never knew her will not know her by these squares. Céline, the twin soul, must reanimate her sister. Thus, I take my pencil, my gouache, my brushes, and my art.

I lift Thérèse from her place in a group portrait; a photograph I took one sunny day in our Lourdes courtyard. Carefully I trace her onto paper— the best. Tenderly I shade her habit, the scapular and sleeves, the white wimple and dark veil. I gaze at her face, broad in life. Her dying took that from her later on. Yet she was tired when she posed that day. Her mouth is strained, fixed. Her eyes are clear but there are shadows and pits below the rims.

My Thérèse. Gently, gently, I caress her facial features into a soft smile. Wipe the gray from under her eye as though it were a tear.

I remember doing such for my sister—my real sister, not a drawn remembrance—all through our girlhood. She would not let me do such acts in Carmel; only at the very last. But then, to my chagrin, I could not make her well.

I take Thérèse from her last formal portraits. She has two months left to live. Here her mouth is a line, dead set. Her eyes are heavy and hooded and dark. She is almost cowed with darkness. I remember her voice, her reprimand to me that "Some things, Céline, are more important than art." The final time, I think, she told me off. I never told Pauline her words and can't believe Thérèse did either, although somehow Pauline always knows when her siblings have argued. At least, she always thought she knew. I take my gouache, and gently dust the likeness into a brighter hour. I reduce the pain in her eyes. I lift the lips and stroke them into a pleasant quiet. Softly curve her chin as though I cup it in my hands. My professed nun's hands, old enough now to be my little sister's mother. Our roles are reversed once more.

I muse, as I work, on how she liked her solitude, but in her dying the opposite was given her. I select another community photograph. Cut her free. Place her peerless in an image of our chestnut tree-lined alley—here where she wrote her last manuscript, weaving our interruptions into words. Glue her in place and leave her in peace. I know, in my heart, that this image will be blessed. It makes her more herself.

My lost twin soul. My friend.

I only want to make her better.

Algiers: Maurice

My formation continues. I swelter in the heat of Algerian days and shiver at night on the wooden boards of my bed. We walk miles, my brothers and I; we reach and preach to the poorest of the poor. My language skills are also poor, but we learn the rudimentary vocabulary of these native souls so in need of God's love and direction. My companions make the life easier; Andrew, Paul—we are apostles of a sort. I like a laugh and a joke as much as in the old days of my soldiering. I write, when the hours in my day and the oil in my lamp permits it, to Mother Agnès at Lisieux. *The Story of a Soul* is never far from my side, my precious letters folded within its pages. I tell her this, and I tell her of the sweet moments of a dawn Mass and an infant baptism. Of how I have shown Thérèse's photograph to the scampering children of this place. They look at her in puzzlement.

"Sister," I say, holding the framed image high. "She is my sister, your sister."

Like a soldier on the frontline writing to his family, I don't tell Mother Agnès of the fetid water and the flies, the chronic risks of cholera and the offhand manner of young souls resistant to our mission.

I look at the photographs of our latest congregation; the powerful, burnished faces of men who have grown up in this harsh, hot land. They stand tall and proud in their herdsman's robes, their eyes startlingly wide and bright. The women are more reticent, bundled in modesty, slim of figure. When I preach, when I try to teach—using my awkward mélange of image, gesture, and word—sometimes I meet a gaze and even share a smile. At such moments more dissolves of my will than I am prepared to acknowledge, even to my superiors. Who learns from whom? Surely it is I, the harborless, celibate man, who am graciously harbored by these wise children of God's world? Where even the children have more knowledge of life than I, who teaches whom?

There is only one soul to whom I confide my flickering doubts, and she listens in silence, and counsels nothing but love. I place her precious photograph, the one she sent me, upon my desk. The sounds of children's play echoes through the compound. She is my saint; I am her knight at arms.

Caen, Convent of the Visitation: Léonie

When the time comes once again for me to make my first profession, I am helped to design a card. I announce my new name and ask for the prayers of my sisters and my new friends. When asked what photograph should go to make up the card, I select one not of myself, but of Thérèse as a novice. In the image she is plump and happy in a way I never have been. She clasps the Carmel's courtyard cross. Her eyes smile at me out of the past. Then I sense her shimmering beside me in the present, and I ask her not to leave me. She whispers that we are bound together by my new name in religion. I imagine a golden ribbon tethering my steps to hers.

I write out my vows to belong wholly to Jesus, vows that, as a Visitandine, I will renew every year. As we cross over into a strange, new-sounding century, I take my name and place as Françoise-Thérèse, a twentieth-century nun in a brave new world.

"You come from a holy family," says Mother Clémence, regarding me over her spectacles.

"I'm the black sheep," I say.

Made welcome through some miracle of mercy in this place, I think.

"You rely on the prayers of your own little sister. I've read her book," says Mother. I wonder if a reprimand is coming, but as always, I'm not sure. "You treat her like a saint, like a family saint," she says. "Sister Françoise-Thérèse, there are no private saints in the Catholic Church. Be careful that the religion you follow is the same as that of your community. Though I grant you that, given the marvelous work she is doing from above, one day you really may have a saint in the family."

Humbly, I bow before this older woman, though a shimmering continues in my heart.

"Thank you, Mother. You are right. I will go to the Virgin and ask her to protect me."

I keep my hands hidden. My right hand touches the little photo in my black habit's pocket.

In Carmel: Pauline

Father Thomas Nimmo sits in the parlor with his chair pulled up to the grille. Under his smart black soutane, one leg is crossed over the other and he leans towards me with a sense of urgency. He is a strange-looking man: angular and slight, ill at ease in his own body, but full of an energy that does not strike me as self-seeking. He has placed his hat on the parlor table, and in his hands are several sheets of closely written paper. Beside his hat is a copy of *The Story of a Soul*. Having greeted each other in the name of Christ, Father Nimmo has lost no time in getting down to business. His accent confirms what his name suggests: he is not a native Frenchman. In fact, I wonder whether Sister Anne, who is with me as tierce, can understand what the good father says at all.

"I am honored to meet you, Mother Agnès. Not only for your own ceaseless work in steering the ship of this holy Carmel, but also because you are—excuse my boldness—in my opinion, the sister of a saint."

I reply carefully, with a measured smile. "This is indeed a bold assertion, Father."

"You are modest, of course. It is one of your many virtues, and of your order. But it is one of my few virtues to be intrepid when it comes to matters of faith. I was called into the Holy Catholic Church, and then into the priesthood, for a reason. I believe that, when I found out about Sister Thérèse and her immense spiritual heroism, I found my reason. I intend to be true to my calling—and to her rightful glory."

As we talk, I begin consciously to entertain a possibility that I have secretly treasured in my heart for several years. It is not merely the personal ardor of this priest, nor the correspondence that arrives daily at our door. It is a sudden memory of being at her sickroom bedside, trying to capture her words as her breaths came hard and labored: this phrase in its perfect clarity, its rhythm like a heartbeat: *I will spend my heaven doing good on earth.*

I stand up, indicating our meeting is at a close.

"Thank you again, Father Nimmo," I say. "I promise you that I will discuss your words with our sisters—and with Sister Thérèse's own family. If a decision is agreed upon, I—" and I call upon my little sister's boldness, and continue, "I will raise the matter with the Bishop of Bayeux. Please pray for us as we place our intentions in the Virgin's hands."

I go to the oratory and tell a weakened Mother Xavier what young Father Nimmo has said to me.

"Agnès of Jesus—you seek my opinion. It is this: the acclaim goes too far. We might as well set in motion some unwieldy process to canonize all the sisters in our monastery, living and dead—and those yet to hear their vocation." And she snorts weakly in derision. "Besides, you cannot be prioress and promote the cause of your own sister!" And then clutches her hand to her jaw once again, a spontaneous confession of her own increasing agony.

*   *   *

Barely three months later, we gather around the infirmary bed. Mother Xavier is dying. And in her dying she has become diminished to an unexpected degree. She lies curled under the sheets as though she has in part reverted to a child again, under the relentless pain of her disease.

"How is she?" asks Céline. "She really wanted us to come to her?"

"Doctor de Cornière says that she is in the final stages."

"Does she suffer?"

Marie answers Céline. "She has refused morphine injections. Also the syrup."

One could accuse Mother Xavier of many failings, but hypocrisy is not one of them, at least not when it comes to the disregard of her own comfort. I look at the unnatural angle of her jaw and the hollows of her cheeks; her aristocratic nose and high forehead: all a parched canvas now for death's gray bloom.

But she is not yet gone. Aware of Céline's entry or of our discreet murmuring, she opens her eyes.

"Dear Mother. I hope that we haven't woken you."

Carefully, slowly, she opens her mouth and shapes a reply. The tumor on her tongue has taken away her life-long facility for a rapier-like response. But still, she responds.

"Agnès. Geneviève. And Marie." Already she tires.

"Please don't disturb yourself," I say. It is a futile suggestion.

"I want to tell you—to ask," says Mother Xavier, and involuntarily she raises her hand to her mouth. Discreetly, Marie moves to her side, and offers her a soft cloth to hold to her aching lips. She takes it, and continues. "I have been selfish, and I have been vindictive. I ask you to f—" She labors for the next word with difficulty. "To forgive." She sinks back into her pillow, closes her eyes, and a thin tear slides from under each hooded eyelid.

We are silent, contemplating the old feuds, the hurts of elections and battles over whose hands should receive the vows of the newly professed. A little spark of indignation kindles itself in my throat. And then it disperses. What are these snags and thorns but evidence of a family of souls? We have lived so closely together for so many years that our branches intertwine, our flowers blend, blessing each other daily.

"My dear Mother, please be assured of our love. We are here—we are all here," I say. And I dare to add, "Our little Thérèse is here for you, too, I'm sure of it."

Although she does not open her eyes, her proud mouth twists into the whisper of a smile. And now Céline speaks.

"We have to thank you greatly, Mother, I in particular have to thank you, for allowing Thérèse and myself to join the Carmel here at Lisieux. Without your generosity I would never have found my home. And Thérèse— she loved you as a daughter loves her mother, as a saint loves one who tested and trusted her extraordinary soul."

And Mother Xavier's lips curve upwards slightly further.

I think to add more soothing words but opt to remain silent. Only the rasping of our patient's breath continues to be audible. Marie looks at me, raises her eyebrows, and makes the sign of fingers to wrist: Should she summon the doctor? But I shake my head. She leaves the infirmary as the bell rings for Compline. Céline, however, stays, and assumes Marie's former place behind my chair, with her hand softly touching my shoulder, as the silence settles on us, and the evening brings its own releasing balm.

In Carmel: Lucie Guérin

High summer in Carmel once more. The world turns and the seasons wheel us into this new century, and I receive Jesus often into my unworthy little heart. With the death of our wolfish Mother Xavier, there is a peace in the convent, but perhaps a dullness also, an increased layer of absence among us, we who remain. As I grow older in body and in my religious life, I realize how much death is a part of life, departures as prominent as arrivals.

But look, I am alive! I see myself in Céline's latest photographs. A grown-up woman, it would seem. Older than Sister Marie-Anges who talks to me so reverently of Thérèse, someone she has never known in life. Céline says she will likely be our next prioress; how important she has become, compared with me! But I am a spouse of Christ, although God knows I am still the little songbird who takes fright even within her haven.

This evening we witness a spectacle at recreation. A great balloon floats right over the convent, and after some hesitation, Mother Agnès permits us to rise and view it from the grounds. We crowd in the half-concealment of the cloister walk, peering up to the strangely inhabited sky. A huge, blue sphere, like an inflated globe, wending its way over Lisieux, and us in its path. How silently it glides! But Céline whispers to me that in the heart of its pendant basket the elevating fire gives off a steady, local roar.

We are transfixed—the small blue world, laced with gold (piping on the fabric, or a contribution of the summer's evening sun?) carries its human cargo: a gentleman standing dark and tall in the sky. He leans to the side of the basket. I shade my eyes from the sunlight and can just make out his top hat.

"Surely, he will fall!" says Anne of the Trinity, sounding more excited than alarmed at the prospect.

"The saints preserve us! A man falling into the Carmel! Sisters, we must fetch the new stuffed mattresses for him to land on!"

This is Sister Aimée, who, still wearing her work apron, looks set to put her words into action on the instant. I am frightened. This man can bode no good, surely?

On it sails, this balloon and its passenger. Can he see us, here below him, a quaint community of nuns who have foresworn the freedoms of the world, and found, by doing so, a loving home? Does he seek such a home, in his secular heart?

Before we know it, the man has sailed out of view in his airborne vessel, and Mother Agnès signals the end of recreation. The sisters turn back, and quiet settles again.

In my choir stall at Compline, I think more about this vision. From the air, what must a man see? A great panorama of the land; our Carmel a shape on a patchwork map; fitting in, with its irregular boundaries, like a jigsaw piece—one of many, but unique. The way a soul may look back on her life, perhaps, as it comes to an end. The patterns of a life revealing themselves in their intricacy, their miraculous fit, visible only to she who rises up, leaving them.

Thérèse, before she died, spoke of an elevator. How she longed for one, scooping her safely and tenderly up to God. Ah, what would she say of this evening's event? My mind wandering idly now, I imagine Thérèse and myself up in a great balloon's basket, holding each other safe and tight; looking down with pleasure from a sunlit heaven.

In Carmel: Pauline

As the summer fades, I go to the parlor to greet Uncle Isidore. Céline and Marie will visit after me. Then he will have what he really desires, some time with his cloistered daughter, who is not well. I have woken up, these last few nights, with terrible anxiety about her health. Francis says little to me after his visits, but I have not forgotten the pattern of my own little sister's suffering: I see much of it replicated in Lucie's pallid skin and incessant coughing. And as a former pharmacist, Uncle will not be deceived as to the likely progression of the disease. Neither will Lucie herself, although she seems to be almost blissful when I visit her.

"Uncle. Your Lucie had a better night. We are all grateful for the gifts you bring her. They make her smile and sustain her soul as well as her body."

I will not tell him about her retching after valiant attempts to swallow food too rich for a nun in fragile health.

Uncle, stouter and grayer these recent years, looks at me and clears his throat loudly. "The new century continues to speed by," he says. "Even the Carmel has seen great changes—our dear Thérèse must be looking down from heaven with astonishment." He refers to the gas pipes and electricity that now warm and light up our community rooms. "And such a young new prioress . . ." He shifts in his seat. I notice he sits stiffly, through a combination of arthritis and unease. "I would have expected you, Pauline, the experienced one, simply to continue in your role as shepherdess."

I decide to be bold. I take a breath and begin. "Uncle, our new prioress Mother Marie-Anges has spoken to Bishop Lemonnier about initiating the cause for the beatification of our Sister Thérèse. She was marvelous about it; far more so than I could have been. She has prayed over the issue many times. And this month we received an equally marvelous reply: the bishop has requested that we forward all Thérèse's writings, and the hundreds of letters and recommendations received by the Carmel over these last years. As you know, they only increase in volume."

Isidore grunts his acknowledgment of this state of affairs. "She continues to charm and surprise, all these years since . . . I will have a saint for a niece."

"You have a saint for a daughter too," I tell him gently.

He looks directly at me, and for a moment I fear his gruff façade may crack to reveal his anguish over Lucie. But his hands reach for his tie and straighten it. He smooths his thinning hair and adjusts his spectacles.

"Do not let her suffer unnecessarily, Pauline," he says to me, his voice thick with distress.

I promise him, with a lump in my throat, and the realization that it is I who am dangerously close to tears.

In Carmel: Lucie Guérin

Nausea wells up from the pit of my stomach. I retch instinctively but have nothing to show for it but some foul sputum. This happens, over the course of the days and the weeks, again and again from summer through to winter. I am no fool and know when tuberculosis begins to show. I have not yet coughed blood, but my throat is raw, and my voice altered, husky and rough, as was Thérèse's in her final illness. By November, I am confined to the infirmary.

"I am so sorry," says Pauline, many times. "We prayed never again to lose a sister in this way."

She has time to be as kind as her heart prompts her be: our new young prioress has entrusted me to her care. These days, her face has softened, as if with love. Céline bids us go upstairs and look out of the upper dormitory windows onto the courtyard. Pauline supports me as I lean against the sill, my short white cape and white invalid's veil protecting me but little from the cold air. My eyes stream. But nevertheless, it is rather wonderful to look out onto Christ. On his stone cross, from this level. I am a little nearer to Him than I used to be perhaps. A little more on His level: I do not even trouble to quash the bold thought. He knows my intentions by now.

Céline arranges for the photograph, Pauline by my side. I feel dwarfed by the wideness of the double windows. A white bird resting on a sill. Perhaps I should sing: a little bird waiting in hope for the sun. Experimentally, I try a few notes of an Advent canticle. Although my voice flutters up and disappears, I hit the notes. I make a sound like a misty wisp of air. Pauline presses her hands, one on each of my upper arms, clasping me like the little mother she is, and leans her head to touch against mine.

"You are a beautiful soul, Lucie. I have always known it. And so, God calls you to Him because you are beautiful. Would you like to respond to Him in song once more?"

"Oh, Pauline—how I would love to. But like this? I do not know if I will ever have the strength again."

"It was a pleasure to hear you just now. Your voice, like your soul, has feathers, and prepares to fly."

"I have loved to sing," I admit to her. "Some nights I think I would be happy, if I could, just to sing until I die."

"It is always hard for our choir sisters to step down from singing the Holy Office. For you it was a double sacrifice, because of your special gift. And it was a sacrifice to us, too." Her words comfort me, as though she has wrapped an extra woolen layer around my body. She continues, her face earnest. "Lucie, you know we have the Advent procession in a week's time." I nod, sadly; I used to love leading the chant to the Child Jesus as we passed his statue in the corner of the cloister. But it is as if Pauline knows what I am thinking: "If you are willing, and God wills you well enough, we will bring the Child Jesus to you. You may sing to Him from the infirmary. It would be a precious gift to us if you could do this, my darling. You know that none of us have the talent with which you have been graced."

She is as good as her word. In December, the sisters in their mantles bear Him to me. At the downstairs window, holding my slim candle, I sing: of my victimhood and the joy of consecrated life. I offer Him everything, knowing my little flame may soon gutter out. I see Pauline and Marie looking at me with shining tears: expressions reserved for sick members of their blood family.

The procession moves on towards the chapel. Sister Aimée touches my back and guides me back to bed.

I know without the shadow of a doubt that I am loved.

In Carmel: Céline

I take her final portrait after the laying-out: such sorrow. Little cousin, you barely felt you were dying, such was your sweet dissolution and the strength of your faith. I turn to Pauline in the choir. We have made it beautiful, with lilies and candles. Lucie wears the white rose wreath of her profession, as do all Carmelites in death. It is their right. Our right. I shiver for a moment, and raise my hand to my scalp, but all I feel is my heavy veil and the warmth of my own head.

"She became more beautiful every year she spent with us," says Pauline. "And her voice—"

"I sometimes thought her whole soul was a lens," I say, surprising myself with my impulse to talk; I suppose this is grief once again, the dissolver of proprieties. "She left her traces of song in the air, imprinting it like a photograph."

"A photograph of what?" asks Pauline the practical.

"Of a soul before God. Or perhaps of love itself," I reply, struggling to put the image in my mind exactly into words. I should draw it instead; filigree silver lacing the night sky. But Pauline is satisfied with my answer for now. She must continue her letter writing, the task that fills her days. Perhaps my picture will be memorial enough for Cousin Lucie. I have an oil painting of her too; a sweet success, capturing her pensive grace. I will gift it to Isidore.

"I must write to Father Bellière," Pauline says to me. "It goes badly for him. He has blackwater fever and I am afraid his strength has failed."

"Does he return to France?" I have a sudden flash of Papa in his final years; of his confinement in the vast architecture of *Bon Sauveur* at Caen. "Will he be cared for?"

"Let us hope so," says Pauline. "Thérèse regarded him as family. Let us continue to pray for him as such."

At Sea: Maurice

I am barely aware of the voyage home. Swaying between sleep and consciousness; fever and chill, my body—broken, how broken since my priesting—lies disconsolate in a small cabin. I am unable to distinguish between the lurches of the ocean and those of my stomach. But what causes terror are the lurches of the mind.

This terror does not go unnoticed. The nursing sister sent to accompany me back to *La Patrie* murmurs quietly to her superiors—captain? doctor? priest?—outside my cabin door. I assume she speaks of me and this rouses in me a certain rage, while at the same time I am oddly reassured. I try to tell her this in a way that would not frighten her. But all that comes out is a guttural snarl.

At times my ocean-borne cell becomes a poor Chiwamben hut, made of hay and reeds. I am reclining on a hard, wooden bench, waiting for David and Basil, my youngest students. I seem to smell them before they arrive: glee, fear, sweat—young boys on the brink of their own worlds. The bench is hard under my back, and I grimace, knowing my mattress in the poor dormitory will not be much better. But as I involuntarily arch my back and stretch my spine, the reeds dissolve and I am faced with white walls. What, am I nothing but a simple monk, dreaming the last decade from my worm-eaten prie-dieu? A monk, a nun; am I even a man? I lift my right hand, suddenly aware of how weak it feels, drop it onto my chest, and push it down my clammy body, checking as I go. As I do so, a shameful memory surfaces in my mind, of stumbling soldiers and a whore opening her legs. I seem to be falling into her once more, my body a wooden strut seeking its groove. A man then. A thing of flesh and blood.

I snap open my eyes; find and focus with difficulty on the small black crucifix on the cabin's wall. Christ is in agony, dying amid the nauseous waves of the sea. I stretch my arms out in union with him. The back of my hand bangs against the cabin wall. I let it slide down to the wall towards my thigh, but my body itself is dispersing as I slip into feverish sleep.

A little later I get out of my bed and stagger to the far corner of the cabin to a small mirror. A man stares back at me, the haggard face of a wild man. More than a wild man, though I am terrified to say it. I am become a mad man. This is why I slip between times and places, ignorant as a beast of my true location. My mind is diseased, poisoned by a blacker water altogether: the bitter waters of despair.

Thérèse comes to me that night.

She has the bold look of her dying portrait. I know the photograph so well I can summon it precisely, even in the midst of my raving. I find myself within the image, kneeling in the Lourdes courtyard to the right of Sister Geneviève, who fusses with her camera. Thérèse looks straight at me as though she had expected me. Her gaze is of infinite pain and infinite love. It is so utterly pure that I cannot meet it for long, and so drop my own gaze to the dual images she holds up in her hands. They are the two pages of her own book of life. The Child Jesus is static in his pose. Next to him, a dying Christ, the battered features and shut eyes of the Holy Face. In my visionary state I recognize the face as my own, the ravaged features I have so recently viewed in the cabin.

The Good Savior.

"Maurice," says a voice within and without my head. I look back to her eyes and wonder if she almost smiled.

Dreams of Saints

1912—1925

In Carmel: Marie

Young Mother Marie-Anges flourishes as prioress. She is as tall as a co-
nifer and radiant as the dawn, and she insists that it is her vocation to
promote the cause of our Sister Thérèse, a nun she never knew in life. She
is not insensible to our recent loss, and embraced me with real sorrow after
Lucie's funeral Mass. But she keeps a clear head, and with her encouragement soon we have a little industry. Pauline, freed from the binds of office,
plans the leaflets, and oversees the reprints of *The Story of a Soul*, Céline the
images. Little Anne of the Trinity and myself sit in the library and answer
requests for prayer cards and pictures. She notes the requests on a large
piece of paper, and I help mark the number of items parceled up and sent.

"We should set up a shop!" says my assistant.

I think to rebuke her but sigh my acquiescence instead. I am too hot
and too tired to engage in a dispute. She is right. We have a burgeoning
business, impractically so. I make a note to speak to Pauline, to ask how she
plans to proceed.

Céline has produced a catalogue of pictures of Thérèse, with one in
particular garnering devotion. I should not say devotion, as Thérèse is
too young and surely too recently deceased to be canonized; attention,
then—the one thing she eschewed in life, as should all Carmelites. Thérèse,
clutching her crucifix covered with roses. Thérèse with her smile, except it
is not quite her smile. She never had in life the rosebud lips Céline bestows
upon her in this portrait. But Céline has a painter's eye and knows what
she is doing. And the requests for pictures, for letters, for relics, pour in.

The bohemian in my soul grumbles from her cavern. *Nothing*, she whispers, *replaces the loss of a goddaughter.*

In Carmel: Céline

Soon I head what in the world would be an artist's studio. My old vocation has flown home to me a hundredfold, as a fluttering flock of portraits. But now my subject is always the same: I have painted my Carmelite sister in heaven and made painstaking collages of her in Carmel. I have created the sweet, triumphant image of her that charms all her new devotees. My Thérèse *aux roses,* scattering petals from roses without thorns. I myself posed for this painting's photographic sketch, clutching a crucifix and a brace of falling flowers; I drew her form from mine, painted her absence over me like a palimpsest. In that photograph, my gaze retains an unmistakable sheen of grief.

I try to brush aside the sadness that she has never appeared to me, in this or any other form; that she left me here; that she leaves me here still. But then I shake myself back to faith. She guided my hand as I painted her—nobody else's. Now she is mine to present to the poor, broken world. I chaperone her from the cloister as she goes out to spend her heaven. And a whisper of Lucie's spirit remains by my side, just out of vision, as I work.

But such is the hunger for images that I make commissions too. Not to the other sisters if I can help it, but to artists of good faith out in the world. To Monsieur Jouvenot I commission one design, to Monsieur Annauld another. We correspond by increasingly brief and terse letters. I insist on seeing the sketches. To both, I make recommendations. I am the twin soul of a little saint—they are not. They do their best to please but will by their very natures fall short. I make sure her face is full and pleasant, her lips delicate, and her hands soft. Even as she travels the world, her mantle must fall fluidly, her habit stay immaculate. The roses must pour down lightly, gracefully. The clouds themselves must reflect her purity and be white and spotless as her soul.

I encounter some resistance. She is too strong, or too sweet. My designs would be misunderstood, be ridiculed: Thérèse at prayer on a cloud looks like Thérèse kneeling on a mushroom, according to Sister Aimée! But I sweep the misgivings aside. Where once I might have caviled at popular portraiture with the snobbishness of youth, now I see the charm of dainty lips and a tiny white hand. She is my sister, and—may God forgive me for so saying—if the world was ever crying out for sweetness, it is now.

Yes, this is my studio. In this one way I lead, and even she must follow.

In Carmel: Pauline

"I know what you are going to ask," I say to Marie as she sits, larger than life, opposite me. For once, I almost see a reflection of myself. She wipes her brow with the back of her hand, artlessly. Her body must prickle with perspiration sometimes, as does mine. As we advance in years, I wonder if she has the same pounding heartbeat and headaches as I do. She moves more stiffly now; I see this even under her bulky habit. "Are you quite well, my darling?"

She smiles in response. "Quite well, Pauline. Although perhaps no longer quite free." She alludes to her childhood nickname in good humor.

"We are all taking on extra work. Thérèse enlists us in her tireless efforts to save souls."

Marie puffs her cheeks out and gives an exaggerated sigh. She raises her eyebrows.

"Anne of the Trinity suggests we might use the new printing company in Lisieux to distribute the leaflets and prayer cards. I think she is right to ask. It is too much for us to do. I have the garden to look after as well, supplies to oversee, and—" She shrugs.

I complete her sentence for her.

"And our primary vocation is, after all, one of prayer, not industry. I agree, Marie. I admire our Mama all the more for living so many years in the world with this burden of commission and distribution, but even she was not without help as a lacemaker. And—" I cast another glance over Marie's round features, unsure of how apprised she is of worldly politics, "France may soon find herself at war, at serious, prolonged war. I have dark dreams—I fear this century may be one of bitterness and conflict, more even than the last. Our little Thérèse may find herself busier than she knew in all her earthly life. If she is to go into the battlefield, we must be her armed camp."

In Carmel: Céline

Oh! It is I who shall find myself in a battlefield, never mind our soldiers! Francis sits across from me in the parlor, his face crisscrossed by the grille. I consider each tiny square of his flesh and features, and how I would paint an oily flush into his portrait. I must have done this for a moment or two, exchanging concerns over the coming war, and Adèle's always-uncertain health, before I fully realize that he is angry. The furrows between his thickset brows are not those of age but of fury. He is as furious as the day he visited my dying sister and found no morphine injection had been dispensed to her, despite old de Cornière's instructions.

"Francis. Won't you tell me what's troubling you?"

"You, Sister Geneviève. You are troubling me! And Pauline and Marie too." His voice booms, filling our sedate parlor.

I open my mouth to respond but can't think what to say. What is this?

Francis opens his bag and draws from it papers. I see they are my pictures of Thérèse, pictures I have worked on long and hard to present her soul as the sweet flower it is. But inexplicably Francis holds them bunched up in his clenched fist, and I fear they are in danger of being crushed.

"Francis, I—"

"Céline, this is unacceptable! It is preposterous! This silly little girl is not Thérèse. I cannot believe you and Pauline are—are *selling* all that is good about your sister as this—this travesty of a likeness. The poor girl had a short life, and a brutal death, and now you—you!—have turned her into a vacuous doll, a sugar pill for all the world to swallow down! The world in all its sorrows is being duped. Céline, I am ashamed, and Isidore is too."

A hot rage rushes its way to my own face, and I feel my cheeks burn. From Francis—Francis, of all people! Isidore is an old man, used to having his say. Yes, I have had my critics. But I had not anticipated this blow from someone who has stirred me, over the years, more than I can ever tell him. I am humiliated, in a way Thérèse never could have understood—and Pauline too will never know. But worse is to come. Having rubbished my art Francis opens his folder one last time and takes out a fresh image. Immediately by the rounded white bloom in the center of the sheet I know what this is: a photograph of Thérèse as a novice, displaying her as unformed, unkempt. There she is, her cheeks full and wide and bearing a childish smile, seeming younger even than her then sixteen years. Father Gombault took this image—alas—upon his brief inspection of our Carmel, back in 1889. Thérèse must have charmed him, in her naive way, or he her. She clutches the pillar of our cloister crucifix as though it were a giant toy; a vertical pillow hugged to herself. This countenance should not be public. I am embarrassed beyond all measure to think that a girlish delight—the sort of looks we shared, in total privacy in our bedroom at Les Buissonets—should be shared with an adult world.

"This," says Francis, heaping shame upon shame, "is the real Thérèse. I cannot think why you resist such a picture of truth."

At Compline, my face is still burning and my heart stinging from his rebuke.

Show me what to do, I pray, gripping my hands together so hard my fingers start to feel numb.

Be grateful, I think I hear her say.

I grit my teeth and offer my shame to God, begging Him to imprint Himself onto my next artwork as though it were Veronica's Veil.

Dream of Céline

That night I dream I drag my easel and its untreated canvas before the oratory altar. Then, after genuflecting, I unlock the door of the tabernacle, revealing a small monstrance within which resides a consecrated host gleaming with light. I retreat to the far corner and kneel down. I see the rays emanating from the monstrance onto the blank white paper, as though God is shaping Himself on its surface, without even the instrument of the brush to assist Him. All that is necessary is to expose the empty space, to drag or push the blank heart before him.

I seem to see the firm, bruised face of a man glowing inside this virgin canvas. The image darkens and strengthens and a great joy washes through me as I witness exactly what I've yearned for. The Holy Face has formed in my soul, as a photograph is made through the exposure of a glass plate to the light.

I wake with a start and, lighting my old oil lamp, go in search of Him, first in the oratory, then in my art room upstairs. My easel is there, but the canvas remains blank. As if it has receded into the microscopic weft of the cloth, the holy image is gone from my sight.

Show me.

The words echo on in my mind; are they my own, or directions from heaven? All day I hug this unmanifest vision to myself, pondering the lesson of its message.

In Carmel: Pauline

The times are intensely unsettled. What wrath has our poor world provoked? Then, struck by a sudden illness as though by lightning, young Mother Marie-Anges sickens and dies.

"I am going to light, to life, to love," she murmurs, her hands stretching out as though to an invisible friend.

I find myself resuming the painful responsibility of office. Everyone, including myself, assumes it will be a lifelong burden now.

Within a few short months the world convulses. The German army invades us through Belgium. France is at war and all our men suffer. Nations rise against nations, and I fear our nation pays the price for a century of insubordination. Feeling helpless, I instruct an extra recitation of the rosary be added to our community prayers, resolve to fast beyond our Lenten season, and to take up once more the discipline, that little leather whip that waits in every Carmelite's cell. There is more than we can know crying out for reparation. I shrink into myself. My temples pulse. I imagine I can hear the ringing of bullets at the military front. Our glorious wheatfields will be flooded in blood. I begin a correspondence with a Monsieur Charles Maurras, who asks for our prayers. His love for the Motherland offers us a steely hope. His movement is not afraid to fight. His poetry makes me believe his soul warrants our support. Marie disagrees, looking askance when I tell her and shaking her head. She has never taken to poetry or penance.

But here is a miracle. According to those who are there, little Thérèse traverses the battlefields. She appears in the war-torn skies; implores the heavens to release her blessings, her roses—and down they pour. She answers prayers at the moment of their uttering. She is like light—gracing, reflecting, intensifying. Unhampered by the mortal body, she has become the saver of souls in extremis. She captures dreams, hearts, sinners, and saints—all for the good God, whose sun blazes through her. Céline paints her next to her beloved Joan of Arc. They are warriors both. I make a decision to catalogue accounts of her appearances. I am still her little mother, although she has far outstripped me in grace and power.

Two streams of correspondence flow into our Carmel. One is the ever-increasing demand for medals, pictures, and leaflets. These we send out, endeavoring to have the day's demands ready for our turn sisters each evening, though Marie and I sometimes work late into the night in my drafty prioress's office. Our tokens fly out like birds over the wounded earth. But a second stream reaches us, full of personal accounts from the front of the conflict. I read many out at our recreations. Others I weep over in private. These are the testimonies of graces received. Many are from officers and soldiers who have seen death in terrible ways, who have faced their own destruction and found themselves desperate for help. Those who have adopted our little sister as their helpmeet have been assisted beyond what is possible. Thérèse strews her petals down from heaven, her love crosses all battlefields and offers nothing but Christ's mercies, even when the battlefields most ravaged are those of the heart.

Look. Here is a letter from a soldier who had long ago abandoned the faith of his childhood. He prayed to Thérèse, and the clouds parted to reveal her looking down from the heavens. She must love the roses and crucifix Céline has pictured her with, because here she clasps them from within her cloudy aureole. And here, look: the witness of an officer who claims he saw Thérèse appear on the churned soil of no man's land, to cradle the head of a dying soldier. He declares that she held the crucifix before the soldier's face, her mantle billowing around her like a cloud of glory. And here: a soldier in the trenches, dreadfully wounded, his uniform soiled and his very cap bullet-ridden, holds up his holy card, our little Thérèse *aux roses*—and declares his pain abated, and his soul at peace.

The letters are hand-written, many shaky, as shaky as her own last written words. The paper is often smudged and sometimes torn. I see thumbprints formed of dust and blood. On one letter the ridges of such a print are so pronounced that I think it an affidavit at the hour of death. But even as I read these letters, I seem to catch a faint scent of flowers.

And then I think of patterns: of Alençon lace, of the painstaking designs from Mama's work boxes, of how she sat at her little round table night after night, lacemaking queen to a whole industry of lacemaking women. I see myself as taking on Mama's profession—I am become a lacemaker, in charge of a vast network of patterns, casting and gathering, rendering and framing. The more I oversee, the greater the returns. The faster I commission and design, the greater the strain—and yet it is the vocation to which I am called. To which I am bound, stitched.

Lacemaking. Stitching, binding, and threading. I pick up the pile of heart-rending letters and hold them in my hand in the quiet of my prioress's office, as though weighing them. The memory flits through my mind of the first editions of Thérèse's writing. A flash of lightning outside temporarily illuminates this sparsely furnished room, with its grand desk, few chairs, and worn prie-dieu in the corner; a storm is coming, a natural one rather than the bluster of the guns. A storm from the heavens. A glorious storm. A sustained shower of roses. A storm of glory.

An idea strikes. I put down the letters and pick up my pen and think to ring the bell for Céline. But I choose to write my plan first, because now I know that this is what we shall do: instead of creating more booklets and devotionals, we will use the testimonies themselves. Immediately I see the completed pamphlets in my mind: testimony upon testimony, with the momentum of the answered prayers of France building up like a legal proof. Proof of what, exactly, I do not yet allow myself to declare. But it does not escape my notice that should a process from Rome be initiated, we now have an abundance of testimony; it reaches the volume of popular acclaim.

Meanwhile, I remind myself, there are orders to place and fulfill. Stocktaking. Finances. Thérèse, the balancer of books. Balancing the books! A skill she never had in life, and one she claimed was of little interest to God Himself. I pull towards me the larger file at the edge of my desk, open it, and sigh—a little with anxiety, and a little with satisfaction. The ledger goes down and over the page, even with my writing—a neat hand that gets even smaller under stress. Mementoes of Thérèse can be purchased in the form of calendars, postcards, souvenir albums, exercise books, writing paper, and blotters. Recent demand has led us to expand into trinkets: lockets, charms, badges, brooches, scarf pins, necklaces, and bracelets. The people love these items. All the little fripperies she loved herself as a child—now she sanctifies them wholesale.

I lift up my hand to brush away the tiniest strand of doubt from my mind, but in the event, I find there is none there. Instead, I think again of a future Vatican audit and the potential for satisfaction our items might offer to a beady-eyed official.

Caen, Convent of the Visitation: Léonie

Mother Clémence comes to me while I sit in the garden after our simple second meal. It is early for my monthly conversation with her, in which we try to trace a little progress in Léonie's soul. The evening is mild. She gestures to me not to get up, but instead sits carefully beside me on the wooden bench. Perhaps she will share a prayer with me for all our gallant soldiers. She smiles. Although there is a tightness to her smile, I do not sense a reprimand.

"Sister Françoise-Thérèse. I am to give you news you may find surprising. Although somewhere in your heart I believe you are already well aware of the state of things I am about to describe."

"Yes, Mother," I say, not knowing how else to respond. Mother Clémence doesn't waste any more time.

"Your famous little sister has been attracting great interest. I have heard today that the cause for her beatification is to proceed at once, now our warring world longs so much for peace. The tribunal will be held in Bayeux."

She pauses and regards me through her black-rimmed spectacles. To say I am astonished is an understatement.

"Thérèse—beatified!" I cannot help myself. "My little Thérèse!"

"Indeed, it seems that this is what the bishop anticipates. Now we have a part to play in this process—you especially, Françoise-Thérèse. I know you never thought you would leave the Visitation grounds again. But your presence is required in Bayeux. You are to give your testimony at the final process."

I look at her in horror. "Mother, do not make me go!"

"I will come with you myself. I have the role of mother in our religious family life. You are a beloved daughter. Besides, I like to think that we are friends, you and I, after our years in this house of gentleness and sacrifice."

"I—I do not know what I am supposed to say."

Of this only I am sure: if there is a wrong thing to be said, I will say it.

"We will plan your answers. Your Pauline has already sent us plentiful notes. The official statement will not be a casual recollection, but that is all the better because your answers will be written out beforehand." This sounds slightly clearer, if daunting. "And we will leave tomorrow. By motorcar. You will have something to write to your Carmelite sisters, after this adventure is over! Rest assured you will be returning with me." Then she smiles at me again, a fuller smile. She adds, "These ten years have seen a blooming of your soul that is all the more genuine for you being unaware of it. I do believe that if the cause continues you will be summoned to Lisieux."

"To Lisieux?"

"Yes, Sister. You may well find yourself summoned to the Carmel. You have valuable testimony to make, and witness to give. See how Thérèse has allowed your life to become just as valuable as that of any Carmelite?"

I think she hides a further smile at my amazement. Soon afterwards she leaves me, having placed her hand briefly on my shoulder, and walks back towards the convent building. I should move too, but remain where I am for a few moments more, digesting this beyond-astonishing news. My face is burning, my hands are clammy. My neck is prickling. But this I offer up.

Lisieux, Cemetery of Champs-Remouleux: Céline

They are digging her up for the Vatican process. Seven years after the transfer of her bones to the rosewood coffin, she is to be exhumed once again from the good earth. The necessary identification of the relics must be made. Pauline gives permission for me to leave Carmel with Sister Magdalene and go in a closed carriage to the cemetery chapel. So it is I pass, weightless, dizzy, like a veiled ghost through the crowds of the faithful. I *am* a ghost; of my own past years as the worldly Martin sister of Lisieux. Here are my unrealized shreds, as housekeeper, artist, mother.

Wife. Henry. In another life I could be caring for our children, our children's children.

I shake myself awake. This was not my calling. My calling is to live, and to witness—fulfilling each task as the sometimes-ghostly echo of a saint.

I am ushered into the small, plain chapel. The remains are laid out before me on fine cloth. The flesh has gone, just as she had predicted; it is a poor coat fallen away. As expected, the new habit we sent seven years ago to clothe her corpse has also disintegrated into soft lint fragments—they will be gathered and added to the holy cards Pauline even now plans to have produced. Thérèse is utterly reduced, a nothing; her skeletal—I barely dare to say it—her skeletal remains are the muted whispers of her earthly life. My hand shakes as I reach out to touch them, bones small and exposed on the altar's linen. I think: this is not a dream, but the task of a ghost.

Sister Magdalene remains in the corner, swathed in the silence of her vows. The scent of the cold little chapel lightens and sweetens, with just the faintest note of violets. I look to Sister Magdalene, but she does not raise her great veil from her face. I am but barely aware of an official entering, and then leaving us alone. We form a strange, silent enclosure of three.

And here is the gleam of the white silk ribbon we sent to her. Like her first grave marker, the white cross in the Champs Remouleux plot, it bears her boldest final declaration: *I will spend my heaven doing good on earth.*

The rosewood coffin is placed before the altar. It has Carmel's coat of arms and a Latin inscription that echoes the declaration I have signed:

> *Hic*
> *Ossa Ancillae Dei*
> *Theresiae a Puero Jesu*
> *Deposita Sunt*
> *Die Decima Augusti*
> *Mcmxvii*

I whisper what I assume is a final farewell to the outside world.

"I will see you again, my Thérèse," I tell her. "You cannot be kept much longer from our Carmel."

In the carriage back, it occurs to me that perhaps she does not fetch me yet for heaven because it is my task to fetch her home first. This thought rekindles something fine and sweet in my soul I had not realized I had lost.

In Carmel: Pauline

She always told me not to be afraid. Not to care so much for my cage, though I am captive in the aviary of Christ Himself. She tells me still. In my dreams she makes more promises than she did in her infancy, extravagant promises of light and peace, the travel and new horizons that were never my lot in this life.

"I have my elevation now," she says.

Or does she say *elevator*, her favorite symbol of Divine Love? A cage in which one might both sing and fly. I wake consoled, but are these just sweetmeats I allow myself in the wanderings of my mind?

It is late afternoon, sweetness fading, when I return to my correspondence. Brother Simeon writes to me with news of another exorcism. A chill strokes the back of my neck, despite my full veil and the muggy summer warmth within the prioress's office as I read his report. He is not a man given to fantasies; in fact, I associate such fantasies more with women than men. I do not, in truth, care for reports of apparitions and possessions. Dreams are one thing. Dreams are enough. But then I think: perhaps apparitions are also dreams. Who can say what is sleep and what wakefulness when the whole of our lives will one day vanish like an insubstantial song?

According to Simeon, the devil is restless. War is one ghastly result, this we know. But there are demons who seek the vulnerabilities of the female form, and these possessions are vile events indeed. Only the purest of men have any hope of fighting such infestations. An exorcist eating his breakfast with gluttony gives Satan's minions their way. But here, too, Thérèse comes with her balm. She is known to the demons, says Simeon, and I believe him. In her trial of faith she sat at the table of sinners where foul and fallen spirits roam: they know of her power. Even her image causes them to sigh in defeat. At the bedside of the possessed, as in the trenches, Teresita, with her roses, has become the instrument of conversion.

The girl's name is Charlotte. Her parents, not known to be pillars of the church, called on the exorcist in despair. After the prayers were said, the book and the candle raised, the crucifix exalted, and Thérèse invoked in the litany, her image was shown to the bound and suffering girl. The shriek of the demons took away everyone's breath. Amid their infernal howls, the exorcist demanded they reveal why they were suddenly so powerless.

It was Thérèse, they said.

The priest asked why.

It was Thérèse. She gave herself up; she was a soul destroyed.

Brother Simeon offers his disingenuous commentary. "Had she been a man, what a priest she would have made, conquering all infidels, all sinners, all doubters, with the high price that she paid."

The demons' phrase slides back into my mind, beneath the tight skein of my wimple's headband. A soul destroyed. The chill creeps down my spine. Oh!—did I help with this destruction? Will I ever be forgiven?

Later I speak with Marie. She comes to evening recreation wiping her hands on her apron, with her face shiny from late labor in the garden. She does more than her fair share, I think; I hope she reaps graces in accordance with her efforts. I bid her read the letter from Brother Simeon. She does so, giving me her nod and downward-turning smile as she digests the information.

"What do you make of the demon's response?" I ask her as she folds up the paper and returns it to me.

"Why should we trust the words of a demon?"

"They are constrained to speak truth at the point of exorcism," I remind her.

Marie looks thoughtful. "Has the girl recovered?" she asks.

I chide myself for my lack of interest in Charlotte's wellbeing.

"Brother Simeon's conclusion makes me believe so." Marie nods, but I feel again the chill that beset me earlier. "But did we do it, Marie? Did we destroy her?"

If I cannot be honest with my older sister, there is no one to whom I can possibly turn. Marie looks shocked at the suggestion. But then she comes close and boldly takes me into her arms. Enveloped, I smell her familiar comforting smell, plus the herby grass of Carmel's little meadow.

"Dear Pauline. Whatever makes you say—"

"We let her come here—so young! I had already broken her heart by leaving her motherless, and then I couldn't stop her being martyred by the strictures of our Rule. And Mother Xavier was so harsh with her. And then, oh, God—she was so young, younger and younger as the years go by, and—" Marie tries to *shhh* me as though I am one of her struggling protégées in the novitiate, but I force the words out, or they force themselves out, commanded by this close company of love, "and after her death—have we—Céline and I—destroyed her all over again with this endless campaign to set a halo around her face?" And then another horrible thought: "Is she even happy in heaven?"

Marie has released me from her embrace, and at her gesture I follow her to the window that looks out into the garden as the light starts to lower.

"Look how it all continues to grow," she murmurs. I look out. It is true. "As long as there is grass, there can be fruits and flowers." I offer her a smile. What she says brings back a little sweetness. "You know how diligently she cultivated her own soul," she continues. "She suffered—how terrible it was to witness. But she never lost her loving nature. You are better at your letters than I, little mother, but I am sure that whatever those—" and she looks as though there is a sudden sour taste in her mouth, "—foul creatures say, they can never uproot her foundation of love."

I drink in her mélange of wisdom as though it is clear water, quenching my thirst. I allow myself to think that behind language—her language, all language—dwells the same elusive light, the same fresh hope.

In Carmel: Marie

Pauline bears the burden of our correspondence. She cultivates many voices in the silence of her office and must untap the right tone for the recipient of each missive. She writes to Léonie with maternal regularity. All the surliness of the past has dissipated. And for months we have been preparing her for the likelihood of a summons to Lisieux. Pauline frets. How will this poor struggling sister of ours cope with the physical and emotional demands of her visit? Céline and I exchange glances as the preparations are made.

"You will know what to do," she whispers to me in the cloister, flouting the Great Silence—not for the first time. "You can give her one of your hugs and some herbs to help her sleep," she adds. "And then you can do the same for me."

I reach out and we clasp hands for a moment, before walking on to the dormitory staircase.

The next day I finish the letter Pauline was unable to complete. Due to time, she claims. Due to understandable hesitation, I think. But I sense that Léonie would like to hear about the exorcism and the description of our little saint as a soul destroyed, yet triumphant still. If anyone is able to understand the destruction of a soul as its own highest offering, it will be Léonie. I pick up my pen and fill the white space my constrained, careful sister has left; I fill it with the story of Thérèse's life after life: her promise to do good on earth fulfilled again and again.

I believe I will see you soon, I finish.

Not in the afterlife, whatever spatial realms that world will offer—but here, in Lisieux: birthplace of callings, birthplace of sanctity, birthplace of reconciliation.

In Carmel: Léonie

It is a dream. Dream enough that I am a professed nun, and now this dream of dreams, when the trauma of war is all around us. I am admitted, as Visitation Sister Françoise-Thérèse, to the Carmel of Lisieux. The side door to the enclosure opens, and—extraordinary moment—three faces welcome me that I have known longer than I have known my own. Then comes softness and the scents of their skin, the press of their bodies, in their brown Carmelite habits, against mine. Their warm hands hold my own cold fingers. Our breath mingles as we kiss each other's cheeks. I forget the years that have poured out between us.

I do not know what to say, but for once it seems that I am not the only one. We all struggle to find the words. This must be a dream from which I shall wake, but for now, I have never felt so welcomed in my life.

Pauline breaks the prolonged moment of bliss. "My darling. Thérèse has worked her most heartfelt miracle in allowing us the grace of your presence." I smile as best I can, though I feel my mouth tremble. She continues, "This is the door through which she came in 1888. Do you remember? You entrusted her to us. And now, she has entrusted you to these same poor sisters of yours."

It is true. I saw her spirit going through it.

"This is a joy I had not thought to have on this earth," says Marie, piously, but her own smile is as full and real as her face in its fraying wimple.

And Céline—my worldly sister, always so much cleverer and more polished than me: "I'm so proud of you," she says. "Look how beautiful you have become!" She plucks at my black sleeve and pulls me close.

It has been seventeen years since we all lived under the same roof, and for seven days I am to be with them again. A week-long holiday in heaven. Just as at Bayeux last year, I am to sign documents in the presence of the bishop and the Vatican emissary. This time I am to speak to them in the presence of Pauline. She assures me that their questions will be gentle. But otherwise, I am my sisters' guest.

It's Marie who takes pains to walk with me round and round the distinctive cloister, its white-and-black mosaic floor now fixed forever in my mind. She shows me each room. The refectory, empty of nuns but full of the smell of vegetable soup. The dark wood-paneled choir, and the little oratory beside it, with its sweet, plump cherubs painted by Thérèse. The chapter room on the first floor, clear sunlight flooding through. A room of vows and faults. The warming room, where I long to merge into the background as she did when she was alive. And then the cells she slept and suffered in. I ghost myself back to 1896 and imagine her coughing secret blood. I imagine her bare, cropped head bent over her handkerchief in the Lenten darkness. Then the antechamber where she trained novice Céline, new in the ways of Carmel. I pause, and picture them there, plus little Cousin Lucie.

"Show me the room where she died," I say.

Marie takes my hand, and we walk down St. Elijah's wide stone staircase and along the cloister to the infirmary of the Holy Face. Outside the air is fresh, and birds cry from the tops of the trees behind us. We reach the infirmary and step into the small, empty room. Firstly, I am aware of the light: fuller even than in the chapter room upstairs. A broad double window stands slightly open.

Marie notices my gaze and says, "We moved her in front of the window that last summer, so she could see the garden."

But now my attention is caught by the bed with its black, drawn-back drapes. Beside it is a large, framed image. I breathe in sharply. A photograph. It is Thérèse. Her face in close-up. She is asleep—no. She is dead. She has died all over again. There is a slight smile playing about her lips. I struggle to breathe. I feel intensely dizzy and raise my hands to my face.

Instantly Marie is at my side. With her arm around me she leads me to the bed, the bed in which Thérèse had lain. We both sit down on its heavy softness, and she gently presses my head to her shoulder. Beneath its coarse brown habit, her full form offers me a long-lost comfort.

"I was there at the end," she murmurs, I think to herself as much as to me. "What Céline captured with her camera is true. She saw God, I am sure of it. He possessed her all her life."

In Carmel: Marie

We rejoice as peace blooms again, and the cause of our Servant of God grows ever greater. But as the new year begins, I sense a sinking of my spirits. Perhaps it is the knowledge that I am unlikely ever to see Léonie again in this life. I seek solace among the white-veiled sisters I love. Not only the novices, but also those deemed of too rough a provenance ever to train for the choir. The gardeners, the cooks and cleaners, those who carry the physical burden of Carmelite life and turn it into a prayer. They remind me of Léonie, and also of myself.

They come in bewildered, sometimes stunned by the turn their lives have taken, and are immediately set to work. I slip into the refectory at odd hours, the hen coop, and the outhouses. There I find awkward Sister Ruth or shivering Sister Domenica. The latter is so stoical, it took me several encounters to determine the cause of her distress. New to our life in common, she did not realize how all the younger sisters' bleeding comes at once, with the waning of each month's moon. I show her where the rags are stored.

"Just take what you need—there's no need to ask permission," I tell her. And then I slip her a packet of my pain-relieving herbs—chasteberry, lavender, cramp-bark—I have taken to making herbal complexes in the potting shed behind our little meadow. "It's your duty to keep as strong as you can," I say, when I see by her frown that she fears self-indulgence. "And that includes taking your share of the morning soup," I add.

I've noticed it's become the fashion for the younger sisters to abstain from this bread-based first meal. Quite ridiculous, in my view. It's not as though they are slimming to fit into the latest fashions, and we need all the energy we can muster in the garden, even if the laundry facilities are part-mechanized now.

Coming back from one such visit in the kitchens, I am summoned to the prioress's office. "Walk with me, Marie," says my sister, indicating we slip through the cloister hermitage and out, unobserved, into the garden.

We reach the end of the chestnut walk and Pauline sits down, gesturing for me to join her on the garden bench. We are near the old cemetery, crosses marking the resting place of our first sisters here. Old Mother Rose-Chrétien rests there, as do other brave foundresses from the middle of the nineteenth century, and those we lost in the sharp years of influenza—Fébronie, Marguerite. There is a small flowerbed behind the cemetery ground proper, beneath which rests Mira, the once-imperious cat of Mother Xavier. I wonder if she prowls and is petted in heaven. But Pauline has her somber look, and is speaking:

"My Marie. I have sad news." She touches my forearm and glances at me. "Sad news in the eyes of the world, I mean. It should not be so for us." She inhales before continuing. "Our Father Pichon has left us. Not for Canada this time. He has left us for heaven."

I feel the blood drain from my face, and I hear myself utter a soft "Oh."

Almire has died. It sounds inevitable but also almost impossible.

For a few fast beats of my aging heart, I am a young woman again, riven with diffuse but painful longing; waiting at the Lambert Factory to see this famous priest; waiting at Calais for his ship to reach port; waiting for his letters, his fine guiding hand. Then I fall back into this too-modern, too-fast-moving present. "How did you hear?"

"I received the letter from his Jesuit superiors this morning. They were kind to write to us. They know what special souls he has guided to our little enclosure." She does not speak of herself, but of the trinity of blood sisters who have followed her to Carmel; I the least of all, Thérèse our future saint. Céline the quixotic, the elusive. I feel her hand squeeze my arm over the rough sleeves of my habit and I turn to meet her gaze. Her gray eyes probe mine as they have over a lifetime. Always Pauline. She speaks again, careful as ever with her phrasing. "I did know how much he meant to you. As a friend, a spiritual father—everything."

I swallow and with my free hand, wipe away disobedient tears.

"What a shame he will not be present for the beatification, and what will come after," I say. I am obliged to say it, as Thérèse is all our daily business, these years. But then I add my true thoughts: "I'm sure he thought of me no more than the other hundreds of souls he guided."

Pauline gives her characteristic smile, warm but repressed. She continues to gaze at me, almost as though we have been apart for a long time.

"Ah, Marie," she finally says. "Is this not like being loved by God? He loves all souls. But each one, having turned to Him, holds a special place in God's heart. Don't you care in this way for all the poor souls you help here?"

Clever Pauline; ever our Mother Prioress. This is her way of thanking me, not for my prayers—basic and hasty as they are—but for my support of our troubled sisters. As she rises, I notice she is old, and stiffening like me. But her own soul, I think, softens, as we journey through time together; she at the helm, and I forever looking to the shore.

In Carmel: Pauline

They are exhuming her for the final time. I cannot be there; just as in her childhood illness, I am promoter of the cause and absent from the process of her recovery. Decades ago, I left her for the Carmel, and caused her to fall into delirium; I could not leave the enclosure to rescue her. All this brave new century I have promoted the cause of her sanctification. I cannot be released to assist in the recovery of her bones from the good earth; they are raised by sextons, handled by priests. But the cycle of history returns her to me in the end. She travels to our chapel in her chariot of glory. She is coming for her crown. The wax statue, the *gisant*, is prepared; the public chapel is rebuilt; the faithful are invited. Her beatification glows like the dawn. Canonization will follow like a blaze of midday sun. I have written the script; I have paved the way.

In Carmel: Marie

In an effort to distract myself from grief, I watch the workmen through the grille dividing Carmel's public chapel from our nuns' choir, lifting the heavy curtain enough to gaze unseen. I should not; but nobody will chide me. They are widening the walls and preparing the alcove for her life-size reliquary. She returns to the Carmel as the canonization is confirmed. Céline has commissioned her image, a beautiful, dreaming doll, as if from heaven itself.

I smell the sawdust and stonedust and the sweat of hard labor; hear the gruff laughter and the sudden pools of silence as they remember where they are. Thérèse's name floats like a feather on their breath. One has invoked her for the restoration of a child's health, another for the return of a brother to the faith.

"My father swears she won us the war," says one, sounding full of youth's confidence. He has a wife of twenty-four, another has a daughter of the same age. One says it is a shame to die so young. Another says it is a strange God who locks up beautiful women. A third makes a noise like a groan or a yawn. There is grunting and nudging. Perhaps I am spotted.

"Careful boys; we are in the presence of the angels. Give us all your blessing, holy sisters of Lisieux!"

I let the curtain fall back and the laborers vanish from my sight like a dream. For the flicker of a second, I worry their cries will seep into the chapel walls and wake her, but then I realize that she has long since shaken off her sleep. It is I who am still sleeping, behind this thick black veil.

In Carmel: Céline

They promise me photographs. Even moving images. It is a new art, these days—quick, and merciless. Subjects are caught off guard, in an instant: looking around with surprise, adjusting their clothes, passing a hand over mouth or brow. Is this how the thief will take us, at the end of our lives? Unprepared? Unanointed? Unforgiven, perhaps? All her life Pauline has feared such a predicament: my thoughts will not be shared with her. And Thérèse would tell me no. His mercy is not only greater than His judgment, it is infinitely quicker. Quicker than light or the click of the camera. I think back to the photographs I took of her, alive and dead. Only a few of them are blurred, as she observed the seconds of stillness required for the equipment of that time. One captures her movement more than the rest; in Carmel's meadow one long-gone July, where she stands with her heavy fork held up, as if in the very action of gathering the summer-fresh hay. For a flickering second, I feel the sun on my face, and the scent of the hay.

Now she is but fragments and must be gathered once again from the earth. I close my eyes and remember her slender bones. I know how the day will proceed. The stone slabs will be raised one by one, and the rosewood coffin recovered from the grave. Blessed by the bishop, it will be placed in its chariot adorned with cotton and silk, with gold, cream, and pink, and with an image of her face, painted by me. Then the walk with the honor guard of thousands, including Adèle, stooped by age and covered in her widow's veil. The pause at St. Pierre's Cathedral and the Abbey School. The slow progression to our courtyard. The white horses robed with cream and gold. Horses not of apocalypse but of sanctification, drawing our family together once more. The bones will be washed and wrapped and placed in the reliquary;

under her sleeping form, the new wax body I have fashioned for her with the life that remains in my still-beating heart.

But no longer, for Thérèse, the tired cotton of her wimple and veil and the rough serge of habit and scapular; she shall have velvets and satin and silks. Our waxwork saint will have a brown silk habit lined with brown satin. I authorized the purchase of the materials, and, inspired, asked for gold thread with which to trim the edges. Her new veil shall be of black silk, her wimple the same in cream. Her mantle I will ensure is exquisite. Rippling ivory silk, with Mama's Alençon lace trimming and wrapping the whole.

At night, in my dreaming, I join her in the empty refectory. She has the latest issue of *Mademoiselle*. Together we leaf through the new patterns and fashions; the twentieth-century dresses she has never known. We are both attracted to a particular gown, one featuring a slim waist and full skirt.

"But Céline," she says to me, "could we not cut these silks more carefully, and get two habits out of the one cloth? Look, turn the pattern sideways and see how much more can be made."

She touches her hand to mine, and I am amazed at its softness, for she has done hard labor here for years.

Caen, Convent of the Visitation: Léonie

I am summoned, as so many times before, to our Mother Superior's office. Mother Christine is a gentle new superior. Still, I know I receive more than my fair share of gentleness. This is another balm that Thérèse has given to me. While her star rises, mine glows feebly in its wake. I am content that this should be so.

I shut the door and move forward to Mother Christine's desk. The open window gives this room the gift of daylight. The plain walls receive a caress of gold. The large wooden heart, symbol of our order, glows above its dark mantlepiece. I pull the chair back, hearing its familiar scrape, and sit. My robes fall into place. I fold my hands respectfully and gaze at them, mildly surprised by their signs of age. These signs have settled, like spots of rain, on all the community's sisters with whom I served my novitiate, and after whom (sometimes, long after) I took my vows of profession. They have settled on the hands of our Reverend Mother too, but her face is still that of a nun in the full bloom of her calling. I bite my lower lip, gently. Much more gently than I used to.

"Mother, I am sorry if I have mislaid Sister Madeleine's grocery list again. I was unaware last week that she left it on the sacristy shelf deliberately. I did not mean to cause our sister distress."

So often I misunderstand what had been said or done. But I am better when I visit with our sick ones. I soothe them as I wish to be soothed myself.

Mother Christine smiles, if a little cautiously. "Dear Françoise-Thérèse, you have done nothing wrong. I have received word from the Carmel of Lisieux, and what they have sent is more than mere words: and it is for you, the sister of a saint."

Carmel. The word is like a bell inside my heart. It has tolled most of my life. The word summons pictures since my visit: I see not just the public chapel, but the cloister, the choir, the cells, the warming room. The infirmary. The garden and its humble hermitage. The scent of meadow flowers.

My mind has wandered and with an effort I return to Mother's office. There is something for me, not just a letter. It is from my sisters in Lisieux. Mother places on her desk a cube wrapped in cream silk. She beckons me closer, and I stand. The sunlight catches the silk as she unwraps it. A wooden box, with almost a fragrance. She gestures me to open the box. I extend my suddenly shaky hands and lift the lid. It is smaller than my palm. Inside—more silk. I am sure that this is something from Thérèse. I look at Mother, who is gazing at the open reliquary, for now I realize that this is what it is. Not something from Thérèse, then. Something of Thérèse.

Unfolding the small square of silk in my hand I am met with a single white tooth. It is Thérèse's tooth. This is my gift, then. It is like a pearl, a perfect little pearl. Like a baby tooth from one who has grown out of childish things.

I cradle my long-dead sister's tooth in my hand. As I do so I feel a shift in all the pulses in my body. I do not think to ask how this gift has come to be sent to me, but Mother Christine breaks the silence by explaining.

"Your dear sister's remains have been recovered, prior to the canonization, Françoise-Thérèse. The Carmelites have welcomed them back. Thérèse is back home in Carmel, my darling. But she is here too. As they prepared the relics, Sister Geneviève noticed that a tooth had become detached from the jawbone. As you know, her flesh had long vanished, such is her humility after death, as before it. Of course, it could have been replaced, tied in with the silks which protect her bones, but the sisters—your sisters in particular—felt that this tooth should be sent to our convent, to be cared for by you."

These words swirl around the air between us. I wait for them to settle and for silence to cover me again. The pearly tooth absorbs my gaze. I imagine Léonie reflected in its littleness, its simplicity.

In Carmel: Pauline

The day has come. We pray with an ease, on light's rivulets; she sends her grace as a floral perfume, both deeply familiar and utterly fresh. Saint Teresita. Little Saint of the Little Way. A storm of glory in a sun-shot hour. I am the little mama of a saint.

Lisieux is a festival. Turn sister Babeth describes the plans for the streets. Processions, banners, and lights. Lights everywhere. Thérèse as a statue with a halo of bulbs. I look at Céline's photographs again. Her camera is a box which has preserved past years like wine. And she such a long time a nun now; my strong girl Céline, with decades of cloistered life inside her. She has become much-ringed wood, like me. Together we have raised our saint on Martin branches, while dear Marie gazes at the forest we have grown. Thérèse is to be sainted in Rome, remembered before a Pope, when in life she was hauled away from one even as she begged for the monastery gate to open and hide her forever.

I walk alone in the cloister in the cool of the early morning. It is a bright spring day, and the early hours are strong with promise. The cloisters are transformed. And yet they remain her cloisters. Folds of white linen are fastened to the ceiling: bright, clean, and pure. Roses are sewn into the cloth for the entire cloister's length. All day the petals will curl and softly drop. They will fall to join their sister roses on the cloister floor. Wreathes adorn the supporting columns of brick. Flowers and light. Petals and linen. I walk, as I have so often, so very often, from the Child Jesus to the infirmary door. My Thérèse, your birth and your suffering; a fold in time, a gleaming sheet. Here, time pools and flows in on itself. Prayer does that to the heart, life's restive wave held in a pleat of grace.

We were invited to the canonization, Marie, Céline, and I, but we take our vows of enclosure seriously and declined the journey, although it would be my and Marie's one opportunity to make the pilgrimage to Rome. Instead, the *Office Central* lends us a transistor radio, and we listen to the service—quite the miracle of the airwaves. From the perspective of eternity, from Thérèse's perspective, we are merely kneeling in the side chapel of the Vatican, behind our veiled enclosure grille. In my heart I am convinced that she listens among us, and, as so often of late, I almost hear her smile.

In Carmel: Marie

In a dream she comes to me, her hair wet and her lips dry.

"I do not know how to be a saint, Marie!" she says. But already her body is so full of light that I can hardly focus on her face.

"You have always been our hope, Thérèse," I say to her. "You did nothing to obstruct His love, and that is all the sanctity you need."

I think I see her smile, and I think I feel her fingertips brushing my mouth, but I wake up in my solitary cell before I can be sure. The air is full of static, as though Pauline has saved up the broadcast from Rome and reset it to herald each new day. My heart is jumping and quivering, as if with some new gift.

Aftermath

1925 — 1945

Caen, Convent of the Visitation: Léonie

I sit in the small office room where post is received and sorted, and various files and forms are stored. Most are too complex for me to be concerned with. Some of the other nuns comment on my exemption from such tasks with envy. To envy my stupidity seems a stupid thing to do, but I can sometimes agree with them in my childish, secret way.

"You see," I hear Thérèse whispering at my side, "remain little, and God treats you with special care. You are given more time with him; more strength to do the little works of love which really count."

"That is the sort of adding up I can manage," I say.

"Oh, I do not tell you to add up your good works," she responds. "That might have been Mama's way; she had her worldly business after all. But the good God is no more interested in mathematics than we are!"

And with that I hear her laugh, gently, like the spirit that she now is. I'm still smiling when I hear the doorbell ring. As I am portress for the day, I rise from my simple sorting to answer it.

I pull back the heavy wooden door to see a priest. He is not a young priest, but I judge him younger than me. He stands in the brisk October air. I notice the watery sunshine at his back, the autumnal colors from the trees in the rue L'Atelier at his back. His face is open and friendly, his brown hair thinning on top.

"Good morning, Sister. I so hope I'm not disturbing you in your work."

"Not at all, Father. My work is to answer the door today. Won't you come in?"

He steps into the entrance hall, and I indicate the visitor's room to his right. "Shall I fetch Reverend Mother? Does she expect you?"

I was not aware of having to prepare for a visitor. I must have forgotten.

"In truth, no, Sister. I did come in the hope of speaking to a member of your community, but I confess I hadn't written in advance." He forces a smile and puts down his briefcase. He fingers the buttons of his black over-coat. "I had great hopes of a short interview with Sister Françoise-Thérèse."

"Oh really? Do you know this sister?"

I buy myself some time. I don't think I've met him before.

"Ah—no, in fact. But as the sister of our new, dear saint, I so wanted to meet her. Imagine the insights—the living sister of a saint!"

I make my decision to hide.

"Father, I'm sorry to say that Sister Françoise-Thérèse is on private retreat. It's not possible to see her today." The priest's face falls, and my confidence with it. I must do something to raise his spirits. "I can tell you in confidence, Father, that you're not missing anything. Françoise-Thérèse is not a sister who is worth much attention. You certainly won't learn anything from her. Better to visit the Carmel in Lisieux—that's where the real saints live!"

I must have gone too far because his expression is one of shock. But I am not sorry. Instead, I exchange imaginary glances with my saintly sister. I feel her twinkling a smile at me, despite her love of truth.

I offer to fetch coffee for the father, but after a failed attempt at small talk he takes his leave. As I shut the convent door behind him, I do not know whether I have committed a sin or an act of humility. Is it possible to do both simultaneously? This idea causes Léonie's head to ache. I return to the office room and recommence my filing.

In Carmel: Céline

Mail awaits me after first collation, a sloppy vegetable stew I have grown used to but will never like. I glance over at Pauline as we gather in the warming room: she has the right to read all correspondence, but with the volume of letters that never cease assailing her I doubt she has thought it necessary to monitor mine. She looks tired, with lips pressed tightly together, and shadows under her eyes that are not merely due to our uneven electric lighting—something else with which I will never entirely make my peace. Every one of us is tired, in fact. To promulgate a saint is no easy work, especially when we are still shocked by the brutality of military conflict in this new age of machines. I wonder if she has heard further of the Virgin's warnings in Portugal. We are not alone in fearing yet another war.

The envelope pulled open, into my lap slide a number of papers, as though unbound pages of a book. Some are photographic plates, and some are printed word. What is this? Another book on Thérèse, it seems. Another rogue voice? It rapidly becomes apparent that this is so.

This Mademoiselle Delarue-Mardrus—I have come across her name before. Yes, a novelist, a lady novelist, one not sympathetic to the Catholic Church but eager to have her say, nonetheless, on matters religious in the modern world, matters, of course, including Thérèse herself. I am not entirely surprised to discover that she has written a book; her second, on my sister.

I still tremble a little internally at these strangers—to the faith, to our family—who see fit to expostulate on a young woman they never knew, and whose purity and love would set them to shame. Truly, this world is a heap of vanities. To think I once longed to set my path into its depths! As I leaf through the extracts, I am affronted by the critical tack they take: Thérèse's real message is coddled by sickly structure; the sanitized edition of her *Story* is wielded by the Carmel as their weapon; we present our saint as though she were a pink *bon-bon*; all pleas to release the true Thérèse fall on deaf ears; all criticism muffled by our dark forbidding veils. Feeling myself redden with rage, I shuffle the pages around on my lap, unaware of other nuns joining us for an hour of pallid chat. I also question why this package of dross has come to me, rather than Pauline herself, or our *Office Central*—surely it was set up precisely to deflect intrusions such as this? But then the photograph captures my attention and I both burn and freeze with its assault on my senses.

It is a photograph of a statue, a statue of Thérèse. But it is not the Thérèse I have labored so long and hard to establish and promulgate, my own Thérèse, my Thérèse *aux roses*. This Thérèse stands sentinel over a pile of discarded toys. An abandoned doll lolls at her feet. This Thérèse is tall and straight as a spire. Her hands are pressed together in prayer. Her head is flung back, and she hungers for the heavens.

This Thérèse is a lightning rod. There is nothing sweet about her.

As an artist, I sense a rending of my vision for which I had not been prepared. I am rebuffed, but more than this: I am challenged. I lift the page and squint at the small-print credit for this statuary gauntlet: one Monsieur Carlo Sarrabezolles has followed authorial instructions. He claims to rectify the Carmel's marring of her soul.

"How much longer must I suffer the blasphemy of fools," I mutter compulsively to no one in particular.

"Sister Geneviève, what is the matter?" asks Anne of the Trinity, once one of Thérèse's most beloved novices. She suffers greatly in recent years with a partially disfigured face; a condition that requires painful daily dressings. She peers over at the pages in my lap. "Have you received upsetting news?" And then, "Oh! It is Thérèse—may I see her?"

But suddenly I cannot bear her attentions and turn rudely away from her. My own mean-spiritedness horrifies me further. I feel the sting of impending tears and crumple the offending photographic image into a ragged ball. Then I do the same for the other, printed sheets, angrily, methodically; until a collection of crushed pages lie at my feet, like so many spoiled white roses.

In Carmel: Pauline

"Monsieur Ghéon has published his book," says Father Coombes. "I am sorry to say that there is another battle to be fought."

I am obliged to take his warning seriously. This priest, who never knew Thérèse, has been our guardian for several years now. He sits across from me in the visitor's parlor. I have an impulse to invite him into the enclosure so that we can walk in our little garden rather than the weary formality of this division between religion and the world.

Even when it is not at war, it seems that the world wants nothing greater than to fight and despoil; since Thérèse's raising to the altar, we have become prime targets. I prepare myself to listen to the latest assault.

"And are we still depicted as madwomen, wedded to our cult of death?"

I sound sharp and I know it. Monsieur Mabille's recent book was a wound inflicted on Carmel. Our only consolation was that, in his specious cause to prove Thérèse a neurotic, he was unable even to identify which Martin sister was which in the blurred photographic gallery at the back of this book. Other titles, too, have come and gone. Mademoiselle Delarue-Mardrus's book flickers at the periphery of my memory like an angry fly. Céline maintained her temper less successfully than I at that literary calumny. I await to hear this new tranche of disparagements. We are, perhaps, less vulnerable than in previous decades. I have authorized the *Office Central* to publish our rebuttals swiftly and prolifically. In this way I flex the reins of power more than is normal for a humble prioress.

"My dear Mother. I am aggrieved on your behalf. Monsieur Ghéon is a man of considerable literary skill." Father Coombes resettles himself in his chair. "He is not crude as was Monsieur Mabille, nor emotionally wanton as Mademoiselle Mardrus."

"Then precisely how does he threaten us?" I ask the question, unsure I want it answered.

"He is another self-confessed devotee of Thérèse who objects to her—her depiction as a passive soul, a sugary confection, where she should, according to his view, be given to the world complete with all the rough edges of her life. And the very human context of the Carmel sisters."

He brushes some imaginary dust from his black soutane as his words settle into the parlor's walls and floor. I straighten in my seat, acutely aware of my lack of stature. I bristle. But nothing of this is a surprise to me.

"He questions our testimony? The sworn affidavits of her sisters in both blood and religion?"

Coombes nods. His dark brown hair is ruffled as though he habitually runs his fingers through it. The heavy black lines of his thick-lensed spectacles frame sapphire-blue eyes. I sense he is tired, stressed perhaps, but will never give up his advocacy of Carmel.

"He does. And you should know, along with dear Sister Geneviève, that he has procured the very fine photograph of Thérèse in her final laying-out and uses it as an example of all that is authentic and defiant about our saint, in comparison to the sweet-faced drawings that he claims no longer appeal to the public taste. He says, Mother Agnès, that you have hampered the power of Thérèse through confining her to a sugary shell. And—I fear this may offend, my dear Mother—he has used this photograph as the frontispiece of his text."

It is only at this point that he fetches a book from his briefcase and, opening it, rests it against the grille's tight squares. In the image, Thérèse lies dead in the choir once more. Her jaw is strong in death as in life. Her brows are firm and dark. Her pale, pale face is framed by her dark veil, and turned away from the lens. I have seen this photograph a thousand times or more, but suddenly I have an impulse to blurt out jagged tears. I grip my wrists under my habit sleeves and bite my lip in a long-practiced gesture of self-control.

"This gentleman does us a disservice. We have all attested to our intimate knowledge of Thérèse and borne false criticism patiently over these many years."

Father Coombes is silent. I find his silence restful.

"What should we do?" I ask, eventually, meaning, *How shall we combat this? Refute it?*

A further pause. I look again at the offending book and its frontispiece, feeling only sorrow for her passing, long ago. Then Father Coombes clears his throat.

"I think, dear Mother Agnès, that it could be time to reevaluate what the faithful need to nourish their souls at this source of grace." Resentment begins again to unfurl in my stomach. But before I can retort that the nuns who knew Thérèse would always be sovereign witnesses over those who did not, Coombes raises his hand. "I do not mean—of course!—to imply that you should retract your testimony, nor dear Sister Geneviève's paintings. But—ah—" and here he visibly searches for the right phrase—"that there is such a wide interest in, and appreciation for, Thérèse and her mission, that we must also consider releasing the full evidence of her spiritual genius. You were guided by heaven in editing the first text of *The Story of a Soul*, I am convinced of it. But has the time now come to allow for the full facsimile printing? Every page of her notebooks?" And as if this is not enough, he braces himself for a further request: "And, forgive me, but I do also believe that now is the time for the photographs to be made available to the faithful. All of the photographs, untouched and entire."

He grips his hands together in his lap. He looks me in the eyes and tries to reassure me with a smile.

"Sister Geneviève will attest that her paintings capture the soul of Thérèse, where a photographic plate never could."

I attempt to defer the decision that, unfairly, rests with me.

"I respectfully disagree," says Father Coombes. "She has captured untold riches with her camera lens. The time may not have been right previously, but now . . ." He spreads his fingers over his soutane and gazes at them. "In this modern age, souls are surrounded by the fruits of photography and are able to respond to the directness it offers. I am sure she can be persuaded of the importance of her own work."

"I'll speak to her," I say.

"Not just our admirable sister's work, of course. We are privileged to have photographs of Thérèse as a child, as a novice . . ."

"I'll let her know."

"And your own permission, for the manuscript facsimiles?"

I feel a twist of pain in my heart. My life's work has been to help my sister to her sanctity. All my old pride at teaching her the faith merges with my editing work and my years of fighting to protect her name and image from defamation. To acquiesce to Father Coombes's request requires a ceding of control like none other. The work I have done to keep her safe . . .

I look again through the grille at my dead little sister. My eyesight blurs and I brush away a tear. Then I know what I will say.

"I agree to your request, Father. I will release the full manuscripts of Thérèse's work. As you know, they are made up of three separate documents, and were reordered to constitute a spiritually beneficial whole."

"Dear Agnès, this is wonderful."

But now I hold up my hand and, for a second, have a vivid memory of Mother Xavier once giving me orders in the middle of the night.

"I have just one condition." He leans forward, eager to oblige me. "This will all be done, and done well, by you. But it will be done in due season, after I myself have left for heaven."

I stare at him, inhaling strongly through my nose, just as Mother Xavier used to do. He opens his mouth as though to remonstrate. But then he shuts it again, and while I know that one battle has been lost, I have the pleasure of this small victory to see me through to the end of my earthly life.

Caen, Convent of the Visitation: Léonie

"Sister Françoise-Thérèse, I do declare you are growing a beard!" Novice Sister Annette whispers to me, tugging at my black habit's sleeve.

Immediately I stiffen in offense. This is the young girl I dared to embrace when I found her in tears during her first weeks here, and she was pleased enough with me then. The experience was overwhelming for me, and I remember it more than my own novitiate lessons. Now, though, I think, *She is getting above herself!* Then I chastise myself. I should not question her intentions so quickly.

I give my usual embarrassed smile when I don't know how to respond to a comment. Then I turn back along the cloister and return to my cell. My needlework awaits me, but first I run my right hand over my face. There are no mirrors in the cloistered life, something that has helped me forget the anxieties over my displeasing appearance, my awkward shoulders and jutting chin. Now my fingers serve as a sightless reflection.

With a worldly horror, I encounter thick, whiskery hairs where my chin begins. And more—single hairs on my jawline and down towards my throat. What has happened? I tug at the worst-feeling ones and pull away some short wiry evidence. All my vanity and pride flair up. Why me? I flick through my memories. Mama was dead before she began to grow old. Aunt Véronique always looked pearly smooth. I have not noticed the other Visitandine sisters with this problem, except perhaps old Sister Perpetua with her arthritic limp and cramped hands. I look down again at the glinting fluff between my fingers. At least it's a bleached white color. Perhaps the cropped hair on my head has turned white too.

I worry away at the discovery.

Who can I turn to? But I am assistant sister in the infirmary and my unformed prayer is answered in the shape of a pair of tweezers from the general dispensary. Several of these items remain in the supplies drawer. I make a guess that nobody bothers to keep an inventory. *I'm not going to dig my way out of the convent like a prisoner with a file*, I tell myself. However, once back in my cell, I experience difficulty in using them. Unused to pressing anything to my face, I slip and gouge myself rather than removing the unwanted whiskers. I sigh. As usual I am only going to make things worse!

Feeling exasperated and in need of comfort, I mention my unsuccessful attempts when I next write to Marie. She has always been the down-to-earth one of us. She helped me when my monthly bleeding first came and frightened me. She did the same for Céline and Thérèse. Now she is like a godmother to all the young sisters at Lisieux, wrapping them up with her practical love.

Marvelously, she writes back to me at once. I guess Pauline didn't even bother to read it, as it is only a letter to me.

> *Dear little Sister,*
>
> *On to the matter of the famous tweezers! You will succeed in this endeavor, just as you have in all others. All it takes is acquiring the knack. Hold the skin of your face taut with the fingers of your left hand and pluck the offending whiskers out with your right! You will soon have your beautiful smooth face restored to you. And don't waste a moment upon scruples. We are expected to be neat and tidy in the cloister, trial though this sometimes is. Besides, we are the family of a saint, one who never had to deal with these issues of later life! We may be required to face visitors and cameras more than the cloistered vocation generally demands. You may wonder if I am familiar with the technique I recommend to you: indeed I am. I am not a good gardener for nothing. Out comes any whiskery crop as soon as I feel it arrive. And speaking of gardens, dear Léonie, we will soon be sending your mother our boldest roses for your little plot.*
>
> *Your Marie,*
> *with all the love in her soul*

I love this letter so much I fold it carefully and place it in my habit pocket, along with my picture of Thérèse and the latest handwritten renewal of my vows. Immediately my veil seems easier on my face and I stand a little taller. The next time I catch a glimpse of myself in the infirmary's glass cabinets, I try a larger smile than normal, one I can offer to those newly moved to the infirmary. I think perhaps I am becoming, if not like Thérèse, then a little like Marie, and this thought gives me immense pleasure.

In Carmel: Marie

I love, these days, to hear from Léonie. She writes to us all, but to me she reveals her fears. I find myself advising her on everything from personal grooming to the niceties of the recreation hour. I find her fun and humble in the midst of her clumsiness. Dear Léonie. She has a little hidden spark of sanctity about her. I am surprised, yet not surprised, when she is blessed one day with a vision of Thérèse's hands. But oh—I rise stiffly these days. I could do with a little saint's hands under my own arthritic elbows, helping me to walk.

In Carmel: Céline

I take the photograph of Cardinal Pacelli. It is a fine spring day. The air is crisp, and the negatives of my light new camera will capture the pale sunshine and the sharp, thin form of this Roman prelate in our little cloister and the severe folds of his robe. The basilica is complete, and Pacelli is here after consecrating the building to Thérèse. The crowd was vast, he tells us. As vast as the numbers who accompanied her bones back to us in 1923. And now her right arm resides in the crypt of her own basilica. The humerus, ulna, and radius, and all the delicate bones of the hand that made her a saint. Dear God—the words she wrote, hunched over that clumsy replacement desk she found for herself in the attic. My heart twists. For the fraction of a second, I remember us both as young girls at Deauville, her right arm linked in mine, the gleaming sun warming us both in equal measure.

I imagine the sunlight shining on her new building, like an image of the heavenly city. I suppose I will never see it. Will her bones miss me there, in their gilded reliquary? But I must not be rude to this man of God. He turns towards the cross at the center of the cloister quadrangle and lifts his face to contemplate the crucified figure at its peak. His features are fine and pale, like a sort of delicate bird, and the lenses of his wire-rimmed glasses glint like two discs, two transfigured hosts. Do they retain what he contemplates, like the camera's lens? What will he remember of our little world?

"Your enclosure is small, Sister," he muses, as though he has heard my thoughts. Still holding my camera, I bow my head in agreement. "And the Vatican is sumptuously large in comparison. But there is something in your life here that is profoundly spacious." He offers me what I suspect is a rare smile. I wait for him to continue. "The hours you spend at prayer—this is glorious labor, dear Sister! I should not say I envy you, and yet . . ."

He trails off. I bite my lip. The Céline of old might let him know just how many of those hours pass in dozing, fretting, awareness of bodily discomfort, or the mental listing of chores. But I consider that he says what he needs to believe and conclude there is no harm in that; it is something very common in religious life. And then, after I have shown him to the infirmary, where he will say Mass and bless poor wheelchair-bound Marie, I think that for all my brittle cynicism, he is also right. Light blesses the waiting soul, even if only a sliver at a time. Forty, fifty years spent in the dark: all given willingly for a brief, searing touch of the sun.

In Carmel: Marie

I am not given to intuition, but this Father who comes to celebrate Mass holds himself in such a way that I dare to consider him a future head of the church. Rather like Pauline, he is full of a light, practiced grace; politely we vie as to who humbles themselves to whom. I am defeated, due to this aching prison of a body. After the Mass he asks after my health, and when I make a mute gesture of frustration at my rheumatic state, he seeks to console me with his account of the day. Now Thérèse's basilica gleams in my imagination, alongside all the other ways and places in which she has received honor from the Church.

My remarkable girl.

He turns around in the infirmary and pauses before the dark bed in which she entered into life. He makes as if to touch its drapes but lets his ringed hand fall back against the drapes of his own cloak.

"Remarkable," he says, echoing my thought. "The discipline and devotion of a young woman. Remarkable."

I appreciate his reflections but wonder if this is really the whole truth. I have the flash of a memory: Thérèse, in her cell, a young novice still, caught leafing through a fashion magazine. Of how she looked up at me and smiled in such a way that I had already forgiven her before I even saw what she was browsing. The impulse of love she stirred: that is the remarkable quality I remember. I dare to think God responded as I. Pauline and the priests, however, are obliged to stick to discipline and duty.

"I am honored by your visit, Father. We have here a little taste of heaven, do we not? Though I think I shall soon be following my little sister up above. Do not forget us in your prayers, despite all the trials to come."

I hardly know to what I am referring, but I wanted to say it; I want this priest to know I am more than an old woman in a dark robe and a wheelchair. I was once a soft blur of love. There was at least one priest who saw me as such.

He bows and gives me his blessing; his dark cloak swishes as he leaves, and the dust motes dance and settle in the sunshine that remains.

Caen, Convent of the Visitation: Léonie

I am awake. Light has just begun to bathe my cell in the gentle way I love. I push my hurting body to get up: I can prepare the refectory for breakfast. I feel as stiff as though I have aged another decade overnight. Perhaps I *have* slept for ten years, and the community has forgotten me.

Don't be so stupid, Léonie, I tell myself, and in shaking my head, cause myself such dizziness that I fall off the edge of the bed and hit the floor.

I am stunned with shock, and then more pain. I cannot lift my arm to pull myself back onto my mattress, or even into an awkward sitting position. I hear a low moan of distress and realize that the person making this sound is me. Something pulls the left side of my face down into an ugly grimace. Despite the coming dawn, cold and darkness creep around the back of my skull and push themselves into my mind.

After the attack, my words come and go. They come and go like sisters, bringing punishment and comfort.

"T—" I manage to say.

The infirmarian brings me a tisane of dried fruit and flowers. I think I am a dried flower myself, pressed between white bedsheets. I have the greatest difficulty feeding myself, as though someone has bound my hands with an invisible web.

I fear Louise; she will scold me should I spill anything. I didn't tell Mama, I try to say, but then I remember Mama is dead, and before she died, she took me back under her wing. It was painful for her because of my jagged bones.

Mother Gabrielle comes to see me with an opened parcel. Her smile is very warm and full of love. I think she has Thérèse's smile, and wonder whether she has been practicing, like I do, from all the photographs.

"From your Céline and Marie," she says, showing me the bouquet, carefully wrapped in clear plastic.

I gesture that I want to hold a couple of the flowers, so she selects for me a white rose and a pink one. I pinch the petals of the pink rose and pull some away from the rest. Shakily I let them drop on my crucifix, already lying by my side on the bed. Mother Gabrielle kisses my brow: she is pleased with my work.

In Carmel: Marie

Resting on my infirmary bed, I start to sense a loosening of my poor old limbs. Is this laughter I hear, or childish sobbing? They look for their godmother. Perhaps it is Hélène, waiting for me to make a space for her in the sheets. Or Thérèse, waiting for me to brush her long hair until it gleams. A sliver of song reminds me of dear Lucie. One more sleep, I think, and then I will rise and take the girls, all of them, into the quiet garden.

Caen, Convent of the Visitation: Léonie

"I am afraid . . . I—I—" I struggle to speak my fear.

The priest at my bedside listens hard; the purple stole around his neck means he must be taking my confession.

"My dear sister. Please do not be afraid. Our God is a God of peace and joy."

It seems to me I have heard, or read, these words before.

"F-Father," I manage. "I have stumbled many times. This does not—trouble me. Thérèse has sh-shown me how."

The priest continues to listen, calmly.

"And now you in your turn show the young sisters that by your trust and abandonment to God, you have learned the one thing necessary."

This I am able to accept. But the fear goes deeper still.

It is the fear of being not just stupid, but mad.

Of confusing past and present, faith and falsehood. Right and wrong.

Of being sent to that place: The *Bon Sauveur*.

To my immense relief, I am eventually understood and reassured. God is merciful to me.

"We would not abandon you, Françoise-Thérèse," says Mother Gabrielle. She sits with me as the light fails and the birds settle to their sleep. "God does not abandon you. Why should we?" She looks at me, and I am able to smile. Mother Gabrielle continues. "The only person who should practice abandonment is you, my dear patient. But this is hardly a new instruction for you."

In her voice, I hear Pauline's toughness, and a shake of Thérèse's sweetness. I gesture to my side table and Gabrielle places the most recent letters from Carmel in my hands, and a photograph from my visit there at my side. Marie secretly clasping my fingers while our portrait was taken. Marie, already released from her body's cage.

But I do not wish to be admitted to the Carmel after death. Mothers Christine and Gabrielle finally broach the subject with me.

"My dear Françoise-Thérèse," begins Gabrielle. "We understand, we more than understand the call of the heart to rest with one's family. Your long years of exile here—"

But I cut her off with a shake of my head. Here is where I have learned to pray so the light shines through my heart.

"God called me to be a Visitandine. This—has been my vocation. I will stay with my community—in death as in life."

My final profession, I think to myself.

I offer my prayers and my petals that day to big sister Marie, asking for help to be true to myself. I feel certain my request is granted.

In Carmel: Pauline

First Marie, set free from her own pain-filled skeleton. Then Léonie, a stroke at the last, dying almost as saintly a death as her little sister. I am left wrestling with my own lingering terrors. But in my dream, it is little Thérèse who appears to me. She is as she was: round-faced, radiant. She looks at me with a gleam in her blue eyes.

"You are growing old, little mother!" she says.

I tell her how happy I am to hear it. I wake up with the sense of having slept in sunshine. But I do not wake to sunlit peace: I wake to war, yet more war, and I flail in vain to understand why I am obliged to remain still in my earthly exile; why I have not yet done enough. The dream assuages the anguish that flickers in my soul; but it is not extinguished.

It is summer, and France has fallen. The Germans occupy Lisieux. Normandy is held shackled and captive. Oh—where is our warrior Joan of Arc now?

"They are a strong force, the Socialist Army of the German Republic. But they will be defeated. We are a weak nation and have been wounded for decades, for over a century. Out of such weakness a little saint has been raised to heaven. We below must offer further penance and—and much greater sacrifice. Heaven and our earthly allies will come to our aid."

I try to rally my nuns with such words, but fear that I fail. In my heart I fear this is more punishment we poor French souls must bear. Then I rouse myself. These Nazis hanker after purity, a purity of blood. It has led to nothing but brutal cruelty. We seek a purity of soul and must be prepared to offer ourselves. This is our heritage, our spiritual bloodline.

In my office I pray that our Carmelite bloodline is spared, and that the blood of our Lisieux neighbors is saved likewise. Reluctant to close my eyes,

I regard my papery hands, the hands of an old woman, and see them grip each other tight.

And then the bombing of the English begins.

Final Battles

1945—1958

In Carmel: Pauline

Hell rains down on Lisieux.

We hear it in the crack and despair of the skies.

We hear it in the crash and destruction of rubble.

We hear it in the cries and agony of our fellow citizens. We see it in their injured, worried faces at the grille.

My own inevitably approaching death pales into the insignificance it deserves.

The bishop visits and urges me to abandon the enclosure and lead my nuns to safety.

"Do not fear that the sisters shall escape the cross, good mother, whatever God leads you to decide."

One day in June we are at Compline. The day is done, and the sky is gently fading into night. Increasingly this has become my favorite time of day. My endless papers are set aside. Daytime, like my very life, is peaceful on the verge of its own dissolution. But as I stand to intone the Magnificat, the unmistakable sound of an explosion assails our ears. It is a bomb, and, although not unexpected, it shocks us to our core. It is perhaps a mile away, perhaps two. Further bangs of destruction and invasion rain down for the space, perhaps, of a Credo. I think as quickly as my stunned mind, my in-grained, narrow round of thoughts, will allow, while my Carmelites gasp and a few of the younger ones turn to hold each other's hands. It must be the railways. The line from Lisieux to Paris is what holds the unholy German presence steady here. This is the English mission to shake them off, but such action threatens to destroy our poor lives too. My heart quickens at the fear of sudden death. The gasps and whispering in the choir confirm I am not alone in my surmising.

But I must not let fear show. I click my fingers with authority and the whispering stops. Then I take my lonely prioress's seat at the head of the assembled rows of sisters and begin the sure prayers of the rosary. Together we recite the entirety of the eighteen Carmelite mysteries, after which the night sky has turned to a velvety blackness and Lisieux has resumed its mantle of silence.

But as we gather for Matins—the most holy, silent of offices—the raid commences in earnest. It is two o'clock in the morning. At Carmel, we are accustomed to chanting at this hour, in the valley of the shadow of night and death. But this is—I cannot smooth the fact into anything else—terrifying beyond all measure of personal distress.

"To our cells!" I hear myself saying, with more authority than I feel. And I add: "You may gather in each other's cells for prayer. It is no sin to seek companionship in such an event as this. But I will not have us all collected together for wholesale destruction."

Even as I speak the bombing continues. I fear more than sudden death. I fear hellfire and destruction here in this little town; here even, in these hallowed grounds. Céline puts her arm around me.

"We must not lose faith, little mother," she whispers. "Though He should kill me, yet will I trust in Him."

I hear myself murmuring in response, as though I am in a chapter meeting and slightly behind myself; a dream self, a ghost revisiting my future.

Would I sacrifice myself? This has been the direction of my whole life. I fear only that my will has been too weak, my little gestures too insignificant.

Would I sacrifice my nuns?

Only you, O God, would call beyond all logic.

Yes, my God, I would sacrifice my nuns, though it crucifies my heart beyond all reckoning.

Then, as with Abraham, God catches and suspends death's arm.

In Carmel: Céline

When the bombing raid sets in, it is the middle of the night. My bones are tired and my mind more tired still. There are no concessions made to age or artistry. Pauline directs us away from the choir; I am not surprised. She is ever pragmatic: she would not have all her daughters burn at once. For burn is what we will all do should an English bomb fall through our roof.

She bids us group together in our cells for prayer. Instinctively I make my way, not to my own poor shelter, but to Thérèse's last cell with its two rooms and its own little relic of her bone wrapped in cloth and preserved in its silver box. I have the key to the cell. Touchingly, novice sisters Alise and Marie-Anne are waiting outside. Marie-Anne, the older, is comforting her younger companion who is weeping.

I usher them inside. We stand, then kneel, together at the little oratory to the Virgin, and I begin with the Hail Holy Queen. As the explosions continue out in the world, I am partially transported back to my own clumsy, angry days in the novitiate. I search, as I had then, for Thérèse's presence and the high spiritual tone she perpetually set, continues to set before me. I am seventy-five years old and still I look for guidance from my long-dead little sister.

A hand on my shoulder. It is Pauline, standing beside me. I look around and up and incredibly she is smiling.

"Come, my Céline. We have work here still to do."

She leads me into Thérèse's inner chamber, where her straw mattress, with its brown woolen coverlet, waits in its corner, and where, under her pillow, we place the many letters that still arrive for her every week. Here, too, is the small, silver reliquary box on a simple low table. Pauline takes the box with both hands, and momentarily lifts it as though it is a flaming torch. She turns and takes it through to the novices.

"Let us ask her for her help." Her voice is quiet but crystal clear. "We have never needed it more."

Leaving Carmel: Pauline

As my body starts to fall and fail me, Lisieux falls harder, fails faster.

I read the reports. The newspapers are supplemented by letters from the *Office Central*. I recognize Monsieur Bernard's hand and utter a swift thanksgiving that he still lives.

"Notre Dame du Pré has been utterly destroyed," I say to Céline and the few sisters I can trust not to slide into despair. "It is very unlikely that the mementoes of Teresita's first Communion remain unscathed. It is very likely that some of our Benedictine sisters have died."

"Murdered by the English," mutters Sister Magdalene.

"Unnecessary words are occasions of sin," I retort, sharply. "They are not the only community to suffer deaths in this current crisis. The Sisters of Providence have been hit by a bomb. It is possible the entire community is killed."

Céline gasps. Novice Alise, the youngest of us, gropes behind her for a chair. But I have not finished.

"The Little Sisters of the Poor have also suffered fatalities, as have the Sisters of Charity of the Refuge."

"They have killed those who help old men, and poor girls who are with child. What kind of deliverance can they possibly offer France?"

I cannot answer Céline's question.

The noise of blast and impact is so sudden that for an instant I believe it is the end and we are dead. Then hideous burning smells penetrate my prioress's office. Due to a lifetime of curbing my natural impulses, I do not rush to the door or crane my neck by the window-slit to see what remains of our beloved Carmel. Instead, I sit at my desk and extend my hands to the others.

"Sisters let us pray. Our community will not desert its vocation. I expect all nuns to continue in the cells with rosary and intercession. When the final sacrifice comes, we will not be found wanting."

I suppress the voice of fear that whispers in my mind: this is no merciful love.

By evening Carmel's outer courtyard has been destroyed in a flash of flame and a black bloom of smoke. The *Office Central* is in flames. The chaplain's house is in flames. The rue de Livarot burns as though it is a pathway to hell. I hold my hands up in a cry of mute anguish. If He wishes us to burn, then we will burn. We are warriors; we will burn with weapons in hand.

"Mother, you must leave the Carmel," says the superior of the *Mission de France*. "Take your daughters, seek shelter in the basilica. There is no hope of surviving this raid."

"I will not leave our Carmel. My vow is more sacred than my life here below."

Lisieux burns. My life is in flames. It is seared back to nothing. I am a girl in St. Jacques's Church. A white sword pierces my heart. I stand in my day dress and black corsage in Madame Besnier's studio. The past burns. The present burns. I bathe Thérèse with a damp cloth. Her forehead burns. Her heart is aflame.

"I am here forever. We will not leave."

Zelo Zelatus sum pro Domino Deo Exercituum.

The superior looks at me through the parlor grille. He all but orders me to leave. I am, he reminds me, the living sister of a saint. I must preserve the community. It is the will of Rome. It is his will. It is her will.

"I will not leave."

"If we are going, then it must be now," says the priest.

He is in such shock that my refusal neither penetrates his mind nor scandalizes his soul. But he proves himself as stubborn as I. More so.

Bombs bring their spherical hells. Hell rains down and down.

You are a toy of the Child Jesus, I once wrote to her. *You are His little ball. See how He delights in piercing you; what sweet breath of love you exhale in return.*

"Mother Agnès, you must hesitate no longer."

I leave the parlor and summon the community.

"We are leaving the Carmel and taking shelter in the basilica of my little sister. We will leave now. We will walk. We will assist each other. Brothers of the *Mission de France* will guide us while we still have light. Their superior awaits us beside the parlor door. Sisters Magdalene and Felice. Take the Blessed Sacrament from the oratory. Wear your long veils and do not delay. And remember, my daughters, that we do not remove ourselves from the battlefield. Our lives are His, and I offer Him my own minute by minute."

I am surprised by the silence and the instant obedience. Of course, I should not be. Thérèse has trained us well, even those who never knew her when she lived. I pray to my little daughter: cover us with your shield and mantle. We have more need of these than roses now.

Leaving by the entrance door I dip my withered fingers in the holy water stoup and bless my dear Carmel. I had not thought to step over its threshold again while still in this life. Now, perhaps, I must die before I can reenter its poor, loved walls.

Leaving Carmel: Céline

We stumble out, blinking rapidly, onto these burnt and acrid streets. The light is not substantially brighter than in Carmel and yet my eyes are seared with its harshness.

The *Office Central* is a cavernous, blacked-out hole. It smolders. My Thérèse *aux roses* has burned there all day—hundreds, thousands of papery prints, dispersed like dead leaves, like seared, burnt offerings. A couple of badly singed images drift cruelly across our path. Come, Céline. Offer each stumbling step.

Lisieux is destroyed indeed. My heart burns with its flames. My heart, in its useless sack of a body, clad in the rough habit I will never get accustomed to. When I entered, I was a young woman with a tall-legged camera. Leaving it I am a chronicler of devilry. But I will never sketch this obscene world. I carry the small silver box which holds a fragment of Thérèse, and a folder of my original sketches for a new biographical project. Pauline has not ordered it; but she has not forbidden it. If I have sinned, then I will repent at my leisure. It will not be tonight.

We did not have time or resources to rescue the bones beneath the reclining wax statue. I utter a desperate sort of beseeching.

"Keep safe. We will return for you. And shelter Marie."

Marie is in heaven, but her bones are in the crypt below. And Lucie, little cousin, who melted almost to a nothing all of forty years ago.

Up the hill to the basilica. At last, we see it with our own eyes: close, and soon to be close enough to touch. How different it is from the domed outline visible on a clear day from Carmel's roof. It is impossibly vast, and visibly stained and scarred with war.

Lisieux, Basilica of St. Thérèse: Pauline

When we arrive, we are a ragtag bunch of women. Disorientated, dirty from the gravel and the smuts of a devastated town. Beyond tired: it is as though sleep is something from our former, sheltered lives. Now we stagger through the interminable paths, the broken paths to our strange shelter. It is our little sister who will shelter us.

Lisieux is a broken town, a deserted city. All who can have fled. Electricity has been substantially destroyed so we are thrown back to our old childhood rhythms of the always encroaching cold and dark. I think wildly, my mind unable to relinquish its habit of community budgeting. How shall we live? Who will feed us? We are indeed a community of beggars now. As we climb ever upwards towards the basilica, I see that it has not been immune from the destructive bombs. Like the Carmel, its approach is now in ruins. Smoke and brokenness replace what was previously—according to the photographs—a wide and welcoming esplanade.

The evening light is dim now. We are veiled and the black gauze of the Carmelite's great veil makes for restricted viewing in the best of circumstances. Add to this my poor eyesight, with decades of peering over letters of petition, all addressed to a little sister long since dead, and no wonder I think I see visions of other realms; I can barely distinguish the dust and smoke from the twists of the dark sky and the obscuration of my veil. We see through the dark, darkly. I reach out to hold the hand of my Céline.

"Little mother," she says, her voice hoarse from dust and exertion. "Let us go through. We are to seek shelter in the crypt."

A shape looms towards us, tall and black. It is a priest, and I sense the exhaustion in his face more than see it.

He leads me, and I lead my Carmelite daughters. We walk, aching, down a wide flight of stairs, with dust still present everywhere. There are loud, unfamiliar, cavernous sounds. I put my hand to a banister and feel its strange shock of cold.

Lisieux, Basilica of St. Thérèse: Céline

I am almost hallucinating. I would not call it a vision, though it is that. As though I have been reduced to the size of a doll, I approach Thérèse's house, this great, gray succor in our devastation. It is bulky, wide, and squat in a way she never was. Pauline—I cannot imagine how her poor body must ache—reaches out and I take her small hand in mine as we approach the damaged esplanade. My great veil is thin enough for me to see through its cotton smuts. Shapes, shapes, as though a moving image palace surrounds us; absorbs us wholly into its projection. Will such things exist in this world one day? People—single, secular people, poor souls without family, without domestic support in this world—stumble towards my sister's great basilica.

"We have evacuated all that we could," explains a young gentleman—a priest?—as he sweeps his arm over the jostling panorama. "Some of these we rescued from the fallen masonry and devastated streets."

I see an old woman with her hands outstretched, a rosary gracing the wrist of her right arm. Then I realize that this woman is, in all likelihood, younger than I. All time and all space are fractured here. I close my eyes and still I see baleful lights and the zigzag of death. Does she come for me now? I do not, yet, want to die. Before I open them again, I see Thérèse, Thérèse not in life or death but as a painting not yet begun; angular, white, and stark, with blues and reds blooming like wounds, or like worlds, around her slender form.

Lisieux, Basilica of St. Thérèse: Pauline

We go to the low, wide space of the crypt. We are led there like the old souls of the gospel. I am led by another, after a consecrated lifetime of leading. I tremble more than I can disguise. There are others—the odor of sweat and fear and injury trouble me more than I can say—but we are led to the front. I push back my veil. The light, though electric, flickers like a fire. Whispers as the paltry congregation parts for us to walk to the front. A wretched sibilance.

"Sisters, sisters, sisters of St. Thérèse."

And a few exhortations.

"Pray for us!"

"Little saint, save us!"

We gather on the right. Céline supports my arm, but my strength is not yet gone. I discern a familiar figure among the distorted proportions of this great cavernous place. The Virgin of the Smile gazes serenely on, just as she had when watching over Thérèse in her childhood and through her dying. One of the sisters—is it Marie-Anne?—starts to intone the *Memorare*. A little pocket of familiarity opens up and we fill it with our breath. Sister Felice comes forward and places the Blessed Sacrament on the wide ledge beside the Virgin. Its silence fills the air of the crypt like a slow exhalation.

Lisieux, Basilica of St. Thérèse: Céline

Pauline wilts with sudden exhaustion once our journey is complete. I will not call it a pilgrimage, but perhaps that is what it is. No rubble has crushed us; no Carmelite has fainted or fallen. There are other religious here; some in visible distress. For now, they keep a respectful distance, but I have a feeling we will come to know each other well enough. Here in this crypt, we are as if cast onto a shadowy plot of earth. Not buried, but planted—transplanted—like seeds. Well, some of us are poor seedlings. We are the withered offcuts from our consecrated grounds.

Some of the secular people are bruised and bleeding. Their shirts torn and their torsos gashed. Women with smut-smeared faces; the compromised still-white flesh of their décolletages indecently exposed.

I think of the Carmelite Martyrs of Compiègne, those sixteen sisters who sang *Te Deum* before they were beheaded one by one at the guillotine. The last, Mother Teresa, stepping bravely up to her death, while the jugular blood of her nuns resanctified the desecrated earth. I have a sudden urge to paint that horrifying scene, slashing the canvas with a gamut of reds. Yes, I would paint it with feeling.

Some younger people are setting out blankets and pillows for us. We will have cushions and soft material on which to rest. I glance at Pauline, sitting straight and empty-handed by my side. She looks so small, but still so sure. I have no doubt she would step up to the same task as Mother Teresa at Compiègne, should God ask it of her.

"All my daughters, if it is your will," she murmurs.

Lisieux, Basilica of St. Thérèse: Pauline

A priest from the *Mission de France* approaches me as we are eating our meagre midday meal. There are some bruised apples for dessert, and I put aside my dry bread, fearing to sin against charity—but my throat cannot accept any more of its sharp fragments, and my mouth feels full of broken brick. The priest's approach is convenient. I shall ask him to hear the community's confessions. I shall go first.

But he looks in a hurry, this tall father with papers slipping from his damaged leather folder.

"Dearest Mother," he says.

Do I know him? Is it Father Roulland, back from his missions? Of course, it is not. I have not lost my wits entirely. This father, or one of his team, helped us to get here, helped to persuade me that we should come here. His reappearance suggests there is news of the Carmel. I doubt that it is good.

"Father. What of our Carmel? I see you have something to tell me," I say to him.

I do not have the energy for pleasantries. My voice sounds strange from the scratches of the bread and the unfamiliar acoustics of the crypt. Luckily this priest is also too worn for bourgeois niceties.

"Yes, Mother Agnès. There has been another raid. It occurred in the early hours of this morning. The allies choose to cause the most destruction under cover of darkness. With the long hours of sunlight, we could almost predict it."

"They too do the devil's work," mutters Céline, who hovers at my side.

I hesitate to agree or disagree. These days, where does the fiend not thrive?

"The cloister and chapel remain undamaged, for now," the priest continues, "but the roof of the turn sisters has not escaped destruction." He looks directly at me, and exhaustion rings his young-man's eyes. "I'm afraid it burns still, and this is the bigger danger."

Beside me Céline gasps. I sense rather than see her covering her mouth with her hand. She does not need to speak in order for me to understand her terror. The fire will spread to the external chapel and destroy the main reliquary. The sleeping wax statue will melt. The marble angels will last longer, although they look as if they are carved of sugared ice. But they too will blacken and wither in the flames the bomb set off.

Thérèse's remains, the bones and flecks of her, will be assaulted by the fire. They will blacken and crack. They will be crushed in the guttering pyre of this terrible war.

Little sister. I would give my old bones for the sparing of those fragments. Little sister, who curled on my lap like a cat when we both lived in the world. Must you now be reduced to a bone in a glass case, a sliver in a small silver box?

A noise behind me brings me back to myself. It is not Céline; she is at my side, hugging herself for comfort and with one hand raised to her brow. It is, in fact, Alise. The desperation of the situation seems to have forged some courage in her. She has heard the priest's speech, and will no doubt have come to the same conclusion as me.

"Dear Mother Agnès . . ." she starts. I turn to her wearily, but kindly. I am still prioress and stand in the role of Christ to the community. "The reliquary chapel is in danger of being destroyed. We must pray to Thérèse—you said it to us yourself. She will petition the help of all the martyrs. Of St. Joan, Reverend Mother! Together they will put out this fire."

She looks at me with a face shining like Thérèse herself. She was born long after Thérèse's death and not long before her canonization. She joined our Carmel a few brief months before war returned to the afflicted nation of France. She has been fearful, weak, and tearful. But never has she asked to be released from her vows—her war-prolonged novitiate. She has a vocation, that one. And now she reminds me of mine.

"Gather the nuns," I say. "We must redouble our prayers and ask Thérèse to raise them even higher."

Lisieux, Basilica of St. Thérèse: Céline

Even when I close my eyes, I experience change. The light in this crypt is dim and deep. My eyelids cover the view with their old, thin skin. Tiny capillaries transport my blood, and the effect is one of a deep maroon, as always. But the quality of darkness is also made up of sound, motions, scents, the toughness of the cool-tiled floor. I sense the devastation spreading far beyond the basilica walls. Pauline calls us to pray. It is a dim deliverance.

In my prayer I experience a flash of reminiscence. I am with Thérèse in the belvedere of Les Buissonets, and, some spring sunset, we are drunk on our own youth, imagining ourselves the twin mystics of our age. I am Monica and she is Augustine. Or is it I who am Augustine, peremptory, troubled, and unruly? What was the book she waxed lyrical over? I remember it; Arminjon, Father Arminjon.

The end of the present world, and the mystery of the life to come.

She would turn a page and read of the ecstatic light displays of heaven. Never did she imagine such displays of hellfire as we have had these last days.

Little novice mistress, tiny chick of a saint: it is not roses we need now, but rain.

Lightning rod of grace, bring your thunder and your storm.

Lisieux, Basilica of St. Thérèse: Pauline

She summoned the wind. I am sure of it. By the end of the day, the crisis has been averted. Thérèse, in league with this great element made up of nothingness: not rain in the end, not supernatural fire, but the wind which dances around life's heaviness and the poor world's obstinacies. The wind which slips under rather than confronts. The wind, the holy spirit of contemplative life. Brother Wind, Sister Gale. The wind has blown the fire in the exact opposite of the reliquary chapel. Her touch, her prayer, her hard-won breath.

Lisieux, Basilica of St. Thérèse: Céline

I hear the footsteps before I see them: five brothers from the *Mission de France*, carefully descending into our shelter. They are dusty and dirty and burdened; four of them shoulder a small coral casket. What is this? A child's coffin? We must expect such atrocities, these days. The fifth brother carries a large box in his arms. Another coffin, even smaller? But it looks familiar. As does the coral casket. Do I slip back in time? Wildly I grasp for an explanation as the brothers turn towards us. I think, or whatever this instinctive version of thinking might be, that these are our little Martin brothers, dead in infancy, retrieved and housed in box and glass. If these really are the end times, then this makes a kind of sense. My old bones creak their agreement.

Then this fantasy vanishes with the last dark vapors of the night. The coral does contain a coffin of sorts, but it is not of little Joseph or Melanie.

It is the inner reliquary of Thérèse. The brothers have rescued her bones from the chapel's wax form and brought her to us. It is two decades since I had seen this casket—compact, gilded, and heavy—and so I knew it and did not know it at the same time. For the first time in many years her skeleton is gathered whole under the same roof.

Then the smaller box finds its place in my memory too. It is the box of Thérèse's manuscripts and of her correspondence we have gathered at Carmel over the years. Letters to me are included in the files, letters from the six years of our separation when she drew me in, ardently, relentlessly, and then left me, gasping for her light.

Pauline comes to my side, and then forward towards the brothers and their gifts—for this is what they now are. Her aged face might be impassive, her stature especially diminutive among all these men, but she is happy. I know this in my core. She goes slowly to the coral casket and for a charged moment lays her hands upon it. Then she resumes her role of perpetual responsibility, and signals for the brothers to take the archive manuscript box to her makeshift office in our corner of the crypt, while Thérèse's remains take a direct path to the altar. I join her and whisper discreetly into her veiled ear: "She will protect us. She will bring us home."

Without turning her head, she reaches for my hand in her practiced way. Before I can continue to speak, the other nuns gather around. I sense we form a body as a whole, with Thérèse once more taking her part—that of love, always and only, in the heart of her church.

Lisieux, Les Buissonets: Pauline

I am slipping into eternity. The real world intrudes and buckles into destruction. What is left is some ideal, or the structure of a long-gone dream. But I am told that the Carmel survives. The wind pushes the fire away. The bombs fall but less frequently. So far, I believe the cloister and chapel are spared. Or does the angelic spirit of the Carmel rise up from her own broken body, ready and able only to ascend to an anticipated heaven? Just as I have decided this is so, Céline shows me the newspapers, complete with photographs taken so quickly that mere hours have passed between incident and the printed witness of the front page.

Carmel is spared. So, too, is Les Buissonets.

Céline sits on my makeshift basilica bed. For a moment we are back in our family roles. I imagine pushing the glossy brown hair back from her eyes, sharing her love of oil paint and bright jewels. Les Buissonets. Then she tells me that is exactly where we shall return. In this strangest of times, in what may yet prove the end times, I am invited back, finally, to my own young womanhood.

Once out of the motorcar, it hurts to turn my neck. I raise my hands to ease the muscles, rigid at each side and above my shoulders. At Carmel I look straight ahead more than I do from side to side: it is our way. But now, I thirst to take in what scarcely seems possible. Les Buissonets restored and frozen in time. Céline is very moved; I sense her breathing, emotional and ragged. I am so much an old woman that my breathing always comes with some struggle. But—oh! Have we reached heaven already? Is the family home, restored to how it was before I left it, our true paradise after all? In the attic I stop to recover from the painful stair-climbing. Here was my room, my attic room. Even the easel is here, with a canvas bearing my simple, early efforts at still life. The birdcage—empty with little door open—and the bench. My little domestic cell as I readied myself to take wing. Thérèse took it over after me—I know from her memoirs. We visit the girls' room—see how I still think of it as that! The twin beds of Céline and Thérèse, each tightly bound by their satin spreads. The prim little dolls. Thérèse's white Communion dress with its pale pink sash. I think I am crying: for her, and for me. What did I know of compassion, really, in those days?

Downstairs all is preserved. Papa's chair by the fire in the sitting room. The round table that was once Mama's at Alençon—I remember this better than Céline. The shifting moods of the kitchens and the gardens. I breathe and breathe to keep myself alive.

Lisieux, Les Buissonets: Céline

There is a sort of blurring in my soul. My eyesight is not what it was, so perhaps my artist's heart makes up the details that I cannot really see, and yet it is the light that is the most evocative of all. I help Pauline visit all the rooms, mindful that she left the world twelve full years before me. I sense, rather than see, how moved she is. In our room—that is, mine and Thérèse's—I look upon the shine of the bed covers, the demure filigree of the wallpaper, the silent, ever-enduring dolls, with a particular wonder. I remember how her absence bloomed in every space when she left for Carmel. How Monsieur Quesnel arrived with his ill-timed proposal that evening. I remember how grateful I was, when Papa fell into his fury, that she could not see her king in such distress. How Léonie and I were the only girls of his to witness the disfigured face, the mental tortures.

The garden. Its neatness greets and disowns me. I spy a life-size plaster cast of teenage Thérèse, begging her father to let her fly from the nest direct to the cloister. Of course, this place is a spot in the pilgrims' itinerary, as much as it is the shell of my childhood. But the light—oh!—dappled and mild, untroubled by the town's devastation, acknowledging me with its warm, weightless touch. With her light, warm touch. How I would like to rewind the years, and dwell once again in a prolonged, hazy dawn.

When it is time to leave, I close my eyes and utter a wordless prayer. I feel only the sunshine, and Pauline's hand in mine, guiding me back.

Lisieux, Basilica of St. Thérèse: Pauline

I ease my hurting old body into the chair and settle in for a time before the Blessed Sacrament. I could be anywhere, but I am sheltering under the vast architectural ribcage of my sister's basilica. She is love in the heart of the Church. Jesus is the heart in this body built of bricks, in memory of her. Already my thoughts, so taut and worn by day, start to skitter into dream. In heaven, do we dream? If not, I will miss my dreaming there. The dreams of a Carmelite are like a stained-glass window, fragmented and illuminating. I must share this thought with Céline; she would understand it more than me.

But then I am approached by Father Bertrand. He emerges into my consciousness out of the sea of civilians who have poured in here at the destruction of their homes and livelihoods.

Father Bertrand looks thinner than at our previous meeting. I suppose there is little chance for bodily sustenance, let alone indulgence for him at such a time as this. Then I notice he holds a gleaming envelope. Something akin to Thérèse's proclamation of canonization that I held in my hands some quarter-century ago.

"Mother Agnès. I am always honored to speak with you. I hope Our Lord is keeping you and the sisters safe, in your time of exile." Yes, yes. I appreciate the sentiments, but so much time is taken in these sorts of exchanges. I understand why those in authority are sometimes seen as curt. I incline my head and wait for him to continue. "I have glorious news from Cardinal Suhard." Does he expect me to open my arms to this news? I cannot think what it could be. Does the Pope, in these troubled times, make Thérèse a Doctor of the Church? That would be miraculous news indeed.

"What glory is this, Father?"

"Your sainted sister is elevated to protector of France, together with the Blessed Virgin and St. Joan. The proclamation is to be made today. You must be very honored."

"Oh!" I raise my fingers to my face. Despite myself, yes, I am moved. This little girl who loved Joan, who loved her own father as a king of France and Navarre. Does she have no limits to her ambitions in heaven? But I cannot let myself dissolve in front of this young, earnest priest. It has long been my belief that if I started to cry, I should never stop. "News indeed," I say instead. "And now I understand—" I raise my eyes to his young gaze, "—how well protected we have been, and shall be so until our return."

Lisieux, Basilica of St. Thérèse: Céline

After the proclamation, time moves quickly and slowly at the same time. We even become somewhat accustomed to our makeshift lives here; a community exiled to this shelter so peculiarly apposite. I grow used to the primary colors and angular lines that have been used to decorate Thérèse's basilica and portray the significant incidents in her life. I do not, after all, need to fear my own portraiture will decline in use. Thérèse *aux roses* is the most successful holy card of this century, I have been told. I start to accept that sweetness and sharpness can each serve their purpose in her depiction. She was acquainted with both in her life, after all.

So many join us here: Germans as well as displaced denizens of Lisieux. They all have their holy cards and their well-thumbed hopes of survival. And so the days pass, like so many beads of the perpetual rosary we have set up in the basilica's crypt. At least three of us—sisters or other refugees from war's destruction—are saying our prayers at all times. In doing this, we offer a work of reparation and reconciliation different, but perhaps not completely different, from our lives of silent sacrifice in Carmel. And the weeks go past; and this summer of war starts to wane like an over-proud youth.

In August, Pauline and I lead our sisters back to Carmel; our Carmel that still stands radically intact like a miracle. The Nazis are defeated. The town is almost entirely destroyed, but the war is over. Ahead of us goes the coral casket in which most of Thérèse's quiet bones still reside. She has dwelt with us all this time, a supernatural pulse within the body of her own shattered town, the battered French nation, the war-torn world.

In Carmel: Pauline

While we sheltered in my little sister's basilica, I received the lifelong vows of our novice Alise. She was ready. She has been tried in the furnace of war, and despite her fears, she has accepted God's hand at every stage. Had I been Mother Teresa at Compiègne, I could not be more pleased with Carmel's newest professed sister, nor could we have felt our life and faith more acutely than if we were sisters at the scaffold in those bloody days of revolution. We tried to keep the ceremony simple, private, as far away as possible from the crowding and instability forced into our lives by this terrible war. I see in her face, so smooth and young, an echo of us all on the days of our nuptial mysteries, the start of our consecrated journeys.

Now back at Carmel I am asked to yield my very self into His hands. My nuns thrive; they bloom like flowers back in their allotted portion of rich earth. Even Céline—she sits with me each day in the sunshine of the garden, which always seems so particularly light and golden. I remember her hand touching mine throughout our lives: at births, at deaths, at blessings beyond measure.

It is hard, having been mother for so long, to offer up first my mobility, then my hearing, my sight; even my lungs decline the earth's oxygen.

"Each day I wonder what else I am to give up," I tell my sister. "But let Him take want He wants, as He wants, when He wants."

She squeezes my hand, and for once, I feel like the younger sibling. I worry, vaguely, about upsetting the community with my imminent departure from this life. I have learned through my own hapless guilt how hard such leave-takings can be. But Céline knows my thoughts without me having uttered them and calms me.

"Everyone loves you," she tells me.

Do they really? All my life I have longed to flee fear's cage for love's blue skies. I try to speak, but even this I find I must offer up.

What a calling is that of a Carmelite: to die young or to live long, each of us blooming according to her season. We have nothing but God; and He is everything.

In Carmel: Céline

After so many decades, Pauline's death seems an impossible thing. Again, the death of my sister, and again, and then Léonie, poor Léonie in her exile. And now my long-standing soul-sister. My darling Pauline. To relinquish her nuns, all her daughters, and go to her rest. And leave: me.

We two have raised Thérèse to the altar: Pauline with her papers, I with my art. We two have survived through two world wars. Pauline and I as old women, even set loose once again in Lisieux when the others had gone. This long-drawn-out late autumn of our lives has had its own savor, one that will not be scrutinized and recorded as were the years of our young womanhood. It has its own gifts of hiddenness, its own losses and gains.

Old womanhood. Something Thérèse never knew. The drying out and slow crippling of the body, that envelope she always mistrusted. She would not have cared about aging the way I cared at the start of it. Oh! She would have made a delightful crone. Her face lined and dry as an old apple. Her eyes become as playful as I remembered them in Alençon.

Pauline in her garden, having given up all: limbs, sight, voice, and finally, breath. I held her hand and her clouded gaze. At five in the morning, in the glimmering dawn, she went to her God. Our little mother Agnès.

Two months on, Sister Augustine comes to me. She is respectful and I appreciate her studied grace. From her habit pocket she produces a silver frame. "Sister Geneviève. You will be lonely now that our beloved Agnès has gone to heaven. We will all be lonely—we have all lost our mother."

I look at her, this young woman who will without doubt assume the position of prioress herself once elections are held. She says the right things. She means well. I squash down an instinctive distrust of her just because she is not my blood sister. After all these years, that impulse still remains.

She continues to speak, so my attempt to smile must have been successful. In her hand she has a picture. Perhaps one of mine? I see the outline of a Carmelite. It will be the oval portrait. Perhaps she would like me to sign it; have her personalized prioress's remembrance, obtained while I still live. I am, after all, the last living relic of a saint. But no, what she offers to me is not my own work, and it is given as a gift rather than a request.

"Céline." (She uses my family name! This woman is not afraid to risk intimacy, to bend the rules when it suits her.) "I would like you to take this photograph and keep it with you. No one deserves more wholeheartedly than you this privilege. Who would refuse you permission to soothe your soul with the presence of your Pauline?"

It is a photograph of my little mother, she who became, in the end, my life partner. Taken perhaps thirty years ago, Mother Agnès holds a book (our little book, no doubt) and stands small and proud beneath the statue of an angel. She smiles, more fully and spontaneously than those old group portraits once taken so painstakingly by me. The capturing of a heartbeat in time. And now, time buckling with grief, given to me.

I place the portrait on a small table in our cell, next to my medicines and my little office, my rosary beads, and the unfinished sketch of a young girl's face, rendered shakily but stubbornly last night.

*   *   *

Father Combes sits in the visitor's parlor, having spent a half hour in prayer at Thérèse's tomb. He speaks flatteringly about the *gisant*, when many have called it a florid labor of past times. He worked with Pauline many times, and I know, from her few comments on their meetings, that she considered him a friend.

"God's hand shines through your designs, Sister Geneviève," he says.

A safe opening gambit, I think. *More than safe.*

"I am only a conduit, Father Combes," I reply. "And then only when called upon."

"You have much to give," he responds, valiantly. "God uses you still."

"I have much to do to earn my crown. The others have all completed theirs."

He knows to whom I refer. Pauline has joined Marie and our little cousin in the vault, under Thérèse's mentorship in death even more than in life. The memory of each is reduced to a name and a set of dates. Together they form a community, in their final, exclusive enclosure. I know it is only a matter of time—very little time, now, surely—before my mortal remains join theirs. And my still-awkward soul, please God, flies up to them ab—

"Dear Sister, I have a final request from you. It is something only you can agree to. I have prayed extensively. I think the time is right."

I wait, with the patience I have learned late in life. The father is a good man; not young and impetuous like some of the visiting priests, inflamed by their own sense of my sainted sister, and begging for any scrap of wisdom I may have, miraculously, been keeping just for them. This man is old, too, and sits with a self-sufficient gravity I like.

"There is a need—a very great need now, I think—for Thérèse's letters to be made available to the faithful."

I suck in my breath. He continues, having launched himself into the subject.

"We must remember, so many have seen terrible things from the recent war. There is a new generation of souls in need of the grace only she can give them."

"But the significant letters are already printed. Long ago."

Even as I say this, I know how Father Combes will respond. He looks straight into my eyes and his thick lenses catch a glance of the light. His face is lined with age, his hair white, and his blue eyes water, but his gaze is confident, and oddly gentle.

"Indeed. And in the past, this has been sufficient. But now, who are we to say what is significant to the work of grace? And, dear sister, why should we limit our saint to the so-called significant? Does she not work her miracles of grace through the least significant of ways? See how Pauline has released the entirety of the first manuscripts to the faithful, now she has flown to heaven."

It is true. She authorized the release of all three original texts before her death. She also persuaded me to allow the original photographs to be published. Times have changed. The faithful are hungry for truth.

"You want everything?"

"The time has come. And it is in your gift to allow this to happen."

I fall silent. The ability to pause is another gift of my old age. In the past I may well have stormed halfway through the cloister by now. I think about the request. It is true that the memento room still houses the box of unpublished letters—or at least fragments of letters that Pauline had deemed unsuitable for the wider world to read. Paragraphs of endearment, as well as exclamations and badly punctuated effusions of a young girl whose heart was full but whose schooling was curtailed. These, we thought at the time of the process, would embarrass rather than edify. We wanted a saint for a sister. So we cut away the juvenile lines and kept the blessings and the signatures. This was a time when I was tasked with image-making, when I cut and smudged her photographs, the better to enhance her heart.

I can still remember Francis's rage at my efforts to suppress the Gombault photograph of Thérèse as a round-faced, eager novice. At the time, I did not countenance his objections as anything other than ignorance and error. I have a little more humility now, I like to think.

"I will consider your request," I say to Father Combes.

"I knew you would," he responds. He smiles. "I would expect no less from you, Sister Geneviève. I only hope I will not put you to inconvenience."

"The boxes are old. They contain cuttings as well as entire pages," I say.

He spreads his hands in a way that is intended to reassure.

"I am a scholar as well as a priest. Such archival work is a joy to me."

I nod and stand up, scraping my chair legs as I do so. Sister Felice comes forward to help me back to my cell.

Later I meditate on my memories of the excised scraps. Some are sweet and frivolous, of course. Others—and here I catch my breath again—are far from sweet. Her trials of faith are well known already: the dark night of nothingness she feared to write of in her final memoir. But still I think the faithful might be startled by the visceral depths of her convictions. *He is a spouse of blood,* she once wrote to me. *Blood is his gift, and his demand.* So much so, I remember, that she wrote her final Credo in her own red ink.

As the sun reaches across the bare floor of my cell, I think the time to entrust her to the world has truly come.

*   *   *

Rheumatism makes it difficult to move. And fatigue makes it difficult to speak. But if I have one duty left, it is to smile when I can. All the years of having my say have made this a less comfortable task than I could possibly have imagined as a young girl, beset as I was even then by death, departures, and internal conflict. Thérèse once counseled me that to smile was an act of love. I believe this, now it is the last gift I can give.

After much persuasion, I allow myself to be photographed in the sunshine of the cloister. I hold onto the railing at its mid-length, and stand, uncomfortably. Sister Marie-Anne wends her way towards me, holding the camera. I focus on her with difficulty. She has already pressed the shutter. So quick, the ticking seconds of my aging world.

Then, as directed, I sit on a chair with the familiar black-and-white mosaic of the cloister tiles underneath. Marie-Anne helps me smooth down my veil. She brings me one of my own portraits of Thérèse, a large, colored oval portrait, and bids me settle it in my lap so that it faces her camera, her lightweight camera that she totes so easily in her nimble hands. She backs away from me while making soothing noises. Behind me is the corner entrance to the infirmary. I smile at the symbolic continuum between her youth at one end of the cloister walkway and the sickroom where our earthly lives will end at the other. She takes the photograph. I cradle Thérèse as a great-grandmother cherishes the generations to come.

I tell her I'd like another photograph where I stand beside my famous drawing of the Holy Face.

"I'd like that too," says Marie-Anne, helping me up, and offering to lead me back to my cell, a new space furnished for me beside, but not officially within, the infirmary itself. "I'll ask Mother's permission. I'm sure she'll agree."

As she settles me in my easy chair, retrieving the blanket from the side table to tuck over my legs, I tell her about how when I painted it, I'd snatch a mere few minutes of sleep on the floor of my studio, a rolled-up cloth for a pillow. But something about her smile, and a persistent mist in my own mind, makes me think I've told her this before—perhaps more than once. Alas! Am I now another Sister St. Pierre, set to trouble our young nuns with repetitive stories and cantankerous ways? But Marie-Anne listens respectfully while performing her practical tasks. Then she offers snippets of the world, the turning world I left so long ago.

"Russia is boasting of space travel again, Sister Geneviève. They have sent up sputniks, satellites that will circle the earth. They say that by doing this they will gain more knowledge of our planet than ever before!"

Marie-Anne smooths down my blanket and places a glass of water on my side table, then drags the moveable floor lamp to the other side of my chair, should I wish to read or draw.

She is expecting more rambling memories from me, but instead I say, "A satellite—a sputnik—oh! That is a good way to describe my life, in orbit around His Face."

The young nun stops and stares at me.

"Go on," she says, astonished that I can still formulate images, connect the new with the eternal.

Thérèse did the same with her divine elevator, but now we reach out into the heavens for our metaphors.

"Yes, Marie-Anne, He is the world around which I circle and spin. It is His Holy Face that draws me into Him like gravity."

And nothing I've said has been so true. I sense the pull of Him, alongside the ongoing flight of myself, just as I once, so long ago, felt the tensions of a call to Carmel and a longing to taste the world beyond its walls. But I do not say this to Marie-Anne. I have courted scandal enough in my overlong life.

So I tell her, "One day soon, when my engine is spent, I shall fall into Him and rest there forever."

She kisses me. She looks genuinely moved and leaves with a smile. As I take my rest my eyes close; I feel the comfort of chair and blanket. I dream, not of falling, but of a gentle dispersal, into the mist and its particles of gold; the warmth of a body dissolved into her God.

Postscript

1982

Lisieux: Lynette

It is 1982, and I am finally ready to go.

I am Lynette, an old woman, though how this should be is not explicable to me. I look back over my life of travels and family and see in my veins her love like faint ink on an old parchment. I live in a world of televisions, colors, meals in packets, and women in business, but my life fades back to the sepia of dream. I am no nun, but I knew their ways: back in the old times when the good sisters were divided between the elite, permitted to sing the praises of the Lord in their Carmelite choirs, and the serving sisters, the less-educated, white-veiled women who exclusively cooked, cleaned, washed, and repaired, and kept the community anchored to its good earth. And then, there were the turn sisters, one or two per enclosed convent, neither of the world nor of the cloister, running errands and working the turn so the shopping could pass from outside to interior worlds through the hallowed contraption at the parlor doors. Aunt Babeth was happy enough, but oh how much happier when—decades on—she was privileged to wear the same habit as theirs.

I was so young, young as Thérèse was young when she first visited the Lisieux Carmel parlor. My aunt loved me, of course, as did all the nuns. They slid the boards and grille back; I was so little, nothing in me could injure their exquisite souls. My boots were patent-clean, and my dress had the best lace and buttons. I was a little lady: little Lyn. I remember Thérèse. Her face indistinct, her eyes bright flames which warm me still. I remember her well. She seemed, with her kindness, to be my friend. I brought her a flower and her heart flew up. I felt her cloaked arms embrace my whole world. I loved

229

to talk, but here there was little to teach, so I said my farewells: "Happiness to all I love!"

Later I learned that she received my words as a second flower and repeated them to everyone she met. Even then, she had started her dying.

I remember her. I have remembered for eighty-five years, through all the public proclamations and a century of pain.

I am the last. And yet I am not.

Afterword

Lynette may have been the last person living to have seen Thérèse, but she was far from the last person to get to know her. Continuing her "storm of glory," this young Frenchwoman who did not even live into the twentieth century remains one of the Catholic Church's best-loved saints. Her relics still regularly travel the world. In 1997, the centenary of her death, Pope John Paul II declared her a Doctor of the Church. Her writings are never out of print, and are also now all available online, along with all extant photographs of her and many other images, letters, and articles, thanks to the Archives of the Carmel of Lisieux.

Thérèse's parents, Louis and Zélie Martin, were beatified in 2008, and canonized in 2016, the first spouses in the Church's history to be canonized as a couple. Their "problem child," Léonie, is currently (2022) being considered for beatification and future canonization.

A Note on this Novel

I do not claim this novel to be entirely historically accurate; I have necessarily been selective in the narrative and its fragmentary progress over a long historical period. For example, I did not include details of Thérèse's beatification in 1923, a step on her path to full sainthood. Thérèse's story is well known among faithful Catholics, not least through her own writing, but perhaps her family members and close associates less so. While I have written and published poetry about her, I have long wanted to complete a fictional reflection of her life, and to recognize the important family members who accompanied and witnessed her childhood, her vocation, and her legacy. While I have drawn on many documented events, major and minor, I have not directly quoted from any letters, or memoirs. I did closely adapt Thérèse's funeral notices, but I created fictional extracts of the many letters that poured into the Lisieux Carmel after Thérèse's life and writings began to be known.

As I stated in the introduction, no character here is meant to be entirely biographically accurate either. Occasionally I have created composite characters and incidents, such as Thérèse's advice to weep into a shell (not given to her cousin but to another young novice, Marie of the Trinity). Furthermore, some names have been deliberately changed, primarily to avoid confusion over the popular French Catholic name "Marie": in particular, Lucie Guérin's character is based on Thérèse's real-life cousin Marie Guérin, and Mother Xavier is based on the redoubtable Mother Marie de Gonzague. Lucie's older sister Adèle was really Jeanne, but I changed her name to avoid confusion with Joan of Arc (or Jeanne D'Arc). In addition, Mother Rose-Chrétien is based on Mother Geneviève (whom I did not wish to be confused with Sister Geneviève, AKA Céline). Aunt Véronique is based on another Céline, Céline Fournier, wife of Isidore.

Needless to say, I mean no disrespect to any character I have considered. On the contrary, I have felt great admiration, affection, and respect for all their various callings and complexities. Many times, I wished I could be friends with each one.

Resources

There are many resources on Thérèse. I am especially indebted to the following:

Websites

The online archive of the Carmel of Lisieux. http://www.archives-carmel-lisieux.fr/english/carmel/index.php/accueil-home

Saint Thérèse of Lisieux: A Gateway. http://www.thereseoflisieux.org/

Nonfiction

Ahern, Patrick. *Maurice and Thérèse: The Story of a Love*. New York: Bantam Doubleday Dell, 1999.

Baudouin-Croix, Marie. *Leonie Martin: A Difficult Life*. Translated by Mary Frances Mooney. Dublin: Veritas, 1993.

Deboick, Sophia Lucia. "Image, Authenticity and the Cult of Saint Thérèse of Lisieux, 1897–1959." PhD diss., Liverpool University, 2011. https://core.ac.uk/download/pdf/80770824.pdf.

Görres, Ida Friederike. *The Hidden Face: A Study of St. Thérèse of Lisieux*. Translated by Richard and Clara Winston. San Francisco: Ignatius, 2003.

Kochiss, Joseph P. *A Companion to Saint Thérèse of Lisieux: Her Life and Work & the People and Places in Her Story*. Brooklyn: Angelico, 2014.

Moorcroft, Jennifer. *Saint Thérèse of Lisieux and Her Sisters*. Leominster, UK: Gracewing, 2003.

Nevin, Thomas R. *Thérèse of Lisieux: God's Gentle Warrior*. Oxford: Oxford University Press, 2006.

———. *The Last Years of Saint Thérèse: Doubt and Darkness, 1895–1897*. New York: Oxford University Press, 2013.

Udris John. *Holy Daring: The Fearless Trust of Saint Thérèse of Lisieux*. Leominster, UK: Gracewing, 1997.

Novels

Hansen, Ron. *Mariette in Ecstasy*. New York: Burlingame,1991.
Roberts, Michelle. *Daughters of the House*. London: Virago, 1992.

Plays

Pascal, Michel. *Story of a Soul*. 2009.

Films

Cavalier, Alain. *Thérèse*. 1986.
Cottafavi, Vittorio. *Il processo di Santa Teresa del bambino Gesù*. 1967.

www.ingramcontent.com/pod-product-compliance
Lightning Source LLC
Chambersburg PA
CBHW071833020726
47502CB00004B/1334